POLITICS
AND POLY

MN BENNET

Copyright © 2026 MN Bennet
This edition is published by M.N. Bennet LLC

All rights reserved. No part of this book may be reproduced or transmitted in any form or by any means, electronic or mechanical, including photocopying, recording, or by an information storage and retrieval system - except by a reviewer who may quote brief passages in a review to be printed in a magazine or newspaper - without permission in writing from the publisher.

Names, characters, businesses, places, events, and incidents are either products of the author's imagination or used in a fictitious manner. Any resemblances to actual persons, living or dead, or actual events is purely coincidental.

No generative artificial intelligence (AI) was used in the writing of this work.

NO AI TRAINING: Without in any way limiting the author's [and publisher's] exclusive rights under copyright, any use of this publication to "train" generative artificial intelligence (AI) technologies to generate text is expressly prohibited. The author reserves all rights to license uses of this work for generative AI training and development of machine learning language models.

Hardback ISBN: 978-1-967397-18-1
Paperback ISBN: 978-1-967397-17-4
Ebook ISBN: 978-1-967397-16-7

Edited by Charlie Knight (https://cknightwrites.carrd.co/)
Cover art by Lina Ganef (https://linaganef-eng.carrd.co/)
Formatting by Mayonaka Designs (https://mayonakadesigns.com/)

www.mnbennet.com/

AUTHOR'S NOTE

Thank you all so much for taking a chance on this story. I had so much fun writing this lovely little poly romance. This was my first poly story aside from *Three Meant To Be* which mostly dealt with the grief of losing a partner in the trio. However, *Politics and Poly* is all about the joy of falling in love with two people who are also falling in love. That was such a fun journey.

It was also incredibly difficult to piece together the plot from three different perspectives and make sure I balanced everyone's story, but I loved every minute. I'm not sure if I'll be writing another poly romance from all three perspectives again. The only grace was following them with a close third POV, but I still had to find their voices as I alternated between chapters.

While this is a romance filled with a lot of joy and humor, there is still a few darker moments along the way. I have some content warnings listed for anyone who needs them.

CONTENT WARNINGS

Violence and fighting
Physical assault
Verbal assault
Homophobia
Transphobia
Queer slurs
Emotional manipulation
Gaslighting
Bullying
Family abandonment
Body dysmorphia
Depression
Anxiety

This is an open-door romance so there is a lot of graphic sex between adults: Kissing, oral, face fucking, throat fucking, gagging, choking, fingering, anal, rimming, first times, rough fucking, threesomes (obviously).

For those who like to know ahead of time, there is no open relationship outside of the throuple itself, no other person drama (romantically speaking), and no cheating of any kind.

Please remember your mental health is important and if this story isn't for you that's completely okay. Your comfort matters. Your joy matters. You matter.

This is for the people who love deeply.
This is for the people who are angry at everything going on around us.
This is for the people who know reading is political.
Words can be a great escape but never forget bigots would ban and burn books every chance they got.

PROLOGUE
RUS

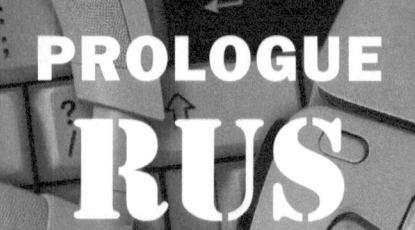

A WAVE of irritation hit Rus as his rideshare arrived downtown. He already regretted paying for the expensive trip from campus, but it was certainly a lot quicker than catching the city bus, paying for the transfer, and still landing on the far edge of nowhere downtown.

Normally, there wasn't much excitement downtown and certainly not too much to do other than check out the oddity stores or stop into a restaurant. He was still a couple of months away from twenty-one, so that kept him out of all the bars and clubs worth going to anyway. Those that didn't card or allowed eighteen and up tended to be overcrowded and underwhelming.

When Rus spotted the people chanting their disgust, it left him unsettled. His confusion twisted into rage and discomfort and secondhand embarrassment as the driver stared at the flock of protesters. They'd lined up across the street from Rus' destination. Since it was a single-lane one-way road, there wasn't much distance between Rus and these unwanted picketers.

"Thanks for the lift," Rus said in a deep, gravelly reply as he slipped out of the car and headed toward the indie bookstore.

The frigid winter breeze tousled Rus' thick, messy brown curls. His hoodie suddenly seemed so flimsy, completely incapable of shielding him from the cold. He wrapped the hood over the left side of his neck, protecting his new tattoo from the chill. He also tugged on his sleeves, keeping his hands warm, and covering his wrist tattoo. While Rus had plenty of tattoos, none of them ignited his frustration quite as much as the one on his wrist.

It read off a date, a remembrance, an acknowledgement that Rus should've willed himself to forget. Valentine's Day had come and gone this year, but he still clung to the emotion connected to that day. He rubbed his thumb over the date inked across his wrist, glaring at the protesters. What in the hell were these people even protesting?

Their signs infuriated Rus, spewing their hatred with every word, using tacky one-liners to spout lies, and chanting bigoted phrases that drew the attention of anyone unfortunate enough to walk down the street.

Cold air slapped his face, and the heat boiling inside him simmered a bit. Only a bit, though.

He really hadn't anticipated the campus Pride Club hosting a small event at a bookstore would garner this much hatred. Personally, Rus only made the trek downtown to support his friend Daysha. She'd organized the event to spotlight historical queer Black figures during Black History Month.

"Please consider stopping inside." A Pride Club member stepped over to meet Rus, handing him a flyer to the event he already knew about.

Considering how flushed her pale face had gotten and the way she huddled tight in her large winter coat, Rus figured she'd drawn the short straw of greeting bystanders to encourage them to drop by the event. A task surely made all the more difficult by the assholes right across the street.

"What the fuck is up with these people?" Rus asked, cupping his hands to spark a cigarette.

He didn't need the smoke, didn't particularly want it, but he did want an excuse to linger outside and gawk at the bigots across the road.

"They're here because of the Drag Queen Story Time," the Pride member replied.

"Wait, I thought today was..." Rus looked at his half-crumpled flyer and read the details.

Yeah, it was Daysha's event.

"The previous event was over a month ago, and they've been coming in droves every few days to protest the bookstore."

Rus scoffed, puffing on his cigarette. "Doubt any of these morons can even read. Sounds like they could use a little story time help, fucking idiots."

The Pride member gave Rus a weak smile, then encouraged him to step inside, but he gestured to his smoke and took a deep drag.

One of the protesters shouted something, and the next thing Rus knew, an empty soda can hit the Pride member on her shoulder. The can clinked against the concrete, and Rus whirled around in a rage, absolutely offended on her behalf.

"It's fine," she lied, tugging on Rus' hoodie. "Go inside. Warm up and cool down."

Rus almost grinned at the humor in her poor attempt to settle him. It almost worked, too, until Rus spotted two more cans kicked off and hidden by the corner of the bookstore. One of these assholes had used this girl, handing out flyers to an event they knew nothing about, as target practice. They used her timidness to continue pushing and poking and provoking.

But Rus was never one to let an insult go unchallenged, despite how provoking a confrontation often led to more trouble.

"Wait," the Pride member called out as Rus flicked his cigarette to the ground, picked up the empty soda can, and bolted across the street.

"One of you assholes dropped this." Rus held up the can, eyeing each and every one of them.

There couldn't have been more than a dozen or so people. A few smirked at Rus, gloating, but others averted their gaze, clearly uncomfortable to be challenged.

"It's mine." A much taller man with a huge gut stepped forward. "What's your problem?"

He looked down at Rus, overconfident and under the misimpression that Rus would hesitate since he barely stood at 5'6, and this man had nearly a foot on him.

"First off, you need to apologize," Rus said, turning the can in his hand so the bottom sat snugly in his palm.

"Fuck off—"

"Secondly," Rus interrupted. "You need to work on your aim, dipshit."

Rus flung his arm upward, giving a demonstration on how to hurl a can. In a swift motion, Rus slammed the soda can into the man's chin with such ferocity, he crushed it flat and sent the man tumbling back into the crowd.

Another man swore at Rus, swinging his sign. All Rus saw was red. He braced his arm to lessen the impact, then snatched the sign away and went to punch the man.

Rus unloaded all his pent-up fury, wrapped in a whirlwind of chaos as

POLITICS AND POLY

protesters screamed and shouted and ran away. Some stayed to fight. Things turned into a cesspool of destruction. Rus kicked and punched at people every which way. He raged and roared. Someone blitzed him from behind, but that didn't stop Rus. It only further infuriated him.

Every time someone struck him, he reached out and swung back. Rus didn't give a damn. He wanted to beat the ever-living hell out of the entire crowd. He kept swinging until sirens blared around him.

CHAPTER 1
DYLAN

DYLAN raced from one end of the venue to the next, double-checking all the little details to ensure everything went off without a hitch. While he hadn't been put in charge of the fundraiser itself, this was the most responsible he'd been for organizing such a big event at Slayer's Brush Art Gallery on behalf of Dorothy's Home.

Turning the small gallery into a suitable locale for a hundred and fifty people plus the caterers seemed an impossible task. Slayer's Brush certainly had the elitist vibe the fundraiser required to attract donors, but Dylan struggled to make arrangements that wouldn't leave their wealthy benefactors climbing over each other.

"Still freaking out?" Kaiden asked, his light voice a bit pitchy as he carried a rather large portrait. "How goes the list of a million and one things?"

"Got it down to a solid hundred thousand."

"Impressive." Kaiden nodded with a congratulatory bob of his head.

Dylan couldn't tell if Kaiden had added some type of glittery gel to his emerald green hair or if the lights added some sparkle. Either way, it looked nice and stylish, like most of Kaiden's getup on a daily basis. From his snazzy outfits to his seamless makeup.

The hair reminded Dylan he needed to do something with his own. His blond highlights were fading, and the roots had grown about half the length of his hair. Maybe he should attempt something a bit bolder, like Kaiden, this time around, but Dylan never thought bold really suited him.

Speaking of bold… Dylan soaked in the bizarre painting Kaiden hung up for display.

"Trust me, this abstract baby is going to create a bidding war," Kaiden said, reading Dylan's mind as he often did.

"You're the expert."

"Exactly," Kaiden said, playfully backstepping with an almost rhythmic shimmy. "So when I tell you this place will hold a hundred guests comfortably, trust me."

With that, Kaiden twirled and kicked his leg high in some semi-graceless version of a pirouette as he danced between a few others helping with the setup.

Kaiden had worked at Slayer's Brush for years, helping with the usual events, and when he recommended the venue, Dylan didn't see any problems until he'd been tasked with all the last-minute to-dos. Suddenly, everything seemed rather pressing, a weight of too many tasks to achieve perfection.

"A hundred and fifty," Dylan clarified.

"Huh?" Kaiden straightened up, adjusting his corset vest, which had wriggled up a bit from his playful jumps and kicks and spins.

Unlike Dylan, who dressed pretty casually most days—finding his button-up and tie a bit overwhelming for the evening—Kaiden always wore something flashy. Usually, a corset vest of some kind. He seemed to have dozens of them in every possible color combination, and he always paired them with a long-sleeved dress shirt, a colorful tie, fancy slacks, and perfectly polished shoes.

If it weren't for Kaiden's goofy personality, Dylan would've felt out of place the moment they crossed paths, but despite his presentation, Kaiden remained pretty down to earth.

"You said a hundred," Dylan elaborated on his comment a moment ago. "It's a hundred and fifty-ish. Also, gotta add in the staff and such."

"Oh." Kaiden's face fell flat. "Well, it'll be fine. People cancel all the time."

"Wait, what?" Dylan asked wide-eyed.

Before he could get clarification, Kaiden rushed off to grab more artwork to put on display for tonight.

"Everything will be fine, everything will be fine, everything will…" Dylan's affirming mantra turned into a mumble as the grittiest of the worker bees made his way out from the back, carrying two of the pillar-designed tables over his shoulders.

Rus Diamond looked like a surly little Greek God hauling those marble pillars. Well, they weren't marble. Dylan wasn't sure what they were exactly, other than Kaiden had suggested them to amp up the aesthetic for the fundraiser. Kaiden always had brilliant ideas. They were basically high tables for guests to set their drinks and plates down from time to time, to congregate with each other, and to spark a conversation with an elegant piece of decoration.

All Dylan wondered was how heavy they were as he watched Rus barrel between people, announcing his presence with an aggravated grunt as he lugged the pillars from the back.

The lights glimmered against the snakebites on Rus' lower lip, which was prominently turned into a frown. A seemingly default scowl for the young man. Dylan attempted to count Rus' piercings, noticing a new one every time they crossed paths. He couldn't help but imagine some purpose behind their arranged locations. Like a constellation splattered across his face. The eyebrow connected to the nose, maybe the nose connected to the lips, the lips reached out to the earlobes, which connected to the upper ear stud. Potentially.

Mostly Dylan just wanted a reason to study Rus' face. A reason to study all of Rus if possible.

He had the cutest curly brown hair. Deep brown and thick curls. And Dylan didn't want to get started on the parallels of curls and chaos and how Rus was an obviously chaotic bisexual. Rus practically wore his sexuality on his sleeve—or more precisely, the neck tattoo he had on display.

POLITICS AND POLY

It was deranged and cute and artistic all at once. A silly goose posed for a threatening attack with a knife in its bill and feathers splattered in the colors of the bisexual flag. The array of pink, purple, and blue reminded Dylan of the bizarre abstract painting from earlier, only in Rus' case, the art made sense and held purpose.

"Oh, honey, do you mind rearranging these?" Jasmine asked with a wave of her hand as she strolled on into the gallery. "I was thinking a bit of a zigzag display to space out the audience."

Rus nodded and went to work, moving the table pillars around, clearly having a strong understanding of the distance between each pillar as he made mental notes on the spacing. That impressed Dylan.

Granted, Dylan was an easy sell, since Rus could quite literally take a breath and mesmerize Dylan with the bob of his Adam's apple and the puff of his chest. And now, Dylan had found himself lost on the flex of Rus' muscles as he worked.

When those piercing hazel eyes flitted up for a moment, locking with Dylan's brown eyes, he quickly turned away. He nearly swiveled into a tumble he moved so fast, but as he composed himself, he shifted his focus onto the person hosting tonight's fundraiser.

Jasmine wore a white dress with golden lacing wrapped around it, adding to this Olympian vibe that'd been created for the evening. The white and gold complemented Jasmine's dark brown skin, and her golden heels gave her a lift, making her a bit taller than Dylan for a change. Not that Jasmine was a short woman at nearly six feet herself. But between the heels and the way she'd styled her braids up into a high bun tied together with golden strands, she appeared to tower over Dylan and everyone else.

Dylan stood close to Jasmine as the pair observed Rus' work.

"How are things coming along, hun?"

"Great," Dylan said, his deep voice squeaking a bit as his self-doubts crept up. "A few hiccups, but easy enough to fix before tonight."

"How's this look?" Rus called out, lifting his T-shirt to wipe his face and revealing his firm, pale stomach and the briefest glint at a tattoo on his hip.

He'd dropped his shirt back down too quickly for Dylan to study the tattoo, having wasted precious seconds lost on Rus' abdomen.

"Looking absolutely wonderful," Jasmine said with a small applause, and Dylan couldn't agree more. Though it wasn't the pillar layout he sought to applaud. "What ever will I do without your assistance, hun?"

"Wither away and hope I end up with another round of community service." Rus playfully punched upward like he was smacking the air.

"Let's hope not," Jasmine said with a small laugh. "They might not let you off so easily next time."

Rus scoffed. "Between eighty hours of community service and their bullshit mandated anger management courses, there ain't nothing easy about that."

Dylan found himself enthralled by Rus' presence. He didn't fluff up his words, speaking his mind very plainly no matter who he was around. The lack of niceties for the sake of politeness exhilarated Dylan, who often found himself placating people's feelings because the alternative seemed too cruel.

It helped that the story surrounding Rus' community service hours got a bit embellished every time someone told it. Dylan knew he hadn't fought off twenty bigots outside the local indie bookstore, but he had fought a handful. Still, he found it impressive as all get out. Rus had this recklessness coupled with compassion that seemed so mismatched, it captivated Dylan.

Admittedly, Dylan spent most of the summer wary of Rus, having little time or reason to spark up a conversation with the guy. However, there was something appealing about the stoic grump who helped around the youth home without complaint.

It was September now, and Dylan had barely gotten to know Rus outside of his volunteering time. He wanted to talk with Rus more than the occasional small talk between tasks around Dorothy's Home. He wanted to get to know Rus before he finished his community service.

Jasmine's reminder was just the kick Dylan needed. Rus' services were coming to an end after tonight's fundraiser; Jasmine kindly offered a bit of wiggle room for Rus to attend and count his presence toward his remaining hours.

That type of consideration was something Jasmine always did, working to uplift her community in any way she could. As a proud Black trans woman of nearly fifty years old, she'd made it her mission to fill the gaps in the system any way she could to keep her community safe. She founded Dorothy's Home for Wayward Rainbows and had dedicated her life to keeping queer teens off the street.

Some only stayed for a night, some only came because they were legally required, such as Rus and his community service, but everyone benefited. Especially Dylan, who found himself saved by Jasmine's group home. It got him off the streets and helped him finish high school. Helped show him his life didn't have to meet a dead end. And when he didn't know where to go after he turned eighteen, Jasmine stuck around and guided him. Hence, he continued hanging around at twenty-six, still helping Dorothy's Home in any way he could.

"All right, boss," Rus said, approaching Dylan and looking up at him. "What're your orders?"

Dylan found himself awkwardly hunching just enough to hide the height difference between them. Not that it did much good. He stood at 6'2", and even hunching an inch or two didn't make up for the fact that Rus barely reached 5'6".

"Um, well, uh…yeah…" Dylan flipped through his to-do list, searching for something Rus could work on.

The only thing Dylan wanted Rus to work on was very inappropriate. Still, he found himself emboldened to make a move. Not now. Goodness no. They were both working.

"How about helping Kaiden haul the art pieces?" Dylan asked. "Carefully, 'cause they're like super important."

"Fundraiser and all." Rus nodded.

They weren't just bidding on art pieces but that was the forefront of the event.

Rus meandered, making his way to the back of the gallery, and Dylan determined that tonight he'd ask Rus out. As friends. A chance to at least get to know him outside of manual labor. After all, if he didn't make some type of a move, he'd likely never see Rus again.

Dylan couldn't tell if he had a crush on Rus because he was like some kind of hot, vengeful, bisexual punk who jumped out of a 1980s rock 'n roll poster or because he actually liked Rus' personality. And he couldn't determine if this was a crush, simple lust, or merely admiration. That was always Dylan's difficulty when it came to feelings. Since hopping into bed came easily for Dylan, he ran off a lot of potential friends over the years. Casual sex rarely stayed casual when someone caught feelings. Unfortunately, it was never Dylan who had them for longer than a fun roll between the sheets.

That was the main reason Dylan had pressed the brakes around Kaiden, realizing Kaiden didn't seem all that into Dylan. Since he didn't want to ruin another potential friendship with casual sex, he sort of friend-zoned himself.

Now, he just needed to figure out if he wanted to be friends with Rus or bang his brains out. Or the strangest of all…go on a date.

"Jeez, you look like you're about to puke."

Dylan nearly jumped out of his own skin, startled by Kaiden's arrival. Honestly, Kaiden had the quietest footsteps in the world, and somehow, he always took Dylan by surprise.

"No, I don't," Dylan protested, feeling a bit queasy by his own determined declaration to ask Rus out.

Unfortunately, Kaiden knew Dylan quite well, and if he stayed, he'd press him for answers. Dylan didn't really date. He didn't really flirt either. It'd been years since he put even the slightest investment of interest or pursuit into a crush. And if he explained that to Kaiden, he'd have to explain a lot more. This was too long of a conversation to have considering all the work Dylan still had to complete.

So, Dylan rushed off to make his way through the insurmountable checklist he'd taken on for the fundraiser and waved Kaiden off to show Rus which paintings needed to be set up.

CHAPTER 2
KAIDEN

SLAYER'S Brush filled up quickly, much to Dylan's dismay. Sure, a packed event meant a great fundraiser; however, the cramped guests quickly turned sour as they bumped elbows with others in attendance. Kaiden couldn't let such a pretty face frown the entire night, so he set out to find his boss.

Alison wore a tight red dress, stealing focus from the artwork as she talked up the venue. She was a big, busty, bold woman who rarely took the sidelines. It was what kept her expensive art boutique in high demand. Unlike Kaiden, who sucked in a sharp breath at the pinch of his corset vest, Alison didn't care about tightening her waist or hiding her gut. She was a very curvy woman with long blonde hair down to her waist.

"Pardon me." Kaiden squeezed through the small crowd, smiling because pretense mattered to Alison more than anything.

Times were always good, even when they were terrible.

"What do you need, darling?" Alison asked, smiling.

Oh, damn. He'd already gotten a darling. She must've been in a mood.

"Things are a little tight here." Kaiden rolled his green eyes around the venue, discreetly nodding. "I was thinking since the back room is a bit bare, we could—"

"Absolutely impossible." Alison held up a hand. "People come here for elegance, not messy storage rooms."

"People also come here to breathe in art and mystique." Kaiden brushed up against his boss, letting his chest hit hers. "Elegance is lost when we're bumping butts."

Alison glowered, her blue eyes appearing all the icier.

"Unless it's the fun kind of butt bumping." Kaiden winked. "Come on, we throw a few decorations up, make it an exclusive tonight-only experience. Behind the scenes. Sneak peek at some upcoming events. Artists no one else has had the privilege to view."

Alison's frown softened, considering. She was a smart woman, smarter than Kaiden, so he knew not to play her so much as play to her ego. If he could convince her this was her idea, she'd gladly take the credit and toss in a few more ideas to turn the makeshift extra space into a success.

"Fine. There's a few pieces in my office," Alison said. "Carefully put them up and make sure the back room is actually clean."

"Will do." Kaiden gave her a tiny salute, much to Alison's annoyance.

With that settled, Kaiden took off to Alison's office to find a few suitable pieces to put on display. Grabbing two smaller portraits, he made his way down a hallway leading to the back alley of the art boutique. If he cut through the crowd to the storage room, he'd never hear the end of it from Alison.

Outside, plastered against the wall, was Rus, who wore a wrinkled dress shirt, baggy slacks, and scuffed dress shoes. Christ, he was a rough sight. Smoke trickled from his mouth, almost artistically, creating a landscape silhouette. Well, at least that was what Kaiden envisioned, seeing mountains with each puff Rus took from his cigarette.

The stench of the smoke nearly gagged Kaiden; he could never grasp why anyone in this day and age would smoke cigarettes, especially when there were much nicer alternatives. The blueberry-flavored vape in his pocket weighed all the heavier as he considered pausing for a puff or two of his own.

Sadly, the buzz of his phone drew him to his other pocket. Ugh. His sister was calling him yet again. He sent her to voicemail. Hopefully, she'd check her texts and realize Kaiden had work. Slayer's Brush had a pretty routine schedule, excluding the monthly event or two, which meant Kaiden was out for the evening and unable to help around the house. A problem for later. Right now, he focused on the fundraiser.

Kaiden approached Rus, figuring since he had hours to work off according to Dylan, he might as well get the storage room set up faster. "Hey, I need your help setting up the storage room."

"No," Rus said, taking a deep inhale of his cigarette.

"Um, yes." Kaiden batted his eyes, conveying his aggravation.

"I was told I just had to show up."

"Unless an emergency came up." Kaiden shrugged. "And look? Here's the emergency. Thanks, friend."

Rus ground his teeth, shooting Kaiden a menacing glare. Too bad all Kaiden saw was an angry purse puppy when he looked down at Rus.

"Come along." Kaiden strutted ahead, walking with a swagger in his hips, feeling a little extra confident with each step.

He hoped to maintain this vigor and pep through the evening. Dylan had pumped his ego pretty high, giving Kaiden far too much credit for suggesting Slayer's Brush as the queer youth home's next fundraiser venue.

All Kaiden had really done was make the suggestion, convince Alison, and rearrange her other events. And contact guests, handle decorations, and fill out the paperwork for write-offs, and… Okay, maybe Kaiden had put some heavy lifting work into this fundraiser.

Dorothy's Home meant a lot to Dylan, and Dylan meant a lot to Kaiden. He didn't have many friends, having lost contact with most of his circle when they went off to college, and he stayed behind to find himself. He had even fewer queer friends. In fact, he had a grand total of one—Dylan.

So, it was important to Kaiden, helping his friend, seeing him smile, and the best way to do that was by making sure this fundraiser went off without a hitch. In order to do that, Kaiden needed to get the storage room set up as a bonus space for the venue, which would go a lot quicker with Rus' reluctant assistance.

Kaiden quickly put Rus to work, moving things around and cleaning up where he could. Little by little, they transformed the storage room into a modestly acceptable space for guests. Kaiden asked Rus to discreetly steal two of the pillar-designed tables and bring them back here, considering them the final touches necessary before unveiling this room.

Guests started trickling into the storage room, taking in the modest display and enjoying the extra breathing space.

Dylan wandered their way, waving over a few of the caterers to fill up the bonus space.

"You're brilliant," Dylan said, giving Kaiden a quick side hug. "Thank you."

"All Alison's idea," Kaiden said with a pointed look, reminding Dylan that if he suggested otherwise, she'd be offended, and as the actual host of the venue, it was wise to stay on Alison's good side.

"How'd you get this set up so fast?" Dylan asked.

Kaiden pulled Rus by his wrinkled sleeve and gestured to the frowning man. As a peace offering, Kaiden grabbed two champagne flutes off a tray from a passing server and handed one to Rus.

"For lying about having to help me."

Rus snatched the glass. "I fucking knew it."

"Well, thank you both," Dylan said, eyeing the guests continuing to funnel into the storage room and easing the pressure of the front venue space.

"No problem," Kaiden said, raising his own glass to cheers.

"It really means a lot that you helped bring this to life," Dylan said, and for half a second, Kaiden prepared to bashfully blush at the compliment until he realized Dylan was speaking to Rus.

Kaiden's face twisted into a disingenuous smile, fighting off a grimace and biting back a few comments. Mostly. "So, what're you planning on doing with all your free time now that you're liberated from all this community service?"

"Not a whole lot." Rus sipped his drink.

"Oh, come on."

POLITICS AND POLY

"Focusing on my classes," Rus said with a snort. "I'm not that interesting."

"Well, there's not much to do here." Dylan ran his fingers through his hair.

It was a nervous act of Dylan's, something Kaiden knew for certain, but he couldn't place the anxiety. Surely, Dylan wasn't still struggling with the success of the fundraiser.

"There's always Himbos," Kaiden said with a shrug.

Rus quirked a brow, raising his eyebrow piercing. The curiosity softened his gloomy face.

"It's the gay bar," Kaiden explained. "Semi queer but mostly gay."

"Meaning?" Rus asked.

"Meaning they do like Sapphic Sunday brunches and karaoke for all on Wednesday night, but they're pushing twinks, leather, poppers, and gloryholes in everyone's faces."

"Plus, all the tourism," Dylan added.

"Tourism?" Rus asked, his face looking even more confused than a second ago.

"Straight girls looking to dance and not get hit on," Kaiden elaborated. "Straight guys looking for free drinks and easy targets from girls who just came to dance."

Dylan nodded with an exasperated sigh. "And the annoying couples looking to show they're adventurous."

Kaiden chuckled. "Exactly."

They weren't usually adventurous. They just wanted to stare at the gays like exotic animals on display. That was the key distinction between an ally and a tourist in Kaiden's mind. The number of times Kaiden had been told to 'slay' by a supportive drunk woman was innumerable. Not to mention, there was always one woman who teasingly warned the gay boys not to flirt with her man, as if either of them were worth anyone's time of day.

"Never been," Rus replied. "It's twenty-one and up, I think, and I only recently turned twenty-one."

"You just turned twenty-one?" Kaiden asked, feigning shock.

"And no fake I.D.?" Dylan tsked. "A lawbreaker like you."

Rus snorted. "You punch one douchebag and suddenly..."

Kaiden side-eyed Rus, green eyes catching the light. "I heard it was waaaay more than one."

Rus counted on his fingers, then gave a sly smile. "Still single digits. I'm pretty sure."

"Well, now that you're finally all grown up, you're going to have to check it out."

"I'm plenty grown."

"Uh-huh." Kaiden nodded, mockingly, playfully, he wasn't quite sure, but the teasing brought a grin to his face.

Rus scoffed. "And how old are you?"

"You never ask an elder gay their age." Kaiden pressed his hands to his chest, dramatically playing offended.

"Twenty-four." Dylan shot Kaiden a judgy look.

"Practically a baby yourself," Rus said, then turned his hazel eyes onto Dylan. "So, that makes you the oldest?"

"Ooof." Dylan cupped his hand over his heart. "You wound me."

"I mean, twenty-six," Kaiden said with a shrug. "You should be applying for gay senior citizenship pretty soon."

"You are toxic."

"The best boys are." Kaiden batted his eyes, feeling feisty the more they bantered.

"Did you do anything fun?" Dylan asked, turning his attention back to Rus. "Since you just turned twenty-one."

"Clearly not," Kaiden said.

"Well, not *just*," Rus elaborated. "My birthday's in April but—"

"That's like a year-ish ago," Kaiden said with a laugh as he counted the actual number of months on his fingers between April and September.

"But," Rus said, clearing his throat with a bit of hostility, "I sort of got into some legal trouble around then, and that pretty much blew my whole summer away. Between community service and driving all the way back home for family time—because God forbid my behavior ruin any family reunions or vacations or blah, blah, blah."

"If you hadn't screwed up, we might never have crossed paths." Dylan had a coy smile.

"Himbos is pretty great." Kaiden's phone buzzed, and he dug into his pocket.

"Minus the tourists, right?" Rus added.

"Exactly. But even they can't ruin the Friday night drag shows," Kaiden said, swiping to ignore a barrage of texts from his sister. "You should check it out."

"Yeah," Dylan exclaimed. "Oh, I haven't been to one of their drag shows in forever."

Not forever. The last time he went was back in July. Kaiden had managed to pry Dylan away from his work at Dorothy's Home. If not for Kaiden, Dylan would pretty much hunker down and work nonstop, relying on his phone for any and all human interactions. Even when they hung out, Kaiden spent much of it helping around at the queer youth home, whether that meant sorting through donations or organizing fundraiser venues.

"You should go this Friday," Kaiden suggested, taking a careful sidestep as he prepared to exit so he could message his sister and do a lap around the venue. If he enjoyed the fundraiser too much, Alison might notice.

"That'd be fun," Rus said.

"Yeah, definitely." Dylan grinned.

"Then again, it is a Saturday…" Rus raised his shoulders suggestively, likely testing the waters on whether anyone wanted to go.

"Remember what I said about tourism?" Kaiden made a face.

"Okay, okay, so Friday it is." Rus dug through his pocket for his phone. "So, should we like meet at the club or like hang downtown beforehand? The food's good there."

"I'm pretty much down for whatever," Dylan answered, taking Rus' phone as he handed it to him, clearly requesting his contact info. "What do you think, Kaiden?"

"What?" Kaiden paused, staring at the two of them. "I was just making a suggestion. I wasn't going to go."

Scanning through his texts, Kaiden read through the increasingly aggressive messages his sister left him. Apparently, he'd flaked on dinner for the family, even though he told everyone multiple times he wouldn't be there because of the fundraiser. Now, if he skipped out on a Friday in the same week, he'd never hear the end of it. His sister usually picked up extra work on the weekends, which meant she'd need someone to watch the kids.

"What? You'd send me there by myself?" Rus placed a hand to his chest, feigning the same phony surprise Kaiden had a moment ago. It pulled Kaiden's attention away from his phone. "What if I get snatched up by one of those hetero tourists? Do you have any idea what they do to bi boys?"

"No, what?" Dylan asked.

"Neither do I," Rus said with a laugh. "That's why I asked."

"You won't be alone." Kaiden gestured to Dylan.

"I don't know." Dylan shrugged. "It's been forever since I've gone to Himbos; I might lose him."

"And I'm just a lil baby, remember?" Rus made his voice light and childish.

Kaiden scoffed. "I guess I can check my schedule."

"Sounds good." Dylan shoulder bumped his friend, keeping Kaiden planted in place in the storage room.

"So, which one of you is buying me drinks?" Rus handed his phone to Kaiden.

"You little scammer." Kaiden rolled his eyes, typing his name and number into Rus' phone before texting himself.

"Damn straight—pun certainly not intended." Rus winked. "It's my first time at the gay club. I expect to be plastered on someone else's tab."

"We'll find you a sugar daddy for the night," Kaiden teased.

"Absolutely not," Dylan replied. "They'll eat you alive."

"Doubt they could handle me." Rus shot Dylan and Kaiden a devious smirk.

Kaiden smiled back, a bit surprised how endearing Rus came across.

It was one Friday night. He didn't have to put his life on hold every single weekend. At least, he told himself that while he figured out what excuse he'd use to avoid his sister's ire.

CHAPTER 3
RUS

THE week dragged for Rus, and every day seemed infinitely further from the fun Friday night he had planned. While his class didn't start until ten, he had barely dragged himself out of bed in time to make the long trek across campus. Technically, he lived off campus, but his apartment complex was actually closer to his class buildings than most of the on-campus dormitories scattered at the far end.

"What are you wearing?" Daysha called out in her judgiest tone.

The expression fell away quickly since she was mostly all smiles all the time.

Rus smirked, half-exhausted and half-amused by Daysha's failed attempts to pick at him. It wasn't every day he rolled out of bed and rocked his pajamas to class. They were comfy and casual, and when Daysha's gaze dropped to his feet, Rus realized it wasn't his pajamas but his slippers that his friend judged.

Giant dragon slippers with floppy wings that bounced on the sides of his feet and a tail connected to the heels. They were ridiculous, and Rus loved them.

Unlike Rus, Daysha wore a plaid blazer and matching skirt with a fancy purple blouse. The vibrant purple complemented Daysha's deep brown complexion, and the outfit itself accentuated her stout, curvy frame. She looped an arm around his as they reached the crosswalk and boldly led him across, ignoring traffic alongside most of the campus pedestrians.

The sun stung Rus' eyes, making him buffer his vision with his free arm, and giving complete control of his welfare to Daysha as she led the way to their class. The history building was one of the least historic on campus, having been built a few years before Rus enrolled. It practically still had that new building smell, very sleek and modern and simple.

Daysha made small talk with Rus before their lecture started up, but even as class began, his mind remained lost on his Friday plans.

All he thought about was the next time he'd see Dylan and Kaiden, finding himself fixated on their conversations during the fundraiser. It didn't help that he hadn't heard back from the court about his finalized paperwork. While he knew he'd checked all his boxes and done everything the DA had demanded, he still anxiously awaited the results. Once they officially dismissed his case, he could put that incident behind him.

"I'm sorry, is this class seriously going to overlook *true* historical heroes just to be diverse?" Emma Alexander asked, brushing a hand through her long blonde hair as she raised it high. The hand was just a gesture to draw eyes to her, as she never waited for the professor's acknowledgement. Nope, she often blurted her commentary mid-lecture every opportunity she could.

Another reason Rus' week dragged had to do with the fact that his history class, 'Hidden Heroes Between the Pages,' took place three mornings a week. This was supposed to be an amazing course for him to share with Daysha. It covered her elective requirements, and it fit into one of the History electives Rus required for his major. It was also nice to take a class that specifically focused on historic figures who were often overlooked or completely cut from standard textbooks.

Unfortunately, Emma also needed the credit for her history major. She was the bane of Rus' existence, intentionally enrolling in history so she could learn to fight back against the "woke" mob she proclaimed wanted to rewrite history without the right lens. And Rus knew she meant conservative with her shitty pun.

"I don't know," Emma said, twirling a pink pen between her fingers. A stylish pen that matched her outfit and had her sorority letters on the tip. "I just find it challenging to fill an entire semester with historical figures while purposefully ignoring the accomplishments of white men. I understand it's not PC to be inclusive to white people anymore, but it just feels like we're going to be missing a lot of historical relevance skipping around to the few moments in history not impacted by successful white men."

Daysha gagged hard, rolling her eyes in the process. When that didn't get a rise out of Rus, she gave him a silly smile to lighten the mood. Not an easy task when Emma was nearby. It didn't work, but he faked a sassy grin anyway. His way of thanking her efforts. It took everything Rus had to bite his tongue, almost quite literally as he ground his teeth. But he'd already been kicked out of the class on two separate occasions for arguing with Emma.

Not that the professor wanted to remove Rus for his disruptive behavior, but Emma cried bias at her removal when the arguments only ever escalated because of Rus' rude antics. It didn't help that he called her a cunt on both occasions—loud, proud, and with a string of other profanities to keep the curse word company.

After ten minutes of back and forth with Emma, whose questions got more obnoxious, the lecture finally continued. Rus knew Emma's only real goal in this class was to waste time and diminish the value shared in this course, all while ensuring she did just enough to pass.

"You know she's only that way to get a rise out of people," Daysha said, tugging on Rus' sleeve to guide him toward the doors opposite Emma's direction. It was the longer way out of the building, but Rus knew Daysha suspected he'd provoke an argument if he crossed paths with Emma.

"Well, it's working," Rus admitted.

He never understood why someone would pick a major for a degree in a field they only ever wanted to undermine. Emma had a few courses she liked, usually led by old, crotchety professors who focused on the standard, whitewashed texts. Still, even so, Emma never held much passion for knowledge, just an interest in poking holes through any discussion that didn't match her beliefs.

Rus thought about his brother, who majored in theology as a way to deconstruct religion, focus on the philosophy of ideology, and fight against Christian nationalist beliefs overtaking politics and policies. Maybe that was the same thing as Emma, only clearly for evil in her case. But even that didn't make sense. His brother never warped what he learned. In fact, he went out of his way to highlight the inaccuracies many churches swept aside when it didn't fit their message of hatred.

Emma didn't want to learn history to amplify historically repressed white people. As if such an oxymoron existed. No, she wanted to master history so she could bury the truths of minorities. She wanted to undermine the impact of BIPOC people, hide the roles of women, and pretend the queers were just roommates, close friends, or anything heteronormative. She was bigoted trash, and Rus despised her.

"I'll be honest," he said through gritted teeth. "I want to punch her in her snide, little face."

"You and me both," Daysha replied. "And about a thousand others."

After they left the building, Rus followed Daysha across campus, letting her lead the way. He didn't have another class for two hours, so he was content wandering aimlessly. Especially since he didn't have much else to distract him from his Friday plans. With the semester only recently starting up, the coursework had remained relatively light. With his community service finished, his schedule remained all too flexible.

"Grab a bite before class?"

Rus wrinkled his nose. "I'm not really that hungry."

"Well, unlike someone, I have four back-to-back classes today, so now or never." Daysha booked her schedule super heavy on Wednesday and Thursday to lighten the rest of her week. Actually, their history class together was the only Monday-Wednesday-Friday course Daysha had this semester, focusing most of her coursework to Tuesday-Thursday or the big three-hour block class that met weekly on Wednesday. It helped lighten the rest of her week for work and Pride Club and pretty much anything else she wanted to focus on.

Rus tried to take part in the Pride Club meetings but found he didn't mesh with the queer campus group as well as Daysha. She navigated the daily politics much more delicately than someone of Rus' brash nature.

There were a lot of great ideas floating around in Pride and some solid members, but Rus found that, as a group, things often turned into this debate on morals, where any misstep was treated as intolerance. Lots of purity politics. It was something Rus had recognized in his behavior once upon a time, finding fault with everyone as a teen for failing to uphold whatever ridiculous moral compass dictated Rus' life. Eventually, he realized there had to be room for mistakes, for growth, and to accept that people had imperfections. He didn't have the energy to argue with Pride members—who he mostly liked despite their virtue signaling—while they turned their compassion into a competition, looking for any flaws in similarly minded peers so they could go to war with them for not being tolerant enough.

Speaking of war, as they made their way into the campus café, Daysha broke away to grab some pizza and sushi, while Rus went for something light and snack-ish. Of course, he had to pick the same salad bar as Emma and her friend Landon.

"Oh my fucking God, look at this dumb bitch," Landon said with a heinous hyena laugh, holding his phone up for Emma.

Landon had a terrible tan of someone who spent way too much time under UV lights. His bleach-blond hair looked extra brassy under the fluorescent lighting, and that made Rus smirk. But it was the colorful yet conservative outfit the pencil-thin Landon wore that confused Rus the most. It was how Rus imagined clowns in cages dressed.

The pair snickered, poking fun at a fat person with vibrant fire hydrant red hair. They kept their clothing masculine and their makeup flamboyant while their features were more androgynous. It didn't take long for Rus to realize Landon and Emma were mocking some enby creator's content. They did ramble, hyper-fixated on something, but Rus hadn't heard enough to piece together the topic of the video. Still, he edged in closer, skulking and furious at Emma and Landon, who mocked the video in full two times over before Landon went to respond in his own recording.

POLITICS AND POLY

"Okay, okay, I know folks are always worried about them sending us to camps"—Landon wriggled vigorously as if that added more merit to his point or undermined the reality that people truly hated queer people in this country—"but lemme just say if they do, please don't bunk me with this weirdo. Like, lock me up and throw away the key, but please keep *that* in a separate cabin."

Emma cackled in the background, the pair making light of the idea of detention centers. A joke in their minds because even the reality of these types of facilities didn't matter to them.

"Seriously, this is why people can't take the gay community seriously," Landon continued, moving closer to the register. "Trans people always do too much; they make it their whole identity."

"All while not committing to an identity," Emma said, careful to keep herself off camera.

"Exactly," Landon said with pitchy agreement. "I can't stand that. Don't get me started on why the T is just there to add tea to our cause."

"Well, it's not really a cause," Emma corrected.

Landon, the obedient trash he was, nodded affirmingly, likely terrified to be perceived as the type of queer person to make it his whole identity. Rus never understood the argument for such things. Of course, there was more to every queer person than their identity, but if they didn't make their queerness part of themselves, embrace who they were, they'd end up a self-loathing cunt like Landon, bending over backwards to please heteronormative ideology. Internalized homophobia was pathetic and disgusting.

Rus nearly cracked his plate as he smacked the silver spoon holding black olives onto his salad. Not that Emma or Landon noticed, wrapped up in the bitchy retorts on how trans people didn't exist in the LGB and why it was important their mental illness wasn't lumped into the community.

A funny commentary Emma supported, all while keeping her face off camera, likely too soft for the mic of Landon's phone to catch. Especially since he felt the need to repeat her points before ending his video.

Yes, Rus had stalked enough of both their social media platforms to know they each painted themselves very differently. Emma offered kind and conservative advice, presenting the perfect picture of compassion—completely opposite of her real-life behavior. Landon, on the other hand, presented himself as a no-nonsense gay man who wanted to show that not all gay people were terrible liberals obsessed with grooming children and making their gayness their whole personality.

Rus hated Landon even more than he despised Emma. The worst kind of gay person was a conservative. Though that held true for any minority who licked at the boots of their oppressor, and believed they were somehow different.

Thankfully, Rus never had a single class with Landon Cross. He'd had the misfortune of watching Landon's hot takes online, finding the algorithm sent him to Landon's videos on more than one occasion, which was his own fault for his obsessive need to know the enemy.

Landon believed that being gay didn't have to be someone's entire personality, a truth warped to serve the bigotry of hiding queerness so as to not offend the straight overlords. Landon's effeminate behavior only further irritated Rus, knowing he didn't appreciate that sassy swagger was only tolerated because hundreds of thousands of queer people fought so he could be so uninformed. Also, despite his fem attitude, Landon suffered from unchecked misogyny. Not shocking, considering he hung out with trad-wife wannabe Emma Alexander, who only wanted a degree to find a man.

"Do you know anything about the queer community?" Rus slammed his tray onto the table, sliding into the booth, and joining Emma and Landon.

Daysha reluctantly followed Rus' lead. The café had plenty of seating, and forcing his way into the same booth would definitely cause problems, but all the same, Rus had had enough of biting his tongue.

Landon rolled his eyes. "I know about the gay community, yes. I know there is a lot of political propaganda to force—"

"What about the L?" Rus jumped in quickly. "Do you know why the L comes first?"

Landon didn't respond, likely surprised by the turn Rus had taken. The biggest issue with Landon was his war on queerness, focused on undermining and belittling the trans communities involved in the so-called LGB.

"Come on, tell me why the G decided to put the L first," Rus said, goading Landon. "I know you're not a history major like your lavender beard, Emma, but surely you can show me what you know about *gay* history. This is one of our most important moments."

Rus wanted to point out Landon's hypocrisy and show his bigotry extended to all members of the queer community. Hell, even the gays weren't safe from Landon, a self-hating gay with enough internalized homophobia to make even the biggest bigots blush.

"I'll give you a hint, it's not alphabetical," Rus teased. "So, why is the L first?"

Landon stayed silent.

"That's so weird." Rus gestured emphatically at Landon. "Here you are advocating the importance of the *gay* community, how it's just the L, the G, and the B, please hold the fucking T. Running your damn mouth about the importance of not lopping orientation with gender mental illness—because you're the kind of dumbass who thinks they'll draw the line at gender dysphoria being a mental illness and won't push homosexuality right on into the *strait*jacket even though they already have, another historical fact you don't know about your own goddamn community—but the strangest part of all this is that you don't know one of the most fundamental aspects of the gay community you pretend to advocate for."

"If you're going to run your mouth about Stonewall, lemme stop you there." Landon held up a hand with a snap of his fingers. "It wasn't as pivotal as the rewritten history would have folks believe. The gay movement actually started…"

Emma nodded in support like she'd coached Landon on his bullshit speech about gay rights like either of them knew a goddamn thing.

"I'm honestly not even sure how you think lesbians played a role in Stonewall, but whatever." Landon shrugged.

"I didn't say they did," Rus continued. "You tied in Stonewall, dismissing a milestone that actually afforded you the right to flaunt your effeminate ass here without getting the shit beat out of you for existing."

Landon gasped, true offense etched onto his face. "See, you are the bigot."

"They always are," Emma added, taking a bite of her salad. "They pretend to care about causes, but they're just looking for ways to bully good people, belittle beliefs, and be homophobic to gays who don't agree with them. It's despicable."

Rus buried his rage, content with continuing his lesson that Landon wouldn't appreciate.

"Let's focus on the L and why it comes first. Way back when the government prayed AIDs would wipe out the faggots of America, they had no one to rely on," Rus said. "That's right, your lovely conservatives were counting the days until every homo met a brutal, agonizing death. And they thanked Jesus for it."

Rus made a mocking cross sign over his chest, then flipped off the ceiling to show Landon and Emma exactly what he thought of their phony deity.

"So, fun history lesson." Rus turned his attention to Emma really quickly. "I know you don't like that kind of stuff, especially since this lesson explains how queer women had an impact on history. Two evils, one stone."

Emma scoffed, doing her best to poorly ignore Rus. It wasn't much, but he knew he'd gotten a rise out of her, and that high would make up for the rough morning of class.

"During this epidemic, where gay men were suffering and dying and being smited by the US government under the guise of God, it was only the lesbians who truly stepped up. They rallied in a way only women can. They came together to donate blood, to offer comfort, to give peace, community, and love to their dying brothers."

Rus let his words soak in, knowing Landon wouldn't grasp the importance of this unity, wouldn't give a damn about the L coming first. He was a conservative gay who hated trans people for making *his* life harder. The type of man who blamed trans people for the homophobia he faced, with no sense or care for where the bigotry stemmed. It wouldn't surprise Rus if Landon were one of those stupid gays who bought into the petty bullshit of being rivals with lesbians, as if such a thing should ever exist in community.

"Sorry, hun. I don't argue with debate bros," Emma said with a spiteful lilt in her cheery voice. "I get that the basis of your knowledge is to pin people down in a verbal altercation where you can feel superior based on your silly little word play, but just because you can talk out of your ass doesn't mean much of anything."

Rus scoffed, sick and tired of morons treating knowledge like a dirty tactic because they remained willfully ignorant. "Other than facts, statistics, truths, literally anything, because—"

"All garbage at the end of the day." Emma shrugged dismissively. "Facts are just well-rehearsed lies, stats are just mathematical propaganda, and the truth is in the eye of the beholder. Jesus knows the doubt in your lies, even if Satan helps you hide it from yourself."

"Oh, fuck you."

Emma nodded, conveying this phony sympathy. No, more like pity, which only further pissed Rus off. He clenched a fist under the table, pressing it hard to his bouncing knee. Her gaze held this satisfied dismissal that only further ate away at Rus.

"Anyway, we should be going," Landon said, feeding off Emma's attitude and adding to his own smugness.

Emma and Landon took their leave.

"Bitches," Daysha muttered.

"Yup."

"You know that whole rise above thing I push for most days?"

Rus nodded.

"You can totally sink to their level." Daysha gestured in Emma's direction. "I'll join you."

"If I knew I'd just get community service again, I'd seriously consider running them both over."

Daysha snorted.

"But alas, I should probably do the mature thing and just hit them with words, even if sticks and stones would be so much more effective." Rus sighed.

As much as he wanted to punch some sense into Emma and her gay prop, he knew it wouldn't make any difference. Fuck. Had he actually learned something from those stupid court-mandated anger management sessions?

CHAPTER 4
DYLAN

DYLAN showered away the grime of a long day at work, then sprayed enough cologne to cover up his three-in-one shampoo, conditioner, and body wash. The facial hair lining his neck had a few odd strays that didn't lay uniform with the rest of his finely trimmed beard, and Dylan took his time clipping them with the tiny scissors Kaiden had bought him.

Honestly, most of Dylan's hygiene routine and products had been at Kaiden's behest. Kaiden had become the fairy godgay Dylan never realized he needed. Granted, Dylan lost interest in all the upkeep of using a dozen different bottles for hair, skin, face, facial hair, sensitive skin, this or that, and whatever else. But there were some things Dylan found himself keeping a routine for.

When it came to his body hair, Dylan let his chest and stomach grow as wildly as they wanted. Same with his arms and legs. He did trim his crotch hairs from time to time. Much like his beard, which itched a lot less now that he didn't let it become unkempt.

After finishing his routine, he'd mostly air-dried, so he tossed his towel in the hamper and threw on a breezy outfit. Since he'd grown up in Dorothy's Home, he learned long ago to handle the lack of privacy any way he could. As a grown man, strutting around in just a towel wasn't going to cut it like when he lived here as a resident.

Dylan checked in on Jasmine, who was unwinding in one of the smaller bedrooms she'd claimed as her own. Only her and Dylan had the privacy of their own rooms, while all the teen residents had to share their space. But Jasmine tried to ensure the bigger rooms in the house went to those who bunked together. Even when she saddled four to a single room, they landed the master bedroom with a built-in bathroom. Everyone compromised in their own ways.

"You sure you're going to be good tonight?" Dylan poked his head into Jasmine's room. "I'll have my phone on if you need anything."

Jasmine waved him off. "Go have fun. What have I said about clocking out?"

"And what have I said about not giving me an actual time sheet?"

Technically, Dylan only worked part-time at Dorothy's Home, since that was all Jasmine could afford. Still, it came with housing and food and peace of mind. Truthfully, Dylan spent way more time giving back to the home that got him off the streets and gave him a chance at a future. But he'd do it for free if Jasmine wanted.

"Just be careful, sweetie," Jasmine said. "I've heard Himbos has been getting hit lately."

Dylan quirked a brow, quizzically.

"Crime, hun."

"Damn wicked gays." Dylan tsked and shook his head disapprovingly before cracking a smile.

"It's not a joke," Jasmine clarified. "There have been muggings, assaults. It's not always safe wandering around the wrong parts of downtown late at night."

"Here I thought Himbos aimed to be one of those upscale clubs."

"You know what I mean." Jasmine pointed a finger, poking Dylan in the chest with her nail.

He rolled his eyes because, as ridiculous as it was, the warning was valid. Sadly, it was the price of existing and the risk of creating openly queer spaces. All the same, Dylan learned how to handle himself in precarious and dangerous elements years ago as a teenager who did what he had to do in order to get by before Jasmine dragged him off the streets and into her queer youth home.

"Now, just because you're being safe doesn't mean you can't turn this into a fun weekend." Jasmine did a little shimmy, enthusiastically smiling. "Take the weekend and really enjoy yourself, sweetie."

"Yes, ma'am." Dylan grinned.

He did have the weekend off, which almost never happened between his side jobs, his holiday hustles, and his position at Dorothy's Home. He took his job almost as seriously as Jasmine when it came to running the youth home, but she'd insisted he spend a little time being free from responsibility.

"Oh my God," a high-pitched voice called out from behind Dylan. "Please tell me you're not wearing that ugly ass outfit in public."

Dylan frowned, taking in the judgmental once-over from the residential fashionista, Miguel Alvarado-Hernandez.

He was a short, slender teen with a bronze complexion, complemented by the oversized powder-pink polo that he kept tucked in the front and hanging out in the back. Did Dylan question Miguel's fashion choices? Certainly, but only to himself. Miguel had already schooled him on trendsetting enough to make his head spin.

"I was just about to change," Dylan said, making his way past Miguel and to his bedroom.

He slipped into some loose jeans and a crop top, which he hoped Rus might like.

"The 80s called and said you're doing it wrong," Miguel announced, inviting himself into Dylan's room.

"The 80s called, and you answered?" Dylan asked, aghast. "Then why do you always send me to voicemail?"

"Fine, the 80s texted," Miguel huffed, then plopped onto the edge of the bed.

Years of living in a home with so many teens rotating in and out had taught Dylan not to expect privacy of any kind.

"So, where you going?"

"Downtown."

"Where downtown?"

"Thinking a biker bar, maybe a pool hall. I might just wander the streets aimlessly singing showtunes."

Miguel rolled his eyes. "Uh-huh."

Dylan searched through his belts, trying to pick one out. Miguel made a face at Dylan's two choices, so he set them down and ran his hand over a rack where his belts hung. It was like a metal detector, only instead of a beep, Miguel's expression softened when Dylan's hand landed on a choice he didn't find revolting.

"So, going out with Kaiden?"

"Yup."

"Again."

"I guess."

"You two hang out a lot."

"When we can." Dylan shrugged. "Our schedules can get pretty busy."

"Must be hard, being away from him and all."

"Excuse me?" Dylan fastened his belt and turned back to Miguel.

"Come on, we all know you two have a thing. Just wondering if you're going to walk on eggshells the entire time."

"A thing?"

"Yeah, he's your situationship."

"I do not have a situationship."

"Oh, so your DL boyfriend?" Miguel nodded affirmatively. "Good for you. Big step."

"Kaiden is my friend," Dylan said, quite slowly in a slightly mocking tone. "Not all queer men need a situationship."

And maybe he'd contemplated a situationship at one point or another with Kaiden, but he really did like their friendship. If Dylan knew the first thing about healthy relationships, he'd have asked Kaiden out a lifetime ago. Now, he was content with their friendship and didn't need Miguel's mockery.

"Yeah, bitch, I know," Miguel replied. "And not all friends need to spend their every waking minute of free time tied to each other, or text bullshit memes at all hours of the day, or—"

"Yes, they do!" Dylan protested. "That's what friendship is."

"Gurl, he could slap you in the face with his dick, and you'd say that was friendship."

"Okay, first off, no one is slapping each other with their genitals," Dylan said with the reddest face—so red, he felt the heat burn from his neck to his cheeks. "Second of all, where in the hell did this come from?"

"Am I the only one who—"

"Hey, what the fuck are you doing?" Chelsea stormed into Dylan's bedroom, arms flailing and bringing the heavy aroma of bleach wafting inside.

Chelsea Blisston used to be one of the sweet, quieter residents living at Dorothy's Home. While Dylan was grateful the timid trans girl had found her voice, he did wish it came with fewer profane outbursts. Thanks to her friendship with the sassiest guy in town, she'd learned to drop a swear word with nearly every breath she took. Miguel, naturally, encouraged the attitude.

"Are you gonna finish with my goddamn hair or sit in here jerking your dick all night?" Chelsea had foil around her hair, currently soaked in bleach products.

"Language," Jasmine shouted from another room.

She was more of a stickler about vulgarities than Dylan, but she also put more effort into getting her teens ready for the world.

"Well, bitch?" Chelsea planted her hands on her hips, glaring at Miguel.

"Oh, yeah, I almost forgot." Miguel slid off the bed, giving Dylan a finger wave goodbye before turning to Chelsea. "You sure you want to go with blue, pink, and purple? I get the whole bi pride blah, blah, blah, but your pasty ass face can't handle those colors without looking like a wrecked ass meth head pop star doll."

"Fuck off, fruitcake." Chelsea shoved a laughing Miguel.

He sidestepped away from her and started twerking. "Not a fruitcake, but a poundcake."

"More like a pounded out cake," Chelsea scoffed.

"You two are about to be a grounded out cake if you don't watch your mouths," Jasmine said from afar, making anyone in earshot burst out into a raging cackle.

With that, Dylan left a little early to avoid any more conversation from the house and considered where his evening with Rus and Kaiden would lead. If he got lucky, he might be able to find someone for Kaiden to hit on so he could figure out if he and Rus had anything in common. Well, enough in common to determine if Dylan wanted more than friendship and more than a casual fuck. Although it had been a while since he'd rolled between anyone's sheets.

He opened an app on his phone, doomscrolling through blank profiles, and contemplating just how much time he had before clubbing.

> Rus: Is it okay if I bring a friend?

Dylan sighed. Was this a friend or a *friend*? He wanted to get clarification, but resigned himself to sending a polite, non-intrusive response.

> Dylan: Of course. The more the merrier or gayer or something holly jolly.

Rus replied with a string of laughing cry faces.

So much for Dylan's plan to break away from Kaiden. If Rus had a friend coming, then this truly was a group adventure. Which was fine—Dylan did want to be friends with Rus. Then again, maybe Rus was bringing a friend so when he and Dylan broke away from Kaiden, all would be well. Or maybe the friend was for Dylan because perhaps Rus had a thing for Kaiden. After all, it was his idea for the clubbing night. Hmmm. Maybe Dylan was overthinking this too much.

He decided to bury the what-ifs and focused on having a fun night out.

The drive to Kaiden's went quickly, but Dylan waited in his car for about fifteen minutes when he arrived. Three cars were crammed in the driveway, which meant the whole house was home. Dylan didn't know if he had the bandwidth for Kaiden's entire family. He texted to let him know he was outside.

> Kaiden: Come on in. Be ready in 10.

Dylan snorted with a tsk of disapproval. That meant thirty minutes minimum. Knowing Kaiden, he hadn't even gotten dressed yet.

Dylan walked up to the house, knocked on the door, and planned on beelining directly to Kaiden's bedroom.

Kaiden's nephews opened the door—seven and nine, if Dylan remembered correctly. All he knew was they were pint-sized and rowdy.

"You got candy?" one asked.

"Money?" the other asked, shoving his brother.

Dylan simply stared blankly.

"Loser."

"You're a loser." The little one shoved his brother.

"Wasn't talking to you, idiot." He shoved him back, and soon, they were running through the house, smacking each other and throwing things.

Dylan learned several visits back that if he froze and didn't respond, they moved on like a T-Rex—or at least how movies made the T-Rex out to be. Who really knew, right?

Kaiden's sister swept through the living room, smacking her boys on the back of the head and yelling at them to go to their bedroom.

"Why are you two still up, anyway?" she shouted. Not that she was entirely wrong since it was almost nine o'clock, but she probably shouldn't be the one asking her kids why they were still awake past their bedtime. Assuming they had a bedtime—Dylan wasn't sure about that.

Sandra stared at Dylan, sizing him up for a moment, and took a long drag off her cigarette. "A little dressed down for a fundraiser, wouldn't you say?"

Was Sandra mixing up her dates, or was Kaiden withholding information? Dylan didn't have the slightest idea, but it cost him nothing to play along.

"I'm getting ready before we head out," Dylan lied with a big ole smile, much to Sandra's disgust.

"Seems a little late."

"We're treating it like a New Year's celebration." Dylan puckered his lips.

Sandra scowled, oozing disgust for Dylan's attitude or presence. She never hid her feelings for Dylan or really anyone, seeing as she found most people irritating, including her own kids.

"Seems you're having one of these fundraisers every other day," she said snidely. "The least you could do is pay Kaiden for his time."

It was obviously easier for Kaiden to ditch his babysitting duties when working, so Dylan shot Sandra a tight smile and nodded affirmingly.

"Darn homeless teens demanding things like food, shelter, hygiene resources, health check-ups, and all that." Dylan's smile nearly folded into a grimace from Sandra's glare. "These fundraisers really are imperative to their well-being."

"Yeah, whatever." She tied her hair back into a tight bun. "What about my well-being?"

Dylan ignored her attitude; he also ignored the sound of a video game blasting from the nearby den. Sandra lived here with her husband and three children, but her husband never babysat the kids on his own. Whether he was working or between jobs, child rearing always fell to Sandra, who often passed it off to her mother during the days and bullied Kaiden into handling nights and weekends.

Since Kaiden lived with his parents rent-free, he made the most of the tough situation. Heat filled Dylan's chest while Sandra continued running her mouth about how inconsiderate Kaiden could be.

The thing that got to Dylan was that Kaiden didn't actually live rent-free. He did all the grocery shopping, paying for the whole household. If his sister bought stuff, she labeled it or bought things outside of Kaiden's diet restrictions. Kaiden helped his parents with utilities, too. He shared his bedroom with his nephews, while his sister only shared her room with her newborn.

"I'm going to go find Kaiden," Dylan blurted, fighting to keep the cheer in his voice.

Life had thrown hell at Dylan from an early age, but he'd learned long ago that smiling through the pain made it easier to bear. Fewer questions, too. But some folks wore on his good nature and made it challenging to stay so optimistic.

He turned to make his way down the hallway toward Kaiden's bedroom.

"He's in the basement," Sandra shouted.

Dylan shuddered, then cut through the kitchen. Since Kaiden shared his bedroom with his nephews, they'd moved some of his belongings into the basement, including his makeup station. Naturally, the family decided Kaiden's lifestyle would be far too confusing to explain to the boys. Men didn't wear makeup, so if Kaiden wanted to continue doing that, he needed a space away from the boys.

Of course, his parents sided with Kaiden's sister when it came to 'lifestyle choices,' rooming accommodations, and all things in general. Dylan didn't think about punching people very often, but Sandra was on his list. Along with her total provider of a husband, who Dylan only ever saw plastered to the couch. Kaiden's parents, too. The nephews on occasion, but Dylan would wait until they were unruly adults. Maybe they'd become better people.

"Die, die, die!" screamed one of the boys as he attempted to shove Dylan down the basement stairs.

Bewilderment stunned him silent, and both boys ran away faster than he could comprehend. Sandra started screaming at them from afar, possibly yelling at her crying baby too, but Dylan didn't stick around to clarify. He made his way down into the house dungeon.

Dylan hated the basement. Originally, when he learned Kaiden's family had moved some of his more flamboyant things downstairs, Dylan encouraged Kaiden to just move into the basement entirely. But as it turned out, this wasn't a livable basement. Dylan swung the door wide open, took a deep breath, and braced himself before heading down the steps. They creaked like a rickety bridge. The hollow gaps between each step sent a shiver through Dylan's body. That subconscious fear of a monster snatching him by the foot and tripping him always put him in a chokehold.

It didn't help that the basement had zero overhead lighting since the electrical had gone haywire years ago. Dylan had offered on more than one occasion to assist. He wasn't an expert, but he'd learned a lot of home maintenance hacks from Jasmine over the years while she kept their last home afloat. Sadly, Kaiden didn't want any improvements made to his parents' place.

He lived here reluctantly, doing his best to save up for his own place eventually.

"You're early," Kaiden said, applying eyeliner.

The makeup vanity had cool lining around the mirror, helping brighten the darkness around Kaiden. He kept a few portal spotlights around the station, using them to scrutinize every tiny detail of his makeup.

"Well, I didn't want to risk being late for the fundraiser."

Kaiden scoffed. "Is she still bitching about that? This is why I said fundraiser. I could be giving an orphan my kidney, and she'd complain it inconvenienced her. And the only reason she's pissed at me is because Mom is yelling at her about watching the boys all day and night, but like, why not make Tommy get off his lazy alpha ass and watch his own kids? Oh, because that's not manly, blah, blah, blah…"

"I know, I know," Dylan said as he leaned forward to position his head in line with the mirror, next to Kaiden's face. "I played along. Always do."

"Thank you." Kaiden puckered his lips and blew a playful kiss at the mirror.

He went back to work, finishing his makeup, while Dylan stood anxiously in the basement. There was nothing in the shadows, but it didn't stop Dylan's imagination from playing tricks and suspecting monsters lurking nearby.

Dylan focused on Kaiden, studying him as he worked on applying his makeup. Honestly, Kaiden was cute enough without all the glam, but he always looked quite majestic after painting his face. Even when he kept his look subtle or natural or whatever the right makeupology term was. Kaiden remained flawless.

"What do you think?" Kaiden asked, framing his face with his hands.

Only his hands were turned in a way that flaunted his pink fingernails. Dylan attempted to piece it together, thinking maybe the blush was pink, but he wasn't sure if Kaiden had put any on. Then he looked for pink accessories. Kaiden wore a black corset vest with silver designs and lacing up the back. He wore a white dress shirt underneath and black slacks. Nothing pink. His lips, maybe? Nope. Not even a light gloss.

"Looks great. Very matchy matchy," Dylan lied, swallowing hard as he awaited Kaiden's reply.

"You think?" Kaiden turned to face the mirror, leaning in close and studying his eyes.

It was then that Dylan noticed the slightest glint of pink on the corners of his eyes, lining the standard black eyeliner.

"Not too subtle?"

"Definitely not."

"Good. I didn't want to go too pink but thought a splash of color would be nice."

"The perfect amount of splash."

"Alrighty, let's get going before you claim I take forever again."

"I wasn't going to say anything."

"You were thinking it." Kaiden gave Dylan a judgy side eye.

"I'd never."

Kaiden nodded, teasingly knowing his friend all too well, then gestured for Dylan to walk up the creaky steps first. Much to Dylan's relief. Not that he believed in monsters, but this way, the shadows wouldn't grab him with Kaiden right there. Though then he'd have to rescue his friend, which would be damn near impossible if shadow monsters were real.

"You are such a baby," Kaiden said, practically reading Dylan's mind in a way only Kaiden ever could.

"Basements are universally creepy. You're the outlier here, not me."

"Uh-huh. I'll ask my sister if she has any spare pacifiers."

"It's not too late for you to drive yourself," Dylan said with a chuckle.

"I take it back, oh brave one, master of all bravery in the world."

"Damn straight…" Dylan playfully shrugged. "Adjacent."

The pair breezed through the house, speaking to no one and stopping for nothing until they reached the car. Dylan always followed Kaiden's lead when it came to family drama stuff, having no real understanding of family dynamics anyway. Then again, seeing how Kaiden's house worked, he wasn't sure their family had much understanding of the dynamics of family, either.

Dylan pushed the musings aside and cranked his car a few times before heading downtown.

CHAPTER 5
KAIDEN

KAIDEN and Dylan stood outside of Himbos, waiting on Rus. While Kaiden did his best to avoid eye contact with folks making their way up and down the busy downtown streets, Dylan held onto a lamppost, casually twirling around it. There wasn't a worry on his face as he scrolled through his phone, absentmindedly dangling on the post.

As Kaiden crept further away, he studied his friend. Always a bit envious of Dylan's carefree nature. Dylan finally looked up from his phone, laughing and searching for his friend. Kaiden stopped in his tracks as he nearly slipped the corner of Himbos club into the alleyway beside the building. It was the perfect hidden nook to avoid passersby.

"What're you doing all the way over there?" Dylan cut through a crowd of strangers.

His steps were effortless. There was a gracefulness in the way he weaved between each person, not disrupting their flow or being deterred from his own. When Dylan reached Kaiden, he snatched him by the arm and pulled his friend away from the alleyway.

"For someone who spends so much time perfecting his look, you sure do tend to hide it every time we go out." Dylan grinned, his goofy expression further illuminated by his big white teeth and devilish, finely trimmed beard.

It was true, Kaiden put a lot of effort into his image. His corset vests were the most expensive part of his wardrobe, and up until recently, he often had to have them taken in or replaced when his sizes changed. But they gave him confidence that he didn't know how to explain to Dylan.

Unlike Kaiden, Dylan let it all hang out. His tight stomach and perfect abs were almost always on display in some type of crop top. In fact, the only time Kaiden had seen him in a full-length shirt was for very formal events like the recent fundraiser or if he spotted Dylan in a work uniform. Even those he'd occasionally modify.

"You're going to be the envy of every guy here tonight." Dylan interlinked his arm around Kaiden's. "In fact, if you're not careful, I'm going to spend the night cockblocking the hotties coming to sweep you up. Can't have you ditching me too early."

Kaiden snorted, rolling his eyes in the process, but allowing himself to be pulled over to the lamppost and overcrowded street.

Kaiden didn't have a perfect stomach, a perfect body. In fact, he had the furthest thing from it. But he'd busted his butt to lose over a hundred pounds and finally take back his life. He really believed he'd finally feel comfortable in his own skin once he lost the weight. And most days, he really did, but with such a drastic loss of weight, Kaiden's skin didn't shrink with the rest of him. The corset vests wouldn't tighten the saggy skin, but they helped give him the waist and illusion he craved. The look he longed for after years of dieting and exercise.

There weren't many people who knew Kaiden before the weight loss. Sure, former classmates, but he didn't hang out with any of them. Old co-workers from the ghost of retail past. And, of course, there was his family, but they knew so little about him in general, he doubted they understood the effort he put into his health journey.

Dylan knew Kaiden at his highest and his fittest weight. The thing that always kept Kaiden close to his friend was how Dylan's attitude never changed. He didn't get nicer the more weight Kaiden lost. Most people weren't directly rude to him when he was fat, but they did pretend he didn't exist. Not Dylan, though. He didn't see Kaiden in a new light all of a sudden. It was comforting knowing Dylan always appreciated him, always saw him for who he was, and always knew how to drag his introverted friend out of his shell.

Kaiden was the introvert who desperately craved being an extrovert, whereas Dylan seemed like the extrovert content with the life of an introvert.

Having spent most of his life hiding under baggy clothes and long, unkempt hair, Kaiden now went the extra mile to stand out. Hair always styled, makeup flawless but not extreme, outfits ridiculously sexy, and even his nails were perfectly polished and on point. All the same, despite peacocking most days, he shied away from the attention he craved. A true enigma, perhaps.

"Aren't you looking all snazzy?" a raspy voice called out, drawing Kaiden's gaze.

Rus approached with a woman.

"This is my friend Daysha." Rus gestured to the woman beside him.

She wore a white dress, accentuating her dark brown complexion. The dress was tight at the top and flowy at the bottom, cut off at her knees. Daysha had a crimson belt that Kaiden suspected was supposed to match her bright red heels and fingerless gloves.

"Love the look," Daysha said, eyeing Kaiden up and down.

"Thank you." He blushed. "Right back at you."

"Yeah, it's really cool." Rus nodded. "I thought that whole thing was for the fundraiser, but it's really…yeah."

"I'd ask you to use your words, sweetie," Daysha said, rolling her eyes so rapidly her lashes fluttered. "But given you're the last living grunge in the world, we can't expect much."

"I was being nice." Rus' jaw dropped, and Kaiden couldn't tell if he was actually offended by Daysha's comment or if the two were joking.

Rus did look like a slacker, wearing a faded band shirt with bleach stains, tight jeans with frayed rips at the knees and thighs, and aggressively large combat boots. Were his feet actually that big?

"The corset thing is cool," Rus said, turning to make a face at Daysha, who merely pursed her lips and side-eyed her friend.

"It's not for everyone," Kaiden replied, understanding his corset vests received more crinkled expressions of disbelief than smiley faces of flattery, but he loved the confidence that came with wearing one. Sure, anxiety too, but Kaiden could never shake away the anxiety. He might as well throw a little confidence in there, too.

They all made their way into the long line of Himbos, paid their cover, and flocked to the bar. Even by nine, the crowd had swelled, making the wait for drinks chaotic. Rus ordered a blue motorcycle and seemed to regret it from the first sip, so he grabbed a beer to join the nasty gin cocktail. Dylan didn't order since he never drank. Daysha got a cranberry vodka and ordered a second one before the bartender walked away.

"Whoa."

"It's been a week," she shouted over the music. "The semester just started; it shouldn't be this stressful."

"Oh, yeah, for sure." Kaiden nodded in agreement, not knowing a damn thing about semesters or college coursework or any of that headache.

He turned to grab his vodka water and squeezed a fruity blue raspberry flavored spray into the drink. He was about to drink his calories tonight and then some. He also suspected that after a sugary buzz of booze, he'd be convincing Dylan to take him for two-in-the-morning pizza. So, being sensible, he kept his calorie count safe during the drinks. Hopefully, he'd dance away his deficit.

The group slowly made their way to a couple of free seats, including a couch that Rus leapt onto, securing a space for him and Daysha.

"So, are you two, you know, like an item?" Kaiden asked.

Rus snorted, pointing a thumb at Daysha. "Am I dating her? No."

"Like I'd date some scrawny, pasty boy with so many anger issues even the drywall punching Kyle's of the world would be shocked."

The way she rolled such a convoluted insult out so quickly took Kaiden a moment to piece together. He still didn't understand the full context, but he laughed with everyone else.

"Like you'd date any boy," Rus quickly countered.

"True, but come on, if I were going to date a guy, I'd have standards." Daysha waved a hand, gesturing to all of Rus. "I can do so much better than this tiny tyrant."

"Not tiny where it counts," Rus boasted.

"OhMyGod," Daysha gagged. "You're giving off small dick energy."

"Wounded." Rus clasped his chest and collapsed in his seat, sinking until his knees reached the floor. "I am moderate, I swears."

The group laughed louder, taken aback by Rus' pinky measurement as he held both together.

"That's a snow day in the South." Rus nodded frantically. "Lots of inches, right?"

Kaiden turned his attention to Daysha, composing himself. "So, you're a lesbian?"

She shook her head. "Ace."

"Ace ace baby," Rus said to the tune of a song. "But she's also my lavender wife in case the world goes to Hell."

"More to Hell," Daysha clarified. "The fire's bearable right now."

Kaiden chuckled, enjoying the conversation, and sinking into this seat as he listened to Rus and Daysha go back and forth for another five minutes, lovingly insulting each other.

"I need another drink," Rus said, guzzling the last of his blue motorcycle. "It shouldn't be this goddamn abomination, but I think I'm starting to like it."

"That's what my folks said about me," Dylan blurted with a laugh.

"Oh my fucking god, Dylan!" Kaiden roared, cackling at the comment. "You can't just casually drop trauma as a joke mid-conversation."

"Is there any other way?" Dylan smirked, goofy and slightly oblivious.

"Oh shit," Rus said. "Are your parents not cool with…" Rus gestured at Dylan up and down.

"Nope, not even the tiniest," Dylan replied. "Part of why I'm so involved with Dorothy's Home."

"Okay, okay." Rus nodded. "I gotta ask. Why name it Dorothy's Home and not Jasmine's Home? Like, didn't she found it?"

"You don't know the story? Okay, I got you." Dylan leaned forward.

"I'm going to get everyone another round," Kaiden said, double-checking drink requests before walking away.

He already knew the reason behind the name. Apparently, Dorothy's Home was named after the phrase "Are you friends with Dorothy?" which used to be a code queer people used back in the 40s and 50s. Dorothy from Wizard of Oz, so it probably had something to do with the whole rainbow shit, or maybe because the Tin Man was played by a gay dude. Kaiden knew the gist; he'd heard Dylan explain it to potential donors more than once.

He also knew Dylan's origin story. Well, the barest of details. Dylan didn't discuss much, but Kaiden had pieced together enough to build a basic timeline. Dylan got kicked out when he was fourteen—or so Kaiden assumed. Most of the teens living at Dorothy's Home landed there after being kicked out by their parents, so it wasn't a stretch to think the same had happened to Dylan. Though Kaiden didn't know much about how Dylan got by until he found Jasmine at fifteen.

Kaiden didn't press about the gap between them. It wasn't something Dylan willingly offered, and when thinking about that time, it seemed to be one of the few moments Kaiden would notice Dylan's smile fall away.

"Hey," said a guy at the bar beside Kaiden.

"Oh, sorry." Kaiden immediately scooted away, offering him space.

"No, I was like, um, saying hi."

"Oh, sorry." Kaiden grinned. "Loud in here. Didn't realize."

"Yeah, very loud." The guy nodded in agreement, moving to close the distance between them. "Trying to grab a drink, then step outside for some air."

"Nice."

"Yeah, but I can't find my lighter. Sucks."

"Yeah, definitely," Kaiden agreed. "I don't smoke. I mean, not cigarettes."

"Oh, okay." The guy paused for a moment, and Kaiden couldn't figure out his expression.

The bartender returned with his drinks, and Kaiden quickly grabbed them and left. When the guy turned to say something, Kaiden pressed ahead. He wasn't sure why this guy wanted to talk to him, but it didn't make any sense.

"Dude, what was that?" Rus asked, grabbing his blue cocktail and biting the rim of the plastic cup. "He was flirting with you."

"No, he wasn't."

"Yes, he was." Daysha nodded. "Even I saw that. He's still staring at you."

"Kind of creepy," Dylan said. "But in a cute weirdo way."

"You should go back and flirt with him," Rus said.

"No, he's just looking for a lighter. He's heading outside anyway."

"Then you can be his hero." Rus withdrew a lighter from his pocket. "Always carry a spare."

"No, it's too late."

"It's never too late." Rus tossed the lighter to Kaiden, which bounced against his palm a few times as he bopped it, trying and failing to catch it.

"I'm really bad at flirting," Kaiden admitted a bit too readily as he knelt to pick up the lighter.

The vodka water with raspberry flavoring had a strong bite and an even stronger boozy afterglow. It made his words spill more freely. It didn't help that Rus kept digging in.

"We're all bad at flirting," he said. "Well, with people we like. If you don't like the person, the banter just pours out, no awkward delay or secondhand embarrassment."

"Truth," Daysha said, lifting her cranberry vodka. "I apparently give off flirty vibes all the time, even when I think I'm just being friendly."

"Oh no, sweetie." Rus patted Daysha's leg. "That's just because you have tits and a vagina. You could literally just stand there minding your own business, and some guy somewhere would assume you're flirting with him."

"Gross," Daysha said.

"And with that beautiful commentary, I think it's time we dance away the awkward." Dylan nodded to the dance floor, which was slowly growing.

Kaiden mostly hated dancing, knowing he lacked rhythm and didn't feel cute enough to pull off awkward movements. Still, he enjoyed the carefree nonsense when dragged out with Dylan, so he let his friend lead the way.

Daysha and Dylan had the most grace, each moving in sync with each other and anyone who joined them for a moment. Rus thrashed about like a wild beast fighting the air. Kaiden recalled briefly learning about mosh pits, where deranged people beat each other up and called it dancing. That seemed very much like Rus' style. Kudos to him; he definitely cleared the floor and made room. Also, despite his chaotic attitude and wild behavior, he looked like he was having a blast.

Kaiden definitely disappeared twice to grab another drink. He wasn't the only one. It seemed Rus required more of his blue motor fuel to kick back. The looser Kaiden got, the easier he swayed, enjoying the loud music and random people bumping into him.

Hours passed on the dance floor, booze blurred the night away, and laughter made for a carefree freedom Kaiden had almost forgotten. Each time he jumped up with Rus, he forgot about his job. Every time Daysha pulled him in to sing lyrics he didn't quite understand, he forgot his sister's complaints. When Dylan dragged him into a dance number his body couldn't follow, he let the nonstop babysitting wash away. It was just a night for him, for his friends, for fun.

Goddamn, Kaiden loved every drunken second of the nonsense.

The lights went up momentarily, flashing to announce the shift in the evening. When everything dimmed again, spotlights went to the stage where a drag queen stepped out. She wore a glittering dress, flowy and big in all the most dramatic ways. Her heels were huge, yet she stepped with grace. Her makeup was vibrant, her hair done up.

"Welcome everyone's favorite queen to the stage!" said the MC who'd handled the music earlier.

"Fuck you, Charlie." Amber Ale pointed at the MC as she strutted onto the stage.

Laughter followed her entrance.

POLITICS AND POLY

"Heeeeeey, you ugly bitches." Amber Ale posed for the applause. "Why are you cheering? I just insulted you."

The roars of the audience increased, accompanied by a few hecklers, but they were drowned out quicker than Kaiden or anyone could hear.

"This is why I hate this goddamn generation," Amber Ale shook her head disapprovingly. "Ugly, dumb, and annoying as hell. But damn, at least y'all know what you're doing in bed."

"Wooo!" Rus shouted alongside a whole slew of hyped, drunken fools.

The more Amber Ale bashed the audience, the more they loved it. She made her rounds, insulting clothing, makeup choices, and even the features of some of the pretty guests in attendance.

She paused at Kaiden, sized him up, then puckered her lips and blew a kiss.

That was probably the most complimentary experience of Kaiden's life. He could call it a night and a win at this rate.

"Bitch, what are you?" Amber Ale sized Rus up the same way she had Kaiden a moment ago. "Is that a duck?"

She pointed to the pink, purple, and blue bird tattoo on his neck.

"Goose."

"Duck, duck, goose motherfucker," Amber Ale shouted. "Why? Why a bisexual goose?"

"'Cause I'm a bisexual dude."

"That doesn't answer my question."

"Then you weren't listening, hun."

"Oooooh, mouthy," Amber Ale said, drawing the crowd's laughter. "I like it. So, are you here with your girlfriend looking for a boyfriend, or here with your boyfriend eyeing all the girl candy?"

"Just here with my friends," Rus said into the mic, a bit breathy as he laughed.

"Hmm. I'm gonna come back to you, sweetie. Can't tell if you're a hot mess or a hot bless me Father for I have sinned." Amber Ale pointed a finger at Rus, letting the spotlight hit him and the whole group, much to Kaiden's dismay. "But I'll get my answer, best believe it, sweetie."

With that, Amber Ale continued her rounds, mocking audience members on the front lines and then introducing a performer. The queen came out, dancing to 80s pop.

During the second performance, Kaiden caught a glimpse of the guy from the bar. He stood alone, nervously sipping his drink, as he eyed the crowd. Kaiden dug into his pocket and fiddled with the lighter Rus had loaned him. It was a waste of time. There was no way that guy was actually flirting with Kaiden. He knew that. Still, he longed for a little flattery, hoped for butterflies of excitement, and wondered if maybe he was wrong and this was an opportunity.

"I'm going to go, um, you know…" Kaiden nodded across the way.

Dylan eyed the guy and turned to Kaiden.

"Okay, okay, have fun," Dylan said. "But be sure to let me know if you need an out. I can be a total menace if needed."

"Me too," Rus chimed in, scowling with a tiny smile. "I'll go all agro."

"I can also offer an out." Daysha pointed a finger at Kaiden, then steered her pointed hand toward the crowded bathrooms at the other side of the club. "But only after I take a piss. Those goddamn cranberry vodkas."

Kaiden made his way through the crowd, politely squeezing between people, and over to the guy from the bar.

"Hey."

The guy nodded.

"Ever find that lighter?"

He shook his head.

"Well, you're in luck." Kaiden held up the lighter. "Maybe we can step out after the show."

"Sure."

They stayed and watched the drag performers come out one by one and lip-sync to a brilliantly choreographed dance number. Amber Ale undermined every queen who came out, reminding the audience she was the only one worth worshipping. Everyone laughed at her caustic comments, grateful not to be on the wrong end of her barbs.

"I'm Kaiden, by the way," he said during a lull between performances.

"James," the guy replied, keeping his eyes fixed on the empty stage and avoiding eye contact.

Kaiden found it a little awkward and a lot adorable. At least he wasn't the only one struggling with small talk for a change.

The pair made their way through the crowded club, and Kaiden handed him the lighter as they approached the indoor/outdoor smokers' section. James took the lighter, stuffed it in his pocket, and led the way further toward the front.

"You don't want to head over there?" Kaiden pointed to the smoker's section of the club. An outside venue that was still walled off by the club. Sort of like an enclosure within Himbos walls.

"Too crowded." James shook his head, leading Kaiden to the front door exit.

Kaiden hesitated, staring at the bouncer and the sign that made it very clear that if you left, you paid for your cover again. No in and out from customers.

"I'll get you on the way back in," James said, giving Kaiden a coy smile.

There was tension in his cheeks, clearly as nervous as Kaiden, so he followed him outside, hoping the cold air would ease his anxiety.

The streets were mostly empty. Kaiden suspected most people were in bars and avoiding wandering for another hour or so. Still, James led the way to the corner alleyway between buildings.

Just as they cut the corner, a bitter breeze hit Kaiden, sending him stepping in close to James. He hadn't meant to brush up against him, but he desperately needed to get away from the wind. Now, they safely stood in the alleyway, away from the frigid air.

James's expression soured at Kaiden's close proximity. He recoiled, arm retreating just enough to shove Kaiden off him. The sudden push knocked Kaiden off kilter. He winced at the jagged lining of the brick wall. His head bobbed back with a sharp, quick crack.

Hate replaced James' coy smile, and Kaiden wondered if he'd become delirious after knocking into the wall.

"Don't touch me, fag."

Kaiden shivered, shrinking into himself. The pain from impact, the humiliation from James' venomous tone, and the fear from the looming shadows turning the corner. Kaiden's breathing hastened, his mind flooded with worry. What was happening? Why was this happening? How had he been so stupid in believing someone actually liked him?

CHAPTER 6
RUS

PIN prickles ran along the short hairs of Rus' arms. He couldn't explain it, but the heat of the club had washed over him in such a way that it created a cold sweat.

"Take this away from me," Rus said, sipping his blue motorcycle with way too much gin. "This antifreeze is gonna kill me."

"Oh, hush," Dylan said with a laugh, disappearing the plastic cup onto a tray one of the go-go dancers-turned-drink server carried. "You okay?"

"No," Rus said, digging in his pocket. "I need air. Fresh air."

"Wanna go outside?"

Rus looked over at the window where the smokers sat enclosed in a tiny pocket of outdoorsy freedom. Only, it wasn't freedom. The club had this wonderful outdoor venue for smokers to get some outdoor space while still within the walls of the club.

They looked like exotic pets on display, covered in smoke, flapping their mouths and waving their hands, and spreading their smoke like a poisonous nausea. It made Rus' stomach twist into knots, almost puking up his nicotine craving. But he buried that putrid feeling and focused on the calm that came with an inhale. Oh, how he wanted the solace of a single puff. The ease of tension as his lungs swelled, the release of stress as he blew out smoke.

"No, it's too crowded over there," Rus said, eyeing the front doors. "Ugh, but they're gonna charge us if we go outside *outside* again, aren't they?"

The enclosure provided a bit of luxury, giving smokers freedom to be outside without actually exiting the club, and it allowed the club an easy way to charge a cover every time someone crossed their threshold. Since they only invited twenty-one and up, they didn't bother with stamps for anyone, and patrons left early at their own risk. Rus gathered that much from the signs posted all around.

Rus could pay another five bucks to get in. But in his drunken stupor, five dollars truly felt like the end of the world. They would bankrupt him. He had to beat the system, defy them, defeat their vicious monopoly on robbing him for wanting to live his life. A life where he'd puff his smokes in peace.

"I know where to go," Dylan said, stuffing his hand in Rus' pocket.

The brief entanglement of their hands made Rus pause. His cheeks warmed, his body stilled, and his eyes locked with Dylan's.

"Follow me." Dylan yanked the pack of smokes from Rus' pants and led him through a dark corridor of the bar to another open venue, which split off to a side area with bathrooms and a "Do Not Enter" doorway.

"That's closed off." Rus hesitated.

"Not scared to break a rule or two, are you?" Dylan waggled his perfectly trimmed eyebrows.

Rus grinned. "Never."

The night was looking up. He hadn't realized how much fun Dylan was, finding him interesting from the start, but too straightlaced for Rus' taste. Danger and defiance appealed to Rus.

Dylan swung the door open, sauntering ahead, and encouraging Rus to follow. They stepped outside on a metallic platform connected to a small staircase leading to a hidden alleyway.

What a true slice of heaven. The moon's light crept through just enough to brighten this secret nook. The alleyway offered a buffer to the harsh wind from earlier. The secluded vibe kept everything silent. Everything except the muffled grunts nearby.

Rus tilted his head as he lit a smoke. His eyes locked with Dylan's for a moment. A second at most. The fear in his sweet, smiling eyes sent a shiver of terror through Rus.

Dylan tensed, petrified.

Rus kept his gaze shifting, following the strange sound, and found a group of men kicking someone crouched on the ground.

Under the darkness, Rus spotted red shimmering against vibrant green hair. He heard the whiny plea of pain. He felt the twinge of guilt for daring to relax.

Every fiber in Rus' body twisted into a state of alertness.

Six men stood over Kaiden, kicking him, laughing at him, beating him. Gay bashers. One was the jock who had flirted with Kaiden. A phony, a villain, a monster who dared to harm someone under Rus' watch.

The booze cleared from his head, and rage consumed him.

By the time Rus clenched his fists, he'd sobered up enough to beat the ever-living fuck out of these monsters.

"Go get help." Rus shoved Dylan toward the door.

The slam startled his crush, which hurt Rus. He didn't mean to harm him, but he needed him awake, aware, actionable.

"Now," Rus demanded.

He didn't know who Dylan could get. A bunch of drunken clubbers wouldn't do much good. Maybe Dylan could convince the bartenders to run outside. From his experience, they were often the most alert during drunken brawls. Surely, they'd be ready for bigots.

Once Dylan stumbled inside, Rus rushed down the steps. He didn't hesitate. He didn't falter. He readied himself for war. Six men against him. He didn't expect to win, didn't expect to stop them entirely. But he had to hope to draw their attention.

All Rus really wanted was to steal their focus. The sounds of pain Kaiden let out were horrifying. Miserable. Brutal. He yelped and cried and wheezed. Rus couldn't stand it, finding every second a misery he'd never escape.

"Get the fuck off him!" Rus barreled ahead, fists swinging as he lunged at two of the men.

He took them down with him, punching the entire time. When they shouted, he smacked harder, demanding blood as his knuckles cracked against their faces.

"Fuck you. Fuck you. Fuck you." Rus wriggled and swung and fought furiously.

The weight of another person twisted him off the two he pinned, so he kicked back. Legs moving in this deranged, methodical nature. Rus didn't have time to think, to feel. Someone hit him. Hit him hard. Hard enough to sober out the last few drops of booze in his system.

It didn't matter. He'd take a thousand punches to protect Kaiden. How dare they attack his friend?

Rus launched himself forward, finding a booted heel to greet his face the moment he gathered his bearings. Again and again, someone kicked him. More than someone. Multiple people kicked and punched him, making it impossible for him to claw his way up.

When he managed to get a swing in, he felt a harsh pelt against his arm. When he turned to look, someone bashed him in the head. When he buried himself, he managed to glance at Kaiden, who had been knocked away from the fight and was out of immediate danger.

Bloody and bruised, filled with fear, but alive.

"Run," Rus gurgled, finding a fist collide with his jaw as he struggled to send that wish.

If he died here, truly died at the hands of these hateful pricks, he didn't want Kaiden to join him. He didn't want anyone to feel this agony.

A moment ago, he was trying to have a cigarette, flirt with a guy he liked, and now he found himself surrounded by half a dozen men beating the ever-living shit out of him because of his existence.

He didn't know for certain why they attacked Kaiden, but he knew the reason the second he spotted them. This was fueled by hate. Their words between brutal strikes made that clear. They hated faggots, they wanted to kill them, to teach them a lesson for breathing, to end their queer plight on humanity.

"Die. Die. Die." The words raged between the assault.

Rus couldn't move, couldn't counter them. They hit him everywhere, again and again.

"Biiiiiiiitch," a queen screamed.

Rus knew her voice above anyone else. She'd spent half her show telling off the audience, introducing lesser queens, and making the night all about her.

Amber Ale's long blonde wig cut through the thicket of limbs, beating Rus. She swung a bat, screeching profanities.

"Get 'em," she shouted, a gloved finger pointing to some dickless prick as a group of queens followed her lead.

Soon, a flurry of drag queens leapt into the fray, beating these bigots back. Fists swung. Heels dug into skin. Queens roared. No one relented.

The men fought back, true menaces to society, refusing to be beaten by creeps in dresses. They shouted slurs and made vicious threats.

The queens fought harder, shouted louder, and swung with more fury.

Soon, preserving dignity meant nothing. They had to preserve their lives. Amber Ale had the girls at her beck and call. None of them relented.

"Get 'em!" she shouted, demanded, ordered with a swing of her bat as the queens raged ahead, beating down bigots with style.

Rus pushed himself up, taking a deep, dreadful breath. His lungs screamed at him, demanded he stop, but he pushed on. Despite the pain, Rus forced himself to his feet, checking his surroundings.

Dylan had arrived—likely the beacon who'd called the army of drag queens to war—and now tended to Kaiden.

Oh, poor Kaiden. Blood soaked his beautiful green hair. Dirt sullied his lovely corset and suit. It pained Rus to see his friend crying in fear. It enraged him.

"You better run, you fucking pussies!" Amber Ale roared loud enough to wake the entire city.

That wasn't good enough for Rus. He hated these men. Not for what they'd done to him. He'd die a thousand deaths at their hands, proud of his valor for fighting back. No. He couldn't let them escape after having beaten Kaiden, having harmed a hair on his head.

"Get back here," Rus shouted, his raspy voice cracking.

He bolted ahead, tearing through the alleyway and giving chase to these bastards, these bigots.

They wouldn't escape.

Rus wouldn't allow it.

He had to stop them.

Had to beat them.

It wasn't fair.

His body ached as he chased after them. His skin screamed as he bolted down the corner. His muscles begged for release as he pushed through the crowd of bystanders.

They weren't getting away. Not tonight. Not ever. It wasn't fair.

Before he could grab them, stop them, they reached a truck and drove away.

"Fuuuuck youuuuu!" Rus roared.

He did his best to study the make and model, the color in the darkness with a few streetlamps to illuminate them.

Dark blue, oldish, and big truck was all he managed.

Rus hated cars. His mom never stopped talking about them, sharing her work life regularly from years of sales. So, Rus did his best to tune it out, not wanting to learn about her job, about his dad's job. Their paths felt inevitable, and he wanted his own. Now, he regretted that choice, wishing he'd paid more attention.

He repeated the few details he had again and again as he walked back to the club, spending the few blocks trying to recall any details he could to uncover these monsters.

Sirens illuminated the street, shining red and blue everywhere. Dylan stood close to Kaiden, who cried, laying there bloody and bruised, doing his best to compose himself.

This night was going to haunt Rus. His bones ached as it soaked into every cell of his being. He'd remember this forever: the night hate won, and the night these cowards escaped.

CHAPTER 7
DYLAN

THE officers approached with a sluggish swagger. Annoyance in their eyes. Dylan hoped this had more to do with the fact that they were aggravated by the tedium of downtown drunken brawls, and not a lackluster performance because they didn't care for the victims of this assault.

Kaiden sat in an ambulance, being tended to by the EMTs. Rus described the truck the men took off in, and he did his best to describe the men, too. Dylan's heart raced, pounding hard as he attempted to recall the details of his own.

It happened so quickly. The most he made out was that they were white, mostly. Probably. It was so dark, and a few wore hoods. It was so dark and brutal and fast.

Taking in the scrapes across Rus' face, Dylan was mesmerized by how much he'd retained. Blood trickled down Rus' forehead, tracing the wrinkles of his scowl as he yelled at the officer.

Daysha waded through the crowd, joining her friend and offering silent support. She didn't speak to the officer; she didn't move much—barely enough to breathe; she just stood there observing the scene unfold.

"You're not listening to me," Rus shouted. "This wasn't some botched robbery. This was a goddamn hate crime, and you know it."

"Been a lot of guys getting held up around here," the officer replied. "They make themselves easy targets walking out alone with a stranger."

"Yeah, made all the easier when the piggies are too lazy to even post up in the area," Rus snapped. "You know, god forbid y'all actually watched an area where crimes took place."

Heat flooded Dylan's chest, thinking back to Jasmine's warning. The few incidents that'd taken place here, the concern she had, the fact he shrugged it off without a second thought. Was this his fault? Should he have warned Kaiden? Should he have suspected the guy flirting with Kaiden? Were there others in the club tonight? How many people were being eyed for an attack? What would've happened to Kaiden if Rus hadn't intervened?

"There's no one in the club that caused a problem," Rus shouted, pulling Dylan from his worries and back to the cold night. "Have you listened to anything I've said?"

The officers went to work clearing out Himbos, closing it early for the night as they questioned everyone.

"How do I make it any fucking clearer to you idiots? You need to be looking for the real perps!" Rus yelled at the main officer he'd been interviewed by. "They took off in a fucking dark blue truck. Six men. Likely overcompensating incels obsessed with their pencil dicks and red hats."

Daysha swept in close, pulling Rus back as he attempted to approach the officer, bombard him with an angry rant.

"Sweetie, you know I love when you abuse your privilege for chaotic good," Daysha said in a concerned hush. "But I'm gonna need you to reel it back, please."

Rus eyed the officers, eyed his friend, and relented.

"Of course." Rus panted to release some of his all-consuming rage. "Sorry."

Dylan hadn't noticed the tension in the officer's stance, the deepened brow of offense, but he quickly picked up on it after spotting Daysha's shaky stillness.

It seemed the officers didn't care how determined Rus was or how vigilant he remained about having his case properly documented. The officers had moved on to an easier target. They held everyone from the club outside in the cold night air, checking I.D.s of all the guests, the go-go dancers, the bartenders. They demanded the drag queens take off their makeup to verify their identities.

They performed a search throughout the entire club, claiming they wanted to find clues, but it was all too clear they didn't give a fuck about the six men who assaulted Kaiden and Rus.

Dylan's blood boiled, watching them intimidate people into emptying their pockets.

"Okay, no—I gotta say something." Rus jerked loose from Daysha, who seemingly gave a look of approval as her tiny tyrant friend bulldozed through the crowd. "No one here has to volunteer for a search," Rus shouted, cupping his hands to amplify his voice. "Many of you are too drunk to understand your rights. Say nothing. Walk away if you want. This is not a police state. This is an unlawful compliance check."

Dylan didn't know the first thing about his rights or if Rus was telling the truth. But considering how the officers staggered about, hesitating on their next move, he suspected they didn't know either.

Unable to handle much more of this, Dylan made his way over to Kaiden, who'd stepped off the ambulance.

"You're going to need stitches," an EMT said.

"I'm fine, honestly." Kaiden handed the EMT her blanket soaked in Kaiden's blood. They'd bandaged him up some, but he was still in rough shape.

"You need to go to the hospital," Dylan said.

"No, I don't." Kaiden shook his head, green eyes locked on the ambulance itself. "I'll be fine."

"You understand you're refusing service," the EMT said.

"Yes," Kaiden replied.

"If it's money, don't worry about that," Dylan insisted.

"Easy for you to say." Kaiden gulped, his eyes dancing about, likely counting up all the expenses.

"There's victims' funds for this," Dylan replied. "The paperwork's a bitch, but I've gotten good at navigating it. They'll cover the cost with or without insurance."

Kaiden lingered, still reluctant as his face squirmed with fear. The healthcare system sucked, and most people didn't know the first thing about navigating it. Dylan had learned every little trick, from free care, itemized billing, flat rate comps, and a thousand other things to ensure the residents at Dorothy's Home always got the treatment they deserved.

"Get on the damn ambulance," Dylan demanded. "Now."

There wasn't much Dylan could do about the six men who attacked Kaiden, who escaped in the night. There wasn't anything he could do about the officers' lackluster attitudes. But Dylan knew his way around the victim resources. The benefit of having a shitty childhood and spending his teen years hustling. Years at Jasmine's side had taught Dylan how to access county, state, and federal resources that the government seemingly went out of their way to hide from their citizens.

"I'll meet you at the hospital soon," Dylan said, helping Kaiden onto the ambulance with the EMTs. "I promise."

As they drove off, Dylan turned to steal Rus away from the officers.

"We're going to the hospital."

"I'm fine." Rus glared.

"Not for you," Dylan lied; he'd force Rus to get looked over once they arrived, but first and foremost, he wanted to make sure Kaiden got taken care of. "Kaiden needs us."

"Right." Rus nodded, then turned his attention back to the main officer he'd spoken with. "Hey piggy, I have to go to the hospital to check on my friend. You know, the one who was assaulted in a gay bashing you did your damnedest to overlook. Don't worry, though. I got everyone's badge numbers, and I'm persistent as fuck with follow-ups. Best believe I will be chasing you and your pension."

"Let's go." Dylan tugged on Rus' sleeve, wincing a bit at the blood soaking onto his friend's shirt.

"Translation," Rus shouted with a cupped hand. "Oink, oink, oinkity, oink, pig fuckers."

The hospital visit was uncomfortable to say the least. Dylan dropped Daysha off first, against both of their wishes, but Rus insisted. He didn't want to drag her there half the night for a couple of scrapes. He also tried convincing Dylan to drop him at the entrance and head home himself, but Dylan refused. This was about more than Rus. Dylan needed to make sure Kaiden was all right, too.

It took hours of waiting with Rus before anyone saw him. Even more hours before Dylan received an update on Kaiden's state. More hours of sitting in a waiting room with worn and exhausted people he'd never seen before, all hoping for some relief in whatever misery brought them to the hospital in the middle of the night. The few times Dylan had nodded off, a sharp crick in his neck woke him up, and he jolted in his chair, startled and tired.

Rus came out first, glaring back at the staff before taking a seat beside Dylan. They didn't speak. They just waited in silence. Though Dylan did notice the edge in Rus' attitude simmered more the longer he stayed next to him. Dylan was arrogant enough to believe his soothing aura might've calmed his friend. But reality sank in, and Dylan suspected Rus had merely tuckered himself out by spewing rage half the night and literally getting into a six-on-one brawl.

"How's your friend?" Dylan asked.

Rus quirked a brow.

"Daysha?"

"Sleeping, probably." Rus shrugged. "Any updates on Kaiden?"

"Nope."

In typical majestic Kaiden flair, he appeared from the sliding glass doors and stepped through into the waiting room area. Only, there was nothing majestic about his entrance. Usually, Kaiden had this knack for appearing when summoned or spoken about, or if he knew some random trivia on whatever topic was discussed in his absence.

It was one of Dylan's favorite things about his friend.

POLITICS AND POLY

Now though, Kaiden appeared worn and exhausted. His eyes were swollen from crying and bruising. Small nicks lined his exposed arms as he'd rolled his dress sleeves up. Even his corset vest hung on him awkwardly. When he approached, Dylan noticed the loops on the back were loose and semi-unraveled. He must've taken it off for his exam and likely lacked the energy to redress.

"How are you?" Dylan rushed to his friend's side, accompanied by a silent Rus.

"Just sleepy." Kaiden tilted his head, almost resting it on his own shaky shoulder.

While Rus didn't speak, his eyes studied Kaiden with this entranced observation. Dylan followed the gaze, taking in all the injuries Kaiden had suffered. They both noticed the red specks in Kaiden's green hair, the funky whirl as the hair on the side of his head had been matted down in weird ways, and finally, they spotted the staples in his head.

"We'll get you home," Dylan said, offering a comforting smile. There wasn't much else Dylan could offer other than support.

"I don't want to go home," Kaiden said, his face tense with unbridled anxiety. "It's late. My family will have questions and opinions, and I just don't have the energy for any of that."

"I understand." Dylan nodded affirmingly.

"Hell, they probably already locked me out for the night anyway."

Dylan fumed at that, recalling the additional deadbolt Kaiden's stepfather installed if anyone came home too late. Sure, they had house keys, but the extra deadbolt ensured Kaiden's parents controlled any evening outings.

"You can crash at my place," Dylan offered.

Kaiden made a face, probably delicately explaining that a house full of runaway teens wasn't ideal. The chaos normally didn't bother Kaiden, considering his own home, but Dylan suspected his friend needed a quiet place to disappear for a few hours.

"Let's just head back to my apartment." Rus shrugged. "It's tiny. Bedroom living room combo place, but cheap and no noise."

"Okay." Dylan nodded, and they left for Rus' place.

Dylan pulled into the apartment complex, following Rus' lead as he helped escort Kaiden up the stairs. The building had this outdoorsy vibe where all the residents' doors were accessible to anyone. No inside passage or hallways. Just a spacious corridor leading from one apartment to the next.

Rus opened his door, leading the way inside, and the tour took all of five seconds. There was a bathroom to the immediate left when you entered, small but accessible. There was a closet to the right, tiny and crammed with boxes and luggage and cleaning supplies. After that single step inside came the bedroom living room combination, which consisted of Rus' large mattress and box spring on the floor, a recliner chair propped up in a corner, a desk with a laptop and textbooks, and a wobbly stand that looked one Jenga piece away from collapsing with the television and game systems in all.

"Where's your kitchen?" Kaiden asked.

Rus took five dramatically big steps—his way of conveying just how small the floorplan in his apartment was—then swung open a door on the opposite side of his apartment.

"Kitchen is a shared common space."

Dylan blinked with a confused expression.

"Cheap off-campus housing comes with some quirks." Rus laughed. "I pay for this space; someone next to me pays for the same."

"Oh." Dylan nodded, gathering the tiny space and shared kitchen made for quite the affordable accommodations.

Honestly, Dylan didn't know much about the expenses of housing outside the mortgage and utilities for Dorothy's Home, where he'd lived since he was fifteen, staying on to work alongside Jasmine. He did know it cost several thousand dollars to move into an apartment, most demanding deposits, first month's rent, and last month's too if their renters had bad credit—or worse, no credit. That never made sense to Dylan, how not borrowing money somehow hurt someone's odds of being good with money.

But he ran several fundraisers over the years to help former teen residents get the necessary funds for housing after they aged out of Dorothy's Home. Not all of them went to college, so that meant they needed some type of housing assistance when they jumped into the workforce world, and while Jasmine couldn't take everyone on as an employee in the way she had with Dylan, she always made sure not to send a single kid out into the world without some kind of preparation.

"You going to settle in okay?" Dylan turned his attention to Kaiden, who seemed to silently absorb the events of the night.

"Yeah."

"All righty then...I'm going to get going."

"Are you crazy?" Rus asked. "I saw those woozy eyes on the drive here. It's almost four. Just crash here."

"Um..." Dylan tensed a bit. "Where exactly?"

"This is a king." Rus pointed a thumb over his shoulder to his bed. "Plenty of room for all of us."

"A king for the short king," Kaiden said, the tiniest bit of sass in his weary tone.

That brought joy back to Dylan, seeing his friend blossom into himself again, even if fleeting.

"And to cater to all the queens I bring back to my bedroom." Rus eyed Kaiden up and down.

"Bitch, you're snarky," Kaiden teased. "Okay, but I'm not sleeping in the middle."

"Guess Dylan gets the middle," Rus said. "Hope you're cool with that."

Dylan found himself too tired to protest, too concerned to abandon Kaiden, and too curious not to spend the night in bed with Rus. Even in such a platonic setting.

"Just an FYI—I'm no fan of suffocating when I sleep," Rus said, carefully lifting his shirt up.

Kaiden made his way to the bathroom and spent a few minutes locked away while Rus stripped down to his boxers. Dylan couldn't help but glance at the skimpy, form-fitting boxer briefs.

"Oh, we're just stripping down." Dylan nodded approvingly, playfully—or at least he hoped it came across as such.

"We're all grown-ups." Rus gave a crooked smirk, then bit his bottom lip in the cutest way. "And honestly, I find it impossible to sleep fully clothed. Unless I'm like pass out drunk or some shit."

"Too suffocating." Dylan nodded.

"But you can totally sleep however you're comfortable."

Dylan noticed the reddish bruising with blue lining along Rus' skin, mainly centered around his torso. It was a difficult sight to take in, the cluster of strikes.

"Does it hurt?" Dylan asked, immediately and perhaps instinctively stepping in closer. "It looks—"

"Worse than it feels," Rus interrupted. "Trust me."

"Was anything broken?" Dylan lightly traced his fingers along the bruising near Rus' ribcage, almost grazing his skin, touching his battered flesh.

"Maybe my ego." He snorted. "I figured five or six douchebags would be light work. Though that might've been the gin talking."

"Or your fists," Dylan teased. "You tend to talk with them a lot."

It was an easy observation to make, considering Rus' outburst over the summer landed him community service hours. However, if those pricks were half as foul as the men who attacked Kaiden tonight, then Dylan figured Rus made the right move. Even if it was the wrong reaction.

Dylan's eyes wandered past the bruises, examining Rus' exposed body. Rus' pale skin made the vibrant tattoos pop all the more. For the first time since meeting Rus, Dylan had a clear view of all of them. There was so much more than the angry bi goose on his neck. Rus had a small pentagram on his chest with what looked like black flames around it. Then there was the sexy set of red lips right along the deep V-cut indent below his abdomen, barely visible above the elastic of his boxers. That one particularly drew Dylan's attention, so he quickly averted his gaze to study the other tattoos. And yeah, Dylan had glimpsed the sleeve tattoos before but didn't realize they ran all the way up his biceps, too.

"Wow, you really have a lot of tats." Dylan eyed the half-naked woman on his right bicep who wielded a bloody knife and wore a skull mask as she lay sprawled out on top of a pile of bones, which stretched down to his forearm. Bright crimson blood splatter framed her black and white portrait.

Somehow, the right sleeve seemed much tamer than the left, which showed shadowy figures trapped in flames with a quote etched into Rus' bicep. The letters looked carved, making Dylan shiver as he read the text. "Do not judge, or you too will be judged."

"I've got a bit of an obsession." Rus smirked, running his fingers over his ribcage, showing off the galactic star shower of a night sky tattoo. "This one hurt like a bitch, though."

"I imagine they all hurt." Dylan grimaced. He'd never cared much one way or the other for tattoos, but there was something cute about the way Rus seemed to paint his body with all the things he enjoyed.

"This one I barely felt." Rus slapped his left thigh, revealing a brightly colored Harley Quinn tattoo. She held a bat and stood over a puddle of blood and green goop.

"What's with the green…"

"She finally got fed up with the Joker," Rus teased. "I need to add some flowers or plants or some shit to show she's moved on and moved up from her previous relationship drama."

Dylan snorted. "Wow. Okay. I liked the movie, I guess."

"Noooo." Rus shook his head. "I mean, they're okay—whatever—but we gotta watch the show."

"There's a show?"

"Yes, hence why I got this version of Harley."

"Oh, so a cartoon show."

"Don't be one of those basic, boring adults who are too good for animated shows."

"No, no, they're cool, I guess." Dylan shrugged. He'd never really watched much television to begin with. Most shows he caught snippets of came from trending clips online.

"You got any tattoos?" Rus asked.

Instead of answering, Dylan followed suit and stripped down to his boxers, which were quite the opposite of Rus'. Dylan had always preferred bigger, breezier underwear, so he often went with the large plaid pairs that Kaiden swore were toxic top undies. But Dylan refused to believe underwear determined someone's sexual proclivities. Although he did attempt to recall what position boxer briefs were according to meme culture. Just for a potential heads-up with Rus, one day, someday, maybe. His tan skin revealed no hidden tattoos or piercings. A few scars here and there, but Rus didn't linger long on any of them as he studied Dylan's form.

And yes, Dylan studied Rus' expression as they took in each other's nearly naked bodies.

"I'm beat," Kaiden announced, exiting the bathroom in his dress shirt and boxers. He gently placed his corset vest on the nearby desk and hung his slacks over the back of the chair.

Rus didn't say anything about the shirt, but Dylan knew Kaiden hated being seen without something to cover his stomach, his chest, his body.

"Dear God, what are those, and where can I get a set?" Rus eyed the elastic straps wrapped around Kaiden's thick thighs.

The muscles of Kaiden's legs flexed a bit as he showed off one of the straps before unfastening it. They hung on his thighs and clipped to his dress shirt, keeping it smoothed out.

"They're called shirt stays."

"How in the hell can something be so appealing and have such an ugly name?" Rus shook his head disapprovingly.

"I don't know." Kaiden slipped the shirt stays off and set them beside his corset vest on the desk. He put his dress socks into the soles of his dress shoes and tucked them under the desk. "I think they were also called shirt garters back in the day."

"Ugh, such a better name, but not nearly slutty enough."

They all laughed at that, silently staring at each other, and perhaps all pondering better names for Kaiden's accessories. At least Dylan contemplated potential names.

"All right," Dylan said, climbing into the bed. "We ready for sleep?"

"Yes," Kaiden said. "Eternal if possible."

"Best I can offer is midafternoon," Rus said with a chuckle.

"Deal." Kaiden slid into the bed, scooting close to Dylan and then apologizing before scooching away some. "I'm a tosser and turner, so sorry in advance."

"It's all good," Dylan said, leaving out the bit that this didn't come close to his worst sleeping accommodations. It didn't seem like an appropriate time to make a silly anecdote about sleeping in the back of a car or on someone's floor or that one stormy night in a cemetery crypt.

"I sleep like a corpse, so you could literally slap me, and I'd snooze through it," Rus declared.

That almost encouraged Dylan to drop his anecdote, but he could tell everyone needed actual rest, instead of idle chitchat before bed.

Kaiden passed out from sheer exhaustion, and Rus seemed to have the annoyingly uncanny ability to just will himself to sleep immediately, which left Dylan awake and alone with his thoughts for well over an hour, with the boys on either side of him.

Dylan watched Kaiden's breathing, taking in every second with his friend, and letting the worry of the night slowly wash away. Guilt still gnawed at him, doubt pressed to his mind, and he couldn't help but think of all the ways he failed Kaiden. He should've jumped in and fought alongside Rus when the men attacked. He should've gotten help faster. He should've raced in once he returned with help. Still, Dylan dwelled on every misstep of the evening, and his mind filled him with horrible scenarios of what could've been.

Kaiden could've died. Rus could've died.

Those thoughts twisted knots in Dylan's stomach.

Rus had slowly wormed his way into Dylan's heart, a curiosity that Dylan wanted to explore. A guy Dylan wanted to know more. A potential...*something* Dylan wanted to make sense of.

All the same, Rus came second to the budding thoughts blossoming in Dylan's overactive mind.

Kaiden kept coming into frame. The worry Dylan had sent a shiver through him. Dylan couldn't fathom life without Kaiden. And as his friend slept beside him, Dylan's mind started wandering to what life with Kaiden looked like.

He'd never seen Kaiden as more than a friend. Occasionally, he'd seen Kaiden as a potential fuck buddy—but that never seemed like something

Kaiden would go for, and Dylan didn't have a great history with casual sex. It usually messed with his friendships.

Still, Dylan's imagination wandered with ways he could have Kaiden in his life as something more. It was a confusing thought experiment, but it certainly helped tire out his overactive brain, allowing him to get a few hours of sleep.

CHAPTER 8
KAIDEN

THROBBING pain woke Kaiden early in the morning, finding the sharp pain of his cuts hadn't lessened with sleep. A terrible creak in his neck made him wonder if he'd slept funny or had taken one too many blows to the head last night. Speaking of, his headache hit hard, and he wished to blame the booze, but knew it was another reminder of the beating he'd taken.

Oh, how Kaiden wished he'd drunk more last night. Enough to perhaps dull the pain of the attack, enough to excuse his stupidity. Why had he gone along with James? Was that even his real name? Unlikely. Kaiden wished he had something to drink now, something to wash away the memories of last night, something to turn his brain into a blurry stew.

"You're awake," Rus said, voice quite hoarse first thing in the morning.

"Eh, sort of."

"Coffee?" Rus asked, crawling out of bed.

He carefully maneuvered so he wouldn't disturb Dylan, who was still sleeping. Kaiden nodded, and Rus slipped out of the single-room apartment and into the hidden shared space where the kitchen was located. The minute or so of silence was nice, but left Kaiden with a vacuum of his unwanted thoughts.

"I left room if you want cream and sugar," Rus said, gulping his own black coffee. After he'd downed half the cup, his bloodshot eyes sprang open.

"No, thanks," Kaiden replied. "I prefer mine black, too."

A lie but a semi-truth he'd grown accustomed to saying. Kaiden preferred his coffee sweet and sugary and plump with a thousand unnecessary calories. Occasionally, he'd treat himself to a decadent mocha and delicious pastry from a coffee shop. But most days, he preferred not burning through his daily calorie intake with drinks or sweet desserts. Especially not when he'd easily gone over his deficit with way too many cocktails last night.

He felt so stupid thinking about his nutrition, given everything that had happened.

Kaiden took a sip of his coffee and nearly choked as he spit it up.

"What the hell is this?"

"Sorry," Rus said with a bit less gravel in his voice. "I only got instant here."

"Blasphemy." Kaiden shuddered.

He set the cup on the nightstand and gestured dramatically, like with enough flair, he'd blow the coffee away in a telekinetic fit and wash away the horrid aftertaste stuck in his mouth. Alas, he had no magical powers or memory-altering abilities, so he calmed after his small fit.

"I'm going to follow up on the police report on Monday if you want to join."

"Join?" Kaiden raised a brow.

"On your report."

Kaiden let out this awkward huffy chuckle and shook his head. It seemed bizarre to follow up, especially when those taking his statement seemed rather disinterested. Not that Kaiden was eager to document his foolishness. Still, this wasn't the first time he'd been beaten up for being gay. Perhaps the worst time. Most of his encounters came from bullies in middle and high school.

"I'd rather not make a big deal out of it."

"Your choice," Rus replied. "But to be clear, expecting authorities to do their due diligence and uphold public safety isn't making a big deal. In fact, it's asking for the goddamn bare minimum, in my opinion."

"I've been down this road," Kaiden sighed. "I mean, not this one, but like we've all been bullied and such. Or most of us. I'd prefer just to put it behind me."

"Okay." Rus gave a stoic nod, seemingly offering not to poke Kaiden about the topic.

Now, if he could only put it all behind him by the time he went home. He knew his family would have questions, concerns probably.

"Aaaaaargh," Dylan let out an exasperated groaning yawn as he stretched himself awake.

His legs kicked under the blankets for freedom; his arms brushed against Kaiden and Rus.

"Morning," Kaiden said, pushing Dylan's arm away.

"What's good about it?" Dylan blinked a few times. "Wait. What? I thought you said good morning."

"What's good about it?" Rus scoffed.

The three laughed a bit, then sat silently in the bed for a few minutes. Dylan checked his phone, likely screening for any calls or texts he'd gotten from Dorothy's Home. Kaiden had learned long ago that Dylan lived for work. But he figured as far as obsessions go, caring about a job that kept kids off the streets wasn't the worst thing.

Kaiden sank into the mattress, wishing he could lay in bed with Dylan and Rus all day. A waste of a weekend, but Kaiden would love some time away from the world. This tiny apartment seemed like the perfect place to hole up in.

"Do you have any coffee?" Dylan yawned.

"Well, I—"

"No," Kaiden firmly answered, knowing damn well Dylan was even pickier about his coffee.

"There's a place around the corner," Rus said. "It's right on campus."

"Is it even open?" Dylan asked, likely suspecting the college was completely shut down on the weekends.

At least Kaiden figured as much. Neither of them had attended college, so their understanding was limited.

"It's open," Rus replied.

"Oh, that's cool."

Kaiden slid off the bed and pulled himself to his feet. The floor bed was far more work escaping than collapsing into the night before.

It didn't take long for them to get dressed. Kaiden needed the most time as he laced up his corset vest. He wasted a few minutes trying to make his clothes a little less disheveled, but last night had taken its toll on more than him. It'd ruined one of his favorite outfits.

He'd mostly washed off his makeup late last night, but in the morning light, he now realized how poorly he'd done. After removing the last bits, he examined the bruising settling on his face and neck. His stomach ached, and his chest burned. There were so many other bruises and cuts and pains to examine, but that was the last thing Kaiden wanted to do.

"Ready." He joined Dylan and Rus with a phony soft smile plastered on his face.

It didn't take long for them to head over to the campus coffee shop. Kaiden felt incredibly awkward in his ruined outfit and visible bruising. When Dylan had perked up with his sweet caffeine treat, he offered to take Kaiden home. Ugh, the absolute last place he wanted to go right now.

"You can chill at my place as long as you want," Rus said, giving Kaiden the ultimate offering he'd gladly accept.

If only he could.

"I have work."

"Seriously?" Dylan stared, perplexed. "Call out. Alison will understand."

"No," Kaiden sighed. "I need the money if I'm ever going to get my own place in a million years."

"Well, the offer's good all weekend," Rus replied. "I don't got shit going on. We can chill with movies or something. Game. Hell, day drink. I might not have a coffee pot, but I do have a nice mini bar setup."

Soon after, Dylan and Kaiden headed out, and he dropped him off at home. Thankfully, his stepfather's car wasn't in the driveway, which meant he and Kaiden's mother had likely gone to the flea market. They tended to make their Saturday mornings all about getting good deals on junk they didn't need and had never wanted before setting foot into the bargain shops.

With any luck, his sister and brother-in-law were still asleep. It was doubtful the little terrors were sleeping, and Kaiden figured they'd have a hundred questions on what happened to his face.

Kaiden slipped inside, bolted directly to his room, grabbed an outfit, ignored the blasting cartoons coming from the living room, and turned into the kitchen to make his way to the basement, where he could get ready in peace.

"Finally home, I see," his sister said, facing away from him as she microwaved Kaiden's breakfast bowls.

Of course, she took them. She'd tossed three in at once, obviously doing her best to ready a meal for herself and the kids. Kaiden rolled his eyes. Whatever. It wasn't the first time she'd taken his stuff without asking, and it wouldn't be the last time. Right now, he didn't have the energy for an argument.

"I see your little fundraiser turned into a rager," Sandra said, waiting for the beep of the microwave. "I unlocked the door for you, figuring I'd be nice despite how you canceled last minute, but you didn't even bother coming home."

"Things ran late." Kaiden lingered in the kitchen, wanting to say something, wanting to explain what had happened, but every fiber of his being told him to just go to the basement and get ready for work. "I'm sorry if Mom had to watch the kids. I wasn't—"

"Jesus Christ, Kaiden!" Sandra locked her eyes onto his, but they drifted, studying his bruised face, his ripped clothing, the specks of dried blood scattered across his itchy skin. "What the hell happened to you?"

His eyes swelled, and he gave a teary response. "I got assaulted last night."

"Oh my God, sweetie, that's horrible." She swept in close, wrapping Kaiden in a rare hug, and pulled him away from the basement door and toward the kitchen table. "How did this happen? Why? What fucking monster had the audacity? Who was there? Was this because of the kids you were helping? Jesus, I know people don't like it, but did they really have to attack you because of a couple gay kids?"

Sandra was still under the impression that Kaiden had gone to a last-minute fundraiser to help Dorothy's Home. Kaiden knew the appropriate response was to keep up the lie, to hold back the details. Mostly, he didn't want to divulge the truth, didn't want to invoke his sister's pity or judgment, but as she sat so close to him, cradling his head as she examined his stitches, Kaiden couldn't keep the words in.

The truth poured out as he released a gasp of sorrow that'd built inside him. "No, we were at Himbos, just trying to have a nice time."

His chest lightened as he let out a sob of pain he'd tried desperately to bury.

"Oh." Sandra paused her examination. "You held the fundraiser at the gay club?"

"There wasn't a fundraiser," Kaiden confessed, lost on the temporary solace he got from his sister. "We just wanted to have a little fun. It was a nice time, but then these guys, they—"

"Well, that's horrible," she said rather flatly, returning to the microwave to grab the breakfast she'd made. "Just awful."

Sandra slipped out of the kitchen, bringing her boys their meal, then made her way back into the kitchen, standing at the counter and eating her bowl.

Kaiden's relief was quickly replaced with dread.

"Shame, you know, those men attacked you." Sandra took an aggressive bite of her egg bowl mix. "But it sure as shit wouldn't have happened if you'd been here."

"What?"

"Just saying. You flaked, you lied, and went where you shouldn't have been."

"I shouldn't have been at a club downtown? A public place where people go to drink and have fun?"

"Oh, come on, they don't just go there for that."

"What are you trying to say?" Kaiden let out an exasperated breath, having no fight in him, and wishing he could take back his foolish confession.

"I don't know," Sandra mused. "Just seems a little bit like karma if you ask me. Which you did."

"Excuse me?"

"I'm just saying. You had a responsibility, and you blew it off to probably, I don't know, blow some stranger." Sandra laughed a little at her own play on words. "Maybe next time, you'll think about that before ditching your family."

"To be clear, your kids are not my fucking responsibility," Kaiden snapped. "My free time does not belong to you."

This had been a battle he'd waged with his sister for years, always surrendering because most of the time, Kaiden didn't care to argue. Kaiden didn't mind being the good guncle. But the more he offered, the more his family expected, the more they demanded.

"Look, whatever. You got drunk, you acted a fool, you got beat up by a couple twinks, or I don't know, the bears? Whichever homos are the tough ones. I say karma has been served, and we can put this behind us."

"I wasn't assaulted by anyone in the club," Kaiden fumed, practically snarling as he spoke. "I was outside, led away by—"

"Ooooh, that makes sense now." Sandra nodded, connecting the dots to whatever bullshit version of events she'd concocted. "You were drinking, having a *gay* ole time, and then you went outside and started bringing that flirt game with drunk guys on the street. I have seen that happen before."

"What? No!"

"It's happened to Tommy plenty of times," Sandra explained. "When it's a girl, I handle it. But those gay boys think they're cute, but that type of shit is not cute."

"I…" Kaiden fumbled with his thoughts, with his words, sinking into a fit of frustration as his sister twisted what little she knew and turned it into a working theory based on whatever bullshit she'd experienced with her husband.

"Just saying, sometimes gays think they're being provocative and funny, but they're being aggressive and gross, giving unwanted attention," Sandra explained like she was the authority on unwanted advances from men on men. "You said you'd been drinking, right? Went clubbing or whatever for that. Just saying, you probably did something to make those guys uncomfortable. Most men aren't like you."

Sandra gestured to all of Kaiden, as if every piece of him had been born wrong. He knew which parts she meant, though. His flamboyant behavior. His gay voice. His love for makeup. His need for flair. His stupid outfits that always drew attention. The wrong attention, according to his family.

Kaiden stared slack-jawed. "Are you out of your fucking mind?"

He didn't have the energy to explain how one of them had lured him outside, how they planned their assault, how they got him alone and away from everyone else before making their move.

Sandra had already made up her mind. She'd filled in the narrative and found a way to blame Kaiden for his assault. This was exactly why he didn't want to follow up on the report, why he didn't want to make a big deal out of it. As much as he hated his sister's reaction, it was normal and expected and not even the worst. Chances were his stepfather would say Kaiden brought it on by never learning how to act like a man. His mother would express how God worked in mysterious ways, and to be grateful He was giving Kaiden another chance. And the police? They definitely didn't give a fuck about what happened. They only cared in shitty TV shows and bad action films.

"I don't have time for this. I have work."

Kaiden spent the next few days working for as long as Alison would allow him. She didn't want him to overexert himself and would've preferred Kaiden take some time to recover, but he assured her work was the best recovery. In a sense, it was. He focused heavily on the distraction it afforded him.

When he got off work, Kaiden spent extra time at the gym. Partially

POLITICS AND POLY

because his injuries required he take it slower at the gym. Mostly, though, he wanted an excuse not to go home, not to offer his assistance.

In the days that passed, Kaiden tiptoed around his house, doing his best to avoid his family and any ungodly remark they'd have. His sister had already said her piece. His brother-in-law would go on not-so-vague tangents about how real men always have to be at the ready and alert to protect what was theirs. His stepfather didn't speak to Kaiden, so nothing had really changed. His mother had a look of pity, but she didn't bring it up when they spoke. She'd likely already gotten a version of the story she preferred from his sister, and there was no point in Kaiden wasting his breath to tell her the truth.

When Kaiden rolled home in the evenings, his mother would plead with him to take over and watch the kids. Reluctantly, he'd agree. It wasn't like he had anywhere to escape.

Well, that wasn't entirely true.

After three days of folding to his mother's pleas and surrendering to his sister's whims of babysitting, Kaiden decided he'd had enough.

> Kaiden: I know your weekend was free but any chances your weeknights have some flexibility?

> Rus: What do you got in mind?

> Kaiden: Anything. You? Dylan?

He'd looped them into a group chat. On the off chance that Rus wasn't up to hosting a hangout, he knew Dylan would always offer him a bed. He'd just have to trade screaming children for angsty teenagers. Dorothy's Home was never quiet.

> Dylan: Down for anything.

> Rus: Swing by whenever.

Kaiden packed a bag with a change of clothes for the morning, which he'd leave in his car. It seemed easier to stay a little too late and ask if he could crash again, as opposed to asking up front. He felt a bit like a creep, plotting his escape from his home, but he needed a night away. Hopefully, Rus wouldn't mind.

It turned out Rus didn't care at all. In fact, he heavily encouraged the sleepovers, offering beers every time Kaiden dropped by. Dylan stayed sober and only crashed about half the time they hung out.

Days turned to weeks, and the month of September flew by without Kaiden having to offer his assistance to his sister once. Between sleeping at Rus', Dylan's, and occasionally locking up and sleeping at the art gallery, Kaiden avoided his home except to drop by, sneak in, grab what he needed, and disappear before his family could complain.

After a particularly exhausting Tuesday, Kaiden languished in the gym shower—his least favorite place to clean off. But honestly, after years of sharing two bathrooms and one shower with his family of seven—well, eight including himself—he learned to get over his public shyness.

Once he'd dragged himself over to Rus' apartment, he found Rus and Dylan sprawled out on the bed, controllers in hand, and eyes locked on the television as they continued playing the same video game they had for weeks now. Something called Baldur's Gate 3—which made zero sense since Dylan hadn't played one or two yet was expected to understand how to play the third game in the series. Rus introduced Dylan to it, and it had turned into their go-to way to pass time in the evening. Certainly not Kaiden's favorite.

"How long is this game?" Kaiden plopped onto the edge of the bed, half paying attention to the screen and half scrolling through his phone.

"Sixty to ninety hours," Rus said rather aloof. "Depends on how much exploration Dylan wants to do."

Rus' one negative quality was his obsession with video games and binge-watching shows. Well, Kaiden enjoyed Rus' taste in media. He just didn't get the obsession with video games. His brother-in-law stayed glued to their couch at all hours, practically living in the living room to the point his parents moved their streaming stick into their bedroom exclusively instead of banishing the douche to his bedroom.

The perk of Dylan's friendship came with the fact that he had never been introduced to video games and thus held no interest in them. And for a guy who rarely indulged in anything much other than fresh air and fundraisers, he'd turned into quite the little gaming junkie since Rus introduced him to this co-op campaign.

"Right now, I'm still deciding who to fall in love with," Dylan explained. "I'm torn between the chatty wizard and the charming warlock. They're both so great."

"You could romance them both," Rus said. "But you'd eventually have to break one of their hearts."

"Boo." Dylan sighed.

"I thought this game was about aliens and killing monsters."

"They're not aliens," Dylan said. "I think."

"I mean, they're squid-faced telepaths who pilot interdimensional flying ships," Rus said. "They're kinda aliens. Jus' a lil bit."

"So, shouldn't y'all be killing monsters, not romancing people?"

"Absolutely not," Dylan said. "I need the perfect boyfriend to save the world with. Otherwise, what's the point?"

"Dating cannot be the point of this game," Kaiden said with a huff.

"Oh, it's definitely a dating sim above anything else," Rus stated. "And right now, I'm torn between my favorite Tiefling muscle mommy or the world's greatest vampire twink with an ass that could end wars."

Kaiden tsked. "Only one man has an ass that could end wars, and he belongs to the Bat family."

Rus nodded. "Fair, Nightwing is glorious, but I'd feed Dick to sweet baby Astarion in exchange for a single snarky one-liner of approval."

"Wait, you'd feed Astarion a dick?" Dylan raised his brows in disgusted confusion. "Do vampires in this game eat body parts, too? Yuck."

"No," Rus said, bursting at the seams, about to break into huge laughter.

Kaiden rolled his eyes at Rus' fidgety, barely contained snorts of laughter.

"We're talking about Dick the character," Kaiden explained. "Comic book superhero."

"That explains it." Dylan nodded. "Not ready for my superhero deep dive yet."

"But yeah, I'd give Astarion pretty much whatever he wanted to hear him tell me he's happy."

"Oh, what about the way he purrs, daaarrrrling, at you," Dylan added with a poor British accent, shoulder bumping Rus. "That's pretty hot."

"It's just a shame the only poly option is with the bear."

"Wait, what?" Kaiden blinked in confusion.

"Druid. He shapeshifts into a bear a lot," Rus explained. "I mean, he's cool and all, but he doesn't do it for me. I don't got the daddy issues for it."

At that comment, Kaiden sank into the bed, locked on his phone while his friends spent the evening lost in a video game. Eventually, it got late, and Kaiden convinced them it was time for something else. Reluctantly, they stopped their game and gave Kaiden free rein in picking a movie.

"I should probably get going," Dylan said with a stretch.

"Oh, hell no." Kaiden playfully popped him on the chest and pushed him back onto the bed. "You made me sit through hours of your game; the least you can do is sacrifice a little sleep for a fantastic film."

"I don't really like cartoons."

"Perfect," Kaiden replied with a slick smile. "It's Claymation. And it's almost Halloween, so you were bound to watch *The Nightmare Before Christmas* sooner or later."

"Wait, you've never seen it?" Rus asked with wide eyes.

"He doesn't watch much TV," Kaiden said almost on top of Dylan's reply.

"I don't watch much TV," Dylan said with a sweet smirk as Kaiden read his mind.

There were few people who knew Dylan so well, but Kaiden had learned through Rus that, despite initial protests, Dylan was much more open to new experiences than previously considered. Kaiden rarely pushed people past their boundaries, figuring if someone showed disinterest, that meant no; however, it seemed they weren't boundaries, merely reservations with some reluctant curiosity underneath.

"This isn't scary, is it?" Dylan asked.

"No, it's for children," Kaiden replied.

"I don't know, it gets pretty creepy." Rus made a face and growled.

Dylan shuddered. "I'm using you as a human shield if it gets freaky."

With that, Dylan grabbed hold of Kaiden's bicep and used his friend as a body pillow while he lounged out on Rus' bed. About halfway through the film, Dylan passed out, which left Kaiden and Rus to enjoy the movie.

"He's going to kill me," Kaiden said, slowly adjusting Dylan's sleeping body in the middle of the bed. "He wanted to go home, and now he's knocked out."

"Meh, when aren't you guys passed out in my bed?"

Kaiden stared at Rus, studying his expression, but finding him difficult to read as he watched the movie.

"Sorry for kind of invading your place."

"You're not invading."

"I mean, kind of. I know it. You were hospitable, and I have definitely taken full advantage of it." Kaiden paused, doing his best to avoid complaining about his family.

He might've relied on his sucky family as a way to persuade Rus into these regular hangouts. It wasn't like he didn't enjoy Rus' company. He did. A lot. But the more he crashed here, the more he avoided his family and problems, the more he felt like a leech in his own right.

"If I had a problem with you here, you'd know it," Rus said, turning his attention to Kaiden. "We haven't known each other long, but do I seem like the type of person to bite my tongue? To politely avoid confrontation?"

Kaiden snorted in response and shook his head.

"Precisely," Rus said with a grin. "You're here because I like your company. I like Dylan's company. It's cool that you're both chill since you're like a package deal."

"Yeah, we've been friends a while."

Rus didn't respond, simply stared silently for a long time. The longest ticking seconds of Kaiden's life.

"Still, it means a lot, you letting me crash here. Sharing your bed, quite literally."

"Well, this bed deserves some action." Rus playfully bucked his hips upward. "At least with a few guys rolling around in it most nights, there's the illusion of something fun going on in here."

Kaiden laughed at that, slapping a hand over his mouth when Dylan rustled a bit in his sleep, eyes fluttering before he buried his head into Kaiden's side.

"Plus, I say pay it forward," Rus continued. "My freshman year dormmate was a total douchebag. Thankfully, I made friends with Daysha, who lived in a campus suite and let me crash on her couch for damn near a semester straight. Luckily, my douchebag roommate dropped out, and then I just casually crashed at Daysha's instead of desperately escaping."

"Sleeping on a couch isn't really the same as giving up part of your bed."

"It is when Daysha had three suite mates who she had to regularly sweet-talk into not snitching to the RAs about my unauthorized sleepovers," Rus explained. "It was a big deal for her to offer me somewhere chill to crash. So, I can offer you the same. I know a little bit of what it's like to live with someone who is insufferable."

Kaiden scoffed. "Surprised you didn't just hit your roommate and knock some sense into him."

"Actually, I got stuck with that douchebag after being relocated and threatened to lose my housing because I might've sort of maybe just a little bit decked my previous red hat roomie."

"Jesus Christ, you really don't believe in using your words."

"There's enough folks attempting peace talks with the fascists; I prefer my support methods as a healthy alternative."

Kaiden smirked at that, honestly wowed by Rus' brazen and bold behavior. Also, a little intimidated by the fact that someone could act so chill one moment, then rush into conflict at the drop of a hat.

"I am getting better at it," Rus said, seemingly reading Kaiden's mind, or registering the slight anxiety on his face. "I just hate evil people with no regard for the well-being of others. But it is a flaw to be controlled by one's rage—or so my therapist has pointed out."

"Therapist?" Kaiden asked. "Court-appointed?"

"No. I mean, I do have court-appointed anger management, or I did, but I've been going to therapy for years."

"Why?"

"To get out my rage. Rawr." Rus grinned. "Now, I try to reserve the worst of it for really awful bigots. That and I don't need anything else on my record since I barely avoided serious charges the last time I punched an asshole."

"I guess I'm just surprised you go to therapy."

"Yeah, everyone should when they need it." Rus shrugged nonchalantly. "I've gone off and on since I don't even know. Probably since I was like twelve or thirteen. My folks are big on that stuff. Exercising the mind, healing the mind, investing in the mind."

He made a few silly gestures at that with flowy arms, perhaps mocking his parents in a playful manner.

Kaiden had never considered therapy before. It wasn't something his family did. Talking honestly to each other was an impossibility, let alone a stranger. Still, he sat with Rus' words during the rest of the film, giving real weight to the conversation.

Heading to the local on-campus coffee shop had sort of become a morning ritual for them. Since Rus had 8 AM classes three days a week, Dylan and Kaiden needed to get up pretty early to head on out. Though there was more than one morning Kaiden overslept, and the duo simply left him in bed unattended. It was an awkward thing, having Rus trust him alone in his apartment with no supervision or accountability. Even Kaiden's parents didn't trust him alone in the house he'd grown up in.

Still, Kaiden ignored his family woes, seeing as there wasn't much he could do about it, and focused on getting ready for the day. Rus had allowed him to leave some of his makeup in the bathroom. It wasn't like Rus utilized much of his counter space. He had a few more hygiene products than Dylan, but overall, Rus was pretty basic about his skincare routine. It was made all the more annoying by the fact that he had damn near perfect skin. Perfect skin he continued coloring on with his random tattoos.

Kaiden focused on getting ready for work, then joined Rus and Dylan on the walk to the coffee shop. Neither of them did anything to get ready. Well, Rus at least changed his clothes and put on a bit of deodorant. Otherwise, he was done with his morning rituals. Dylan, on the other hand, wouldn't even bother getting ready for the day until he returned to his place at Dorothy's Home. So, his morning ritual of getting ready for the day didn't really start up until about ten or eleven, depending on when he wandered home.

"You two could be so put together," Kaiden sighed as he brushed by Dylan. "If, of course, either of you bothered putting yourselves together with any effort at all."

"Meh." Rus shrugged as he held the door open for Kaiden, who waltzed right up to the barista and put in an order for the three of them.

He had Dylan's fancy mocha order memorized from years of friendship, and learning Rus' order hadn't taken too long either. He liked his coffee black and bitter like his soul, or so he professed. Kaiden believed Rus to be anything but bitter. Well, maybe to jerks who deserved it.

Once he'd gotten the orders, Kaiden made his way to a corner table the duo had procured for them. Dylan wiggled in his seat while sipping his super sugary mocha with the lightest dash of coffee inside. It was mostly a caffeinated chocolate milkshake at this point. Rus did his sleepy gurgle of annoyance, then took a gulp of hot coffee. This was his real morning ritual. He wasn't much of a person until he'd had his first cup of coffee.

The door jingled as new customers walked inside, catching Kaiden's eye as they wandered toward their table instead of the growing line.

An effeminate guy dressed in the preppiest polo, clashing shorts, and insultingly rugged sandals sauntered over, accompanied by a very well-dressed petite blonde with a horrendous spray tan. It was too extreme, too out of season, and not at all blended with her makeup. Kaiden bit his tongue, having a thousand tips on how to improve each of their shitty try-hard looks, but finding both already nauseating. Though that might've had to do with the snarl Rus let out when they approached.

"You're that guy who got the shit kicked out of him for—"

"Get fucked," Rus spat before the girl could finish her statement. Her hateful insult.

But the damage had already landed. Kaiden clammed up, lost in the realization that despite not wanting to press charges or make a big deal out of his assault, people still ran with the story. Between online trending videos and so-called newspapers, there had been enough of them to drop his name and picture that did the rounds in town. It was horrible knowing that if someone searched up his name online, they'd find articles and images of his assault. It would follow him forever, always at the top of the search engines.

"Don't worry, Emma," the gay guy said while batting his eyes. "Rus is all bark and no bite. Probably why he got the shit kicked out of him, too."

"Fuck off, pick me," Rus snapped.

"Don't speak to Landon that way," Emma retorted. "I swear, the way you—"

"Sir, yes, sir," Rus interrupted, straightening up in his chair and giving Emma a salute before flipping her off. "Anything for you, Commander Conservative Cunt. And while I know you'd love to spell those Cs with Ks, you'll just have to keep crossing your fingers that the kappa kappa whatevers sorority you're in update their name."

Emma furrowed her brow, and the deep creases in her face were amplified by her overly tanned skin.

"Well, well, well, if it isn't my favorite bitchy bi boy," said a Black girl with a familiar face as she strutted over and side hugged Rus, who responded with a polite morning growl.

Between Rus' scowl and the girl's side eye of disdain, Emma and Landon took the hint and wandered away to a corner booth of the café.

"Daysha, right?" Dylan pointed, and the name quickly returned to Kaiden.

He always struggled learning names, whereas Dylan could meet someone for five minutes and have half their life story memorized in his vault of a mind. It probably had to do with how many teens shuffled in and out of Dorothy's Home over the years. Or maybe Dylan was just smarter. Kaiden wouldn't be too surprised by that.

"So, are we just going to pretend like that whole scene didn't happen?" Kaiden asked, gesturing to the empty space where Emma and Landon had stood a moment ago.

"That's your best bet," Daysha replied, tapping Rus on the shoulder. "Unless you want to be like this guy, provoking them into an argument every time they appear."

"It's not my fault," Rus said. "They're ignorant and evil and deserve to be mocked."

"And I have missed your vicious mockery as of late," Daysha said, eyeing Kaiden and Dylan. "Especially, since y'all have been holding my buddy hostage."

"Sorry about that," Kaiden said with a chuckle, letting the stress of their last encounter wash away.

Tension still ate away at Kaiden. Thankfully, his friends noticed. They didn't make a big deal out of it but offered solace. Dylan gently shoulder-bumped Kaiden, and Rus pressed his knee against Kaiden's under the table, each offering a subtle way to soothe away the stress.

"So, you coming to the Pride Club event?" she asked, eyeing her friend.

"Huh?" Rus did a poor job pretending not to know what she was talking about, then returned to sipping his coffee.

It hadn't taken long for Kaiden to realize Rus scrunched his face when he was genuinely confused and stared out blankly into the void of the world when faking it.

"There's a Pride party?" Dylan asked with a glint of excitement. "That sounds awesome. Is it only for students?"

"No," Daysha said. "It's just hosted by us. Pride Club likes to organize a few fundraisers every year, and work with local communities to raise donations."

"I'm in love with your club already," Dylan said. "When is it?"

"It's tonight at Himbos." Daysha nudged Rus. "And I've only told him about it like a hundred times."

"Oh, yeah," Rus quickly covered. "But we're not going to be able to do that on such short notice. We were going to, um…"

"We were going to—*um*—nothing," Kaiden jumped in, wondering why Rus felt the need to hide this, to play it off.

He stared at Rus, trying to understand where this came from, but when he caught a quiet Dylan with a pensive expression in the corner of his eye, Kaiden had his answer.

"We'll see you there tonight," Kaiden declared.

Rus and Dylan remained silent, though their tense expressions said so much.

"Fantastic," Daysha replied before a barista called her order. "I've got to get to classes, but I'll be seeing you all there. Can't wait. Bring your money."

Rus scoffed.

"It's a fundraiser!"

"Yeah, yeah." Rus huffed.

"I hope it goes well." Dylan sipped his drink, keeping his eyes fixed on Rus. "So, what movie is on the agenda tonight?"

"No movie," Kaiden interjected, then raised his hands to silence both of them. "Did you not hear me? We're going to the fundraiser. We're watching drag, we're celebrating, and we're having a good time."

"I'm not really that into clubbing late into the night," Rus said. "Not on a weekday."

"Your first class tomorrow isn't until eleven," Kaiden replied. "We're going."

"I don't know." Dylan shrugged. "It's sort of last-minute."

He quickly returned to his drink and averted his gaze from Kaiden.

"I'm not doing this. I'm not letting what happened there control what I do." Kaiden's body trembled as he spoke. He was grateful Dylan and Rus took his feelings into consideration. He admired them for it, for caring in a way so few did about him, but he wouldn't let this become his story. "I'm not letting one incident control my life, my future. My fucking fun! We're going. We're going, and we're going to have so much fun tonight, we completely forget what happened last time. It'll be all, gay bashers who?"

Dylan and Rus made a face, each of their eyes wide with shock and perhaps concern.

"Shut up," Kaiden blurted. "I heard it. I was trying something out, it didn't work, pretend it never happened. I'll have a better catch phrase tonight."

He wouldn't, but he would have fun tonight. That much was determined.

They headed downtown around nine, finding the special drag show performance for the Pride Club fundraiser was already underway as they arrived. Much earlier than Himbos usually performed, but since it was for an event that sort of made sense. Kaiden skirted by the Pride fundraiser tables, dropping a donation into one of their offerings, but leaving before someone could chat him up.

Festive decorations lined the walls from cobwebs in every corner to dangling skeletons with obnoxious twinkling lights in their ribcages.

"Leave it to the gays to start celebrating the day October hits," Kaiden said with a small smile.

"If they were really festive, they'd have started decorating back in July for Summerween," Rus shouted.

"For what?" Kaiden shook his head in protest, but Halloween did seem like the one thing Rus put real effort into.

For starters, he had a slew of horror films at his place that he always tried to trick Kaiden and Dylan into checking out. Secondly, he'd already pulled out his slasher hoodies and seemed to have quite the collection of horror apparel in his closet.

Himbos was much more crowded than usual, especially for a Wednesday. Kaiden tried to enjoy the performance from a distance, mind recalling the frenzy the drag queens went into the night of his assault. It filled Kaiden's throat with a lump, his nerves getting the better of him, the more people walked by him. Every time someone paused and stared, he wondered if they knew what happened. How many people knew? Did anyone know? Did anyone even care? Kaiden believed he was being dramatic for no reason. No one cared. No one even remembered. It was a million years ago. Well, a month and some change, so he didn't understand why he was hanging onto it so much. Especially right now.

"You good?" Rus placed a hand on the small of Kaiden's back, guiding him through the crowd and toward some free seats at the bar.

"Yep."

"What'cha want?" Dylan asked, flashing some crinkled bills like a big spender with his singles and fives. "I'm buying."

"Um, nothing right now," Kaiden replied.

"I'm good."

"You're not going to drink either?" Dylan asked Rus.

"No, not feeling it."

"Have a drink," Kaiden insisted. "Have several. Have that awful blue motorcycle brake fluid cocktail you had last time."

Rus gagged. "Ugh. Never again."

"Come on, have a beer."

"No, I'm not feeling it." Rus continued eyeing the dance floor, scoping out the club, and analyzing every single person that made their way by them.

It made a pit of regret sink into Kaiden's stomach. Maybe this was a bad idea. Dragging them out to Himbos so he could prove that he could have a fun time. Meanwhile, it left Rus and Dylan playing bodyguards all night on his behalf.

"You know, Dylan doesn't drink," Kaiden explained. "But you're welcome to drink. Please, please, please, do not keep your wits about you on my behalf. I'm fine. Everything is fine."

Kaiden didn't know exactly how much he believed his own words, but he did know he didn't want to give control over to what had happened last time. More than anything, Kaiden wanted to bury that memory, bury it deep and pretend it'd never happened. He also wanted to stay vigilant on his own behalf. After last time, Kaiden wouldn't walk into something foolish. He wouldn't require protection because he wouldn't make that mistake.

"I'll have whatever you're having," Rus finally said.

Kaiden scoffed. "You're impossible."

He most certainly wasn't drinking. It made his inhibitions too loose, and he couldn't chance that. Gah, the guilt ate away at Kaiden, the way he perpetually blamed himself for what had happened instead of directing that blame on his attackers. The self-loathing and regret he had for dragging his friends out tonight.

"I'm going to go to the bathroom," Kaiden said, raising a hand to stop Dylan, who moved like he was about to follow. "Alone."

Well, as alone as anyone could get inside a crammed club urinal. After washing his hands, he noticed a guy making eye contact with him. Kaiden averted his eyes and speed-walked out of the bathroom and back toward the bar, where Rus and Dylan were propped up.

"Hey," the guy from the bathroom grabbed Kaiden by the arm. "Quick question."

"What the fuck?" Kaiden jerked away.

"Sorry, man, uh, I was trying to ask you a question about your outfit."

"Huh?" Kaiden's heart hammered in his chest.

"Yeah, the corset. It's really cool. Just wondering where someone gets a guy's version like that."

"Oh, yeah. It's a corset vest. They're mostly custom." Kaiden pulled up his phone, showing some of the websites he used. "You'll need to do really close measurements, though. Like precise."

"Okay, okay, very cool." The guy nodded. "Shit, they're pricey."

"Very, but worth it. Plus, once you have a few, you can make adjustments and tweaks to change up their looks without buying a whole new outfit. It's not as hard to customize them as you might think."

The guy stuck around, asking more questions. Well, shouting them mostly until the drag performance wrapped up and the music settled for a beat. During that lull, the guy moved in closer, and it seemed much of the crowd drifted deeper onto the dance floor.

"You wanna head out there?"

"Huh? Um…" Kaiden cleared his throat.

"To dance?"

"Actually, um, well, you see…"

"Get lost?" Rus seemingly materialized out of thin air, hand back to the small of Kaiden's back.

"Sidetracked," Kaiden replied, taking an easy breath.

As the guy who'd stopped Kaiden a moment ago went to introduce himself to Rus, he found himself abandoned with silence. Rus turned away, ushering Kaiden alongside him, and returning to the bar where they'd sit and watch the night unfold without actually participating.

Kaiden was completely fine with that turn of events and rather envied Rus' ability to dismiss another person without second-guessing their feelings. Chances were, Kaiden would've continued the conversation for the rest of the night just to be polite. He might've even reluctantly stepped out onto the dance floor. Okay, probably not. Usually, he didn't care how bad his moves were, but right now, every little thing made him question himself, his decisions, his everything.

"Okay, we came here to party," Dylan shouted over the music. "Let's go be himbos for a night. No booze required for a good time."

Without asking for permission, Dylan grabbed Kaiden and Rus by their wrists and dragged them onto the dance floor. Yep. One of the rarities in the world that could make Kaiden dance—Dylan's persistence.

Kaiden could attempt to protest, to explain for the thousandth time how dancing made him feel awkward, but Dylan seemed determined to wash away Kaiden's anxiety. What better way to distract from his discomfort than by giving him something different to cringe about? Kaiden followed Dylan's lead, shaking away his nervousness, ignoring his own lack of rhythm, and laughing loudly at Rus' terrible routine. It was the kind of dance that was so bad it almost looped back around to incredibly cool.

Dylan took hold of Kaiden's hips, guiding the sway of their bodies and forcing him to step with purpose. It wouldn't stick. Dylan had worked with Kaiden on his dance moves time and time again. Still, Kaiden let loose and followed Dylan's lead, jumping between him and Rus whenever one of Rus' bizarre routines actually made room for a partner.

Finally, for a few songs, Kaiden lost himself to the motion and the crowd. It was too loud to overthink. It was perfect. He danced away his stress, lost between Dylan and Rus, the two men who'd become pillars in his life. Both of them held him up the past six weeks, kept his head above water, and provided the support he needed to escape the pain eating away at him.

Kaiden didn't face his trauma head-on, preferring to bury it, avoid it, ignore it. And while that might not have been the best solution, it was the path he needed to follow right now.

Dylan and Rus didn't force Kaiden to confront his pain; they just helped him dance it out. They provided him with a safe space and solace. They were the best part of Kaiden's life.

CHAPTER 9
RUS

THE night turned into a blur between the drag performances, the loud music, the crowd of bodies, but Rus relished what sense he made of the small parts. Kaiden had declared this a night to wash away the memory of their last outing, and Rus hoped that in some small way they'd achieved his wish.

"Okay, okay, they're putting lights up at the bar," Kaiden said with a heavy breath, pulling away from the dance. "Which means they're about to do last call."

"Yikes," Dylan said with a playful shiver. "It's past midnight? Does that mean I'm a pumpkin again?"

"That's the carriage, not the princess," Kaiden corrected.

"Really? Shame." Dylan grinned. "Because I like to let people ride me."

They all laughed, and Kaiden nudged Rus and Dylan off the dance floor.

"Say your goodbyes, it is way too late."

Rus made his way over to Daysha, who had started disassembling a booth with some of the other Pride Club members.

"Heading out," Rus said, wiping sweat from his brow. "Hope your event killed it."

"Hmmm, since we're raising funds for starving kids across the world, I hope we did the opposite of killing it."

"Yeah, yeah." Rus retrieved his wallet and handed Daysha forty bucks before she could press him with a late-night discussion on morality.

"I see why you've been so busy as of late," Daysha said, tucking the cash away.

"Huh?"

She eyed him from head to toe and then craned her head past Rus and over to Dylan and Kaiden. "Got a little crush, huh?"

"What?" Rus blanched.

"I saw the way you were looking at…um, well, honestly, both of them."

"Okay, so *maybe* I've thought about Kaiden once or twice." Rus cleared his throat. "But I might've also been thinking about Dylan."

"At the same time?"

"Well, not at the *same* same time, you know?" Rus responded, a bit flustered and trying to make sense of his crush. Crushes.

"Flip a coin," Daysha suggested, somewhat aloof.

"You're the worst. You realize that's not how feelings work."

"You realize you're asking an ace chick for romance advice?"

"What? It's a wide spectrum."

"And I'm on the dead-end side. No butterflies, warm and fuzzes, and certainly no interest in smooches or cuddles or rubbing bodies together."

Rus rolled his eyes. "Point made."

"Why don't you just try both?"

Rus snorted. "They aren't ice cream samples."

"Of course, not. More variety there," Daysha said, focusing on disassembling her station. "Just grab one of them tonight, pull him aside, and give him a kiss. See if you have those electrical sparks or whatever. Then excuse yourself, grab the other one, and test out his lips."

"With another kiss?"

"Or whatever else you wanna try." Daysha shrugged. "I know where those dirty lips of yours have been."

They both broke out into laughter, and Rus nudged Daysha, playfully knocking away her concentration from her game.

"You are terrible at love advice."

"And you're terrible about following your heart." Daysha's matter-of-fact comment stumbled Rus.

She'd been friends with him since orientation, when they mockingly joked about all the campus policies and were both annoyingly too edgy to care about the school spirit of the college. That evolved over time, much like their friendship. In fact, Daysha was the person on campus who really knew how little Rus dated, how he avoided it after the messiest high school breakup ever. Still, he chased his feelings most days, but unfortunately, his follow-through often fell short.

It was easier not to take a chance on romance than to risk it.

"You ready?" Dylan squeezed Rus' shoulder as he wrapped an arm around him. He held Kaiden in the same embrace with his other arm, ushering the trio out of Himbos and into the streets of downtown.

Maybe it wasn't a risk. Maybe it was a chance. An opportunity. A possibility. Only, Rus didn't know with who.

He kept close to Kaiden and Dylan, carefully eyeing the street as they barreled out into the night. Downtown had mostly died out at this point, with drunken stragglers roaming from one greasy restaurant to the next, slowly pouring themselves into rideshares, or simply passing out on a friend's shoulder.

Kaiden's smile kept Rus afloat. Seeing the joy of the evening had taken hold and kept him vigilant. All Rus wanted was to ensure this night would be cemented as fun. Mostly, he wanted to keep his friend safe, wash away the bad taste of bitter memories, and swim in this good time a bit longer.

"A perfectly drama-free evening," Dylan said with a bit of a swagger.

The sway of his hips kept Rus' attention fixed.

"No drama at all."

"I can wrangle up a little drama if anyone wants," Rus said, mimicking Dylan's swagger.

"Wrangle?" Kaiden asked. "You a cowboy now?"

"Maybe I always was," Rus said with a dreadful Southern accent while tipping his imaginary hat.

They all broke out into laughter, following Dylan back to his car, where he drove to Rus' apartment to close out the evening.

When they arrived at the complex, Rus caught Kaiden lingering, staring at his beat-up car.

"Come on in," Rus insisted, then turned his attention to Dylan, who still sat in his car. "It's late. Sleepovers are no biggie."

"Hmmmm." Kaiden pondered loudly. "On the one hand, I do have work in the morning, so I should head home. On the other hand, I'd rather not get yelled at for slipping through a window again."

"I can't believe you have to break into your own home." Rus scoffed.

"They keep it locked and tight for safety."

"But they know you break in," Rus added. "What's the point then?"

"The point is obstacles." Kaiden gestured with arms, quite dramatically.

"The point is your family is a bunch of bags of dicks," Dylan retorted.

"I concur," Rus teased.

It didn't take much to convince them to come inside. Everyone made their way inside and sat on Rus' bed, much like they always did, with the television on in the background as they unwound from the evening.

Rus kept his attention discreetly fixed on Dylan, who was lost in his phone, smiling so deeply it brought out his dimples. Kaiden, on the other hand, seemed lost in thought. The evening had gone well, more or less, but Rus worried Kaiden pushed himself to go just to prove it wasn't a big deal.

"You okay?" Rus nudged Kaiden.

"Yep."

"You sure?"

"Uh-huh."

"You have fun?"

"Meh."

"Noticed you got a little flirty for a minute, then just sort of fizzled."

"Ouch. I fizzled out?"

The awkward sound Rus released made Kaiden grin, and even drew Dylan away from his phone.

"No, I just noticed there was that guy you were chatting up, then sort of broke off the convo midway."

"He wanted to dance. I wasn't feeling a dance," Kaiden explained with a defiant huff. "Well, except when Dylan dragged me out, but how could I possibly say no to Dylan?"

"Okay, cool. I mean, I had no problem playing buffer," Rus clarified. "I just want to make sure you're not avoiding guys because of what happened. Like avoid them because they're not your type all day long, just I would hope—"

"It's not that," Kaiden said. "That's completely out of my head."

"You sure?"

"Yes, I mean, maybe not all the time, but that wasn't why I was dodging the flirty guy on the dance floor."

"Okay, then why were you dodging the flirty guy on the dance floor?" Dylan asked, locking his eyes on Kaiden in this suggestive, authoritative way.

Rus felt the pressure of their friendship, the way Dylan could ask so much with a simple look. Meanwhile, Rus still found himself in the learning stage, trying to decipher each of their quirks, mannerisms, inside jokes, and so much more.

"Okay, embarrassing, and I've never said this out loud…" Kaiden took a deep, sharp breath, holding it for a beat as he hesitated with his next words. "I've never actually kissed a guy before. Or anybody, really."

"What?" Rus and Dylan blurted at the same time.

"How did I not know this?" Dylan had this baffled expression that Rus tried to gauge, tried to read. "But you've… I mean, there was… I could've sworn…"

"So, you're a virgin?" Rus asked so quickly, he couldn't bite back the words or the unintentional judgy tone that accompanied them. "Not that that's a big deal. I mean, virgins rock. It's why they're sacrificed. And they survive the horror movies. Weddings have a whole archaic color-coded system for them. Also—"

"Stop." Dylan playfully slapped a hand over Rus' face.

"Sank ooo," Rus muttered in a muffled voice, grateful for Dylan's intervention and the gentle touch of his palm on Rus' lips.

"To answer your question, I'm not a virgin," Kaiden said. "Not since I was like twenty. But I am a twenty-four-year-old lip virgin. Or not lip virgin 'cause, you know, oral, but like I'm a lip kiss or kiss lip virgin."

Dylan slowly lowered his hand, the gears in his head slowly piecing together the new info. "I can't believe I didn't know that."

"I never said anything. It's embarrassing."

"Not at all," Dylan said. "But how does that work exactly?"

"Well, I'm not exactly a catch, so I'm not swimming in dates or anything." Kaiden paused long enough to eye Rus and Dylan, and Rus gathered from his stern stare that he wasn't fishing for compliments and didn't want Rus to throw in some polite commentary, so he stayed quiet and listened. "I've never been in a relationship. Not even those bad middle school relationships where you get together in first period, then send a breakup note through a friend during lunch or some shit. I've just never done the whole dating thing. Yet. It's coming. Once things are right."

"Why aren't they right?" Rus asked, genuine and curious.

"I mean, there's lots of reasons. It used to be my weight," Kaiden explained. "I used to be really fat. Like really, really big. And there's nothing wrong with that—plenty of folks get action and are happy with how they look, no matter their size. Good for them, honestly. I wish I could be one of those guys rocking out the thick daddy vibes. But some of us put value in every extra pound…or actually, we take away value in ourselves for every extra pound. And to be clear, I had a lot of extra pounds. So, naturally, I never dated anyone in high school. No one after high school. Then, when I finally lost the weight, I guess I didn't feel that much better about myself."

Kaiden shrugged, tightening his stomach with a short breath and a pinched expression.

Rus didn't understand Kaiden's obsession with being so skinny. Especially since he'd spent his entire life trying to bulk up. He'd kill for Kaiden's thick thighs and broad frame.

"I guess it kind of still is sometimes," Kaiden continued, running his fingers along his elegant corset vest. "This helps. Helps me feel more like how I want to be seen, but underneath it, things are rough."

"No, they're not," Dylan said. "You lost over a hundred pounds. That's fucking amazing."

Rus' eyes bulged, stunned and impressed.

"You're sweet, but please don't invalidate my feelings." Kaiden gave a tiny shrug. "It's okay not to be happy with your body. It's okay not to have body positivity in yourself, just because someone else said we all look perfect just the way we are. It's not fatphobic to be disappointed in my looks. I've been down that road, losing the unhealthy way, hating myself for the wrong reasons—"

"There's no right reason to hate oneself," Dylan interjected, then mimed a zip of his lips.

"True," Kaiden replied. "But it's okay to want more. And I want more. Which is why I've been on the correct path to weight loss, you know that. My fitness game is better than yours. Better than most of those red pill alpha wannabe douchebags."

Dylan nodded.

"Well, I'm damn impressed," Rus said.

"Thank you." Kaiden gave a soft smile. "I'm happy with the journey I'm on now, and proud of how far I've come. How I've stuck with it and learned healthier choices, not just starving myself. I just hope one day my body reflects the journey, shows all the hard work and dedication and definition I've put into it."

"So, no dating until your body is a ten?" Dylan asked, leaning down on the bed and propping himself up with his elbow.

"No, I'm actually probably kind of mostly sort of really okay with how I look when it comes to dating," Kaiden said with a sour expression. "Okay, maybe a few things I'd need to sit down and discuss with the guy beforehand, but yeah. I'm good with how I look. Mostly."

"So, why no dating?" Rus followed up.

"You haven't had the displeasure of stopping by my house," Kaiden said with a chuckle. "It's a disaster. It's hard enough finding a guy to meet for a hookup when I can't host, how the heck am I supposed to date someone? Introduce them to my entire family? My family, who doesn't even want me hanging a rainbow flag up, let alone have a guy over there."

"Fuck them," Rus said sharply.

"I still don't understand how you've never kissed anyone yet have fucked." Dylan gave an inquisitive look. "How does one pull this off?"

"Easy," Kaiden said. "Guys don't give a fuck about kissing."

"Not true," Rus said. Kissing was his favorite part. Granted, sometimes it wasn't always about kissing on the lips, or at least not those lips, but he liked the simple pleasures of pressing his body against another. The joy of tasting someone, the sensations of their body reacting to his touch.

"Well, the guys I've messed around with haven't," Kaiden explained. "It's weird making the first move when meeting up with someone for, you know."

"If you can do it, you can say it," Dylan said.

"It's hard dating because I live at home and I can't exactly bring a guy there. It's not easy meeting guys out in the world either, like you never know if they're gay or polite."

"Ain't that the truth?" Dylan high-fived Kaiden.

Rus had never really thought about that struggle. When it came to guys, he hadn't dated any. Not seriously. He hadn't dated anyone seriously since his high school girlfriend. Things ended rough and sort of zapped out all his emotional bandwidth. It helped that the college scene embraced casual flings and hookup culture. But he'd grown bored of those things, finding sex didn't fill that empty void his last relationship had left.

"So, when it comes to meeting guys, I turn to apps."

Dylan hissed. "The devil's playground."

They all laughed.

"Exactly," Kaiden said, stifling his laughter. "Most guys there are just looking for hookups, and at first, I just sort of wanted to experience something, anything, so I agreed to hookups. Unfortunately, most guys don't wanna kiss. They just want to jump straight to business—pun intended."

Rus quirked a brow. "Pun?"

"Most dudes on a hookup app are on the DL. Masc acting, straight men." Dylan used air quotes around 'straight'. "Those guys don't kiss as much because they don't want to be perceived as gay."

Rus was baffled by the notion. "But sticking their dick in a dude or having a dick poked into them is totally hetero?"

"Prison rules." Dylan shrugged. "And before you say it, yes, it applies. They're in a prison of their own making as they bastardize their life to live some heteronormative nonsense."

"I will never understand the fear of being bi," Rus said with a tsk. "Well, aside from the fact that everyone assumes you're lying because you want attention, or you're really just gay. Guys figure you'll run off to marry the first chick that offers you a baby, while girls assume you're thinking about dudes all the time, and everyone is certain you're an absolute slut. Monogamy is off the table—because, you know, total whore. Then there's bi erasure. Oh, and we're chaotic gremlins. But that last part is totally true."

Rus giggled at his own rambles, letting them roll off his tongue like an unwanted weight.

"Okay, maybe the bi label isn't that easy," he said with a grin. "But to just spend your whole life deluding yourself into thinking you're straight? I don't have the energy to gaslight myself that much."

"I think we all lie to ourselves about something." Dylan had a very stoic expression, which Rus studied, following his gaze that held Kaiden's bright green eyes.

"Welp, I can't do anything about DL dudes, sleazy hookup apps, or your horrible family—unless you want me to punch, that I can totally do," Rus said, cheeriness in his voice at the offer.

The silent seconds where Kaiden contemplated with the slyest of smiles made Rus' heart flutter.

"No beating up my family," Kaiden said. "No beating up anyone."

"Fiiiine," Rus said with a sigh. "But there is one thing we can fix tonight."

"What's that?"

Rus scooted closer to Kaiden, closing the distance between them as they sat on the bed.

"We can get you that first kiss."

"What? Really? No. How?" Kaiden's face turned bright red.

"I'm sure after waiting this long, part of you—even subconsciously—has been holding out for the perfect kiss." Rus placed a hand on Kaiden's shoulder, gently squeezing. "But you should know, the perfect kiss doesn't come right away. It takes practice to know what you want and what you can offer. It takes patience to find the right lips."

"Oh."

In the corner of his eye, Rus found Dylan captivated by the bold action. Rus didn't want to overthink his actions, didn't want to overstep them either, but he found himself entranced by Kaiden's raw vulnerability. He found himself compelled to test his curiosities. And maybe, despite her joking, Daysha had a point.

"Are you comfortable with a kiss?" Rus tilted his head, leaning in closer to Kaiden.

He smirked at how quickly Kaiden stopped breathing, like he'd somehow disappear if he stayed perfectly still.

"Yeah, I guess. I mean, are you comfortable? It's kind of—"

Before Kaiden could ramble his way out of this moment, Rus pressed his lips to the other man's. And yes, Rus knew that somehow, he was taking advantage of the situation, testing his own curiosities in the process.

The smack of their lips filled the quiet room. The smallest of nervous giggles escaped Kaiden's mouth before Rus drew him in entirely. Since Kaiden had no experience, Rus led with his tongue, guiding their mouths in this moment, using his piercing to tease Kaiden, and his hands to adjust Kaiden's head.

Each second that ticked held a tiny infinity that Rus would carry with him. He held Kaiden's first kiss—quite the responsibility. It was a bit messier than he'd intended, but Kaiden lost himself in the passion, and Rus found himself falling into the embrace. Part of him wanted to push Kaiden down onto the mattress, to straddle him as he taught him his first kiss, to taste his excitement as he grinded against the other man.

Instead, Rus pulled back, remembering they weren't quite alone in the room, and a kiss transformed into a make-out session might be harder for friends to brush off.

"Wow. That was just… Wow." Kaiden blushed, breathless, and fumbled to compose himself.

"Now, you two should kiss." Rus gestured to the space between Kaiden and Dylan.

"What?"

"Absolutely," Rus continued. "If you've only been kissed by one guy, you have nothing to really compare it to. Now, a sample size of two isn't much, but it'll prepare you for the next guy you meet on the devil's playground."

They all laughed again, but this time, Rus caught the edge of nervousness in both their voices, working so hard to hide their anxious anticipation.

"Oh, I'm so done with apps."

"All the same," Rus said. "It'll get you that much closer to the perfect kiss."

Dylan scooted over, sitting up crisscrossed in the process. His left knee brushed against Rus' leg, rousing a spark of desire in him. How he'd like to taste Dylan next, but he deluded himself into believing this was a moment for Kaiden. It was as much a moment for Rus, an experience, a craving.

The yearning in Dylan's eyes when they locked onto Kaiden suggested as much held true for him, too.

"Just a reminder that a kiss can be everything or nothing at all," Dylan said. "Between friends, they decide."

Rus watched the intensity in both their expressions, the chemistry that sparked in the air between them, the unspoken consent with a simple graze of Kaiden's fingers over Dylan's forearm.

It was as if this was the first time these two had truly seen each other. Truly experienced these feelings with each other. The calmness before their lips met seemed friendly and playful, but there was a silent sizzle, a pop in the atmosphere as their mouths pressed.

Their kiss came with a passion Rus hadn't noticed between them until just this second. The gentle smack of Dylan's guiding lips, the curious exploration of Kaiden's tongue. A soft caress as fingers trailed up arms, leaving a wake of excited goosebumps.

It seemed Rus didn't need to test his curiosities out; he could see where the real passion lay.

"Well, that was certainly something." Kaiden smirked, eyeing Dylan, then Rus, then the space between the three of them.

An infinite space in Rus' mind, feeling like an interloper in his own apartment.

"Now, you two have to kiss." Kaiden gestured between the pair. "Fair is fair."

"What?" Dylan asked, grinning wide and goofy and adorable.

"Um, this was more of a learning experience," Rus said, trying not to quash the moment. "Not really a—"

"It's a kiss off," Kaiden said.

"A what?" Rus and Dylan asked in unison.

"It's like arm wrestling, with the strongest person landing on top."

"Kissing is nothing like arm wrestling," Rus said.

"Well, damn, then I'm doing it wrong. Guess I have more to learn, so I should probably watch the pros this round."

Rus was unsure why he resisted the idea of sharing a kiss with Dylan. Maybe it just felt awkward, encroaching on the sparks he'd seen between Kaiden and Dylan, even if the pair had missed them.

"It's a little like arm wrestling." Dylan puckered his lips dramatically, seemingly taking nothing seriously in the best way possible. "But the best lips don't always land on top."

Rus snickered.

"In fact, sometimes…" Dylan teasingly raised his brows as he leaned in closer to Rus. "They're best served by—"

Rus rushed in, slapping his lips against Dylan's, silencing the other man as he tasted every unsaid joke Dylan now kept to himself.

Where Rus moved with a gentle, guiding touch with Kaiden, he now used a more assertive and demanding approach. Dylan didn't simply submit, following Rus' lead. Oh no, he practically bucked against Rus as he adjusted himself, moving his lips and body in tandem. Both resisted the urge to collide into one another. To slam into a powerful embrace as they shared this moment. Rus felt the tension in Dylan as he fought as hard to keep the kiss just a kiss, much like Rus did.

When their lips parted, he panted, eyes locked onto Dylan for a moment, yet still instinctively drawn to Kaiden. Somehow, testing his curiosities had worked out perfectly, except for one small problem. He liked them both but worried they might actually like each other.

CHAPTER 10
DYLAN

WHAT started as a curiosity for Dylan, a surprise sprung on him by Rus, had transformed into a fast-growing desire to continue. Without a second thought, Dylan wrapped a hand around the back of Kaiden's head, pulling him into a second kiss.

"What are you…" Kaiden panted between the smack of their lips, perhaps instinctively drawn to follow through on their kiss.

"Just having a little fun," Dylan said, incapable of taking anything too seriously, treating anything with the heavy weight of real passion.

All the same, he found himself yearning for Kaiden, craving Rus, drawn into a tug of war with his body's desires.

He turned back to Rus, kissing him once again, and leaning back onto the bed in the process. Rus didn't require any guidance. He followed suit, crawling on top of Dylan as they continued kissing.

It was late. Dylan was exhausted, yet he found himself in this euphoric state, compelled to follow this through, to chase this carnal pleasure, and see where it led.

As he continued kissing Rus, Dylan spotted an anxious Kaiden in the corner of his vision. With a firm grip, Dylan guided Kaiden's hand closer. A part of Dylan wanted to run his hands along Kaiden's broad chest, unravel the laces of Kaiden's corset vest, but he knew his friend too well. Kaiden would never allow such things, far too self-conscious. That didn't mean they couldn't all have fun, though.

Kaiden followed Dylan's gentle instruction, and they ran their hands alongside each other up Rus' side. Soon, Rus broke away from Dylan's mouth and found his way back to Kaiden's, drawing him closer until they were kissing. It allowed him the chance to caress their bodies, move them closer together, squeeze between their embrace from time to time, locking lips with each of them.

Dylan had had a few threesomes over the years. Hell, Dylan had had many sexual experiences over the years, from blowing rockstars to banging truckers and even testing out kinks he'd never before conceived of. But none had left him this jittery with excitement, this breathless with anticipation, and this eager to please his partner.

That was because Dylan stuck to one simple rule when it came to sex: keep it casual. Feelings messed up everything. It certainly made his life harder when he was younger. But now he'd found himself in a good place, a stable sense of self, and he'd wanted to explore possibilities.

"Wait." Kaiden pulled away from Dylan's mouth. "This is…this is a little much."

"Okay, we can slow down," Rus said, still softly rubbing his hand against Dylan's thigh. "I'd say you're ready for any kisses that come your way, though."

Dylan smirked. Kaiden didn't.

"You all right?" He sat up, trying to evaluate his friend.

"Fine." Kaiden withdrew emotionally and physically as he retreated to the edge of the bed. "It's late. Very late. Tonight was a blast, though. Like in all the best ways, seriously. Really. You know? But I've got work killer early. I mean, I planned on going out, but like now it's almost two, and I think I should head home."

"What? No." Dylan moved to stop Kaiden as he rushed to slide on his shoes. "It's way too late to drive home."

"Not really." Kaiden gave a forced smile. "My secret window makes everything easier. Plus, work early. But you guys should totally continue the kiss off. Or whatever off. Have fun, really. Seriously."

And just like that, Kaiden left. Practically fled, according to the swirling thoughts in Dylan's head. His heart hammered, and his throat constricted. Suddenly, the realization of what they'd done hit him.

"I know he said we could continue," Rus said, almost startling Dylan from the inner workings of his mind. "But maybe we just chill?"

"Yeah…" Dylan pondered his friendship with Kaiden, his lust for Rus, his mixing feelings for both. "Yeah, that sounds good."

"Sorry if I made things weird."

"You?" Dylan shook his head. "Not at all."

"No, I'm pretty sure I did."

The silence between them turned awkward, and it seemed neither guy knew how to break the tension. Each slid into the bed, and despite usually sleeping in the center, Dylan scooted himself to the far edge—in Kaiden's regular spot. Now, the middle had transformed into a vacant chasm.

Dylan lost himself in doubt. This was why he kept intimacy casual and with strangers. Somehow, he'd turned a tiny crush on Rus into a whirlwind of events, making out with him and his best friend. His only friend, really, other than Jasmine. But she was really family at this point.

Was it a mistake to lean into Rus' little kiss-off game?

Kaiden ran away, so clearly this was the wrong move for him. Rus didn't want to continue, probably because he only started this to pursue Kaiden—not Dylan. Now, Dylan lay awake, wondering if he ruined two friendships by pushing boundaries further than they were willing to go.

Maybe if they'd stopped at one kiss each, the singular curiosity, then everything would be fine. Awkward, but in a funny anecdote sort of way. Not in a run-for-your-life and escape kind of way.

Dylan tossed and turned throughout the night, thinking about the taste of Kaiden's lips, the grind of Rus' body pressed against his, the way he craved them both so much in that moment. The way he might've ruined things with both over such a small moment.

The persistent buzz of Dylan's phone on the nightstand woke him earlier than he'd wanted, especially after such a long night out.

"Hello," Dylan answered in a hoarse, scratchy voice.

"Where are you?" Jasmine asked frantically. "I know you're not always here, but I thought with the kids' appointment this morning—"

"Oh, shit." Dylan sprang out of bed. "So, so sorry, Jasmine. I completely blanked. I'll be there in fifteen. I didn't miss it, did I?"

"No, but you're cutting it close."

"Don't worry. I got it."

He'd found himself so distracted by wanting to ensure Kaiden had a good night out after everything that had happened, he spaced on his calendar events. It didn't help that he spent half the night pining for two men who he wondered if he should've kissed or not.

Would he regret kissing them, or would he have regretted never kissing them? Dylan didn't have time to dwell on what was or what might've been. He had to go.

Rus rustled awake as Dylan scrambled to get dressed.

"Damn," Rus said with a gravelly rasp. "Everyone's fleeing the apartment. Starting to get a complex."

"It's not that," Dylan said with an awkward smile. "I have an appointment. Well, the teens have an appointment, and I'm their transportation."

"Understood."

"We'll talk soon. About everything," Dylan assured Rus. "Including the other fleeing, if you're open to it."

"You also thinking about how fast I scared Kaiden away?"

"You?" Dylan laughed. "Pretty sure it was me."

"Nah, you're his bestie. I'm just the creepy guy trying to mash faces with both of you."

"Not at all." Dylan smiled sincerely as the weight of anxiety lifted off him. "So, you did want to kiss both of us?"

"I mean, I basically initiated the make-out session. Well, you might've pushed for that, but I got us started."

It seemed Rus held the same concerns, and maybe just maybe they were all in their head a little too deeply on last night's events. A simple conversation could clear this all up.

Dylan checked his phone and slipped his shoes on. "Shit. Talk soon. Promise."

Dylan rushed out of Rus' apartment, driving home as quickly as he could. He'd completely spaced on the dental appointments. It was hard enough for Jasmine to balance appointments for twelve teens; she didn't need the added stress of their transportation falling through.

When Dylan was a teen resident at Dorothy's Home, seven was the max. Also, the home they had at the time wasn't half as nice as the place Jasmine got a few years back. After ten years of rundown houses, with makeshift bedrooms made out of basements and walk-in closets, and sketchy neighborhoods, Jasmine finally got the funding to purchase a new home fully up to code and spacious enough to keep two teens to a room for a change.

Dylan could drive through the neighborhood a million times and still feel out of place in this suburban beauty. While he was proud Jasmine had gotten this place for the kids—for him too, as a staff resident—he often felt she'd brought them somewhere they didn't belong. They were a Jenga piece being wedged into a scenic puzzle.

Speaking of out of place, the first thing Dylan spotted when he drove up to the house was a neighborly conversation between Jasmine and one of the suburban Karens who'd declared herself the self-appointed president of the non-existent HOA. She, like many of the suburban Karens, made it her goal to protect this neighborhood from outside threats. Despite living here, she never recognized Jasmine, Dylan, or any of the teens as members of her neighborhood.

Suburban Karen wore an unshapely dress that boxed away her slender frame. Almost as unshapely as her perfectly straightened blonde hair. It hung lifelessly, rocking back and forth between her shoulder blades. The heavy make-up she wore added a bit of color to her face but didn't detract from her porcelain complexion.

"Afternoon, ladies." Dylan's cheeks strained as he forced a smile. Few people got under his skin, finding it easy to ignore jerks, but something about Suburban Karen's antagonistic persistence wore on Dylan.

"Glad you're here," Jasmine said with a strained smile of her own. "They're inside."

"Can you please pay attention when I speak to you?" Suburban Karen asked, snapping her fingers in Jasmine's face.

The sudden shift in Jasmine's demeanor was obvious. All the same, aside from an aggressive stare, she did her best to curb her anger for the insulting finger snap.

"Someone is running around this neighborhood vandalizing homes, destroying private property, and—"

"And that sounds like something that doesn't concern me or my children."

"It's convenient that it hasn't happened to your home," Suburban Karen said.

"It's convenient it hasn't happened to any home on our block, or the next two blocks over," Jasmine countered. "In fact, if I recall, someone said your house has been targeted three times now."

"Makes me wonder if maybe they're only aiming for the bitches who run their mouth," Miguel said, announcing himself as he strutted down the driveway and toward Dylan's car.

Snickers from two other teens living in the house trailed behind Miguel. Dylan did his best not to join in with the laughter at Miguel's bold and abrasive entrance, instead focusing on ensuring he grabbed everyone with an appointment this morning.

Chelsea strutted alongside Yazmin, her vibrant bi-colored hair sparkling under the sunlight.

Yazmin had a deep amber complexion, complemented by the white jersey she wore to show off her school spirit. Unlike most of the teens in Dorothy's Home who did their best to blend, Yazmin worked hard to leave her mark by joining every varsity sport she could land. Volleyball, soccer, and track team. It kept her busier than most and often left Dylan playing chauffeur after practices and games when needed.

Most of the kids just wanted to survive high school, finding themselves thrust into a new district and a confusing home after losing their old life because of a lifestyle their parents refused to accept.

Not Yazmin. She'd apparently been very active in athletics at her last school until she'd been outed as the lecherous lesbian in locker rooms. Between teammates who feared her, a school that didn't support her, and a family that refused to accept her, it didn't take long for her to find her way at the doorstep of Dorothy's Home.

Thankfully, the high school all the teens attended now had a very strong anti-bullying policy and had grown to accept students from all walks of life. Mainly due to a decade of persistent community campaigning by Jasmine, who made herself vocal at every single PTA meeting.

"How dare you speak to me that way?" Suburban Karen's offended expression mixed with furious contempt as she locked her eyes on Miguel.

"And how dare you offend my eyes with that tacky ass dress and heavy blush that does nothing to hide that corpse-like face you're walking around with." Miguel didn't mince words with anyone. It got him in trouble at school on more than one occasion. With staff and students. It didn't make him any less mouthy; in fact, it only added to his cutting comments.

Dylan didn't have to strain to smile now, giving Suburban Karen a big ole grin as she absorbed the depths of Miguel's insults. Honestly, she was quite fortunate that they had an appointment to keep; otherwise, Miguel could fill his entire morning picking this headache of a woman apart.

"Good luck," Dylan mouthed to Jasmine, who simply gestured for him to get out before her headache got any bigger.

Miguel had taken the passenger seat, leaving the girls to cram in the backseat. The drive quickly turned into a chaotic whirlwind of chatter.

"And where were you last night, mister?" Miguel asked, pointing his phone like a mic.

"Out."

"With Kaiden?"

"No," Chelsea said. "He's always hanging out with that juvie dude."

"First off, his name is Rus, not juvie dude. Second, he was never convicted of anything," Dylan said. "Third, juvie is for children."

Chelsea tsked. "He looks like a child."

Miguel smacked his lips in response. "Don't be talking about my short king like that."

Dylan focused on the road, ignoring their back and forth. It became clear that Miguel had a crush on Rus. It seemed everyone did.

"So, what'd you do that had you out all night?" Miguel asked, turning his attention to the girls in the back seat. "You know, Dylan's been MIA from the house quite a bit lately. Always out and about, living his best life and having sleepovers God knows where."

Chelsea and Yazmin 'ooooed' in the back seat, followed by some lewd gestures. When Chelsea made gagging noises, the cacophony of chaos caused Dylan to lose sight of the road and suddenly slam his brakes at the intersection.

"Fucking hell," Miguel shouted.

Dylan's heart pounded, pumping adrenaline through his stressed veins.

"Q and A is over," Dylan said. "Just be quiet, please."

"Welp, we can cross back shots off the list of what you were doing last night," Miguel said with the smuggest flair of sass. "Because no one laying it down is going to be this wound tight."

"Yup," Chelsea and Yazmin asserted in unison.

Thankfully, it didn't take much longer to reach the dentist's office, and they sent Miguel in first to have his braces adjusted. Chelsea and Yazmin lost themselves on their phones since the waiting room was flooded with small children. It offered Dylan a bit of peace. He used the time to check his own phone.

He sent Kaiden a text, which almost immediately showed a "read" message below. No surprise. Kaiden had a habitual need to read and respond to any message as quickly as possible. This anxious quirk Dylan had always found cute.

The floating bubbles of a response danced on Dylan's phone for the better part of a minute. Hell, he spent so much time staring at their rhythmic bounce that his screen actually turned black in the process. When Dylan swiped his phone back to an open screen, he found the bubbles had vanished. The message remained on read, but Kaiden didn't respond to the simple check-in message.

That didn't bode well in Dylan's mind. Kaiden could be having a million feelings about their friendship right now, about their kiss, and for the first time in the three years since they'd known each other, he was dodging Dylan.

With no response, Dylan followed up with Rus from this morning, figuring he'd be leaving his first class right about now.

> Dylan: Sorry about rushing out this morning.

> Rus: Totally get it. What happened exactly?

> Dylan: Dentist appt. Had to take some of the teens.

> Rus: Aaaaaaaah. Makes sense.

Dylan sat quietly, contemplating, searching for the right words to send his next message.

> Dylan: I've been hanging out with you and Kaiden so much I've sort of lost track of what's going on at home.

> Rus: Is that a bad thing?

> Dylan: *shrugs* no but also maybe? IDK. Last night was great until well...

> Rus: Regrets?

> Dylan: No?

> Rus: It was a bad move on my part. I had a crush and I tested a boundary. Now I'm worried I pushed too far.

> Dylan: Crush? On Kaiden?

It made sense. Rus swooped in real fast to make a move on Kaiden the second an opportunity presented itself. And when Kaiden made a request for Rus to kiss Dylan, he obeyed almost immediately.

> Rus: Both.

That made Dylan's heart flutter. Then the flutter quickly twisted into knots that turned into a pit weighing on his stomach.

> Rus: Hanging with you and Kaiden has been awesome. And I like hanging out with both of you. A lot. A LOT. I kind of got a crush but didn't know what to do with it. If I should even do anything with it. Then last night I sort of said fuck it and went for it.

> Dylan: Bold.

> Rus: Stupid. You saw Kaiden literally flee my place at 2 in the morning.

> Dylan: :/

> Dylan: Not stupid. Unexpected.

Bubbles danced, then stopped as Rus clearly contemplated what to reply with next.

> Dylan: I think we just take a few days to reflect on what happened and see where we land.

> Rus: Meaning?

> Dylan: Meaning do we have the awkward conversations about feelings. In person. No texting crush vibes. OR do we have the talk about staying just friends who occasionally on very rare occasions in the most casually occasional kind of way make out.

Rus sent a barrage of crying laughing emojis.

> Rus: I think you have a point. I'm gonna use this weekend to head home. Clear my head.

> Dylan: Makes sense.

They continued texting for a bit, sending silly GIFs until Dylan was called back by the dentist to discuss Chelsea's cavities. He started checking his schedule and writing down information to relay to Jasmine.

Afterward, he returned to the waiting room as Yazmin was finally called back.

Dylan wondered what the result of a few days to reflect would be. In what direction would his feelings settle? Part of him wanted to explore this curiosity with Rus. Another part of him wanted to find out where his feelings for Kaiden had been this entire time. It was as if one moment he was looking at his best friend and the next, he was lost in this deep, sweeping desire to explore everything with Kaiden.

Maybe friendship was the best route. Dylan couldn't fathom deciding between Rus and Kaiden. He also couldn't imagine dating one of them and staying just friends with the other while the three of them hung out, casually ignoring the night they all made out.

Worst of all, Dylan worried that this time of reflection might reveal that Rus and Kaiden had a stronger crush on each other than on him. Maybe their connection worked better. It made more sense to Dylan since he couldn't sort his feelings out for the life of him.

That pit in his stomach twisted tighter as he realized he'd have to be okay with it. He'd have to be okay with their feelings or risk losing two friendships.

Fuck, Dylan regretted so much.

CHAPTER 11
KAIDEN

IT was the most awkward and arousing experience of Kaiden's life. He lay in his bed, wide awake and ignoring his morning errands in favor of a small existential crisis. For the life of him, he couldn't get the memories of that night out of his head. The smell of Dylan's sweat and cologne, the taste of tobacco on Rus' lips, the firmness of their bodies pressed against his, the excitement in their gaze, the curiosity in their eyes, the hunger in their expressions.

The most maddening part of this was that Kaiden didn't have anyone to talk to about it. If he were to talk to anyone, it'd be Dylan. But he couldn't exactly discuss how hung up he was on Dylan's kiss with Dylan, especially since he found himself entranced by Rus in equal measure. It wasn't just the kisses. The touches. The passion. It was the kindness, the consideration, the sincerity in who Kaiden was and how he ticked.

When Dylan texted Kaiden about hanging out this weekend, he seriously considered it. Especially sinceRus had group texted he'd be out of town this weekend, some college three-day weekend trip home. If Kaiden were going to work up the nerve to talk about these kisses, these feelings, it'd probably be that much easier to just talk to one of them at a time. Then again, could he really talk to Dylan about these bizarre blossoming whatevers?

Kaiden couldn't figure out what to make of his feelings for Dylan or Rus. The idea of Dylan being anything more than a friend was difficult to comprehend. It wasn't like Kaiden hadn't considered it. Oh, he'd most certainly daydreamed about Dylan once upon a time. He was funny and flirty. Mostly, he was nice. It didn't hurt that he was adorable to look at and had no qualms about showing off his tight stomach at pretty much every opportunity.

But Dylan was out of Kaiden's league. Truthfully, Kaiden didn't believe he had any prospects to offer anyone. Sure, he'd lost weight, he'd jumped on the fitness train, but the insecurity of his skin still followed him. The inner fat boy still haunted him every time he stared at his reflection. And Kaiden really tried to see himself for who he'd become, to take pride in the accomplishments he'd made.

Kaiden just couldn't celebrate one tiny victory when he had so many other faults. Sure, he gained control over his binge eating and worked out regularly to get into some semblance of shape, but he still blundered a thousand other things. He lived at home with his family. He had a job he enjoyed, but not one that paid well or came with benefits. His car was garbage and cost more to keep running than the damned thing was worth. He wasn't smart enough for college—hell, he barely managed to graduate from high school.

It just didn't make any sense.

Why would Dylan or Rus be interested in Kaiden?

He had nothing to offer them. No charming personality, no good looks, and certainly nothing materialistic.

He worried the kiss was pity. And that made facing either of them again that much harder. He didn't want to drag Dylan or Rus down, didn't want to hold them back, and somehow, he felt like he now stood in their way.

An awkward, silly conversation that turned into a wonderful kiss, followed by an enchanting kiss, met with the most spectacular five minutes of Kaiden's life… But now he believed himself an intrusion on what was clearly palpable chemistry between Dylan and Rus.

Speaking of intrusions, the loud creak of Kaiden's bedroom door alerted him to the presence of someone approaching.

"You're actually home for a change," Kaiden's mother said, standing in the doorway with a basket of laundry.

He didn't reply, lost in his thoughts, twisted up in his feelings, and lacking any real outlet to divulge them.

His mother invited herself into his bedroom, much like she always did, and started to fold clothes. Not Kaiden's clothes. Nope. She never volunteered, and honestly, most of his wardrobe required a gentle touch from the suits he had to the corset vests he'd handwash or occasionally send out for drycleaning if he could afford such luxuries. No, the laundry belonged to his nephews, and their dressers ate up a good chunk of space in Kaiden's bedroom.

"You've been going out a lot," she said, tucking away a pair of pajamas. "Partying? Clubbing? Anything risky like last time?"

Kaiden scoffed. His family only brought up his incident as a warning about the dangers his lifestyle brought. After the heated argument with his sister, he learned not to engage when someone in his family made an offhanded quip. It was easier to nod and ignore than speak and educate. None of them were interested in learning a goddamn thing.

"It's been challenging watching the boys day in and day out."

"Yeah, grandkids can be a handful."

Kaiden knew exactly where this conversation was heading—a guilt trip. His mother had used them time and time again when recruiting Kaiden into helping with things that shouldn't have been his responsibility.

"It's put a lot of pressure on your sister," his mother continued. "With work, the kids, saving up, especially with so many unforeseen expenses…"

Kaiden did his best to tune out his mother. It pained him to ignore her plight, but the thing was, it wasn't her plight. It was Sandra. He'd gone out of his way to help for years without asking for a thing in return, even letting the subtle homophobic attitudes in the house slide. But after their argument, he realized there was nothing subtle about her bigotry, her disdain for his lifestyle, her disgust.

If she wanted to blame Kaiden for his own assault, then he'd continue refusing his assistance. He sure as hell wasn't going to give up his evenings and days off to watch his nephews and baby niece when their own father couldn't be bothered to sacrifice one night to watch them.

"Your father and I were—"

"Stepfather," Kaiden corrected.

"We were discussing how you're not contributing anymore." His mother stopped folding a pair of jeans midway, practically using them as some type of buffer to shield herself from Kaiden.

She hated conflict almost as much as he did, which was why she always sided with the majority, and why Kaiden almost always got left on the outside of any argument.

"Not contributing?" He sat up, offended at that notion. "I do all the grocery shopping. I'm the only reason we have any streaming services in this house. Pretty sure the electricity is still in my name because John can't—"

"You know how difficult things have been for your father," his mother interjected, nostrils flaring, and eyes already watering.

"Stepfather," Kaiden snapped, refusing to let his mother slip in the familial term like it meant a goddamn thing.

John had made it clear from every skipped school event, every field trip form left unsigned, every doctor's visit he'd forgotten, every bully he supported to knock some sense into Kaiden, and a million other tiny horrors that he didn't consider Kaiden family. He was simply the unwanted toddler from a bad marriage. Sandra was his only child, and Kaiden found himself reminded of this fact every day of his life.

"At least he's here," Kaiden's mother said, drawing him away from buried childhood nightmares. "Unlike you, going out every night, leaving us to fend for ourselves, exploiting our good grace."

"Exploiting?" Kaiden scoffed. "I share a room with my fucking nephews."

"More like you take away from a room your nephews could have."

"Excuse me?"

"Sandy has been working so hard to give them everything she can, just like me and your father try to give you kids everything we can," his mother spoke with a tremble in her voice, puppeteering some rehearsed speech, no doubt. Only Kaiden couldn't discern if this was a speech she'd practiced herself or been coached on by John and Sandra. "We all just feel that if you're going to continue living here, refusing to contribute, to help, then you should be paying rent."

"For half a fucking bedroom?" Kaiden rolled out of his bed, gesturing to all the toys strewn about, the bunk beds, the crammed closet, and every other bit consumed by his nephews. "I'm sorry, a third of a fucking bedroom."

"Do not swear at me." His mother jabbed her finger in the air. "It is not my fault you're sharing this bedroom. If you didn't like the arrangement, you've had years to save up and get your own place. But wait? Can't do that, can you? Not when you're floating between jobs and partying it up."

"Floating between jobs?" Kaiden snapped. "Do you mean the job that fired me because my car broke down, and no one here would take me to work? Or maybe the job that was a thirty-five-minute commute—on a good day—but wouldn't give me more than twenty hours a week. Maybe you mean the job where Sandra came in with her kids and caused a scene. Gotta love family drama on the clock. That made for a fun resume update."

"I'm not letting you drag me into an argument," his mother said calmly. "I just wanted to let you know your father and I have discussed this. Moving forward, you will be contributing your fair share."

"Okay, so what exactly are you charging me per month?" Kaiden asked, whipping out his phone and pulling up the calculator. "Because I'd like to start making some deductive calculations. I sure as shit am not helping with utilities and food on top of rent for a half-bedroom and some goddamn basement storage."

"If that's how you feel, then maybe you should leave."

Kaiden tsked. "And go where?"

"Exactly." His mother grabbed her laundry basket and shot him a cold glare.

Kaiden was at a loss, completely adrift with no idea what to do next.

POLITICS AND POLY

Every fiber of his body wanted to scream, to rage against his family and their constant war against him. Another part wanted to flee, to find the people who made him feel seen, safe, and sane.

But he couldn't go running to Dylan or Rus, not when he was still lost on the dilemma of what they meant to him. What they meant to each other. He needed time to think, to figure out his feelings, to let them realize their feelings. He was certain they liked each other, and he started to spiral, worried perhaps he was the singular obstacle standing in the way of Rus and Dylan from taking the next step.

CHAPTER 12
RUS

RUS didn't know what to do with himself, so he used the three-day weekend to drive home and finally took his mom up on an impromptu trip. She'd begged him to return home every chance he had since enrolling in college, and after his assault at Himbos, she'd pleaded even more. Hell, she threatened to drive up to the college herself, speak to the local authorities, and put pressure on them for results in the type of way only a mother could do.

Unfortunately, his parents had also decided to use this particular three-day weekend as an escape from their routine. They were out of town, leaving Rus mostly alone except for his older sister, who locked herself away in her bedroom.

Rus was hoping for a distraction, clarity, a chance to work through his thoughts, maybe talk to his mom vaguely about what was happening. Instead, all he got was a quiet house to ponder and overthink what happened between Dylan and Kaiden. More like what didn't happen.

Unable to sleep and in no mood to drink, Rus decided to step outside for a smoke and wander old trails to clear his mind. These haunts used to be an escape so he could have a cigarette without getting in trouble, to smoke a joint without getting a "back in my day" commentary on the wild 80s, or maybe even make out without worrying about a sibling snitching and busting open his bedroom door.

The trails were great for hiking, which meant lots of strangers passing by, so Rus and his friends all learned which off-road paths to wander when looking for a bit of peace and quiet.

He made his way through the woods, deep in the darkness, with only the moon's light peering between pockets of trees to guide him and muscle memories to lead him. Eventually, he found his way to a favorite haunt. A broken-down playset. The pony spring riders with faded colors and cigarette burns around the eyes. The sandbox dirt had finally grown over with more plants than the actual forest floor around the sandbox.

All Rus cared about was the swing. He carefully rested on the weathered seat and finished his cigarette.

"Ikky!" squealed a high-pitched voice.

Rus balled a fist, then buried his annoyance for the worst nickname in the world. To any bystander, they'd assume Ikky was icky, and the person shouting at him wanted to imply Rus was gross in the most juvenile manner. Unfortunately, it was so much worse than that. Nope, she was one of the few people who knew Rus' full name and taunted him with the worst nickname ever.

The teachers who knew Rus' name never had the chance to share it in class since his scowl and quick protest always interjected their attempt. His parents stopped using his full name when he declared he would only be known as Rus henceforth. Yes, he used the phrase 'henceforth' in his argument, attempting to sound grown at the age of nine. Then he proceeded to give the entire house the silent treatment until everyone abided by his choice. His brother broke that pact once on Rus' tenth birthday and got a black eye and two missing teeth. Baby teeth, but the point was made.

"What brings you to my neck of the woods?" Lana Alvar took delicate steps between the thin trees.

Her flowy pink blouse had a white glow to it under the starry night. The frayed edges of her short shorts barely peeked out from beneath her top, leaving her legs exposed. She'd tanned a lot since the last time he'd seen her.

As she stepped between the trees, she gripped one, running her fingers along the bark before swinging a bit. The slight twirl around the thin trees helped launch Lana forward with her last few steps.

Chaotic and reckless, just as Rus recalled.

Lana barreled ahead, colliding with him and nearly knocking him out of the swing as she turned Rus into a seat of her own. Straddling his waist, she balanced herself on the rusted chains of the swing.

"Well?" She let out a heavy exhale, blowing her blonde bangs out of her face. It'd been a long time since Lana was a blonde. Rus liked it along with the pixie cut she'd gone with.

Rus craned his neck and groaned. He couldn't tell if Lana was flirting or teasing. With her, it was never so simple. Part of what kept him locked in her orbit for so many years. First loves were the hardest to quit. Even if she was the absolute worst fifth-grade girlfriend in the world. Breaking his heart over lunch and then ignoring him until seventh grade. But that rekindled spark kept him fawning until ninth grade, and at her side until senior year.

Chances were, Rus would still be attached to Lana if she hadn't disappeared to Europe shortly after graduation without so much as a goodbye kiss. When she returned two years later, he'd created a new life at college. Though occasionally, in moments like this, he questioned those choices.

"You're no fun anymore," Lana said, sliding off Rus and plopping into the swing beside him.

When the entire set shook, both of them clutched their chains like it'd make a difference if the bars collapsed around and atop them.

"That freshman fifteen is hitting me hard." Lana laughed, pretending her weight had any true role in this decrepit swing set's rumble.

Lana was a tiny thing, shorter than Rus by several inches, and very slender. Still, for such a small thing, her legs extended quite long and graceful as she kicked back on the swing.

"You're in college?"

"Community college," she replied. "Nothing fancy like you, darling."

"No, smarter," he said with a chuckle. "You'll get a real skill and none of the debt."

"Well, I always was smarter than you."

"That how you knew I'd be out here?"

Lana smiled, hiding her devious expression behind the rusted chains of her swing. "True love's spark gave me a sign."

"Lying ass." Rus snorted.

"Okay, maybe your sister texted."

"Snitch."

"Total bitch," Lana replied. "It's why I love her more than you."

It seemed Rus and Lana had worked their way past the screaming stage of their breakup. He called her every name in the book when she returned, not so much a word, or an explanation for why she'd taken off. He supposed he knew the answer already, but it still hurt that she had abandoned him.

Rus stared at the tattoo on his wrist, the Valentine's Day he'd never forget. Not for a million lifetimes.

"Where's your head?"

"Lost on Lana." Rus puckered his lips and pressed a hand to his mouth, dramatically blowing a kiss.

"Damn straight."

"Ugh, never straight."

"True. Even your dick is curved."

"Seriously?"

"What?" Lana shrugged. "It's a good thing."

"Uh-huh."

Lana kicked herself closer to him, using the momentum to nudge Rus. He played into it, swinging wonky himself, and soon their legs ended up intertangled as they weaved back and forth on the swings.

Their laughter echoed in the woods. Rus' heart pounded so loudly, so loudly he couldn't hear anything else. It allowed him to fall back into old memories. Love and loss and life and Lana.

Somehow, their rusty chains ended up twirling round and round each other until Rus and Lana were face to face, breathing heavy, and lost in each other's eyes.

Lana leaned forward, lips almost grazing against Rus' until he pulled away.

The silence was awkward, chilling even on such a warm night. It took seemingly forever for their swings to untangle from each other, eyes meeting every time they twirled around, slowly unwinding and returning to their own space.

"Smart call." Lana chuckled, staring up at the moonlit clouds. "We never work, do we?"

"Unfortunate but true."

"I'd burn the world for you, darling."

"And I'd hand you the match, love."

"Is there someone else?" she asked.

"Maybe I'm just not that into you."

"Wounded." She gasped, feigning insult.

"And yeah, there is sort of someone." Rus awkwardly shrugged, like he was weighing things. He was, in a sense. Weighing how much of his life to elaborate. "Sort of some*ones* else. Plural. It's weird."

"I'm intrigued."

"There's these two guys, and I don't know… I like them both, but…"

"Why choose, darling?" Lana raised her brows. "And if they find out, just remind them you're not monogamous until there's a solid convo stating otherwise."

"No, not two guys like that." Rus rocked his head side to side, trying to find the words. "Like, we all kissed. Not at the same time, but sort of. In the same room, together, back and forth. There was a chance of more. Between the three of us."

"Oooooh." Lana's eyes went wide. "Poly boys. Fun. I am so jealous, darling."

"Don't be," Rus said. "I'm not sure what to do. Like, I'm not sure if things fizzled out because, you know, logistics or it being overwhelming or whatever…"

Rus worried that maybe Kaiden or Dylan or both of them just weren't into him. Maybe Rus was just the necessary conduit to spark the romance they'd been tiptoeing around. They'd been friends for a while. So long, they never realized how they felt for each other. Maybe Rus was getting in the way of what they could have with each other. He didn't want to be an obstacle to their romance, but he also didn't want to step aside. Not either of them. Rus wanted both of them.

"Did you consider just talking to them both about it?" Lana asked, pulling Rus from his thoughts.

"Yep, then I ended up coming home for the long weekend."

"Coward."

"You're one to talk." He regretted the comment the second it left his lips, resenting why he couldn't just let things lie between them. He always dug up the past with Lana, and she always chased a different future. They just ended up locked in a weird present.

Lana made a gun gesture with her hand, placed it under her chin, and pretended to fire. "That was a critical hit."

"Sorry, couldn't resist."

"And we were being so civil."

"Perish the thought." Rus gestured dramatically, placing a hand to his forehead. "It's so very unlike us, I had to fix it."

Lana laughed, soft yet carefree. She took one final swing, then jumped off and landed with a firm stance, showing she hadn't let herself slack off even if she didn't train as much as once before.

Part of Rus wanted to ask everything she'd been up to since last they spoke. Well, since the last time they shouted at each other. But if he unraveled the mysteries of her days since his absence, he'd spend all night entrapped. All weekend. Unable to tear himself away and return to classes.

"Well, I think you should pursue this little polycule," she suggested. "You only live once; you might as well love as many people as you can."

"It's just kind of complicated."

"The best romances are." Lana leaned in closely, lifting her knee and setting it on Rus' thigh. Her lips almost pressed against Rus' but she pulled back right as she exhaled.

It left a shiver of reminiscence. Rus contemplated for a fraction of a second what life with Lana would be like. In moments like this, he wanted it with every beat of his heart, but Rus reminded himself that those feelings were fleeting. They were bad together. Quite literally. Rus brought out the worst in Lana, and she ignited his fury for others like no one else.

They'd ruin each other and the world around them if they tried again. Some loves were best left in a memory, reminiscent of the possibility, but mindful not to live the tragic reality. Love couldn't always fix broken people, and they were two very broken people.

"Glad you came back, Ikky." Lana backstepped, sauntering away into the woods.

The moonlight illuminated her footsteps, and she twirled around one final time, waving goodbye before disappearing into the dark.

He savored the silence, the quiet, the chance to consider what he wanted and how he'd go about getting it.

Rus wanted Dylan. Rus wanted Kaiden. Rus wanted them to want each other. Most of all, Rus wanted them to want him.

CHAPTER 13
DYLAN

DYLAN texted Rus off and on during his weekend trip, but let him focus on some important essay when he returned to campus. Honestly, Dylan needed a bit more time with his feelings. Well, he needed a bit more time with the perfect bubble of possibilities. Until he knew for certain how everyone else felt, he could daydream about all the positive outcomes.

It sucked that Kaiden continued dodging Dylan, giving short replies to any message, and insisting he was too busy with work to hang out.

So, Dylan focused on his work all Monday, running errands, fixing broken equipment, and pretty much anything to distract himself. Then he prioritized cleaning on Tuesday. Jasmine let him be but reminded him not to clean too thoroughly, as house chores were divided among the residents. She was a stickler for day-to-day life skills, knowing each of the teens would have to fend for themselves soon enough. By Wednesday, he'd taken on the highly dreaded task of inventorying all the recent donations. It was a mountain of work.

After realizing no amount of busy work would settle his nerves, Dylan reached out to Rus again, planning a meetup on Thursday. Once he'd cleared the air with one person, he could theoretically work on sorting things out with Kaiden, too.

Dylan drove to Rus' on Thursday, a little after lunch, to give him a chance to finish his classes. Feeling a bit antsy, Dylan casually walked around the apartment complex. He hopped onto a wheel stop in an empty parking space, extended his arms wide, and walked along the concrete slab much like he walked a plank. The asphalt became lava in his mind, and Dylan carefully jumped to the next wheel stop, wobbling a bit, but catching himself before tumbling to the pavement.

"Aren't you quite the acrobat?" Rus called out.

His sudden arrival startled Dylan, and his footing slipped. Dylan braced for an embarrassing and painful crash flat on his ass, but instead found himself swept into a secure embrace.

"Careful," Rus whispered in his ear. "What would you have done if I wasn't here?"

Dylan smiled, lost in the warm hug of Rus' arms.

"Well, I obviously would've been fine, considering I was just waiting until you got here to stage my very own damsel in distress moment."

"Clearly." Rus grinned, helping Dylan properly stand before releasing him. "Since you didn't cringe when I caught you, I'm hopeful for our conversation."

"Yeah?"

"Yeah." Rus shrugged sheepishly. "Mostly nervous."

"Why are you nervous?" Dylan asked, fighting the quiver in his voice.

Did Rus have to break the news? Was he going to try and awkwardly steer their brief make-out session back to friendship? Dylan wouldn't be upset by that. He swore to himself he wouldn't be. Friendship was something he could definitely do. He was lucky to have Kaiden and Rus in his life as friends. And truthfully, dating was horrifying. He had no idea where to begin when it came to dating and relationships, so why was he yearning for one with Rus so badly? With Kaiden?

No. Dylan needed to put that out of his head before he found himself swept away by daydreaming again. Right now, he needed to play it cool and salvage his friendships. He already knew those worked. No point in ruining a good thing over a silly fantasy.

"I like you," Rus admitted. "A lot."

"Really?" Dylan quirked a brow.

"Yeah, and not in a friendship sort of way," Rus clarified. "I mean, I do like you as a friend. But I also like hanging out with you. Which I suppose friends do, too. Um, well, it's just when I think about you, I don't just think about friendship. I think about you. Kissing you. More than kissing you. More than moreing with you, if you catch my drift."

"I may have a vague inkling of what moreing is in this situation." Dylan chuckled. "I might also be thinking about moreing with you too."

A rush trailed along Dylan's skin, sending a surge of excited goosebumps that made him involuntarily shudder. That little tremble of excitement quickly twisted into one of dread when he realized these reciprocated feelings meant Kaiden would be crushed.

It wasn't as if Kaiden couldn't handle Dylan and Rus dating, exploring this possibility, but surely after sharing a first and second kiss with them both, Kaiden would be left feeling like an outsider, an unwanted consolation prize. It dawned on Dylan that this was the real reason Kaiden avoided his friends.

"It's going to crush Kaiden," Dylan muttered.

Betrayal ate away at him and devoured all the joy he had swelled with a moment ago. It also left him with this sinking regret. Regret that he was missing something. Missing Kaiden. Missing the possibilities with Kaiden.

"Why?" Rus asked. "I might have moreing feelings for him, too."

Dylan didn't find the silly little wordplay funny anymore, too consumed by guilt and confusion.

"I figured you felt the same," Rus said.

"For you, yes."

"For Kaiden."

Dylan stared, dumbfounded. What was Rus getting at?

"That kind of puts us back in the same situation."

"Yeah, I spent the last few days sort of pondering the same thing, until I had a lovely chat with my ex."

"Oh?"

"She's wise beyond her years," Rus said with an eye roll.

"Yeah?"

"She reminded me poly exists for a reason."

"Wait, what?" Dylan had a vague understanding of polyamory, which extended to an open relationship. "So, how open exactly are you thinking?"

Rus snorted. "What?"

"Poly's just dating around, right?"

"I mean, in some cases, sure."

"Yeah, so it would be us dating each other, but we could also date Kaiden? Or would it be like I date you, but you date Kaiden, and Kaiden dates me?"

"Yes and no," Rus replied. "It wouldn't be open perse. It'd be more like expanded. Instead of a couple, we could be a throuple, so we'd all be dating each other."

"A throuple?" The word sounded hilarious and bizarre all at once, but Dylan did find himself intrigued. "Consider me piqued."

"Hey, throuples are becoming way more common these days," Rus said with a playful shoulder shrug. "And honestly, in this economy, a throuple is practically necessary for basic necessities."

"Oh, yeah. I could probably get a nicer ride with three incomes," Dylan teased.

"Nah, for luxuries like that, living the high life with a new car, you'd definitely need a bigger polycule. Like an octa-couple, octa-ouple, octa-gon-l-ouple. Coupl-a-gon… No, that doesn't work." Rus lost himself in the word play of combining octagon and couple into some terrifyingly massive dating pool.

"I don't want that." Dylan shook his head.

"The nice life or larger polycule?" Rus asked, stepping in closer.

Somehow, even as he looked up at Dylan, he possessed this domineering presence. Rus' authority sizzled in the air between them.

Dylan gulped. "No big octopus polycule thing. Just the throuple."

"Octa-cule." Rus smacked his forehead at the realization, then smiled at Dylan. "And good, because that's exactly what I want."

That still presumed the potential third in their arrangement was on board with such things.

"How about we message Kaiden?" Rus held up his phone, revealing the group thread.

"It would be hard for him to dodge both of us," Dylan replied. "But he's probably just going to say he's busy at work."

"He still works at that art gallery, right?" Rus commented. "What's he even do all day? He never really talks about it except when they have some party he's forced to work."

In which case, Kaiden would complain nonstop about his million and one tasks to complete before whatever fancy gala was scheduled.

"Mostly cataloging stuff by day," Dylan replied. "Maybe showings to potential buyers, but that's more Alison's thing."

"So, then maybe we just drop by," Rus said. "If he's actually busy, we won't pester him, but if he's not, he won't be able to deflect either."

"Sneaky." Dylan smirked. "Let's go."

CHAPTER 14
KAIDEN

KAIDEN found himself lonely this last week. Alone and lost in his thoughts, with only work serving as a reprieve from the anxiety in his life. Home had become a battlefield of expectations from his family. He pushed back, and they collectively pushed back harder until they'd shoved him to the ground. The gym had turned into a chore, no longer an escape of endorphins.

Worst of all, he kept dodging Dylan and Rus. He was unsure what to make of things, but he knew the second he leaned on them, they could very well push back just like his family had. Kaiden knew that wasn't true, simply an irrational fear eating away at his thoughts. Dylan had proven himself time and time again, and Rus hadn't been in Kaiden's life long, but he'd already shown himself to be a true friend. Still, not knowing how things were with his friends seemed so much safer than finding out. Kaiden could only handle so much devastation in his life at a time.

"Is this what you do all day at work?" Rus asked, startling Kaiden. "Doomscroll and avoid group texts?"

Kaiden blinked a few times, baffled by Rus and Dylan's arrival. They'd pranced right into Slayer's Brush, walking through the empty gallery and all the way to the counter in the back near the door to the stockroom.

"What're you doing here?"

"We had a meeting of the minds," Dylan replied.

"And of the hearts," Rus added with a twinge of a playful smile growing on his face.

He always looked so much softer, sweeter when he smiled. Though he certainly rocked the default stern scowl he had most of the time.

"You've been avoiding us," Rus continued.

"No." Kaiden stuffed his phone into his pocket, then went back to reviewing documents on his computer. "It's just been hectic lately."

"So, about our little make-out session," Rus said, bluntly moving them right into the awkward conversation Kaiden had tried his best to avoid.

"We've been talking about what happened between us the other night," Dylan said, standing oh so close to Rus.

Kaiden could practically feel the chemistry oozing off them, the sizzle of their barely tamed passion, and he knew they'd shown up at his job to break the news to him. They were into each other. It was so obvious. In fact, Kaiden couldn't believe it'd taken him this long to realize Dylan had a thing for Rus. Well, usually Dylan didn't dance around feelings. He just sort of made a move on someone and then moved on. Clearly, Rus was special.

Who was he kidding? Of course, Rus was special. There was this passionate and powerful energy constantly flowing off him. Kaiden would be jealous if he weren't so entranced.

"I already know you two have a thing," Kaiden said dismissively. "I'm not trying to avoid you because of it. I really have been busy, but also, I didn't want it to be weird between us. The whole kiss-off thing. It was fun. But it was just—"

"We like you," Dylan and Rus blurted in unison.

Kaiden paused, confused and concerned. They liked him? Why? Were they messing with him? Was he misinterpreting the meaning? Like could mean a million different things. Positive for sure, but not necessarily attraction.

"We all needed a little time to process our feelings," Rus said. "Figure things out, see where we all stood."

"Uh-huh." Kaiden blinked.

"It goes without saying, but I'll say it anyway," Rus said with a smirk. "We're friends. We want to stay friends. But now we find ourselves in this potential entanglement."

"Meaning?" Kaiden needed Rus to just spit it out, say what he meant, what they meant. He looked to Rus, then Dylan, then the precarious space between them.

"We want to date you," Dylan said. "Assuming you want to date us."

"Huh? How in the hell would that even work?"

"Poly," Rus said rather aloofly.

"I'm sorry, but we're all supposed to date at the same time?"

"Yes," Rus said. "Of course, that is only if there's a mutual attraction toward us."

"Wait, what?"

"We don't want to pressure you," Dylan said. "But we didn't really have much choice since you've been dodging us."

"Yeah, sorry about that. I was confused." Kaiden grimaced. "Still am, sort of. Mostly."

They both skirted around the counter, easing their way to the same side as Kaiden, removing his buffer.

"Okay, I get you guys wanting to date, I really do," Kaiden said, gesturing to and between them. "And I kind of sort of get why you're trying to include me."

"Oh?" Rus cocked his head.

It was not a curious tilt but a confident one. He already had some annoying rebuttal to whatever Kaiden planned to say. Kaiden could feel it in his bones. The most irritating part was that Kaiden wasn't even sure what his next words were going to be, so it made Rus so damn smug.

"You don't want to ruin our friendship," Kaiden said, stumbling over his own thoughts. "I get that, really, I do. So, you're trying to include me as you guys pursue your thing. But I'll be fine, honestly."

"If we liked each other and didn't like you, don't you think it'd be easier for us to just not include you?" Rus asked.

"Well, yeah, but we already kissed, like the three of us, so you need a cover."

"Why not just pretend we're all friends?" Dylan asked, then pointed to himself and Rus. "And we could just secretly date."

"Well, yeah, there's that too. But maybe I'd be suspicious."

"So, in your mind, the only plausible way for us to date each other," Rus explained, referring to himself and Dylan, "is for us to pretend to want to date you too?"

"Yeah, obviously."

"Is us liking you that hard to fathom?" Rus asked. "Dude, who the fuck tanked your self-esteem?"

"His family," Dylan said with an angry edge.

"No, it's not that," Kaiden protested. "It's just…I'm me, and you guys are you."

He couldn't put it into words. But Dylan was bold and charming and aloof all at once. And Rus was assertive and captivating and sweet, all wrapped together. Whereas Kaiden… Kaiden was anxious and meek and lost. They were both gorgeous men, but Kaiden had a million flaws with his body. No matter how hard he worked, he could only do so much to fix them.

"How would all of us dating even work? Like kissing? I mean, we sort of made that work. Ish. But that was also like exploratory. How the hell does kissing with all of us work? Do we tap out? Are there timed sessions? Should I…I don't know, play on my phone or something when it's not my turn? Are there turns? Is that weird?"

Dylan rushed into Kaiden, the suddenness of their chests pressed together made Kaiden's heart patter. The way his hand brushed against Kaiden's face as he cupped it around the back of Kaiden's head made his cheeks burn. Then the swift smack of Dylan's lips against Kaiden's twisted his stomach into knots. Nervous and excited all at once.

The tension in his back eased, the stress carried in his shoulders faded, and suddenly the knots in his stomach released into a flutter of eagerness washing over his skin.

"Relax," Dylan panted between kisses. "We don't need all the answers right now."

"That's the point of dating," Rus said, appearing beside Kaiden.

They'd pushed him away from the safety of his counter and toward the wall. Rus slipped in, lips rougher than Dylan's, but his tongue was so much sweeter. Kaiden ran his hands along each of them, unsure what to do, but loving the feel of muscles in his grip as he kept kissing Rus. Soon, Dylan's teeth grazed Kaiden's neck, nibbling and teasing his skin. Hands caressed him, hips bucked against him, mouths moaned with satisfaction.

Kaiden pulled away long enough to watch them kiss, to taste each other, to entertain him with their beautiful expressions lost in the ecstasy of this embrace. But neither offered Kaiden a long reprieve, drawing him back into these sweet kisses.

If his corset vest didn't pinch against his lower back from the awkward press of his body pinned to the wall, Kaiden would've sworn he'd fallen into a dream. No way had this happened. The two most amazing guys in his life wanted him. No, they had him. Completely. Entirely. He'd surrender himself here and now without a moment of hesitation.

It simply didn't seem real to believe he was on the verge of losing every comfort in his life, to suddenly having more than he could ever have hoped possible.

Passion swept through him. Kaiden licked Rus' neck, running his tongue along the silly bi goose tattoo while Dylan kissed Rus. Kaiden's hand slipped under Dylan's crop top, fingers gently tickling the hairs of his stomach, of his chest, and the slightest caress as he reached the nipple.

Dylan growled, snatching a handful of Kaiden's hair and swallowing the yip Kaiden released as he kissed him. Bit him. Tasted his excitement. Rus didn't surrender Kaiden so easily, pulling his gaze back down and tugging on his lower lip before aggressively kissing him.

"Okay, okay, okay..." Kaiden pushed Dylan away, gripping his shoulder with one hand, then moving his other hand to block Rus, who readied himself to fill the space between the pair. "We seriously have to stop. If Alison checks the cameras to see me making out with two dudes, she'll probably fire me."

"She'll probably promote you," Dylan said, noting her very sex positive attitude.

"Well, I can't exactly gamble with my income right now."

"What's going on?" Dylan asked, eyeing Kaiden up and down and in a way that just made the words pour right out of him.

"My mother started charging me rent," Kaiden said.

"Seriously?" Rus scoffed. "Did she finally give you a full room?"

Rus didn't know everything about Kaiden's home life, since he avoided the topic as much as possible, but it had slipped from time to time how crappy his living situation had become when he would express his gratitude to Rus' flexible accommodations of allowing Kaiden to crash at his apartment from time to time.

"I decided to just move into the basement."

Dylan silenced a yelp and gave a full-body shudder, making no effort to hide his hate of the creepy crawly basement. It was disgusting, had a mildewy smell that clung to his sheets—and remained the only reason Kaiden hadn't given up his upstairs closet to keep his wardrobe safe from the horrible stench.

"How much are you paying?"

"One fifty," Kaiden said with a long lull. "A week."

"Are you fucking kidding me?" Rus blurted. "For an extra two fifty a month, you can rent a place at my apartment complex. Hell, they even include an eighty-dollar utility credit."

"Don't worry, I've got a plan." Kaiden forced a smile.

No, that was the wrong word. He didn't force a smile, not with Rus and Dylan. He fell into the smile, and it helped wash away the anxiety he'd carried since his mother approached him, since he started dodging his friends. Correction, his boyfriends. Well, Kaiden supposed they were always his boy friends, since they were always boys and always his friends. Now, he lost himself in silent musings of entertainment. So much so, he found Rus and Dylan observing his giddy nature with confusion.

"I'm coming up with a plan."

"What is it?" Dylan asked.

"It's a secret."

"Secrets aren't healthy for good relationships." Rus moved in, playfully prodding.

"Mystery keeps the romance alive." Kaiden smirked. "I'll fill you both in once it's more than a daydream. Fair?"

Rus and Dylan eyed each other, then nodded at Kaiden. Having them both on his team could be something Kaiden could happily fall into; however, having them team up against him could end badly for him. They'd force him to appreciate himself, much like they did upon their arrival. They might very well force him to acknowledge he mattered. That'd be rough to figure out.

"Well, my apartment is always open if you need an escape."

"Yeah, and we've got a free room for the week," Dylan said. "We still have an empty bed since Jamal moved and Tasha's gone this week for some JROTC competition, so her room is available if you want some space."

"Thank you," Kaiden replied, grateful they were willing to offer him escape, offer him refuge. "But it's kind of weird staying at my boyfriends' places since we just started dating, like, you know, five minutes ago."

"Boyfriends?" Dylan's eyes lit up. "I could get used to that."

The joy etched onto his face made Kaiden's heart patter. The immediate acknowledgement and comfort both of them had with Kaiden casually dropping the word "boyfriends" made him giddy.

"You've crashed at my place like a hundred times," Rus retorted. "Not weird at all."

"Yeah, that was as friends."

"We're still friends," Dylan cut in.

"Yeah, but now we're also more than friends."

"Which should make it even easier to stay the night," Rus added.

Now, they both moved in closer, boxing Kaiden back into the wall where they'd locked lips with him a moment ago. They were doing it. The teaming up thing. They didn't even realize, but they were already working together to poke holes in Kaiden's logic. Two boyfriends might end up being more work than Kaiden was prepared for.

"I'm good where I'm at," Kaiden said. "Plus, I already paid for the month, so I'm getting my rent's worth."

"You paid ahead of time?" Dylan made a sour face, likely thinking of how many times Kaiden had given them money for a utility bill ahead of time, only to watch John piss it away.

"I just wanted to get everyone off my back while I planned." Kaiden shrugged. "It was the push I needed to finally get out."

"You're going to explain this plan eventually, right?" Rus pointed a finger. "I don't like being left out of the loop."

"Oooooh. Such a controlling boyfriend, I don't know if I can handle that."

"You're going to have a lot to handle, buddy boy." Dylan grinned.

"Okay, you two have to go," Kaiden said with a chuckle. "I have work."

"Depends." Rus stood firm, refusing to budge despite Kaiden's gentle push.

Dylan followed suit, even folding his arms.

"Seriously?" Kaiden huffed.

"Are you going to stop avoiding our texts?" Rus asked.

"Obviously."

"Good," Rus said. "Are you going to hang out with us? No being too busy?"

"I mean, I am busy, but yes, we can hang out," Kaiden answered. "In fact, why don't you two pick a day for a real date?"

"Oh?" Rus quirked his pierced brow.

"Yeah, official date night. Sounds like something we need."

"I'd be down for that." Dylan nodded. "I can't remember the last time I went on a real date."

Kaiden smiled, shooing them out of the gallery. Truthfully, Kaiden had never gone on a date. Not once in his life. Not even some sad, sappy middle school kind of sort of maybe a date. Nope. Kaiden very much stayed on the sidelines of his own life, watching everyone else live.

He should've been terrified of the prospect after he sent Rus and Dylan on their way. A date, a real date, a real first date, a real first-ever date, should've left Kaiden quaking in terror. But he simply buzzed throughout the rest of his workday, texting the group chat when things were slow, and fantasizing about what to expect on his night out with Rus and Dylan.

The idea alone brought comfort, excitement, and joy. For the first time in a long time, Kaiden was eager to see what came next, because he knew he'd get to find out with Rus and Dylan at his side.

CHAPTER 15
RUS

RUS' history professor for the "Hidden Heroes Between the Pages" had wrapped up the lecture early in favor of offering the students time to quietly collaborate and discuss an upcoming research project. Rus was still buzzing from his recent relationship…was it a relationship? His dating situation at the very least had kept his interests captivated.

"I have to tell you something exciting," Rus whispered to Daysha.

"Oh?"

Between his dating news and the joy of October officially marking the calendar, Rus buzzed with excitement. Since it was the greatest season of the year, Rus actually dressed up. Today, he wore a bloody, oversized sweater that said "I'm Fine" in carved lettering.

"I'm seeing someone," he quietly continued. "Well, someones."

Daysha quirked a brow, her face completely confused.

"I took your terrible but apparently not-at-all terrible advice."

"My advice?"

"To kiss Kaiden and then to kiss Dylan," Rus explained. "Maybe not in that order. Well, it was for me. Your advice didn't really specify any order."

"My advice was a joke."

"Welp, jokes on you because now your bi bestie has two boyfriends that you're going to have to hear about all the time."

"Ooookay." Daysha side-eyed Rus. "How is that any different from you talking about your crushes nonstop? At least now I won't have to hear about celebs you'd smash if you crossed paths because they'd definitely be wowed by your… Hmmm. Charm? No, that can't be it."

Rus tsked. "I just wanted to prepare you mentally for me being utterly insufferable and talking about guys all the time."

"You realize just because I don't date doesn't mean I'm allergic to the discussion."

"I know, but I also know when I'm single, I find people blabbing about their relationships annoying."

"But I'm a better person than you, obviously." Daysha smirked. "So, tell me everything. Minus squishy bits touching. That, I am allergic to. Unless it's in a BL book."

"Relationship?" Emma scoffed, leaning forward in the seat behind them and intruding on their conversation in only a way she could.

Rus had nearly forgotten she'd taken the seat behind them. Most lectures, she made her presence known almost immediately with cutting commentary and rude questions, but other days, she sat in abject silence until she found the right moment to strike. Why she felt the need to sit nearby Rus so often, he had no idea, but he suspected it was some type of irritating power trip.

Her long blonde hair draped her smug face, and Rus contemplated yanking a strand if only to twist that hateful gaze into shock.

"Dating around isn't a relationship, even if you use some sad gay label to say otherwise."

"No one asked you," Rus snarled in a breathy whisper.

"In fact, dating two men is sort of proof there's nothing serious about your *romance*," Emma said with this condescending giggle. "This is why gays are terrible for the world. They mock tradition, they take nothing seriously, they spit on sacred values, and then they gloat about it in public to rub it in everyone's faces."

"There's no gloating," Rus replied, biting back a thousand cutting words he sought to add.

"Yeah, we're having a private conversation." Daysha pointed to herself and Rus. "You're the nosy bitch, quite literally, forcing your way into our conversation."

"Because you're loudly talking about immoral and disgusting things when we should be focused on our research projects."

"And what are you even going to research on?" Daysha asked in a loud, furious hush. "You hate all BIPOC representation, you adamantly believe queers of history are lies and propaganda to disparage the dead, you think every woman's achievement in history is used to silence the 'real' male accomplishment. So, what the fuck are you even researching?"

She summed up every thought Rus had. It still irked him to no end that Emma took this elective purely to incite discourse in the class.

"I'll be doing a counter essay on the real hidden figures of history," Emma boldly stated. "The white Christians who are slowly being erased from textbooks because of DEI history initiatives."

"You seriously don't even give a fuck if you fail this class, do you?" Rus asked, truly astounded.

"I've actually already started writing out my appeal if the professor unfairly demonstrates biased bigotry against me for my political and religious rights." Emma primmed her shiny, blonde hair, practically posing with pride. "Honestly, if you're going to just date around, you should—"

"Why would I even listen to you?" Rus asked, having a sudden realization about his most irritating, unwanted nemesis. "You're a woman. And by your very hateful definition of women—which you constantly voice, loudly at that—they shouldn't have opinions. So, why the fuck would I listen to a goddamn thing that comes out of your trashy cherry-picking Christian mouth?"

Emma glowered, her face scrunching into something methodical and likely intending to argue her way around her very own stupid logic.

"I'm just surprised you're not more ashamed of yourself," Daysha cut in. "You're like twenty-two, college educated, unmarried and single, career-driven, and quite opinionated."

Daysha counted off each achievement on her fingers, hurling them like insults. Then she made a nasty face, utter repulsion in her eyes.

"Jesus must be so disappointed in you."

"Wait, career-driven?" Rus asked somewhat sarcastically. "I thought her whole trad wife sales pitch fizzled out when her followers learned she was a sad, single college girl and not a 1950s homemaker?"

"Oh, it did, but grifters always find a scam."

Rus nodded, playfully agreeing.

"Now she mostly does Lives with red pill podcasters, arguing about the 'woke' mob and bragging on how she's surviving her liberal indoctrination."

"And not one of those proud good ole boys wants to make you an honest woman?" Rus asked with a sassy twang to his voice. "Pretty pathetic if you ask me."

"No one fucking asked you!" Emma blurted, caught off guard by her own rage.

Rus slid down in his seat, snickering at Emma's outburst. He did his best not to look at Daysha, who followed suit, and they both kept their eyes locked on the whiteboard as their professor turned his attention to their area.

Emma stormed out before the professor even attempted to understand the situation.

Daysha and Rus stayed silent for the longest minute of their life, waiting for their professor's ire to lessen.

"Also, I should mention," Rus leaned over, whispering, "we have our first date night planned."

"Exciting, but how's that work logistics-wise?"

"We all show up, eat food, chat, go to a movie, then—"

"Absolutely not," Daysha interrupted. "Movie first, so you can avoid bathroom breaks from your full belly meal, and also, it'll give you something to chat about."

"About going to the bathroom?" Rus scrunched his face.

"No, you weirdo. About the movie. You see the movie first and can talk about it at dinner. Also, you won't have to step out of the movie midway for a potty break. I mean, unless you order a super-giant soda."

"You could've explained that better."

"You could've honed your critical thinking skills; we all could've done something." Daysha did a hair flip, intentionally swiping Rus across the face. "But seriously, how are the logistics going to work?"

"Meaning?"

"Table or booth?"

Rus shrugged.

"'Cause if it's a booth, someone is going to be left out. Table is the best bet," Daysha said assuredly. "Also, who's paying? Split three ways? Not the worst, but—"

"But nothing."

"Oh, yeah, for sure." Daysha waggled a finger at Rus. "No butt stuff on the first date. But—pun absolutely intended—how is the butt stuff going to work?"

"I thought you didn't like talking about the squishy bits?"

"I mean, on my terms, it's cool. Plus, I'm super curious," Daysha said. "Is it going to be like a conga line of fuckery or more like a wrestling match where y'all tap in for each other?"

"Huh?"

"You know, two-on-one. Whoever gets pinned spends his time getting tapped, and—"

"And we're done." Rus pulled out his laptop, deciding to make the most of this research time provided.

"I guess my imagination will just have to fill in the blanks."

Rus' imagination also started filling in blanks. He couldn't help but heavily contemplate his date. It'd gone from a fun, simple way to spend the night with two of his favorite people, to a weight of concern and stress that if everything didn't go just right, then…

Then what?

He shook away the thoughts. Daysha had inadvertently gotten into his head, but he wouldn't let that deter his plans. This was going to be a great night.

Although he did text his boyfriends about switching movie times earlier, so they could have dinner afterward. And he'd be sure to insist on a table over a booth.

Rus released a deep breath, exhaling the festering anxiety before it had a chance to take root.

Since Dylan and Kaiden didn't share Rus' enthusiasm for Halloween, he toned down his outfit for the date and picked out a casual black polo shirt and gray jeans. He did, however, add a colorful orange tie and some *Nightmare Before Christmas* knee-high socks, which he kept bunched around his ankles. He preferred thicker socks with his boots, anyway.

Dylan and Kaiden arrived together, making their way up to Rus' apartment to greet him.

"You could've just texted me to come down," he said.

"Well, then you'd have to carry these the entire night." Dylan flashed a bouquet of red roses from behind his back.

"He was feeling quite festive." Kaiden revealed a second bouquet. "Do you mind if I put them in water before we leave?"

Rus sniffed the flowers, surprisingly a bit giddy at the idea of someone bringing him flowers. It was weird. Rus never considered himself the sentimental type for something so simple, yet the excitement on Dylan's face only further exhilarated Rus.

"Yeah, I don't have any vases or anything."

"Shoot." Dylan smacked his forehead. "I knew I forgot something important."

"No worries at all," Kaiden insisted, rushing off inside with both bouquets, determined to find the right glass to turn into a makeshift home for the evening. "We can grab something later."

"Sorry, I should've thought about the vases." Dylan grimaced. "I was trying to be nice and ended up making more work."

"No," Rus protested. "It was sweet."

"I'm loving it," Kaiden chimed in. "No one's ever brought me flowers before."

"Me either."

"No one's ever really gotten me anything just for the heck of it like this." Kaiden sniffed the roses, lost in his thoughts, and Rus could see him slipping into the self-doubt he tried to keep tucked away.

"I'm glad you like them," Dylan said with a soft smile, a leading smile meant to steal Kaiden from his mind. "I hope to get you many, many more silly little gifts to show you how special you are. Both of you."

Rus' heart fluttered at that comment, and he studied the tension in Kaiden ease as the smallest of smiles crept onto his face.

With that, the trio headed out for their unconventional first date. Rus found himself more and more eager, and the night had only just begun.

The date night had started off a bit tense in just the right kind of way. Dylan wanted to enjoy something explosive, while Kaiden wanted to watch some dreadful romcom, but Rus managed to sway Dylan's vote by convincing him that horror was basically frightening action.

That was, in fact, not the case. Dylan spent the majority of the film with his head buried in Rus' shoulder, complaining about the gore. Meanwhile, Kaiden sat on Rus' other side and turned out to really sink his teeth into the blood fest.

"Oh, you stupid, dumb bitch." Kaiden tsked. "He's really going to check out the noise. This dumb motherfucker deserves…"

He spent the bulk of the film critiquing the characters and tricking Dylan into turning his head back to the scariest parts.

"No, no, no," Kaiden said. "The music's a clear indicator that the suspense is over. You can trust—"

"FUCK." Dylan slapped a hand over his face right as a machete sliced through a guy's chest.

After the movie ended, Rus stepped outside for a smoke, which he didn't have to rush through since Dylan wanted to walk off a bit of his anxiety. The boys looped the theater parking lot twice before Dylan's appetite returned. Though that might've had more to do with Kaiden mentioning the potential horrors hiding between the poorly lit vehicles. Dylan kept close to the streetlights and hit the automatic locks on his car the second they all stepped inside.

They drove to a nearby restaurant that Rus and Dylan had previously discussed. Kaiden made it clear that he was fine dining anywhere, but Rus knew Kaiden tracked his nutrition more closely than he or Dylan, so they picked a chain place that had all their nutritional facts on an easy-to-find website.

It also helped that this was a bit cheaper than other restaurants, and Rus didn't know the etiquette for tonight's date. He wanted to be ready to pick up the check if need be. The few times he'd hung out with a guy on a sort of date night, the check always leaned his way. Rus didn't know if that had to do with his bi status being equated with masculinity or his gruff attitude being deemed check worthy.

Rus nervously flipped through the menu. "I have to be real; I haven't been on an actual date since high school."

Maybe that wasn't entirely true. Rus had casually hung out with people over dinner or coffee or private study sessions. Sometimes, the get-together turned into something fun but never anything serious. Rus hadn't done anything serious since Lana.

Dylan muttered a bit to himself, counting off on his fingers.

"Yes," Rus said with a light laugh. "It has been a long time. Four years give or take a few months."

"Oh." Dylan's eyes widened. "I wasn't... I was actually... Well, yeah, I guess that is a long time. Why the big gap?"

"My high school sweetheart was a pretty heavy romance," Rus said, averting his gaze from Dylan and Kaiden. "Serious in a big surrender kind of way."

"What happened?" Kaiden asked, soft yet inquisitive.

Rus put his hands in his lap, rubbing his thumb over the Valentine's Day date tattoo on his wrist. "It just got complicated."

"Fair enough."

"Well," Dylan cut in with enough cheer to drown out the somber silence, "I was actually trying to do my own countdown on last dates. Mine landed somewhere in high school, too, which has been a wee bit longer since you."

Rus smirked. "True, old man."

Dylan gasped, slapping a hand over his chest. "You wound me."

"Old people are pretty delicate," Kaiden added.

"And you have the audacity to join him?" Dylan feigned shock, letting his jaw fall slack. "The betrayal."

Kaiden and Rus locked eyes, laughing together in this tiny, uncontrollable fit. It didn't help that Dylan continued playing this offended old person role.

"Well, if anyone gets to be nervous about the date, it's me," Kaiden said, steering the conversation from laughter back to a bit of levity. "It has been a while for both of you. A bit longer for some…"

"Jerk," Dylan whispered in a ridiculous hush.

"But this is my actual first date."

"It's all of our first dates," Rus clarified, wanting to squash any concern Kaiden might've had over him and Dylan perhaps hanging out on a date night without him.

"No, I get that," Kaiden said with a breathy sigh as he fumbled for words. "I mean, this is my actual first date."

"Oh." Rus didn't know how to respond, suddenly feeling he'd dropped the ball on something so casual.

He shouldn't have fought so hard for the horror film. He should've suggested something a bit fancier for their dinner afterward.

"Hey, it turns out patience is a virtue, or what the fuck ever." Kaiden shrugged, then gave a big goofy grin. "As far as first dates go, landing two hotties is pretty, well, hot."

And just like that, the tension at the table washed away.

They ordered food, made small talk, and fell into a comfortable rhythm. Rus talked about his classes, venting a bit about his upcoming midterms. Dylan mostly shared anecdotes about things the teen residents had been doing around the house or at school in a very mother hen kind of way.

Kaiden went over his workout regimen, explaining all the complexities of transitioning between leaning down and then bulking up, all to maintain a healthy frame.

"So, what is a healthy body type?" Rus asked, taking a big bite of his greasy burger.

"Depends," Kaiden said with an awkward chuckle. "Everyone's built different. It took me a long time to realize I would never have a twink figure no matter how much I dieted."

"That was not dieting," Dylan interjected, blushed a bit, and turned his attention back to his sampler platter—because he wanted a little taste of everything tonight.

"No shade, it's fine," Kaiden said, poking around at his grilled chicken and veggies. "I was definitely on the starve-yourself diet when Dylan and I first met."

"Oh." Rus set down his burger; the tension had crept its way back into the conversation.

"But me, being the amazing person I am, helped Kaiden find a better plan," Dylan added. "Well, mostly I just nagged him."

"More like he slowly introduced me to people that Jasmine knew—because she knows everyone," Kaiden clarified.

"She really does." Dylan grinned. "If networking paid."

"It does," Kaiden said matter-of-factly, gesturing to nothing, but clearly pointing out how Jasmine's whole career revolved around networking and raising funds for queer people in need.

"Well, yeah, I suppose," Dylan said, picking up a southwest eggroll and drowning it in ranch. "But not officially or anything."

Kaiden and Dylan started playfully bickering back and forth, and topics of lost days and old acquaintances came up. Suddenly, Rus didn't understand a word that came out of their mouths. They spoke English, the words themselves registered in Rus' head, yet no matter how hard he tried, the context eluded him entirely.

"I swear, extraverts have it so easy," Kaiden said, eyeing Rus, and almost immediately noticing the tension.

POLITICS AND POLY

Rus didn't want to appear awkward, but he could feel it on his face, in his reserved pose.

"You all right?"

He enjoyed the conversation, enjoyed seeing more and more layers of Kaiden and Dylan every time they hung out, but with that also came the revelation that they knew each other so much more than he ever would.

"Just sometimes feels like I lose myself around your inside jokes," Rus said, ignoring the pinch of guilt for being honest. "It's a good thing you guys have. Clearly, you know everything about each other. I just have to catch up, you know?"

"There's a million things Dylan doesn't know about me," Kaiden said. "Trust me."

"Oh, yeah?" Rus asked. "Like what?"

Kaiden went to speak, then paused. Lost in his own mind, he couldn't seem to muster an example.

"It's not a big deal," Rus said. "Really, it's cute. And I don't feel left out, just realizing it's something I have to learn to go with the flow of."

"Kaiden doesn't know how or why I ended up at Dorothy's Home," Dylan blurted, then immediately rushed to down his soda.

"I mean, I figured things with your family weren't great…" Kaiden said with a sheepish shrug.

"Yeah, something I think we both resonate with." Dylan gave a coy smile, a bit forced, or so Rus thought. "My family was shit. My dad knew I was gay before I even understood what the word meant, and he tried like hell to beat it outta me."

The table fell silent, creating this bizarre contrast with the noisy restaurant. Everyone and everything around them bustled, but they remained in this quiet bubble.

"That was probably not appropriate date talk stuff. Definitely not first date talk." Dylan's cheeks twitched as he fought to keep a smile.

It was something Rus had grown to learn since meeting the rather jovial guy. Dylan rarely had a sour expression, but he rarely had a genuine smile either. The real one often came when no one was looking, no pretense or expectations. And almost always over something silly. Playing video games, sure. Making a proper movie prediction, definitely. Talking Rus out of picking a horror film, absa-fricken-lutely.

"I'd like to think we're a bit past first date convos," Rus said, clearing the air a bit. "And as far as inappropriate, that's just people's way of boxing up topics, and cutting out the truth."

"I don't think I fully understood that," Dylan said with a light laugh. "But it sounded like support."

Honestly, Rus didn't fully grasp it either; his mouth moved faster than his brain pieced together his own thoughts. All that mattered was he hoped the words brought Dylan a bit of comfort.

"I was fourteen when I ran away. Almost sixteen before I stumbled onto Jasmine," Dylan explained. "A lot of rough months."

"You never really talk about this stuff," Kaiden whispered.

"Hence why I picked it," Dylan replied. "Gotta find something you didn't know, prove Rus wrong."

"You don't have to," Rus said with a nervous lump in his throat. "I didn't mean to…"

"Nah, it's good to air out old wounds, my therapist would be proud."

"You go to therapy, too? Jeez." Kaiden quirked a brow. "I didn't know that either."

Rus and Dylan shared a silent look and a soft smile.

"Not anymore, but off and on over the years when the ole mind needs a bit of a tune-up." Dylan chuckled. "Things with my family sucked kind of like with yours."

Dylan gestured to Kaiden, who nodded knowingly, and Rus had no way of relating. His parents had always supported him and his siblings. Any choice, any lifestyle, and belief. Even if it didn't match their ideology. They led with love and support, and Rus whispered a silent 'thank you' to his parents. Sure, they wouldn't hear him, but he'd be nicer to them the next time he visited, something to show he was grateful for how lucky he'd been.

"My dad was a piece of work—is, I suppose." Dylan shrugged. "Not really sure if either of them is still alive or not. I assume, but you know…"

Dylan trailed off, lightly touching on how his father treated him, how his mother avoided making waves, and how his home was anything but a home.

Kaiden had turned his attention, staying quiet and simply letting Dylan speak. It was another thing Rus had grown to learn. While Kaiden didn't always have the words for people, whether the topic veered into something serious and emotional, such as now, or simply something light and trivial, Kaiden did possess a communicative expression. Rus always felt the sincerity in his gaze, the curiosity in his smile, the kindness in his soft nods.

Rus attempted to follow suit, and they both listened to Dylan pour a piece of his soul out over dinner in this light-hearted 'let's not make a big deal out of my trauma' kind of way.

"I think the worst part is that as much as I don't want them in my life, a small part of me still wishes they'd change their mind one day and decide to be a part of my life." Dylan shrugged, his shoulders far too stiff to convincingly act aloof. "At least I don't hate them anymore. Jasmine and about six different therapists helped me work through those issues."

Rus' breathing hitched as Dylan recounted the barest of details. Nothing explicit, nothing to elaborate on the horrors of his home life, the hell of getting by on the streets, but his mood lightened when Jasmine came up, and his journey turned into something positive.

"Could've been a hell of a lot worse," Dylan continued. "There aren't a lot of homes geared toward teens. Not places that actually care. Even fewer that focus on queer youth. And probably only one place in all the world with someone as stubborn as Jasmine. She doesn't give up on anyone, even when they don't want the help."

It was hard to imagine Dylan being reluctant or inconsiderate or abrasive, but his conservation tiptoed around his less-than-appreciative teen attitude.

They sat and listened and chatted and fell into casual conversation all over again. Rus found himself entranced by the men who'd invited him into their lives and hoped to grow closer with them.

CHAPTER 16
DYLAN

THE initial dread of spilling a bit of his truth had fizzled away before they'd even left the restaurant. Kaiden always had a way of making words pour right out of Dylan, to say anything, share anything, and know he wouldn't end up judged. His past wasn't necessarily a topic he intentionally avoided, merely something he believed too much of a downer to discuss. Though he'd come to realize all too quickly there was no topic off the table with Kaiden or Rus. They both carried such curiosity and compassion. It emboldened Dylan to think or speak anything on his mind, from the silly to the somber.

After they left, Dylan drove everyone home, starting with Rus. He figured Kaiden could use the buffer before returning to his place, given the headache his family had brought him.

"No one's going to walk me upstairs?" Rus asked, coyly hiding his lips behind the collar of his shirt. "I do hope I get home safely."

With a grin, Dylan slipped out of his car and opened Kaiden's door to drag him along too. Rus lingered at his door, fumbling with keys as he recapped the night. Since casual chitchat quickly failed them, Dylan kissed Rus goodnight, slow and passionate. Suddenly, Rus managed to unlock his door despite his attention fixed on Dylan's lips.

When Kaiden shifted awkwardly beside them, Dylan yanked him by the tie and turned his attention to his other boyfriend. His best friend. Fuck, how he loved having Kaiden in his life this way, loved exploring this newfound journey together, loved every little surprise Rus brought into their lives.

Rus stepped into the tiny apartment, and Dylan backstepped with Kaiden in tow, their mouths still pressed together. Dylan led Kaiden's lips, guiding their mouths and slowly pushing him back to the bed. Rus plopped down first, watching them kiss, but Dylan soon followed after, dropping beside him. He held out his hand, awaiting Kaiden's decision.

Kaiden stared down at Dylan, and for a moment, he worried he'd linger above and find some reason not to join them on the bed. Instead, he carefully knelt and crawled between Rus and Dylan.

The three pressed against each other, lips smacking back and forth, and Dylan lost himself to the bliss of their kiss.

Before long, Kaiden rolled on top of Dylan, straddling his waist and kissing him. Rus nibbled on Dylan's neck, teasing him and surely on the verge of leaving a hickey.

"Don't mark my neck too badly," Dylan said between kisses, losing himself on Kaiden's mouth.

"Just gonna spell my name out," Rus teased, licking and sucking on Dylan's neck.

"Can you even fit Russell on his neck?" Kaiden chuckled.

"My name's not Russell," Rus said with a slight scoff.

"Seriously?" Kaiden tilted his head, leaning against Dylan's shoulder. "What is it?"

"I'll only tell if I can spell it out on Dylan's neck."

"Absolutely not," Dylan declared, sweeping his arms around Kaiden and pulling him into a closer embrace. "Use Kaiden as your canvas, that's what I'm planning anyway."

And with that, he shoved his tongue down his boyfriend's throat before he could protest. Kaiden giggled and playfully resisted, giving Rus a look as he went to move his hickey attention onto him instead.

The sweet kiss goodnight had turned into a full-blown make-out session with Dylan and Rus focusing their attention on Kaiden in equal measure. Kaiden wriggled a bit, ticklish from Rus' touch, from the graze of Dylan's hands swishing along the delicate lace of Kaiden's corset vest. Oh, how he wanted to rip through the fine fabric, but he resisted. In return, his patience paid off with Kaiden arching his back at Dylan's touch. He continued straddling Dylan's waist, lips lost on each other.

When Rus' hand met Dylan's, he gently guided him to the strings of Kaiden's outfit. The pair locked eyes for a moment, each taking their time with Kaiden, and their gaze said everything since words were lost to them. They worked together, unfastening the strings of the corset vest, preparing to take this night to the next step.

"We can't just hook up on a first date," Kaiden said, taking a breathy pause as he pulled his lips away from Dylan.

It made him hunger for Kaiden all the more.

"Says who?" Rus asked, curiously cocking his head.

The way he questioned people always drew Dylan in. Rus never asked out of confusion, out of some need for clarification. No, his look often came with an assertive demand. He sought justification in the answer, certainty from whoever he questioned.

"It's just not what people do," Kaiden said, fumbling with his words. "Right? I mean, is slow the norm?"

Dylan lowered his hands, still craving Kaiden's touch, and fueled by a desire to rip off their clothes. "Is slow what you want?"

"No. Not at all. I don't think so, anyway, but I'm not the best judge on dating rules."

"Me either." Dylan smirked.

"To be clear, we can go as fast or slow as you're comfortable with," Rus replied. "As all of us are comfortable with. No pressure."

"Plus, I think those *rules* you're so worried about apply to couples, not throuples," Dylan added.

"And I've never been one to follow unprecedented societal norms just because it's what everyone else does," Rus commented. "Fuck everyone else."

"Well, hopefully not everyone else," Dylan teased. "That's a lot of dicking even for me."

Kaiden snorted, then covered his face as his cheeks burned bright red.

Rus rolled his eyes and grinned. "Anyway, what matters is what we want."

"Well, yeah, that's true." Kaiden rocked his head side to side, calming down. "I guess I just don't know the rules, the proper steps we're supposed to follow. If this is going to be successful."

"Successful?" Dylan asked, his smile growing bigger. "It's not a test. We don't need a score to maintain a passing grade."

"Thank God," Kaiden said. "I always failed those."

Dylan pressed his forehead to Kaiden's, stealing him from his thoughts. He knew all too well how quickly Kaiden could dwell on something.

"Test or not, we do need a healthy relationship, right?" Kaiden sulked a bit.

"I think a healthy relationship involves an emotional bond, right?" Dylan asked.

"We're already there or on our way," Rus added.

"And there are plenty of first date hookups that turn into committed relationships where they sort of fill in the details of connection as they go," Dylan continued. "There's no one-size-fits-all."

"Yeah, that's true." Kaiden pondered.

"But we can stop, we can figure this out on another date night." Dylan puckered his lips, giving Kaiden a sloppy kiss before releasing his timid boyfriend.

"The important thing is that we make our rules," Rus said, delicately brushing a hand along Kaiden's bangs to help swoop the gelled hair back in place. "We decide what our relationship is. No one else. This can be whatever we want it to be."

With that, Kaiden swooped in, kissing Rus passionately. The grind of his body drew Dylan in, but he resisted. He lay back on the bed, watching his boyfriends lock lips, watching Kaiden quickly strip off his corset vest while Rus slipped off his shirt.

Kaiden paused, taking in Rus' slender, muscular form. "Is it okay if I keep on my shirt?"

Dylan ran his hand along the silky dress shirt. "Absolutely."

"We make the rules," Rus replied. "You set your own boundaries."

"Good." Kaiden smiled, unfastening Rus' jeans. "Well?"

Rus sat up some and unzipped his jeans, pulling them down to reach his knees that sank into the mattress. His bulge caught Dylan's eye, and when Rus slipped down his boxer briefs, a beast of a thing flopped out.

"Christ," Kaiden said wide-eyed, taking the words right out of Dylan's mouth.

Rus had a big dick. Bigger than Dylan's. From his somewhat colorful history of casual encounters, Dylan wagered Rus was somewhere close to eight inches. Clearly, he wasn't short everywhere.

Kaiden stroked Rus' semi-erect cock, still straddling Dylan while he worked. Kaiden locked his eyes onto Rus, who released a soft groan as Kaiden continued rubbing his hand up and down the shaft, following the slight curve of the cock that leaned a bit left. Pulling back the foreskin of Rus' uncut dick, Kaiden leaned down and took the head into his mouth.

Dylan remained entranced, watching Kaiden bob his head up and down onto Rus' dick. He bucked a bit, instinctively mimicking Rus' movements. Dylan found himself throbbing harder the longer he kept himself contained. Before he knew it, Kaiden had adjusted himself, running his hand up Dylan's pant leg. Fuck. The way he took his time as he brushed past Dylan's erection only made him ache more.

For someone who professed having the least experience, someone who only ever had a few boring hookups that lacked passion, Kaiden moved between his two boyfriends with an expertise. He continued sucking Rus' cock, slurping and taking him in a bit deeper each time until he returned to the head, using the reprieve to likely breathe. All the same, he kept moving his hand up Dylan's pants until he reached the button to unfasten them. In a quick motion, he unzipped them and yanked at the band of Dylan's boxers ever so slightly.

Dylan assisted, sliding his pants and boxers down his thighs halfway and fishing out his dick.

"Fuck," Kaiden panted as he took in the sight of Dylan's dick, then returned his gaze to Rus' cock for a moment. "I'm surrounded by giants."

Dylan snickered. He wasn't as big as Rus, but he'd certainly been complimented on his thick dick plenty. While Rus easily had an inch or two on Dylan, who sat somewhere between six and a quarter to six and a half if he stretched the measurement, Dylan's dick was much wider in circumference. So much so, Kaiden seemed to use his hand to gauge the size. Each slow stroke helped take the width of the beast into account.

Kaiden soon shifted his position, sprawling on his stomach and lying between Dylan's legs as he went to take the dick into his mouth. Just the head for now. Dylan tensed, taking in a shaky breath as Kaiden wrapped his lips around the tip, swirling his tongue around the head.

"Argh," Dylan groaned, running a hand over the back of Kaiden's head and encouraging him to take in just a bit more.

Dylan wanted to feel the warmth of Kaiden's mouth, but he knew from previous experiences that few mouths could accommodate his girth.

Kaiden took in another two inches, holding there as he slurped. Spit ran down the base of Dylan's dick, and Kaiden used his hand to stroke the full shaft. Dylan was in heaven. Kaiden focused his efforts on teasing the tip while jerking the rest of the dick.

Rus had moved up on the bed in the few moments that'd passed. He stayed on his knees, still standing taller than anyone else, since Dylan had slipped lower into the bed on his back. Rus grabbed two pillows and propped them behind Dylan, angling him upward ever so as Kaiden continued sucking him off.

"Open up," Rus demanded, setting his beast of a cock directly in front of Dylan's mouth.

Obediently, he opened his mouth to take in Rus. Whether because he'd already warmed up with Kaiden or simply had a more aggressive stance on oral, Rus slammed in fast and hard. Dylan gurgled and gagged but found himself locked in place.

Between the intense pleasure of Kaiden working him over and the hot control of Rus ramming his dick all the way down his throat, Dylan lost himself. He choked on the dick, taking it barely halfway down. Rus gripped Dylan's head, easing him further as he thrusted into him.

Dylan panted, gasping as he took Rus in further each time. He bucked, partly because he couldn't wriggle loose from this position, and partly because Kaiden's warm mouth stole his attention.

Rus continued face fucking Dylan, finding a rhythm he really liked, and taking full control of Dylan's head as he satisfied himself.

Soon, Dylan lost himself to it, lost himself to his own pleasures because all he could fixate on was the haggard, excited breaths Rus released. Dylan pressed his hands to Rus' hips, steadying his thrusts and taking back just enough control to handle the beast reaming his throat. Dylan soon found himself in a steady motion, bucking to push a bit further into Kaiden's mouth and relish the sensation while managing to maintain a strong hold on Rus.

He continued choking on Rus' cock, willing himself to go deeper each time to satisfy him. Rus' movements became a bit erratic the more he pounded into Dylan's throat. Eventually, he cupped his hands around Rus' ass, guiding him into taking more control. Rus didn't question Dylan's adventitious offer. He mounted Dylan's chest, riding his face, and ramming his cock all the way to the base.

Dylan gurgled, unable to handle it for long, but incapable of protesting, of moving. He lay there lost in Rus' assertion, taking each inch to the fullest, and panting with relief when Rus pulled out long enough for Dylan to steal a breath before choking him on the entirety again and again.

"Fuck, I'm gonna cum." Rus snatched Dylan by the hair, holding his head in place. "You ready for this?"

Rus looked down at Dylan with his mouth open as he took wispy breaths. Dylan merely gagged in response, adjusting himself ever so to take Rus deeper.

"Argh," Rus groaned, his body convulsing atop Dylan.

A warm spatter hit the back of Dylan's throat, and he swallowed. Rus' thighs trembled. Dylan relished the sensation and missed the pressure as Rus climbed off him. But he found himself renewed by Kaiden's oral. Dylan lay there, taking tight breaths as he got closer and closer to climaxing.

Rus brushed Dylan's sweaty bangs back and leaned in for a kiss. Dylan lost himself to the moment, savoring every second.

"I'm going to…" Dylan wheezed, then bit down on Rus' lower lip. "Fuuuck."

Kaiden continued working his hand up and down Dylan's throbbing shaft, holding the head in his mouth as he swallowed each explosive burst of Dylan's climax. His hips bucked as his body twitched with excitement.

"Goddamn," Kaiden said as he massaged his fingers under his chin for a moment. "That thing could break my jaw."

Dylan chuckled, pulling Kaiden up and closer to him. Kaiden lay in Dylan's embrace while Rus rested beside them, sitting up. Unlike Dylan, who still lay there fully exposed, Rus had pulled up his boxer briefs but allowed his pants to slip past his knees before taking them off and tossing them to the floor.

"Now, you gotta decide which one of us you plan to face fuck," Rus said to Kaiden, who merely grinned in response.

"Oh, yeah," Dylan added. "I want a piece, but I also want to see what Rus' head game looks like."

Rus snorted in response.

"I'm good right now," Kaiden replied.

"Seriously?" Dylan quirked a brow.

"Yeah, I've always been more of a pleaser anyway."

"Okay, but just so we're clear," Dylan said, squeezing Kaiden into a tighter hug. "It would please me a lot to suck you off."

"Okay, okay," Kaiden replied, trying to squirm loose until Rus joined in, piling on top of them both and pinning Kaiden to the bed.

It didn't take long for Dylan's exhaustion to wash away as he lost himself in this play-fighting meant to wrestle Kaiden into submission on the mattress while he wheezed for mercy between his giggle fits.

CHAPTER 17
KAIDEN

KAIDEN awoke to the light peck of Dylan's lips pressed to his own.

"Go back to sleep," he whispered. "Just wanted to give you a proper goodbye."

"Huh?" Kaiden opened his eyes with a squint to find Dylan rushing out the door. "Where's he going?"

"Said Jasmine needed him," Rus answered as he rolled over and filled the empty space in the bed.

Kaiden found Rus' touch sweet, the gesture itself of moving closer to remove the gap between them. When Rus wrapped a thigh over Kaiden's legs, his heart fluttered in anticipation, reminded of all he'd explored last night.

The taste of Rus and Dylan still filled his mouth, and the idea that he'd been intimate with them both at the same time made him buzz with excitement. Perhaps just oral, but it was still a big step. A big lots of things. Well, one big thing in particular. Something Kaiden considered as Rus' rather large member pressed against him this morning.

"I've never really done the morning after," Kaiden playfully joked.

Well, he tried to play it off as comical, but he really had never experienced waking up at a hookup's home the following morning. On the rare occasion that Kaiden messed around with another guy, it usually resulted in a quick finish, awkward farewell, and a likelihood that he never saw that profile online again. Whether from the guilt of the closet or the boredom of Kaiden's performance, after getting off, the guy in question usually blocked Kaiden.

"Here's hoping for lots of morning afters." Rus kissed Kaiden, a light peck much like Dylan's quick goodbye.

Then Rus buried his head in the crook of Kaiden's neck, giving a little primal growl as he snoozed.

"Hell, maybe even some morning fun," Rus said with a breathy tease.

"Oh, someone's looking for a little relief first thing?" Kaiden grinned, running his fingers through Rus' curly hair.

His hand slowly trailed down Rus' body, relishing his firm muscles. Rus had the most compact, yet very sturdy, build. Like a tiny little tank.

As Kaiden's hand worked its way down to Rus' waistband, he paused. Every part of him wanted to reach down and stroke Rus' massive cock, to take it back into his mouth, to feel it hit the back of his throat as he worked to get him off, but something was missing in this moment.

Dylan.

"Can we even..." Kaiden's hand retreated. "I mean, are we allowed to mess around without Dylan here?"

"I don't see why not," Rus said, rolling off Kaiden and propping himself up on a single elbow. "So long as we're not exploring with someone outside the three of us, then I think we should be allowed to interact with each other however we feel."

"Right," Kaiden said with a hesitant nod. "It's not like it can always be the three of us together. My job, Dylan's very busy career, your whole school thing."

"I don't think it's so much about scheduling intimacy, but merely enjoying each other's company when we're together," Rus elaborated. "I would personally have no problem with you and Dylan messing around without me because I trust you two still want me there when I'm absent."

The words made sense, yet for the briefest of moments, Kaiden lost himself to the insecurity of Rus and Dylan having fun without him, of them realizing how happy they could be without him.

"None of that," Rus said, cupping a hand under Kaiden's chin.

"What do you mean? I'm fine." Kaiden averted his gaze.

"You're lost in your head, probably questioning where you fit into this."

"No, I'm not." Kaiden grimaced. "Is it that obvious?"

"It is when someone is paying attention, and if you haven't noticed, I pay attention to you," Rus explained. "Dylan pays attention to you. We do this because we care about you. So, whatever is spiraling in your head right now about not fitting in, ignore it."

"Right," Kaiden said, a bit more confident. "So, as long as we're not intentionally leaving a partner out, it's okay to be intimate? I mean, we didn't know Dylan was rushing off first thing…"

"Exactly, but if, for example, you and Dylan continued messing around without me, then there would need to be a discussion."

"Right," Kaiden said with a light chuckle. "Because what's the point of being a throuple if one of them is always being excluded?"

"Then it's just a messy couple with no understanding of having adult conversations about feelings."

Kaiden tried to ignore the doubts that lingered in the back of his head, telling him he didn't quite fit with this relationship. His thoughts were his worst enemy, and he wouldn't allow his own insecurities to sabotage his best relationship. His first and only relationship, but still… Rus and Dylan were always honest with him, direct, sincere. These doubts came from years of watching the relationships between his family and the years of feeling uncomfortable in his own skin.

"Is it okay if we wait for Dylan before deciding anything?"

"I think that's a brilliant idea." Rus gave Kaiden a sloppy kiss on the cheek.

While Kaiden believed Dylan would be fine with the idea of their throuple occasionally coupling off in the absence of one member, he wanted certainty in that decision. Dylan meant a lot to him, and he didn't want to even accidentally betray his trust.

After all, Kaiden had quickly learned that he didn't know Dylan as well as he once thought. Dylan had shared a very personal piece of his history with Rus and Kaiden. It was more than that, though. Dylan could keep any darkness of his life secret for as long as he needed. Whatever made him comfortable was fine by Kaiden. But there was more than that, more than Kaiden realizing he still had so much to learn about Dylan.

If Kaiden had to predict his best friend's feelings a few weeks back, he would've called them entirely wrong. It was bizarre, the switch from platonic to romantic. It didn't feel forced, but it still came with this unexpected flutter.

Kaiden wondered if he'd have to learn Dylan all over again, and that excited him. Learning what made Dylan tick outside of friendship, learning what made Rus tick, learning how to please them both.

Kaiden's phone buzzed, and he checked to see several early morning missed calls from his mother.

"Ugh." He ignored them, then rolled over to face Rus. "You know, I am comfortable with you and Dylan messing around without me. In fact, I think it might be entertaining to see you two go at it."

"Oh?" Rus gave a coy smile. "A little voyeurism? I can get behind that."

"I'm just curious to see how it'll play out," Kaiden said. "I mean, I know we're not there yet, intimately, but I'm more of a bottom. People pleaser to the extreme."

"You'd be a support healer all the way," Rus said, making some game reference that Kaiden only half grasped.

"Anyway," Kaiden said, rolling his eyes because he was not being dragged into a video game conversation. "Dylan is mostly a top from what we've chatted about. And you strike me as... Well, it's just you give off top energy."

Rus broke out into laughter. "So, you wanna see us fight for dominance?"

"Just curious who would land on top is all."

"Maybe we'll just take turns plowing you." Rus grinned.

Kaiden's entire face burned, blushing uncontrollably. While the idea of being the treat between Rus and Dylan sounded hot, he'd also struggled to suck both of their cocks last night. He could only imagine how much taking both of them back-to-back would feel.

"So, where's this top energy coming from?" Rus asked. "Is it my big dick, or my bi status? Not sure why folks always think bi boys are somehow manlier."

"Not sure how being the top is somehow manlier," Kaiden retorted.

"Touché."

"Sorry for assuming you're a top," Kaiden said with a smirk. "Shouldn't have stereotyped you."

"Never," Rus said, smiling back. "But I am a top, so you were right."

"I knew it." Kaiden poked Rus in the chest. "That is, of course, until Dylan has his way with you."

"Oh? Now, you're doubting my top energy conviction?"

"No, but I know Dylan has flipped many men over the years, which is why I don't mind sitting on the sidelines from time to time if I can see how that'll all play out."

"Nah," Rus said, rolling over and facing away from Kaiden. He pulled his boxer briefs down just enough to reveal the top of his right ass cheek, showing a shiny rainbow die. Only it had more than six sides. It seemed to have twenty or more. "Anyone who's gonna tap this ass is gonna need to roll a Nat twenty for sure."

"I don't know what that means, but I'm guessing it involves a lot of luck."

"Precisely, skill be damned." Rus rolled back over. "If I'm getting my back blown out, then the dude doing it just got lucky bending me over."

"So, do all of your tattoos have such deep meanings?"

Rus pursed his lips, contemplating. "Yes and no."

Kaiden tilted his head, leaning closer and showing his intrigue.

"I try not to take anything too seriously, but I enjoy humorous meanings." Rus pointed to his bi goose neck tattoo. "I'm a big believer in Pride, but you know, having fun with it."

Kaiden ran his hand over the angry goose with a knife in its bill, smiling. Delicately, he traced his fingers down Rus' chest, examining the pentagram tattoo over his heart, then moved his fingers along the fiery tattoo of Rus' right arm.

Kaiden studied the exquisite artwork of fire, the silhouettes of so many people burning, and the jagged text of a quote that said so much and so little.

"Do not judge, or you too will be judged," Kaiden read off the words.

"Yeah," Rus sighed. "I went through an angry ex-Christian phase."

"Really? That's surprising."

"Me being angry?" Rus scoffed. "When am I not?"

"No. The you being religious thing."

Kaiden had never been into religion. It always seemed to point out how he deserved the lot he got in life, and asking questions about it only caused problems. It didn't help that his family was lazy in their convictions. They rarely attended church, never read scripture, but always pulled out the importance of God when judging the gays. Or any group, so long as it didn't condemn the rest of the family in the process.

"My folks believe very much in letting their kids learn spirituality on their own terms," Rus explained. "They let me attend when I had a friend who pushed me into Christianity. But eventually, I found him to be hypocritical and the bible itself to be flawed beyond repair."

"So, you got this tattoo?"

"Mostly I just like the flames." Rus flexed his bicep and forearm as Kaiden continued trailing his fingers down Rus' arm.

He traced the lines of the muscles until he reached Rus' wrist and paused at the tattooed Valentine's Day date.

"Anniversary?" Kaiden asked. "I suppose that's better than an ex's name."

"No," Rus answered. "I mean, it's sort of connected to my ex but... Okay, well, weirdly, all the men in my family were born on holidays."

Kaiden listened attentively, not sure how this tied to Rus' ex.

"I was born on April first, which is why my life sometimes feels like a joke," Rus said with a laugh. "My dad was born on Father's Day, which changes every year, yada yada, but it's a big deal to him. His sign from the universe that he was meant to be a dad or whatever. My granddad was born on the fourth of July, which is why he's such a patriot and why we don't waste our breath on that red hat cunt. My brother was born on New Year's Eve. Got some uncles with major holiday birthdays and weird, unknown holidays. Like some of those military remembrance holidays conservatives always complain about needing but never remember the fact they have existed for fucking decades."

"Interesting." Kaiden scrunched his face a bit pensively. "How is that connected to your last relationship exactly?"

"Ah, yeah," Rus fumbled for his words. "You ready for a big, ugly truth bomb?"

"Always," Kaiden replied with a bit of intrigue, and a twinge of concern. Mostly, his attention remained rapt.

"I was a high school statistic," Rus said. "Lana got pregnant our junior year. It was a whole mess of a thing. She chose to keep the pregnancy, and we went back and forth about being parents. I was excited, ish. Nervous as fuck, too. But in the end, Lana chose to put the kid up for adoption."

"Oh," Kaiden said, unable to muster anything else.

He expected… He didn't know what he expected from this truth bomb. Something about his previous relationship for sure, but not something tied to a kid. Rus had a child. Or he had had a child.

"Were you okay with her giving up your kid?"

"That's the thing; he was never really mine," Rus said with a sad smile. "He always belonged to the couple who adopted him. Just like I always belonged to my parents."

Kaiden stared silently, processing.

"It's where Lana got the idea," Rus explained. "I'm adopted. My folks are amazing, and I was very lucky. Not all adoptions are… Hmm. That's a whole other tangent. Let's just say that just because someone wants to be a parent doesn't always mean they should."

Kaiden sat up, crisscrossing his legs and offering Rus a spot on his lap. He took the offering, laying his head on Kaiden's thigh and staring up at the ceiling.

"It messed with my head, having the kid but not having him. Like, I don't regret it now, but in high school, I was mad at everyone. It didn't help that Lana iced me out afterward, dealing with her own baggage for sure. Then she left and toured Europe to find herself."

"And that's why you didn't date anyone for such a long time."

"I had to find myself, too." Rus stared up at Kaiden, his beautiful hazel eyes a bit glossy. "Turns out, I'm slowly finding myself in you and Dylan."

"You're sweet."

"You're comfort."

Kaiden leaned down, kissing Rus' forehead and enjoying the silence together.

Their moment was quickly interrupted by a swift succession of buzzes from Kaiden's phone.

"Ugh." Kaiden grabbed it, swiped away from the flurry of texts, and switched it to silent.

"Who's that?"

"Stepfather."

Rus glowered.

"Ready for my truth bomb?" Kaiden asked with a chuckle. "It's not nearly as serious."

Rus' expression shifted to something calm and curious.

"The electric is due," Kaiden said. "They need money to pay it."

"They can go fuck themselves," Rus retorted. "Didn't you just pay for the month?"

"That's for room and board." Kaiden scoffed, hating how much he spent to share a room. More like to hide in the basement at this point. "Honestly, if I don't pay it, it'll screw me over, too. Trust me, no electricity would suck. I've done it before."

"I hate your family."

"Me too," Kaiden replied a little too casually.

It almost frightened him how easily that slipped out. He paused, trying to think about what he loved from his family, moments or bonds or something significant. He truly couldn't find anything of importance that linked him to those people other than blood and pain and hate.

"I've always had to cover utilities," Kaiden explained. "My stepfather pisses through money the second he gets it, so there's never anything left when due dates roll around."

"You should leave."

"Easier said than done."

"The apartments here are way cheaper."

"They're for students."

"No, these are off campus," Rus countered. "They give students a nice discount because we usually pay for the whole semester. It really depends on a person's financial aid package, but yeah. They rent to anyone, though. Most of the folks living here are just looking for affordable housing. This is the closest thing to it."

"Yeah…"

"Look, I'm not suggesting you move into my place; that would be weird and a little too soon. But the complex is huge. Like, seven apartment buildings huge."

And each three-story building housed close to thirty residents.

"Weird? Psst. I practically live here already," Kaiden said with a laugh.

"Truth!"

"But I'm going to pass on the complex," Kaiden answered. "I have a plan. It's just going to take a minute to come together."

And he did have a plan. He just didn't know if it was possible, truly possible, on his own. But Kaiden wanted to prove he could do something on his own. That he didn't need rescuing, and he didn't need his family.

"Promise you won't let them walk all over you?" Rus scooted away some, then pulled Kaiden down so he'd lay beside him again.

"I promise."

"Good, because I'm one flippant comment away from popping everyone in that damn house of yours across their smug little faces."

Kaiden burst into laughter, burying his face into Rus' chest. "I would pay to see that."

"Free of charge," Rus said, slapping Kaiden's butt. "Well, not entirely free."

They fell into each other, cuddling the entire morning away, enjoying synchronized breathing and the silence of content comfort in each other's arms.

CHAPTER 18
RUS

RUS hopped out of the shower and used Kaiden's blow dryer to air out his curls. Normally, he didn't care about such things. But he wanted to enjoy every second of the day in his costume, which meant he needed to dry off quickly to get dressed.

Thankfully, Kaiden didn't mind bringing a few things over to Rus' apartment. Not that he ever took Rus up on the offer to leave whatever oddities there that pleased him. Kaiden believed in boundaries and somehow thought that, by letting his stuff pile up at Rus', he'd be overstepping them. Rus would have to work on that, get Kaiden to see that was what folks in relationships did. However, that would have to come after celebrating Halloween.

First came the red contacts, then the fangs, and finally he clipped on his little elf ears. They blended with his perfectly. He'd have to thank Kaiden for that, since he picked them out, claiming the pair Rus wanted didn't match his complexion enough.

Next, he grabbed his outfit, a perfectly tailored dress shirt, pants, and boots to embody Rus' favorite murder happy vampire twink. After getting dressed, he added his belt and a realistic fake dagger, then finished off the ensemble with an expensive white wig. Courtesy of his mother, who loved cosplay almost as much as she loved her children.

Rus stuffed his laptop into his satchel and headed out the door to classes. The first year on campus, Rus considered himself too cool at eighteen to dress up for the holiday. Did it matter that Halloween was his absolute favorite day of the year? No, not when his very sophisticated adult ego was at stake.

It ended up being his biggest regret. It also ended up being how he met Daysha, who dressed all out as some fairytale princess who carried a giant mallet with spray paint on the front saying 'Not Your Damsel,' and she proceeded to bop the ground between her and any guy who got too close.

Close to half the campus dressed up, from those showing off the assets they planned on bringing to whatever party they attended, to others who hid behind masks while causing chaos in the form of mischief and silly pranks.

"Aren't you a little too old to be dressing up?" Landon asked with sass in his voice and swagger in his hips.

"Aren't you a little too fruity to be dressing with that aesthetic?" Rus eyed Landon's outfit up and down, always perplexed at how hard he tried to flex as some type of frat guy fuck boy.

Personally, Rus didn't give a fuck what anyone wore. Someone's aesthetic could fall wherever they felt most comfortable, but Landon had gradually, quite literally, straightened up his wardrobe since Rus had the misfortune of meeting him their freshman year.

Landon's face turned sour, and he craned his neck to really revel in the height difference he had on Rus. A truly transparent jab that brought a smirk to Rus' face. He knew full well he was a tiny tyrant who fumed with fury at any little injustice that crossed his path, but Rus never worried himself over being short. Over the years, he never bothered defending himself to those who made their jokes on something he couldn't control, allowing their insults to go over his head, so to speak.

With a smile on his face and a pep in his step, Rus swaggered away. He definitely added a bit more flair to his step, trying to emulate his favorite character. After all, if he was going to be a sexy vampire twink, he had to do the part justice. That meant more than dressing for the role.

"Don't you look fabulous," Daysha said as they met after classes for a late lunch.

"Of course I do, darling," Rus said, poorly imitating the British accent of his character.

"Oh, you sweet thing, at least you got the outfit right," Daysha replied with a perfectly posh accent.

Speaking of outfits, she'd shown up in a stunning white and gold dress that'd been ripped to shreds and covered in blood and dirt.

"Pretty fancy zombie."

"Zombie prom queen," Daysha clarified. "My mother took it upon herself to buy me this dress in case I wanted to look nice."

"Nice for the right guy, I'm guessing." Rus snorted, making his way through the café line.

"Or the right girl." Daysha shrugged. "At this point, she's so desperate I don't end up alone, she doesn't have time to be homophobic."

"I mean, it's still homophobic. Acephobic? Just plain ole queerphobia."

"Meh, it's whatever." Daysha grabbed a sweet treat to add to her tray. "I posted a video this morning on how to turn designer into decay, and I'm still waiting for her response."

"She might be stunned speechless."

"My mother? Never."

"So, any big plans for Halloween, or was shredding mommy's money the main agenda?" Rus asked as he led the way to a free booth.

"Himbos with a few folks from Pride. I think they're hosting a costume contest if you're interested."

"Maybe, I will be downtown." Rus shrugged. "Kaiden's taking us to some fancy gala, and we're going to wander a bit. It should be fun."

"Us?" Daysha pursed her lips. "So that means the whole boyfriends plural thing is working out?"

"Yeah, it's been nice," Rus answered. "The real test will be the next few weeks. Lots of holidays and I'm gonna have to go home quite a bit."

"Worried they'll be happy without you?"

Rus paused. It genuinely wasn't something he feared. Though the idea didn't thrill him, he didn't want Kaiden and Dylan to put a stop to things every time Rus had to leave town.

"More worried I won't be happy without them."

"Awww." Daysha took a big bite of her burger. "You're disgusting."

Rus ended up taking a second shower early that evening before Kaiden and Dylan arrived. It turned out his costume was not as light and breezy as one might think, and the weather hadn't exactly gotten the memo that Fall had rolled in. Nope. It was hot and muggy most of the day, but thankfully, as the sun set, the lightest of breezes kicked in.

As someone knocked on the door, Rus fumbled to throw together the last touches of his costume before answering.

"Well, well, well, don't you look lovely," Kaiden said, tipping his bright pink cowboy hat.

While Kaiden stayed true to his heart, wearing a corset vest, he'd picked a costume that worked well with it. His hat and boots were bright pink, while the rest of his western getup was white with dark brown. Almost. The lace lining of his vest matched in a similar pink.

"Darling," Rus said in his poor accent. "You look delicious."

"Always do." Kaiden's cheeks burned bright red at his own bravado, but Rus really enjoyed it when inadvertent confidence slipped from Kaiden.

He stepped inside, making room for Dylan's grand entrance. Only Dylan slinked up wearing a plain black shirt and some ripped jeans.

"Seriously?" Rus quirked a brow.

Ignoring Rus' question, Dylan revealed two single black roses.

"For you, my lovelies." Dylan handed Rus and Kaiden each a rose. "Careful, they still have their thorns."

"You didn't consider getting some without thorns?"

"On Halloween?" Dylan pressed a hand to his chest, feigning shock.

Rus chuckled in response, awaiting Dylan's outlandish reasoning.

"Perish the thought," Dylan said. "Tonight's a night when sweet, lovely things should be a little scary, and very dangerous."

His grin almost charmed the irritation right out of Rus. Heck, he almost outright swooned, but Rus sniffed the beautiful black rose and gently set it on his desk with Kaiden's rose. Then he turned back to Dylan and frowned.

"And what lovely thing are you supposed to be tonight?"

"A superhero." Dylan shrugged.

"Where's your costume?"

Dylan huffed. "You're as bad as Kaiden."

"He's the worst when it comes to dressing up," Kaiden explained. "Outright refuses. I'm surprised he even spun this story of being a superhero."

"Because neither of you would stop badgering me if I didn't pick something."

"You didn't pick anything," Rus said. "You can't just say you're a superhero and not show up in a costume."

"Personally, I think it's an affront when you could be rocking sexy spandex," Kaiden added. "You realize this is like one of my last free nights for the foreseeable future?"

"Huh?" Rus turned his attention to Kaiden.

"I landed a retail gig. It's only part-time, but it's over the holidays, so I might as well just blow my brains out now."

"Damn, and you're still working at the gallery?"

"Uh-huh, full-time. Hence why a hammer to the head would probably make the next two months easier."

Dylan folded his arms and pouted. "You could skip the whole sixty hours a week of work and—"

"Sixty-five to seventy, if I'm unfortunate enough to be that lucky," Kaiden interrupted. "But I need it if I'm going to save up to get away from my family."

"And when they find out you're working a second job?" Dylan asked. "What's to stop them from magically increasing your rent?"

"They wouldn't do that," Rus stated, genuinely stunned by the prospect. "Would they?"

"They won't have time because I'll be out of there soon enough."

"Because you have a plan to move out," Dylan said with a surprisingly surly expression.

"The very secret plan you won't tell us anything about?"

"Why are you ganging up on me?" Kaiden turned his attention to Rus, who wanted to pry a bit more for answers. "We should be ganging up on him for no costume."

Kaiden gestured to Dylan, who sighed. Rus rocked his head back and forth, conceding to challenge Kaiden and return to hassling Dylan.

"You two are the worst." Dylan dragged himself over to Rus' desk. He grabbed a marker and a sheet of printer paper, scribbling on it. After he'd finished, he took a piece of tape and stuck the page to his chest.

"Not all heroes wear capes," Dylan read off his little message. "Or spandex, I guess."

Rus wanted to smile at that, at the added extra effort to placate him and Kaiden.

"Come on, we have a party to get to," Kaiden declared.

It didn't take long for them to get downtown, but it took nearly forever to find a parking spot. They settled for an expensive parking garage on the fifth floor of a building with a broken elevator.

Thankfully, Slayer's Brush was close, and the event itself wasn't nearly as stuffy as Rus anticipated. Most of the guests wore their fanciest outfits and tossed on a simple masquerade mask to make it a costume, but others seemed to enjoy the holiday as much as Rus.

Unfortunately, it didn't take long for Kaiden's boss to rope him into a checklist of tasks. He abandoned Rus and Dylan to handle a few administrative things.

"I can't believe the hoops he goes through when he's not getting paid," Rus said, swiping a champagne glass and almost snagging a second before he recalled that Dylan didn't drink.

"Alison's always been good to him," Dylan said. "Plus, Kaiden loves this artsy stuff."

"Really?"

"Yeah. He still drew a bit when I first met him," Dylan continued.

"What happened?"

"I think he's just gotten a bit busy with life."

After an hour or so of circling the event, Rus went out for a smoke. He took his time, savoring each deep inhale as he let his gaze drift to everyone who wandered downtown.

Kaiden and Dylan soon rushed outside, giggling, each of them grabbing hold of one of Rus' arms before carting him away.

"Come on," Kaiden insisted. "I'm not working tonight."

Kaiden stepped out ahead of Rus and Dylan, ushering them away from the gallery, when suddenly, a crowd of people ran by him. They pushed and shoved their way through, knocking Rus away from Dylan, who snapped, and Kaiden, who shouted.

By the time Rus gathered his bearings, the laughing group had cut a corner, howling and causing chaos elsewhere.

"Fucking idiots!" Rus roared.

He turned to find Kaiden had been knocked over. Instead of getting up, Kaiden remained frozen, taking shaky breaths and holding tight to the pavement.

"It's okay." Dylan gently rubbed Kaiden's back, a soft soothing motion until the fright had passed.

Kaiden didn't show it much, didn't speak about it ever, but from time to time, the horror of what happened to him the night he was assaulted still haunted him.

Rus crouched down beside Dylan and Kaiden, leaning all the way to the ground so that his eyes would meet Kaiden's.

"You're okay."

"I know." Kaiden took a deep breath. "I know."

"Take your time."

"Sorry."

"Don't be."

After another minute or so, Kaiden finally composed himself enough to stand. He pressed his back against a nearby light post and kept his attention vigilant on all passersby.

"You wanna head home?" Dylan asked.

"Absolutely not." Kaiden exhaled. "I just need a minute."

"Take as many as you need."

Rus stayed close to Kaiden as he calmed down, walking beside him all the way to Himbos, where Kaiden declared they were there for a good time.

"Someone get me a shot to clear my nerves, and then we're dancing."

Dylan obliged, returning quite giddy with some neon green shot.

Soon, they made their way to the dance floor, where Rus focused on clearing others out of Kaiden's path, giving him the freedom to relax. Not long after, the drag queens performed, putting on a spectacular Halloween show before announcing the costume competition.

By the time they'd left, most of downtown should've cleared, but the chaos of Halloween kept everyone out, causing a bit of mischief.

"Anyone else hungry?" Dylan asked.

"Starved," Kaiden replied.

Rus wasn't feeling anything but wandered alongside them both as Dylan led the way to a place that he declared had the best pizza in the city. A tiny hole in the wall with barely enough space to step inside and pay. It was even more crowded with the thicket of drunks waiting for their food.

Rus and Kaiden waited outside while Dylan braved the crowd.

"I hear you're a bit of an artist," Rus said, sparking a cigarette.

"An exaggeration."

"Why'd you stop?"

"No time, really," Kaiden replied.

Rus gave him a stern look, a pressing stare, and it didn't take long for Kaiden to buckle.

"I get consumed by passions," Kaiden replied. "Art meant a lot once upon a time, but I spent all my free time living for it, focused on becoming... I don't even know. Something better than what I am."

"You seem pretty great to me."

"I wasn't always." Kaiden shrugged. "When I started focusing on fitness, I just kind of lost the time for it."

"Found a new passion?"

"Kind of. Fitness means a lot to me, it really does, but I don't obsess over it the same way. I mean, I did in the beginning before I learned to enjoy the journey of health, as opposed to the destination of fit."

Rus smirked.

"Dumb, I know, but it rings true."

"Not dumb at all," Rus said. "Why don't you try to make room for both now?"

"Between work and my family, I barely have time for anything."

"Alrighty, who is ready to have their mouth blown?" Dylan left the pizzeria with a stack of six single-slice triangle boxes.

"I think you mean minds," Kaiden said.

"I said what I said." Dylan grinned.

"Hey, if something's getting blown, I don't want it to be my mouth or my mind," Rus clarified.

Kaiden chuckled, nudging Rus in the ribs.

"Trust me, your mouths will weep with joy."

"I don't know if I want my mouth to cry." Rus stared at the pizza boxes.

"Why didn't they just give you a normal box?" Kaiden asked.

"They only serve by the slice," Dylan replied.

They wandered back to the car. Rus piled into the backseat with Kaiden, while Dylan secured the pizza up front, declaring the slices had called shotgun long before either of them.

Rus rested his head on Kaiden's shoulder during the drive, studying the side streets and back roads Dylan took on their leisure ride through town.

Once they got to Rus' apartment, they quickly made their way inside, where they unwound a bit with Dylan playing Baldur's Gate 3 on the edge of the bed. He played one-handed as he scarfed pizza down. Rus enjoyed a slice of pineapple and chicken pizza and rested on the other end of the bed with Kaiden.

After finishing Kaiden's crust, Rus stood up from the bed and brushed the crumbs onto the floor. "I'm gonna go change before I get sauce all over my outfit."

"Nah, it'll totally work," Dylan said, focused on killing goblins. "Just say it's blood."

"For what I spent on this costume, my Astarion is far too fabulous to spill even a drop of blood."

"Wait, you can't get undressed now." Kaiden tugged on Rus' belt. "Not without a little vampire fun."

"Oh?"

"I feel like you deserve a prize."

"A prize?" Rus stared down at Kaiden, who slipped off the bed and stared up at him while on his knees.

"Yeah, for being best dressed."

"You really should've entered that costume contest," Dylan said with a mouthful of pizza, and his eyes locked on the TV screen. "Bet you'd have at least placed."

Rus boasted, puffing his chest out and running his hands over the fine fabric of his top.

"So what kind of prize are you thinking?" Dylan asked, completely oblivious to Kaiden, who slowly unfastened Rus' slacks.

"One where you'll definitely wish you put a bit more effort into your costume," Kaiden said, flinging his pink cowboy hat off and at the TV.

"I don't know." Dylan shrugged. "Seems like a lot of work for—"

"Oh fuck," Rus groaned as Kaiden wrapped his lips around his cock.

"Well, damn." Dylan turned back.

"You just going to sit there, darling?" Rus asked in character, running his fingers through Kaiden's hair.

His head bobbed up and down, taking in a bit more of Rus each time.

"Absolutely not." Dylan tossed the control aside and rolled off the edge of the bed.

As he crawled over to them, Rus half expected Dylan to pull off Kaiden's jeans, tossing them next to the pink boots he'd already set in the corner. However, instead of working Kaiden's cock over, Dylan crawled behind Rus and played with his ass.

"Hell," Rus whimpered at the suddenness of Dylan's tongue tickling his hole. "I've never, uh…fuck…"

His legs trembled as he stood there with Kaiden sucking him off and Dylan teasing and tasting his hole.

The wobble in his stance didn't go unnoticed. Rus felt Kaiden shift just enough to wrap his arms around Rus' sides, offering a bit of reinforcement. Dylan didn't help, though, merely playing with Rus' cheeks like putty as he dove in, licking his ass.

Rus had never had a rim job before, let alone a rim job while getting a blow job. He'd only eaten ass a handful of times himself, and truthfully, he didn't grasp the appeal. That all changed with Dylan's technique, the way his hands kneaded his butt, the way his tongue moved with precision. There was a gentleness with how he lathered his hole with long licks, and an aggressiveness with how he poked his tongue just enough to enter Rus.

At first, the sensation consumed him in the best way, warming his entire body and leaving his muscles weak. But whether from the alertness of standing at attention or the way Dylan's tongue pushed in deeper, Rus nearly jumped from the startling sensation.

"Whoa, was that your tongue, or are you using fingers now?"

Dylan pulled back but still kept his hands on Rus' cheeks. "No hands, promise. If you're not cool with a little prodding, I can stop, though."

"No, no, you're good," Rus panted. "Just unexpected."

"Trust me. Ride the wave, sweetie."

Rus had been very forward about his lack of bottoming experience, and as far as Dylan and Kaiden knew, Rus held no interest in bottoming. Not entirely true. There was a small curiosity, the tiniest of desires, but he'd always assumed the top role. Staying strictly top came easier.

Plus, much like now, there was a certain vulnerability that came with surrendering control. All the same, he rather enjoyed handing the reins over to Dylan and Kaiden, allowing them to dictate his pleasures, work him over to full satisfaction.

They continued for some time, the muscles in Rus' legs grew tired, but he found himself floating at the same time. He couldn't explain it or comprehend it. Part of him would much rather lie back and bask in these vibrant sensations. But the longer he stood there, the more minutes that passed, the more Rus found himself lost to the pleasures. Time didn't slow, despite finding himself lost in this moment, Rus noticed nearly fifteen minutes had gone by.

Electrifying tingles trailed along his skin. Pulses of excitement sent his mind surging far and wide. Every time he took a deep breath to bite back the exhilaration, his body stirred. Restless and quivering and on the verge of...

"Fuuuck." Rus bit his lip. "I'm gonna, I'm gonna..."

Between the way his body quaked from Dylan's mouth, to the stimulation of Kaiden's very strong head game, Rus knew he'd cum any moment. Kaiden stroked the full length of Rus' shaft, focusing on the head of his cock by rotating his tongue.

Rus bucked a bit erratically, unable to help it as he came closer and closer to climaxing. Dylan didn't relent, merely grabbed hold of Rus' hips and shoved his face in deeper to continue eating Rus' ass.

It was intoxicating.

Rus' little thrusts must've been Kaiden's cue because he did his damnest to deep throat the entirety of Rus' cock—nearly taking in the whole thing.

"Goddamn." Rus slapped his hands over Kaiden's face, enthralled by the feeling.

When Kaiden pulled back to breathe, Rus chased the high for a half second but let him go. Well, he would've if Kaiden's hands hadn't moved so insistently. While he couldn't keep himself in place, Kaiden signaled permission by squeezing Rus' hands until they pressed to Kaiden's head.

Rus' teeth chattered as he sucked in a deep breath and rammed Kaiden back down his shaft. The gurgle enticed him, so he relented just long enough for Kaiden to take in a wispy half breath while his lips were still tightly wrapped around Rus' dick. Then, Rus shoved him back down, pushing forward at the same time. He humped Kaiden's face, shoving his cock as far down his throat as possible.

Each thrust put Rus into a deeper frenzy until he couldn't contain himself. Without warning, Rus shot his load down Kaiden's throat, releasing a gasping growl with each shot into Kaiden.

"Oh, damn." Rus wobbled a bit, releasing Kaiden, whose eyes were glossy with tears. "You okay?"

"Hell yeah." Kaiden wiped away the spit running down his chin and eased back just enough for Rus to move forward.

He took two steps and collapsed onto his bed, panting with satisfaction. But it appeared Dylan wasn't finished with him quite yet, returning to his ass and continuing to tease his hole.

Rus lay there, lost in the soothing sensation washing over his entire body.

CHAPTER 19
DYLAN

JASMINE had certainly noticed the shift in Dylan's demeanor over the last few weeks. More and more of his free time had been spent away from the house, always with the same people. Now, if it'd just been Kaiden, chances were she wouldn't have suspected Dylan had gotten romantic. Or maybe she noticed his feelings for Kaiden long before he did himself.

In either case, the time he spent with Rus piqued Jasmine's curiosity. She asked if they were dating. Dylan sort of awkwardly dodged the question since yes, he was, but he didn't want to elaborate on his poly relationship quite yet. Moreover, he wanted Jasmine to meet Rus outside of his community service obligations. If he planned on declaring his relationship, he wanted Jasmine's blessing.

So, he arranged for a dinner and game night date to bring Kaiden and Rus over, not too big a challenge since Jasmine hosted family dinner every night of the week, with weekends allowing flexibility for anyone who wanted to go out or just pick at leftovers.

Kaiden pulled up to the house, parking on the street, and walking up with a semi-reluctant Rus. It wasn't the dinner itself, but Dylan could tell Rus didn't much like the dress shirt and tie Kaiden had undoubtedly forced him into.

Dylan smirked. Dressing up was not a requirement—they kept things very casual at the house—but Kaiden likely sensed Dylan's nerves to make a good impression and played his part well.

"Thank you," Dylan mouthed, to which Kaiden gave a sweet smile in return.

"I can stay for dinner, but I have a shift over at—"

"Is the gallery doing something this evening?" Dylan interrupted.

"Not the gallery." Kaiden stretched his cheeks into a forced smile. "Retail. The joy of holiday presales."

Dylan cringed. He very much admired Kaiden's determination to save up for a place of his own, so much so that he'd taken on a second job, but he also hated how reluctant Kaiden was when it came to accepting a little help.

Honestly, Dylan couldn't imagine the stress of balancing two jobs at once. His gig at Dorothy's Home consumed most of his time, though he never really considered it *work* work. He never clocked in or out. He never had to worry about his schedule. Mostly, he just ran errands, arranged moves, organized fundraisers, and helped the teens with schoolwork. Dylan felt more like a chill guncle around the house than a busy worker bee. Even on days when he juggled a hundred different tasks.

It all came down to supporting the house, and that was what mattered to him the most.

Dylan invited Kaiden and Rus inside.

"About time you got here," Miguel greeted them as they walked inside, his eyes locked onto Rus. "How are you this evening?"

"Fine."

"I'm not sure if we were ever formally introduced."

Rus shrugged.

"I'm Miguel Whitley Alvarado-Hernandez, but everyone just calls me"—Miguel made a loud smacking sound with his puckered lips—"m-wah."

Dylan sighed. No one called Miguel that, despite his very desperate efforts to make it his official nickname. Truthfully, his middle name started with a J, but that wouldn't work for his little kissy-faced flirtations.

"How about a tour?" Miguel stepped closer, and Dylan blocked his path.

"I was just about to introduce him to everyone."

"Waste of time if you ask me." Miguel walked away, lost in a conversation with Tasha before long.

"Not to be that person," Rus said, quirking a brow in Miguel's direction, "but was that kid just flirting with me?"

"Yes," Dylan said with a sigh. "He sort of does that with everyone. Don't worry about it. He's harmless, and his crushes are pretty fickle."

"I'd wager short kings are trending or something," Kaiden said with a light laugh.

Dylan smirked, knowing Kaiden had been dragged into a conversation about Miguel's many online crushes, and his type changed as frequently as fashion trends. The number of men Miguel liked could fill a 365-day calendar thrice over.

"I'm not that short," Rus said. "Just so we're clear, I'm average height."

Dylan eyed Kaiden, then they both looked down at Rus, then up at each other with wicked little smirks.

"Uh-huh," they said in unison.

"Oh, fuck both of you."

"One of these days," Kaiden teased.

After that, Dylan gave Rus a tour around the house as he introduced him to the residents. About halfway through, Rus appeared frazzled. Even Kaiden seemed a bit perplexed by who was who. It wasn't easy learning the names of twelve teens, especially when half of them were eager for conversation.

Jasmine gave a warning call for dinner, loudly announcing they had five minutes. Dylan went to wash his hands, telling Rus that this was his last chance for a smoke break until after dinner. Jasmine tried to keep dinner very official, no leaving the table until everyone else, and ensuring the teens participated in conversation. She liked engagement.

Chelsea and Yazmin carried in large bowls of side dishes while Jasmine brought in a tray of pork chops.

"It's nice of you to join us again," Jasmine said, inviting Rus to take a seat near her.

Dylan ended up sequestered on the foot of the table between Miguel and Tasha, where he normally sat, though he'd planned on bringing his boyfriends closer to his side. Instead, Jasmine got ahold of Rus, and Chelsea dragged Kaiden into helping set the table.

"Just sit down," Dylan whispered as Kaiden placed a basket of rolls on the table. "You're a guest."

"I don't mind helping." Kaiden shrugged, then scurried back into the kitchen to assist.

It seemed every time Kaiden came over, he jumped in for something, whether washing dishes or organizing donations or setting the damn dinner table.

Once everything was arranged and everyone had taken their seats, Jasmine invited Rus and Kaiden to dig in, letting company fill their plates first.

"So," Chelsea said, scooping herself a large portion of mashed potatoes. "You know Mrs. Helix, Hendrix, Hydraulics? Whatever, the old hag down the street who pretends she's still in college?"

"What'd that stupid ass bitch do now?" Miguel asked.

Jasmine snapped her fingers. "Ut-uh. None of that. Reel it back, real fast."

Miguel huffed, then sarcastically pretended to reel back a fishing line to pull his profanity in. When Jasmine disregarded his flair, he shifted to another preferred tactic of his. Miguel had a silent stare off with Jasmine until he either grew bored or quietly surrendered. Dylan smirked, knowing Miguel only relented because of company. Sometimes, guests could bring out his more provocative streaks, but perhaps he didn't want to chance Jasmine's wrath in front of his crush.

Either way, Dylan gave Rus a tight smile and then Kaiden an awkward grin. Kaiden understood the chaos in the house all too well and handled it well enough. Hopefully, this first dinner wouldn't scare Rus away.

"You were saying, Chelsea." Jasmine nodded for her to continue her story on their vile neighbor.

"Oh, well, nothing much. Just her and the platinum Karens were all huddled together, trash-talking per usual, but when we walked by…" Chelsea said with a wave of her hand, gesturing for Yazmin to pick up the story.

"They feel for us, naturally," Yazmin said with a pitchy, sarcastic lilt. "As they hold a special place in their hearts for all unhoused people, but—"

"Megh," Miguel interjected. "I fucking hate that term. What the hell is wrong with just saying homeless?"

"Some people find the term homeless dehumanizing," Dylan explained, hoping Jasmine wouldn't need to redirect the blatant profanity a second time. Personally, he didn't understand the appeal of saying unhoused either, but he supposed it didn't hurt anyone, so it didn't matter.

"Those people would be stupid cunty twats," Rus said absentmindedly as he sawed his pork chop.

The table went silent, and only the screechy clink of Rus' knife and fork hitting his plate could be heard.

Chelsea and Yazmin snorted, turning to each other and whispering.

Miguel smirked, leaning closer to the table. "Oh, do tell."

"Huh?" Rus blinked a few times, then scrunched his face, unsure of himself momentarily.

Dylan grimaced, let out a sigh, and twisted his frown into a slight smile. "You have quite the opinion."

"Quite the opinion indeed," Jasmine added, eyeing Dylan.

He so rarely brought people to the house, finding the presence of acquaintances could be difficult for the teens to cycle through. If Dylan brought someone to the house, they were a true friend. Or at the very least, a proper donor. In years past, he'd only ever brought Kaiden around the house, and it helped that Jasmine knew him before Dylan had even met him.

Kaiden was an easy sell around the house. He was polite, soft-spoken around large groups, and kept his opinions PG-friendly. And sure, the teens were all about vulgarity when the mood hit, but the point of being an adult was not to fan that behavior. Or so Dylan believed.

Of course, Rus would have a strong opinion on any controversial subject with the vocabulary of a sailor.

"Please elaborate," Jasmine insisted.

Rus chewed on his pork chop, taking his time.

"The phrase unhoused is designed to shift the blame of homelessness away from the individual and focus on the socio-economic factors," Rus explained, already losing Dylan a bit. "Great in theory. If that were the true agenda, I could almost be on board. Unhoused is supposed to remove the stigma. But why the fuck would a homeless person care about the stigma?"

He paused, silently apologizing for his profanity with a soft expression directed toward Dylan.

"Perhaps the unhoused population who seeks to pull themselves up and would prefer to avoid harmful stereotypes," Jasmine added, answering Rus' rhetorical question.

"Yes, but unhoused carries its own stereotypes. Worst of all, unhoused is deliberately designed to diminish the horror of homelessness and make it more palatable to those throwing around terms the majority of them have never experienced."

Jasmine locked in on this. Dylan studied her curious expression, the way her shoulders eased. In one simple statement, Rus had shifted Jasmine from going on a polite offensive to a calm dialogue, one where she'd listen with interest. Jasmine never bulldozed into an argument. She explained to Dylan years ago that the only way she could engage in a healthy dialogue with someone who opposed her was to lead them to her argument. Anything else and she'd be deemed hostile, aggressive, unhinged, loud, and so much more. So, Jasmine worked twice as hard to subtly approach her point on a topic. Of course, this didn't come with every conflict, simply the ones she needed to win for the sake of Dorothy's Home.

"People who use the term unhoused aren't trying to give more humanity to homeless people; they're trying to wash away the bitter taste the word homeless leaves in their mouths. They don't like the guilt it carries, the way they benefit in a capitalistic society while ignoring an entire population of people every day," Rus explained. "It's easier to disregard them, create stereotypes on drug abuse or crime, anything that shifts the blame to them—the homeless population. It also helps to assume they're all con artists, pretending to be homeless while panhandling a nice 100k tax-free salary every year. Yes, there was a rare instance where that happened once for certain, so let's assume the worst in every single homeless person."

"Well, that's quite the tangent," Jasmine said with a light laugh. "You seem quite opinionated on the subject."

"I'm too opinionated on too many subjects," Rus said, tearing into a piece of his pork chop. "And I easily get off topic from time to time. The point is, unhoused is just gentrifying our vocabulary to make wealthy people feel less uncomfortable when they discuss unsavory topics. This is partly because of social media and algorithm suppression. For example, saying killed as opposed to the absurdly palatable term unalived. Saying graped because let's ruin fruit and turn SA into a rhyming punchline. Even mentioning race or queerness of any kind knocks a post down. And don't get me started on how cringey it is to even say PDF since these internet assholes banded together. Apps have trained us to edit our language or risk losing our voice altogether, but that's a whole other story."

"I'd be very curious to hear more about it," Jasmine said, taking a sip of her drink. "Perhaps at a future dinner."

Rus nodded, then returned to his plate. Dylan smiled at him, smiled at Kaiden, and took an easy breath.

Miguel leaned over to Dylan and whispered. "My future short king is on fire. Even got Jailor Jazzy's approval."

Dylan sighed. "It's never happening."

Miguel tsked and rolled his eyes. "Wishing on my downfall only makes me stronger."

Shortly after dinner, Kaiden bid his farewells and left for work, while everyone else set up for game night. While Jasmine would gladly drag everyone into the living room to play board games, card games, and anything else family-oriented, she often reserved the game nights for rare occasions. At most, a once-a-month event.

"Hope you're not too competitive," Dylan whispered. "The house rules kind of get chaotic with these games, and winners are sort of determined on who can argue their point the best."

"Sounds like my kind of game night," Rus whispered in response.

"Thank you for coming." Dylan lightly pressed his knee against Rus' and sank into the bliss of sharing a little piece of his home with someone he cared about.

CHAPTER 20
KAIDEN

KAIDEN spent the week on cloud nine, practically floating into the gallery every morning despite working an additional twenty-five hours a week in retail hell and dealing with Alison's incredibly sour mood. She rarely smiled leading up to events, and the impending Thanksgiving gala served as a way for the super elite to celebrate in style while also being charitable.

Honestly, October, November, and December were about to piledrive Kaiden's free time with all the soirées he had to account for at the gallery. Thanks to his part-time gig, he'd even cut back on his gym routine. Not too much, though, since he found joy in working out.

It was all about to pay off, though, quite literally. He'd survived Alison's wrath, he'd crawled through the first two weeks of juggling his new retail gig, and he'd mentally prepared himself for the upcoming horror of holiday sales.

"The catering service sent over a revised menu for your approval, I've sent invitations to your exclusive donors, and there's a few documents that need your signature."

Alison made a garbled sound in response, keeping her eyes locked on her computer as she typed a flurried response to some benefactor.

"Just a reminder, I'm not going to be in tomorrow," Kaiden added.

"Which you approved because—"

"Why are you still talking?" Alison paused her message, looked up at Kaiden, scowled, then returned to her email. "And make sure the truck isn't damaged, or there will be hell to pay."

"Of course." Kaiden nodded, backstepping out of the office.

She might've been a headache during galas, but she'd already been very flexible with Kaiden's schedule since he needed to fit his part-time gig into his daily routine. Plus, she even let him use the work truck for his own personal needs.

When Kaiden finally got home, he went directly to the basement. He wanted to pass out after a twelve-hour day, to crash, to immediately sleep because tomorrow meant freedom.

> Kaiden: You still able to help move tomorrow?

> Rus: You still not giving us an address?

> Kaiden: Nope.

> Well, yes, I'm not giving you the address. It's a surprise.

> Rus: Then right back at you.

> Dylan: Wait. What?

> We're surprising him? With what?

> Shit. How do you unsend to the group?

> Kaiden: You can't. I already saw the message.

> Rus: We're not surprising him. YES we're helping him.

> Dylan: I'm confused.

> Kaiden: He asked me a question, I answered yes. He said right back at you.

Dylan sent a flurry of GIFs with wide-eyed stares and slow blinks. Some had "huh" written in bold caps.

Rus followed up with a crying laugh emoji.

> Kaiden: Just please get here earlier. The sooner I'm out the sooner I'm free.

> Rus: Of course.

> Dylan: Bright and early. 😊

Kaiden stayed up late scrolling through videos and sending at least ten different absolutely hilarious posts that he needed Rus and Dylan to watch immediately. The group chat was nice when it came to sharing videos. Rus sent nearly as many as Kaiden. The two of them always responded with a laugh or a one-liner in response, whereas Dylan never acknowledged the videos.

Social media had never been his thing. Many of the videos were locked behind login screens to apps Dylan always downloaded and then deleted from his phone. So, Kaiden found this little connection that only he and Rus shared quite entertaining. Especially since he could still share it with Dylan, and now he had to deal with this insufferable spam from both his boyfriends.

The next morning, Kaiden woke up and cooked himself breakfast. His scrambled eggs sizzled quickly, and he quelled them with a slice of pepper-jack cheese. While Kaiden didn't like adding milk to his eggs, he did enjoy the creamy spice of the right piece of cheese. He added some already-cooked sausage crumble to the mix and took one look at the mildewy veggies before tucking them back in the crisper.

Usually, Kaiden kept the fridge tidy and organized the produce on the sides, so they'd be used quickly. But in the last few weeks, he'd dropped every responsibility he'd taken on to benefit the house. Kaiden prioritized himself.

"If you're going to use someone else's food, you could at least make them breakfast too." Sandra glowered, dragging her feet across the kitchen floor.

Kaiden didn't know if the scratchy sound came from her old slippers rubbing against the linoleum or brushing against the dirt tracked into the house by his nephews on a daily basis.

It didn't matter. Kaiden took a deep breath and ignored his sister's jab. He could prioritize himself without being a selfish dick. He'd made his family thousands of meals over the years. He'd ignored the complaints about his cooking, the disappearing meal prep boxes he'd arranged for the week, the ingredients used and left out to spoil because someone couldn't be bothered to put back a bag of deli meat. There were hundreds of examples funneling through his head, opportunities to counter, to protest, to argue.

But Kaiden didn't want to pick a fight. He wanted to quietly disappear and move forward with his life.

Sandra intentionally poured Kaiden's black coffee into the sink and rinsed his mug before setting it on top of the mountain of dirty dishes. Then she made herself a cup, using the last of the coffee. Of course, she forgot to tuck the creamer back into the fridge before leaving. Kaiden left the creamer where it was but double checked to make sure the fridge door was sealed. He stood by the table, too wound up to sit, and scarfed down his meal.

Normally, his sister moved through the house like a chaotic whirlwind first thing in the morning, preparing her kids for the bus, and screaming at her husband until he woke up. This morning was just as loud, just as chaotic, but ticked by so much slower. It seemed every minute lasted an eternity, and Kaiden wondered if Rus and Dylan would arrive before his sister left. Then he'd be forced to hear about it from her.

Thankfully, Sandra dragged her family out of the house, and Kaiden had a bit of privacy. His mother had already gone off to work. John worked nights, and based on the empty beer cans littered across the kitchen table, he'd be out for the count this morning.

Kaiden went to his nephews' bedroom, the room he'd finally abandoned, and started packing up his belongings. He brought the boxes to the front hall and set them by the door, then made his way to the bathroom and did a quick sweep for his belongings. By the time he'd finished, his phone buzzed with a text from Dylan. They'd arrived.

"Hey," Kaiden answered the door with a finger pressed to his lips. "Stepfather is sleeping. Should be out cold, but I don't want to hear his rambles if he wakes up and catches me taking my stuff."

"Let him say something," Rus scoffed. "I got a few choice words for your family."

"Tempting, but you talk with your fists too much, so…" Kaiden pursed his lips and gave Rus a peck, followed by giving Dylan one too. "Thank you for dropping everything to help me move."

"Of course," Dylan said, revealing a vase filled with a bouquet of pink roses.

Kaiden found himself enchanted by the lovely gesture. A sweet housewarming gift Kaiden would treasure, especially noticing the art of the vase. It was gorgeous and far too expensive for Kaiden to ever consider buying. He spotted it on one of their outings and refused to consider buying it despite Rus and Dylan encouraging the frivolous purchase. Kaiden did his best to avoid trinkets that didn't provide immediate value. Money was far too tight for frivolous or sentimental things.

"Thank you," Kaiden said, almost collapsing into putty. "Let's put them in the truck and get everything else packed up quickly. I already know where I'll set them."

Kaiden directed them to the basement, where they'd grab the rest of his belongings, while he carried the vase and flowers down the street to the truck. Yes, he'd parked his boss's truck at the end of the block. Chances were his family wouldn't have noticed a random truck parked on the street, and pieced together that it came from the gallery, but Kaiden wanted to avoid any and all questions.

It was petty, packing up and leaving in the dead of morning without a word. But he'd exhausted himself on one-way conversations and guilt trips and pointless debates. All he wanted was to be on his own.

Rus and Dylan piled boxes into the back of the truck. Well, mostly alone. He could make room for his boyfriends. His friends. They were the most reliable people in his life.

Kaiden's stuff proved easy to move. He'd packed most of it away before Rus and Dylan came over. He left behind his dresser and nightstand. Both were mostly filled with his nephews' belongings at this point anyway, and he figured the little guys could use the furniture more.

"You sure you wanna leave the bed behind?"

"Absolutely." Kaiden made a sour face.

He'd had that creaky, squeaky twin mattress since he was fifteen years old. Every time he considered replacing it, something came up, funds ran low, or he simply couldn't bring himself to waste money on another dreadful twin bed. He wanted a full, a queen, a king. Anything with real space. Mainly, he just wanted space, something he never got in this home.

"Be careful, please." Kaiden directed Rus and Dylan with the only real furniture he needed help moving.

His vanity desk and collection of lights and mirrors had really started piling up in the basement. They'd become his very own treasure trove, a safety net when hiding, and the perfect makeup station when putting on his face.

Even so, Dylan managed to Tetris everything into the back of the truck, while Rus did the heavy lifting.

Kaiden climbed into the truck, Dylan ended up wedged in the middle seat, and Rus tried to light a smoke until Kaiden snatched away his lighter.

"Alison would kill me."

Rus sighed.

"But don't worry, there's a nice little patio at my new place with your name on it."

"So, we finally get to see the new digs, huh?" Rus raised his eyebrows.

Kaiden drove through the city and a little more out of the way than he preferred. It was definitely bordering on the other side of town from Rus and Dylan and work, but he'd already accounted for the extra travel time. In the end, it'd be worth it.

While the pride he initially held for his accomplishment kept him buzzing from the day he signed the papers, it did fizzle out a bit as he pulled up to the trailer park.

"I know it doesn't look like much," Kaiden said, driving down the main neighborhood street before turning onto one of the dirt roads. "But—"

"But nothing," Dylan said. "I've helped move a few former residents out into these parts. One of the few spots without a deathly rent."

True. It also proved to be one of the only rental places that didn't require proof of income three times the rent or a co-signer with a high credit score.

"Yeah, folks don't think much of trailers," Kaiden added. "But it's pretty sturdy, I think."

"A home is a home is a home," Rus said. "And it's all yours."

Kaiden pulled into the patch of dead grass that constituted his current driveway. They went to work, bringing boxes inside, piling them up in the empty living room. Aside from a few basic necessities and some kitchenware, Kaiden hadn't gotten much to spruce the place up.

"It looks a little rough right now, but I'm getting tons of stuff soon," Kaiden said, believing he could turn this trailer into a real home.

Despite how small it appeared on the outside, there was a lot of room within. The front door led to the living room, which connected to the nearby kitchen that had a ton of cabinets and counter space. On either end of the trailer was a bedroom, each of them big in its own respect. The smaller bedroom didn't have a walk-in bathroom like the master, but it still had a full bath in the tiny hallway beside it, which connected back to the living room. All in all, the place could easily house more than just Kaiden, but it was just Kaiden's. He let out a small smile. For the first time in his life, he had space that belonged to just him. No sharing, no compromising, no making do.

"I like it." Dylan grinned.

"Thank you," Kaiden sheepishly replied, always unable to truly accept a compliment.

The three of them worked to carry in the boxes and a few belongings Kaiden had managed to get together. With everything piled up in the empty living room, Kaiden suddenly found every doubt he'd repressed creeping back up. Everything he had ignored because he was too busy and exhausted working toward this very goal.

"I know moving into an empty trailer on the other side of town with almost no savings or safety net seems rash, but I didn't want to spend another six months planning, scraping, and doing it the so-called smart way. I didn't want to lose out on this trailer. Sure, it's not fancy, but it's solid and it's safe and it's mine."

Rus and Dylan didn't respond; they merely stared at Kaiden, which only made him more anxious.

"Maybe it would've been smarter to save up longer or rent a room with some stranger, but I couldn't do that. And I couldn't stay where I was. Every day in that house ate away at my sanity, my happiness, my belief," Kaiden said, pouring out all the reasons this was the right choice and not some impulsive mistake where he'd fall flat on his face in a few months. This had to work. It just had to. "If I stayed another month, I'd start to think it was impossible to ever claw my way out. I just needed to go."

Now Kaiden rambled away his own self-doubts, his own insecurities. What he spewed came from a need to reassure himself more than to validate his choice to Dylan or Rus.

"No having to deal with a house full of judgy, whiny family members. No last-minute babysitting. No unexpected bills I need to cover. No hiding who I am in my own bedroom. No tiptoeing around people. I get to be me. If that means I work a shitty part-time job over the holidays, fine. I get to make the choices to support my life in my home for my goals."

Dylan cracked a smile and approached. "Can I speak?"

"Not if it's to poke holes in my decision or note how impulsive it was."

"No holes, no poking. Well, unless it's the fun kind of poking," Dylan said, wrapping his hands over Kaiden's arms.

Kaiden let out an exasperated chuckle. "Okay."

"I'm proud of you." Dylan's smile grew. "And if you're happy, that is literally all that matters to me. I'm just here to wave my Kaiden flag of support."

"Personally, I think it's badass," Rus chimed in, pressing a hand to Kaiden's lower back. "You saw what you wanted and made it happen. On your own."

"Thank you." Kaiden tilted his head, pressing it against Rus' as a small gesture of gratitude and affection for his kind words.

"My boy's a bad bitch," Rus said with a grin. "I couldn't be happier."

"Shut up." Kaiden nudged Rus.

"Tour?" Dylan asked, slapping a hand on top of a stack of boxes.

"Well, there's the guest bedroom, which will probably turn into Rus' smoking room during the winter."

"Please," Rus scoffed. "Like a little chill's gonna stop me."

"Maybe a gaming room," Dylan said with wide eyes of excitement.

Kaiden dismissed the idea. They could keep the gaming to Rus' apartment.

"This is the living room, obviously." Kaiden gestured, then pointed through to the kitchen and dining room, which meshed together in this very spacious open-floor plan.

"It's like five times the size of my apartment," Rus said, following Kaiden through the kitchen.

Kaiden showed them the washer and dryer hookup.

"I can get you a real good deal on those," Dylan said. "Jasmine knows everyone when it comes to furnishing a place. I'll ask her about couches and stuff."

"Definitely a TV," Rus added.

"Oh, yeah."

"Please, don't," Kaiden insisted.

He didn't want to be a burden when it came to getting his place together. Unlike the teens Dylan worked with, Kaiden was an adult and needed to prove he could do this like one. It might be the first time in his life he'd made the difficult decision to stand on his own two feet.

"You gotta have a TV," Rus said. "It's practically a necessity."

"That's what my phone is for."

"You'd honestly be doing us a favor," Dylan said. "Jasmine pays out the ass on storage units, but if we don't hoard it, we lose out on a lot of really good stuff."

"Like?" Rus asked.

"Richy riches will donate entire furniture sets in great condition simply because it's out of style," Dylan said. "Jasmine knows who to schmooze when it comes to grabbing them up. Better than some charity thrift store that'll jack up the price and only donate a penny on the dollar to those in need. Plus, a lot of the former residents get to live in style once they move out."

"Nice." Rus nodded as Kaiden led them into the master bedroom.

While Kaiden hadn't gotten any real furnishing, he did buy an expensive blow-up queen-size mattress.

"I'm getting a real one soon, but this bad boy is top of the line. I might keep it in the guest room." Kaiden plopped onto the mattress, showing how sturdy it was. "Seriously, it's good stuff."

"This is so impressive," Dylan said, bouncing onto the bed beside Kaiden. "You are pretty damn amazing."

"I got lucky—"

Before Kaiden could continue diminishing his accomplishments, Dylan kissed him, tender and sweet and slow. Then, of course, he took it all away by shoving Kaiden back onto the air mattress.

"I think you should show us how top-notch this bed is," Dylan said, climbing on top of Kaiden.

"Is it safe for three people?" Rus asked.

Kaiden snickered, lost in the sweet kisses Dylan left across his collarbone.

"It's safe for four, five, maybe even six, depending on the size," Kaiden said with an excited growl as Dylan continued nuzzling deeper into the crook of his neck, teasing and tasting him.

"Ooooh," Rus said, jumping onto the mattress. "Four or five, huh? Are we not enough for you?"

"Insatiable." Dylan bit the air with a taunting expression.

"You're too much," Kaiden said with a breathy sigh as Dylan worked his way down his waist.

Dylan didn't mess with the corset vest. Between Kaiden's comfort level and the many straps, it was easier to ignore. Instead, he unfastened Kaiden's belt and pulled down his pants.

"Fuck," Kaiden groaned.

In one quick motion, Dylan swallowed the entirety of Kaiden's cock. As Kaiden lay there, lost in the pleasure of Dylan's warm mouth, Rus crawled over to Kaiden, kissing him. It turned into a frenzy of desires. Kaiden's hands were lost in the sudden embrace of Rus' body as they wrapped around each other, but every part of him wanted to grab hold of Dylan too—at least his head. Snatch his hair back, something. Anything. Dylan continued working to take the full length of Kaiden with each bob of his head, making it impossible not to come closer and closer to climaxing.

Kaiden moaned, releasing the ecstasy into Rus' mouth; he bucked his hips, thrusting deeper into Dylan's throat.

"Wait, hold on." Kaiden pushed away just enough to stop from cumming. "I was really close."

"You want to stop?" Dylan asked, wiping his mouth.

"What? No, I mean, you want to…" Kaiden paused, finding Dylan and Rus both seemed on board with continuing, much like Kaiden himself, but he wanted to explore something more tonight. "I was thinking maybe we could…you know. And if I…now, then I won't want to…you know."

"You gotta say it." Dylan had this smug little smirk that practically drove Kaiden up the wall.

He was an adult, surely, he could say it. He had said it. They'd discussed it previously, which was why they all got tested to make sure their intimacy didn't bring in anything unexpected, and when they took things to a further level, everyone would be aware of each other's status. Since no one came back positive for anything, they were fine without added protection. Still, Kaiden found himself nervous working up the courage to discuss advancing their relationship.

"I was thinking of sex," Kaiden said sheepishly.

"You mean anal?" Rus asked. "Because technically speaking, oral is still—"

"Yeah, yeah, yeah, whatever. It's all sex." Kaiden waved a hand to shoo away the lecture. "But I was thinking maybe if everyone is comfortable with it, we could explore something more."

"Hey, I'm on board for any ass pounding," Dylan said with a minxy expression, letting his eyes fall on Kaiden and then onto Rus, quite suggestively.

"I'm also on board with giving, not receiving," Rus clarified. "Sorry, love."

Dylan made a playful pouty face. "Someone get me a D20, I wanna test my charisma."

Rus broke out into laughter.

"I'll be back in a few minutes." Kaiden pulled his pants up just enough to excuse himself before either could protest. "You two continue, please."

He left the bedroom and made his way to the guest bathroom, where he'd stored a few prep supplies in case things ever got to the next level. Mostly, they'd stuck with kissing and oral and the occasional rim job. But—pun intended—since they were going further, Kaiden wanted to make sure he was ready for the fun without worrying about any mess.

Not that Kaiden was too worried, since he kept a high fiber diet for general health reasons, with the added benefit of ensuring a safe bottoming experience. Still, he preferred not to chance anything his first time with Dylan and Rus. Christ, he wondered if he'd be taking both of them? Probably not at the same time, surely. As he worked, fantasy turned into anxiety. They weren't small guys, and Kaiden didn't exactly mess around regularly.

"Fuck." Kaiden gulped.

After he cleaned himself up and readied for any possible direction this evening might go, Kaiden undressed somewhat. He kept his corset vest and dress shirt on, but he removed his slacks and even his boxers because why not be a bit bold? Before he fully undressed from the waist down, he considered keeping one fashionable accessory, and then went to retrieve a bottle of lube he had tucked away behind the mirror in the medicine cabinet. Then he made his way back to the other side of the trailer, where he found Dylan and Rus making out on the floor as they stroked each other.

Kaiden cleared his throat loudly, almost wishing he hadn't interrupted the show, but he posed in the doorway all the same.

Rus' eyes lit up at the sight of Kaiden's shirt stays. "The sexy garters!"

"The what?" Dylan asked. "Sorry, I'm too lost on the sexy man parading around half naked."

"Or half dressed," Kaiden teased, taking a dainty step or two into the room.

Rus and Dylan kept their eyes trained on Kaiden. It was intimidating and intoxicating all at once.

"Just a quick reminder," Kaiden said, eyeing them both on the floor below him. "I told you the bed is very durable."

"Maybe we have some *very* un-durable plans." Dylan waggled his eyebrows.

"Is that even a word?"

"Durable is," Rus said. "Pretty sure all words are words so long as you say it with enough confidence."

"I don't think that's how—"

Dylan and Rus each snatched one of Kaiden's arms and dragged him to the floor before he had a chance to ramble his way into a random debate. He laughed with a gasp as he fell on top of them, grateful for their intervention and for their united force in bracing his impact.

"I brought stuff if anyone is, you know, feeling, I don't know, stuff and such…"

"Dear Kaiden, are you coming onto us?" Dylan asked suggestively.

"No, I just want to be ready in case we…me…you…anyone really, wants to you know."

"Hmmm…" Dylan purred against the back of Kaiden's ear, nibbling on his neck ever so. "And what might you be ready for?"

"Well, I'm ready for anything, really."

"Anything?" Rus asked, his lips were close enough to taste. "That's quite the offering."

Kaiden leaned closer, kissing Rus, losing himself in the moment. Dylan's hands moved behind him, caressing him and sliding his fingers under the shirt stays in a teasing way. When Dylan reached his hand around Kaiden's shaft, he growled into Rus' mouth.

"You seem quite eager," Dylan rasped into Kaiden's ear, tugging on the lobe.

"I am," he whispered in response.

"Nervous?"

"No," he replied far too quickly, which made his voice crack.

"It's okay to be nervous," Dylan said, teasing him with each breath that hit Kaiden's neck. "I want to make sure you're ready, you're comfortable."

"I want you to fuck me," Kaiden panted, anxious and excited and wound up with a million different feelings. "I want to feel both of you. Want to please both of you."

"That can be arranged." Rus kissed Kaiden's neck, just under his jaw.

Kaiden glimpsed Dylan retrieve the lube and went to turn his head further when Rus stole his attention with another kiss. The mixed sensations left him lost in a delirium of excitement and a frenzy of awkward exposure. As much as Kaiden felt confused and unworthy, he also sank into the comfort of being surrounded by those he trusted more than anything.

A cool splash of lube trickled down his crack, quickly warmed by the gentle touch of Dylan's hand. Kaiden moaned, pulling his lips away from Rus' mouth, as Dylan inserted a finger. Maybe two. It was a lot, but he knew it wasn't Dylan's cock. No way had a beast like that slipped right in without protest.

Much as expected, Dylan took his time fingering Kaiden, lubing his hole, and readying him. Kaiden leaned forward, almost bending entirely over despite Rus being directly in front of him. Not that Rus protested, in fact, he stared down at Kaiden with quite the voracious appetite.

"Well, well." Rus unfastened his belt and fished out his dick, lightly slapping Kaiden with the head. Kaiden opened his mouth, sticking out his tongue as Rus continued stroking his semi-erect cock and smacking Kaiden with it. Kaiden groaned from Dylan's sudden withdrawal, and that prompted Rus to shove his cock into his mouth.

Kaiden gagged and gurgled and allowed Rus to take immediate control over his head as he attempted to bob fast enough to keep up with the insatiable desires. Meanwhile, the girth of Dylan's cock rubbed against Kaiden's exposed crack, the lube warming as their skin buzzed from the contact.

It wouldn't be long. Kaiden knew any second, Dylan would push in, and the mere thought excited and terrified him—so much so, his throat tightened. It made it impossible for him to take Rus' dick any further. Choking more than anticipated, he spit out Rus' dick and panted.

"Sorry, I just need a second."

"No worries, baby." Rus ran the length of his dick along Kaiden's face, teasing him with the head.

He'd bring the tip close to Kaiden's lips, then pull it away.

"You ready?" Dylan asked, running his hand up Kaiden's back until he reached about midway.

Kaiden arched, not an easy feat with his corset vest, even if he'd loosened it a bit when he stepped out earlier.

Dylan followed Kaiden's prompting and pushed the head of his cock inside him. The immediate burn sent a shiver of pain surging through him. Kaiden let out a whimper.

"Relax." Dylan trailed his hand over Kaiden's lower back, holding him steady as he kept his cock in place.

It sat inside Kaiden, merely an inch or two, but enough for Kaiden to ache already.

"Focus on Rus and just relax your body," Dylan instructed, moving his hands down to Kaiden's hips and rocking forward ever so.

Kaiden groaned, opening his mouth in the process, and gratefully accepting Rus' dick. The giant member constricting his throat muscles definitely distracted him from the massive shaft shoving its way inside him.

"And we're in," Dylan growled.

He rested a hand on the back of Kaiden's head, his body stretched out on top of Kaiden entirely.

"You hear that, baby?" Rus asked, tilting Kaiden's head just enough to look up at him.

Kaiden's eyes watered from how deep Rus had shoved his dick.

Soon, Dylan began to thrust, taking slow strokes to ease his way deeper into Kaiden. Each pump came with a rhythmic grunt of satisfaction as Dylan quickly increased his pace. The further he pushed his cock into Kaiden, the more he believed it'd rip him open any second. Pain consumed him; even as he worked on Rus' dick, the distraction became impossible.

The carpet offered the briefest of distractions, rubbing awkwardly against his knees and palms as he tried to stay firmly planted. Still, the ebb and flow of being spit-roasted jostled him in place.

Just when Kaiden thought he couldn't endure anymore, just when he thought he'd buckle, when he'd need to pause, his body warmed in an entirely new way. The pain that'd radiated throughout every cell of his being had washed away, now replaced by this euphoric pressure. It struck everywhere, gliding across his skin and melding deep within his muscles.

Rus pulled out of Kaiden's mouth as he moaned with pleasure. Dylan pressed his chest on Kaiden's back and clasped his hand underneath Kaiden's chin, turning his head to the side. Kaiden's lips met Dylan's, and the pair lost themselves in each other's thrusts. Kaiden groaned into Dylan's mouth, and Dylan growled right back at Kaiden. Each pump made Kaiden's dick grow harder. Each buck of Dylan's hips slapping against his skin sent an electric shiver of excitement. Each smack of their lips drew Kaiden deeper into the bliss of ecstasy.

"You're such a good boy," Dylan panted, gently grinding against Kaiden, and pushing his cock in and out at a steady rhythm.

"Probably the best boy," Rus said, grabbing Kaiden on either side of his head and returning his gaze directly ahead.

Rus pushed his dick up to Kaiden's mouth, and he greedily accepted, struggling to swallow as much as possible while Dylan continued ramming him from behind.

Kaiden lost himself in that second, stretching his jaw to further accommodate Rus, who bucked faster and harder. Dylan's skin smacked against Kaiden, Rus' fingers gripped a fistful of Kaiden's hair. It seemed they both moved in unison, slamming as deep into Kaiden as they could from either end.

As Kaiden tilted his head to the side to make room for Rus' curved cock continuing to slam hard into the back of his throat, he glimpsed the guys in the corner of his eye. They'd lifted one of their arms each, extending their hands to each other, and interlocking their fingers.

They grunted; eyes locked onto each other as they rammed into Kaiden. They were gods to him, glorious and triumphant. Kaiden let out muffled groans as Dylan thrust into him harder, his gurgles difficult to hear with Rus shoving in and out of his mouth.

Dylan took his free hand, slowly sliding it down Kaiden's back and wrapping his fingers through the loops of his corset vest. He pushed Kaiden into a deeper arch and then seemed to tug on the strings. The pulls were commanding, guiding Kaiden, who remained in place but still attempted to follow Dylan's unspoken instructions.

Rus wrapped a hand underneath Kaiden's chin, encouraging him to take in more of his dick. As he fought to wedge his dick in deeper, Kaiden gagged.

"Good boy," Rus growled, using his thumb to wipe away spit running down Kaiden's chin. "Keep it up."

"You ready for this?" Dylan asked, slapping Kaiden's ass. "Huh?"

Kaiden couldn't speak, not currently, but he gurgled and attempted to nod, much to no avail. Rus commended the effort, gently massaging Kaiden's neck before moving his hand back underneath his chin to hold Kaiden steady as he bucked forward at full force to brutally face fuck him.

"Goddamn right you are." Dylan pumped into Kaiden erratically, freeing his hand from Rus, and now focused on keeping a firm grip on Kaiden's hips. "Fucking take it."

Dylan pulled out just long enough for a warm spurt to hit Kaiden's exposed hole. He moaned with Rus' dick deep into his mouth and whimpered as Dylan pushed back inside. Thankfully, Dylan's thrusts had slowed, but he continued pouring the rest of his load into Kaiden.

Rus let out an aggressive grunt, pushing Kaiden off his dick and stroking himself until he finished. Kaiden closed his eyes. A warm burst hit his cheek, then a second, and the third seemed to jet across his entire face like a string splattered from chin to forehead.

"Fuck," Rus panted, rubbing the head of his dick along Kaiden's messy face, spreading his seed everywhere.

As Kaiden lay there, lost in the ecstasy of their completion, he prepared himself to ask for a towel when a lubed hand gripped his cock. He shuddered, keeping his eyes firmly shut to avoid getting cum in them, but he curiously reached to find Rus still kneeling above him.

"You love it, don't you?" Rus said, running his hands down Kaiden's shoulders.

Dylan stroked Kaiden faster, focused on the nerves at the head of his cock. Kaiden bucked a bit, drawn into the sensation, and without warning, he shot his load.

"Fuuuuck."

"If you think that was good, just wait until round two," Dylan said with a chuckle.

"Gah, please tell me round two is not tonight."

"Well, we've got to see how you handle Rus dick up your ass while taking mine down your throat."

Kaiden let out this exasperated laugh. Part of him eagerly wanted to see the same; another part wanted to rest.

"Can someone at least get me a towel first?"

"Sure thing." Rus stepped away for a moment.

Kaiden felt Dylan's presence, his face approaching, even with his eyes closed tight. Their lips met, and Dylan kissed him with no concern for the cum.

"You were brilliant."

"Careful," Kaiden said with a smile. "Flattery will get you everywhere."

"That's the plan." Dylan kissed him again, and Kaiden lost himself in the rush that a part of him wanted to ramp up this next round immediately, but he figured his boyfriends would surely need a little time for themselves to recover.

"Can we please move this to the bed for round two?" Kaiden asked. "The carpet is really hard on my knees."

"I suppose," Rus said, delicately placing a towel over Kaiden's face. "But if it pops, I'm not taking the blame."

The three of them laughed, lying on the floor together as Kaiden gently rubbed his face clean.

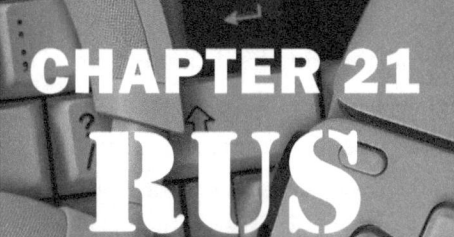

CHAPTER 21
RUS

THE next morning, Rus woke up to find Kaiden retrieving his clothes and heading into the shower. Dylan had sprawled out across the air mattress; his arm pressed heavily against Rus' windpipe. After rolling Dylan off him, he brushed the sleep out of his eyes and tried to adjust to the brightness of the room. Kaiden's place got a lot more sunlight than his tiny apartment.

Once the shower turned off, Rus half expected to catch Kaiden traipsing out dripping wet, but minutes ticked by before he stepped out fully clothed in his compression tank, slipping on his oversized work shirt.

"Sexy top."

"Right back at you." Kaiden winked.

Rus paused, realizing he had slept shirtless, and then the joke dawned on him.

"Nice."

Kaiden tugged on his loose-fitting shirt. "Unfortunately, they have zero style."

Without his corset vests, Rus figured the compression tank offered Kaiden a little comfort. He wanted to comment on how Kaiden didn't need them, didn't need to hide and change in the bathroom of his own home, but he understood that Kaiden still struggled with his body image. Yes, he'd grown to accept himself, but Rus worried Kaiden would always believe others wouldn't accept him. Rus wanted to find a way to convince Kaiden he was comfortable with his appearance in the fullest sense.

Kaiden kept the double doors to the master bedroom wide open as he strutted into the neighboring kitchen and started cooking. There was a pep in Kaiden's step as he tossed flour into a mixing bowl. The sizzle of the pancakes carried a fruity, sweet aroma that roused Rus out of bed. Kaiden shimmied with a bit of swagger as he grabbed plates.

"Well, isn't this a treat?" Rus said, staring at Kaiden's ass.

"They're protein pancakes, so they're good for you, too," Kaiden replied, completely oblivious to Rus' wandering eye.

"Hey, if you need some extra protein, I've got you covered."

Kaiden made a face, clearly not amused. Then he pointed the spatula at Rus. "Maybe for lunch if you're lucky."

"Ooooh."

"Depends how I feel after retail hell." Kaiden stacked pancakes onto plates and carried them into the bedroom. "But y'all are welcome to chill here. Internet is up. Wi-Fi password is on the box. Fridge is stocked. I'll be back around two."

"Cool."

"Normally, eating in bed is not allowed."

"Even ass?" Rus playfully retorted.

Kaiden made a face, trying his hardest not to laugh. "Anyway, feel free to eat in bed since I'm seriously lacking furniture, but please don't spill crumbs."

"No worries." Rus took his plate.

Kaiden stared at the sleeping Dylan and then looked to Rus. Since Kaiden held two plates, Rus shook Dylan.

Dylan woke up but remained groggy the entire time he ate breakfast. He managed one coherent sentence, and that came with a mouthful of pancakes.

"Thank you," Dylan said as he took a big bite.

Kaiden grabbed everyone's plates and tossed them in the sink. He quickly walked back into the bedroom and gave Rus a kiss, then followed up by giving the very sleepy Dylan a peck goodbye.

"You two try to have some fun while I'm gone."

"Not too much fun," Dylan groaned, still waking up.

"I don't know, maybe a little too much fun will wake you up."

Rus snickered and waved goodbye. He sat on top of the covers for a few minutes, scrolling through his phone while Dylan snoozed beside him.

Eventually, Dylan yawned and stretched wide to wake up his sleepy body. "Plans?"

"I'm probably going to shower."

"Oh, now that's a fun plan." Dylan grinned. "We can get dirty and squeaky clean all at the same time."

"We?"

"Well, yeah. Wouldn't want to run up Kaiden's water bill his first day," Dylan insisted. "It's conservation."

"Uh huh." Rus rolled his eyes and hopped out of bed, swaggering as he made his way across the bedroom.

Dylan rolled out of bed, intentionally letting his large plaid boxers hang low, exposing the deep cut line of his hip.

They made their way into the master bathroom. It was a huge walk-in space, much larger than Rus' bathroom. While the trailer might've looked quaint on the outside, it was anything but inside. The shower itself was massive, with a tub almost as large as a jacuzzi.

Dylan dropped his undies and turned on the water before walking over to the sink and gargling a bit of mouthwash. Rus joined him in that, figuring he still had smoker's breath. After he rinsed his mouth clean, he went over to the shower.

Rus tested the water, and when it seemed warm enough, he hopped inside, making room for Dylan, who immediately soaked underneath the spray. He shook his shaggy, wet hair and grinned at Rus.

"That'll wake you up first thing in the morning."

"If you're trying to wake up, maybe you need a cold shower," Rus teased, moving his hand over to the nozzle.

"Don't you dare." Dylan swatted Rus' hand. "It'll wake me up for sure, but it'll put this guy to sleep."

Dylan's eyes wandered down to his semi-erect cock.

"We wouldn't want that, now, would we?" Rus stepped closer, looking up at Dylan.

"Not at all." Dylan kissed Rus.

His stubble tickled Rus. They took their time kissing, letting the water run over them until steam filled the shower. Eventually, Rus broke away long enough to grab some body wash.

"Gotta get clean too," Rus said, rubbing the soap onto Dylan's hairy chest and stomach.

He had fun lathering Dylan's body, covering him in bubbles with a hint of coconut aroma. When Dylan turned around, Rus took his time with his back, eyeing his bubble butt the entire time he worked.

"Let me get you," Dylan said, retrieving the body wash and rubbing it in, paying extra attention to the tattoos. Rus didn't have the heart to tell him that it wasn't necessary, so he just let Dylan work cleaning away at each one with more effort than the last.

"Turn around," Dylan instructed with an almost commanding voice.

Rus obeyed. Dylan soaped up Rus' back, massaging his muscles and taking his time.

"That feels really nice." Rus rocked his head back, letting the water soak his curls.

Dylan continued soaping Rus up, even turning them to get away from the direct spray, then worked his hands lower. As his hand crept closer to Rus' crotch, Rus reached out and guided the direction.

"Ah, damn." Rus let his hand fall and allowed Dylan to stroke him.

When Dylan's other hand cupped his butt, Rus curiously turned his head back.

"I can stop any time you like," Dylan whispered, running his soapy hand over Rus' cheeks.

Rus stood taller in response, almost arching his back. But he didn't speak; he couldn't find the words.

Dylan's fingers gently spread Rus' cheeks, and one of them traced the rim of his hole teasingly. This went on for some time. Rus half expected Dylan to drop to his knees and bury his face into Rus' ass. Instead, he continued playing with his hole, exciting Rus with each brush of his finger.

When Dylan's hand retreated, Rus almost bucked in protest, swept away by the moment, but the quick intrusion of a new sensation startled him. Dylan pressed the head of his cock against the entrance of Rus' hole.

Rus vibrated with anticipation. He turned his head, meeting Dylan at his shoulder as the pair kissed and grinded against one another. The exhilaration left him breathless, but he was too hungry for Dylan's mouth to stop. They locked lips as Rus let Dylan pin him to the wall.

Fuck, how it turned him on so much. Part of Rus wanted to brace against the shower wall and push back onto Dylan, explore this tiny throbbing ache, but another part of him shook the fantasy away.

As curious as Rus might've been, he was nowhere near ready for something like that. Even the slightest pressure against his hole held this tingling ache he didn't feel prepared to take.

"Sorry, but I'm not getting dicked down for the first time in a shower," Rus said with a cocky laugh.

"Hey, we can step out, and I can rail you into the floor," Dylan whispered, somehow even cockier. "Would you like that?"

Rus' skin tingled. Fuck, he really would like that. Dylan's touch was electric.

"And if you're worried about it hurting, I can be oh so gentle when I pound you."

"That sounds quite contradictory."

"Not when you know what you're doing." Dylan bit Rus' earlobe, tugging just enough to tease. "Don't worry."

Dylan took a step back, standing underneath the full blast of the water, and grinning as Rus turned to face him.

"When you decide you're ready to get fucked, I'll be here."

"Yeah?" Rus stepped underneath the blast of water, kissing Dylan, and was tempted to tease a bit more. Still curious where things could go.

"Yeah, and with any luck, Kaiden will get quite the show." Dylan stroked Rus as he kissed him back.

"Hey, we can give him a show this afternoon," Rus said, licking Dylan's Adam's apple.

"Oh?"

"Yeah, so long as you're willing to bend over."

"Hmmm," Dylan growled. "Tempting. But if you're gonna fuck me, I'm definitely going to have to break you in first."

"That so?" Rus lightly bit Dylan's neck.

"A big dicked stud like you? Hell yeah." Dylan shot this minxy expression. "Chances are you don't even know how to fully swing that behemoth."

"I do just fine, ask Kaiden."

"Well, after you've taken a proper pounding, you'll learn a thing or two." Dylan continued gently tugging on Rus' cock. "Trust me, your stroke game only gets better after you take a good dicking."

Rus kissed Dylan, if only to shut him up. His words were silky temptations, but Rus wasn't ready to take such a bold step.

The pair panted as they made out, each jerking the other in the shower.

CHAPTER 22
DYLAN

"I'M surprised you didn't invite either of your boys over," Jasmine said, pouring them each a glass of sweet tea after wrapping up their Thanksgiving dinner. "Kind of figured things were getting a bit serious."

Dylan quirked a brow but didn't reply. Truthfully, he was exhausted since he'd been helping get everything ready with Jasmine. She'd dragged him out of bed at five in the morning to start prepping. Considering it was barely past four in the afternoon, he was ready to pass out entirely. Instead, he continued rinsing dishes before stacking them into the dishwasher.

"So, is it serious?"

"Yeah, ish." Dylan shrugged. "But Rus had to head home for the holidays, so I figured we'd keep it low-key. No need to rush everyone into family holidays."

"You don't want to meet his family?"

"I honestly haven't really considered it."

"Oh?" Jasmine retrieved a small bottle of booze from her purse, a giddy expression on her face as she poured it into one of the glasses. "Time for a little tea and tequila."

Jasmine's face suggested the tea would come from Dylan more than the glasses of sweet tea on the counter. She had her inquisitive face on.

POLITICS AND POLY

They didn't keep alcohol in the house with so many teens floating about. Yet they managed to always find a bottle of something every few months. This wasn't contraband, though. Oh no, this was the fancy tequila Jasmine liked every now and then.

"So, is Kaiden dropping by later?" Jasmine asked, stirring her glass. "This will be the first year he's not enduring his family celebration, right?"

"Yeah, add that to the list of things I'm thankful for this year," Dylan said as he wiped down the kitchen sink. "But he's working today, so again, we're just keeping it casual."

Personally, Dylan liked celebrating Thanksgiving with Kaiden and would've loved to add Rus to the mix, but with both of them creating conflicting plans, Dylan settled into the routine of the holiday. He focused on the house and kept things simple.

"Alison has him working the gallery?" Jasmine tsked. "She's not even in the country."

"Retail hell," Dylan said, explaining Kaiden's desire to earn a little extra this holiday season since he'd moved into his own place. "And before you say anything, yes, I told him about our extra furniture in storage. He's very much of the persuasion to prove to himself he can do this on his own."

"Hmmm, well, remind him that support does not detract from independence," Jasmine said, sipping her drink. "It's a big step getting your first place."

"I guess." Dylan shrugged.

"It's a big place, isn't it?" Jasmine asked, offering Dylan the other glass of sweet tea, hold the liquor.

"Meh. Biggish," Dylan said. "Two bedrooms, two baths, so I guess kind of. More space than he needs."

"But enough to invite others over."

"Well, yeah, but even Rus has company, and he lives in a little box of a building."

"You spend a lot of time at their places. Sometimes more there than here."

"I don't think I spend that much time with them," Dylan replied.

"More than I've ever seen from you before."

"Too much time?" Dylan's chest tightened, wondering if perhaps he'd dropped the ball somewhere, if maybe Jasmine was using her tea and tequila conversation to allude to Dylan slacking around the house.

Had he forgotten any appointments recently? Were the residents noticing his absence? Were his sleepovers affecting how the house ran?

"If there's something I did, please—"

"You haven't done anything," Jasmine said with a light laugh. "You're the perfect person to keep this place running."

Dylan released his anxious breath and relaxed a bit.

"The fact is, it's a lot of work to keep this home organized and successful," Jasmine said, locking her gaze onto Dylan. "I closed a few chapters of my life to help others write their own stories. That was a decision I was completely fine with, but it's still a lot to ask for of others."

Dylan understood that in a sense. Until Kaiden and Rus, he hadn't had the best of luck navigating romance, often ignoring possibilities because it complicated his routine.

"You've put your life on hold since you were seventeen," Jasmine explained.

That was a weird way to phrase it. Dylan never considered it a pause in his life, more like a chance to actually dive into his life.

It took Dylan a year of living in Dorothy's Home before he felt safe. Took him another year in the house before he truly accepted himself. Once that happened, he buried himself in outreach activism, doing everything to help the home gain visibility. His senior year of high school was a terrifying one. His grades were just okay at best and frightening at worst. College seemed impossible. Careers seemed insurmountable. Life away from Dorothy's Home was a daunting hill. Helping around the house was a dream, and Jasmine gladly made room for him to continue helping.

"I was okay with that because you needed that. I've watched you ignore your own desires for over a decade now, focused on this house, the people living here, the community that rallies around us, but never yourself."

Dylan shook his head, dumbfounded.

POLITICS AND POLY

"So, now that I see you exploring your feelings, finding someone—someones—who make you happy, I want you to know it's okay if that happiness takes your life in a different direction."

Dylan didn't understand what Jasmine was saying, where this was coming from, or why she thought his relationship changed anything. Kaiden and Rus had never once stood in the way of his work.

"It's not a bad thing." Jasmine smiled, big and genuine, yet it seemed cruel all the same.

"Are you telling me to move out?" Dylan's voice trembled. "To quit?"

"No, sweetie. You're welcome here as long as you want. Personally, this house runs so much better with you in it." Jasmine gently pressed a hand to his shoulder. "But as long as you are hiding in here, you're putting your life on pause."

Jasmine released Dylan, finished her drink, and tossed it in the dishwasher before hitting the start cycle.

"I don't want you to miss out on something great because you've put obligations ahead of your happiness. The only person you're obliged to is yourself, Dylan."

With that, Jasmine took her leave, and Dylan attempted to process even a fraction of what they'd discussed. His life with Kaiden and Rus had kept him afloat for months now, so much so that he didn't realize the ground beneath him was shifting. All Dylan had ever known was Dorothy's Home. It was his only safety in this world. Did he really want to step away from the house? But what if Jasmine had a point? What if retreating into the program prevented him from finding happiness?

Would it be fair to Rus or Kaiden to string along their relationship? Was it a relationship if he couldn't truly commit?

Dylan lost himself in his thoughts, aimlessly cleaning the kitchen and touching up the same areas again and again in his little daze. His phone pinged, alerting him that the group chat had a new message.

> Rus: Hope everyone's Thanksgiving is going well.

> Only half tempted to blow someone's brains out.

> JK.

> JK to JKing.

> Seriously too much family interaction.

> Kaiden: Oh no.

> That sounds exhausting.

> Family can be a headache.

> I'll gladly take the chaotic Karen's out for the best price over dealing with mine.

> Rus: You're still working?

> Kaiden: Yup. Took an extra shift since no one wants it.

> $ Holiday pay baby $

Kaiden followed it up with some GIFs of guys throwing money around. Dylan gave a weak smile, finding Kaiden's enthusiasm for working on one of the worst holidays endearing. If only Dylan had the strength to jump into the conversation. Instead, he just read through their messages, dwelling on his recent conversation with Jasmine.

> Kaiden: Why's your family driving you crazy?

POLITICS AND POLY

> Rus: They keep asking me if I have a girlfriend.
>
> Half tempted to drop the bomb of two boyfriends just to see my uncle choke on his turkey.
>
> Kaiden: Your family isn't cool with you being bi?
>
> Sucks.

Of course, Kaiden could connect with hateful family members, people who never truly accepted him. It was something that drew Dylan to Kaiden. Not that his struggle was uncommon from most queer people, it was how he handled it. Most of the time, Kaiden ignored his family's barbs, offered them love and support and compassion despite them lacking much of any for him.

Kaiden's kindness always drew him in. An enviable trait in some instances.

Dylan's chest heated, thinking about his own family's disgust with his sexuality, a family that made it clear at thirteen that if he stayed there, he'd be straight or in the ground. Memories of his past clawed from the shadows of his mind, and Dylan worked to push them back down. Dylan didn't dwell on his past, on a family that hated him, on a life he abandoned when he was far too young to make such decisions. Those memories had gone from festering nightmares to faded scars in the back of his mind. No, these fleeting recollections rarely came, but damn if they didn't hit him when he was already down.

Truthfully, Dylan didn't ponder on his family much at all anymore. They rarely haunted him after working through the guilt and hate and confusion. The fact was that he only really considered Jasmine to be family. Jasmine and every kid that passed through the halls of Dorothy's Home.

That was part of what made potential changes so difficult. He'd lived with Jasmine since he was fifteen years old. He'd worked toward making Dorothy's Home a success for almost a decade. It was hard to imagine life moving on to something else.

Dylan shook away the thoughts and returned to reading the group chat, hoping to work up the nerve to respond to anything. He scrolled up, having missed a bit of the chat while lost in his past.

> Rus: My family is chill but we're hosting *extended* fam for 🦃 day

> Let's just say half my relatives are cunts and the other half are worse

> If I push back, it'll just end up in some discussion on the gay agenda which will turn into liberal conspiracies that will then spiral into why women shouldn't vote and will end on how Jesus is American and God only loves white people.

> I'd rather not end up with a lecture.

> Or to punch someone.

> Again.

> Kaiden: Yikes.

> Try not to start any fights with your family.

> Rus: I never start them.

> Buuuuuut…

POLITICS AND POLY

Rus sent a semi-blurry photo of his family members lining a table. Easily ten people, and it appeared that half the table might be missing. He used the edit feature on his phone to circle one member in red. This person scowled from all the way at the other side of the table at Rus.

> Kaiden: Awwww. Someone didn't get the wishbone.

> Rus: Yup. And he's still mad I decked the halls with his face a few years back.

> It's why we keep Christmas closed. Immediate fam only.

> But we still host Thanksgiving every four years like the Olympics.

> I'm only here cause we're hosting.

> Kaiden: Every four years?

> Rus: Mom alternates with my aunts

> Kaiden: Aaaah. Makes sense.

> Sucks you're stuck with annoying relatives.

> Glad most of your family is okay with the gay.

> Well the bi in this case lol

> Rus: Yeah, I'm definitely planning on bringing up the topic of my relationship over Christmas.

> Fingers crossed my folks will be too preoccupied with gifts to care too much.
>
> Kaiden: You think they'll freak out a little?
>
> Rus: Worse. They'll be super chill about it and badger me with a million questions.

The texting conversation quickly devolved into silly jokes and random thoughts.

Dylan wanted to be as casual about their relationship again. But now that he had questions about things he'd never considered, the long term, the possibility of change, such drastic change, Dylan didn't know what to do with himself.

CHAPTER 23
KAIDEN

IT was incredibly difficult working sixty-plus hours a week, but Kaiden was a few short weeks away from having basic furnishings and a nice little nest egg. Well, an emergency fund that'd cover him for an unforeseen expense. Basically, he liked to keep two grand in his savings at all times, and his move had depleted everything and then some.

Between the calls Kaiden made to caterers for Alison's next event, he let his fingers wander to the group chat. Rus seemed very active, but Dylan was quiet. Quieter than usual, too. But Kaiden ignored it, consumed by the arrangements of the upcoming winter showcase. There were some new artists she planned to unveil. Once upon a time, Kaiden dreamed of being one of Alison's newly discovered gems. He'd fantasize about Alison peering over his shoulder one day while he was sketching, find herself mesmerized by his natural talents, and immediately demand he partake in one of her galleries.

Of course, that daydream quickly dwindled away since Kaiden stopped making time for his artwork. Although, since he had a bit of freedom, maybe he could pick up old passions again. Especially considering he didn't have to contend with his family for space or privacy or a moment to think when he got home. Two jobs definitely left him beat, but there was a certain peace that came with passing out when he got home with zero obligations to cook for others, clean up someone else's mess, or babysit his sister's children.

"Where the hell have you been?" Sandra materialized at the front door like some vile specter who'd sensed his avoidance.

"Fuck," Kaiden muttered.

He'd anticipated his family realizing he moved without a word, but he'd braced himself for his mother's guilt trips, not his sister's outbursts.

"You realize by dodging Mom and Dad, you're screwing everyone over, including yourself." Sandra beelined through the empty gallery.

"Huh?"

"It's the fourth. Rent is due on the first," Sandra snapped.

Technically, rent had a grace period until the fifth, which was probably why she'd tracked Kaiden down today.

"It's bad enough I had to scrape my tips together for the internet," Sandra continued her tirade. "Do you realize how inconsiderate that is?"

Yes, Kaiden knew exactly how exhausting it was covering the utilities or suffering without them. Not that internet was essential, but honestly, since they lived in a dead zone and every nearby neighbor locked their Wi-Fi, a connection to the online world seemed rather vital most days.

As Sandra continued spewing cruel comments, jabs at Kaiden's selfish behavior, and insults about his laziness, he realized something. Somewhere between professing his lack of effort to help around the house and demanding he pay his fair share, it dawned on Kaiden that his family hadn't noticed he moved out.

They must've just assumed he was staying at friends' places lately. It wasn't outside the norm, especially after his sister's opinion on his assault. He hid at Rus' apartment most days. But even then, he still often came home late in the night just to sleep.

Had they really not noticed his absence? His missing belongings? Technically, he did leave behind some of his furnishings for his nephews, but still. All his most important possessions were gone. Had his move really gone so unnoticed?

"You can get the fuck out right now." Alison stood overhead, her presence radiating authority.

Kaiden didn't turn to face her, didn't want to see the rage in her expression. After so many years at this gallery, Kaiden had done well at keeping his family drama away from his job. His stomach twisted in knots, reminded of how many jobs Sandra's drama had cost him over the years.

"And who the fuck are you?"

"I'm the bitch who's about to walk down these steps and slap the attitude right off your face," Alison said with the most composed and threatening tone Kaiden had ever heard. "Now, get the fuck out of my gallery before I drag you out by the hair, and if that shitty dye job stains my fingers, I'll slap you a second time for the inconvenience."

"This is between me and my—"

"This is between me and my gallery." Alison strode down the steps so quickly, Kaiden believed she might tackle Sandra. "You ever step foot inside my shop again, I will beat the ever-living fuck out of you."

Sandra wasn't the type to back down from a confrontation, but she mostly kept her altercations verbal. Since Alison stood about a foot taller and clearly had fifty pounds on Sandra, she did the first smart thing in her life and walked away.

"Fuck you, Kaiden," Sandra spat. "This is how you treat your family?"

"Keep walking, raggedy bitch." Alison crossed her arms and glared.

"This is why you're alone. You're a worthless, selfish coward," Sandra shouted as she reached the door. "You'll always be alone, you fucking fraud!"

Kaiden didn't correct Sandra, didn't point out that he had not one person but two who cared for him. All he wanted at this moment was to get his sister to leave the gallery before she caused more problems.

After the longest minute of silence, Kaiden finally looked over to his boss.

"I am so sorry about—"

"Shut up." Alison raised a hand to urge his silence. "Did you make a big deal when my ex stormed in, causing a scene?"

That was Kaiden's first year, and he did, in fact, make a big deal out of the person trying to stab several portraits on the wall. He'd never seen someone so enraged after a heartbreak.

"I mostly just panicked," Kaiden admitted.

"People suck," Alison said with a soft smile. "We can't control the actions of others, only how we respond."

Alison didn't always show it, but there was a kindness in her. She often went out of her way to help others with grand gestures or small deeds.

"Anyway, get back to work." Alison sauntered away. "Don't think this family drama excuses that to-do list. If I have to come back down here, it better be to sign off on a seating chart and not beat one of your dumbass relatives black and blue."

"Thank you."

"Whatever."

Kaiden went back to work, invigorated by the unwanted drama. So much so, he finished his tasks and set out to accomplish a few extra things around the gallery, perhaps to show gratitude for Alison's assistance or merely remind her how useful he was most days.

Still, his sister's words stuck with him over the hours. Somehow, she seemed to know him so well for someone who knew so little about him. No, Kaiden wasn't alone, but he was a fraud in some ways. Ways that started to haunt him the more he dwelled.

In the days that followed, Kaiden kept busy and a bit anxious for more unwanted visits. Thankfully, his family stuck with rude texts and nasty voicemails, which made his life bearable. After the first one from his stepfather started up with a list of profanities, Kaiden simply deleted them without listening. All except for one.

His mother had left him a single voicemail that pierced at his heart. Part of him wanted to believe she left something kind, seeking to smooth things over. Another part of him believed she intended to yell at him too, guilt him over the scene his sister had caused, or worse, hate him for abandoning his family. Kaiden did the only sensible thing he could: he ignored the message until he had the strength to decompress.

Instead, he focused on the men in his life. The group chat had gone quiet until Rus hopped in and asked if they wanted to come over. Kaiden agreed, but noticed Dylan's response was rather curt. No bubbly comments or silly questions, just a simple one-word acceptance.

When Kaiden got to Rus' apartment, the pair relaxed in bed for well over an hour. Kaiden semi-napped as Rus played his video game. When Dylan arrived, the vibe changed almost immediately.

The anxiety oozing out of Dylan needled at Kaiden, so much so that he stood up and attempted to calm him while he paced around the apartment.

Dylan eventually settled in one spot. He shifted anxiously over by Rus' desk, unable to relax. It didn't take him long to share his hidden worries with them, fears he'd unlocked over Thanksgiving, and things he'd never taken into consideration once they started dating.

"Yes, I wanted to explore these feelings," Dylan explained. "But my biggest concern was ruining our friendships if things weren't reciprocated. Now? Now I know there are so many other factors that I never even considered."

"Like what exactly?" Rus asked, taking a cautious step toward Dylan.

"What happens when we want to move in together?"

"My trailer's big enough for three. Hell, probably more." Kaiden shrugged. "And we could always look for a bigger place somewhere down the line. Far, far down the line."

"But I can't abandon my home, my career," Dylan said, his face spiraling in unknown worries. "I wouldn't be as involved if I moved away…"

"Who says we have to live together?" Rus asked.

"That's what will happen the more serious we become," Dylan answered. "It's how relationships work, and I think it's why I've avoided them. I've always known to some degree how they would turn out, how I'd have to choose between taking care of Dorothy's Home or… I don't even know. Start over? I don't want to live somewhere else, to work somewhere else."

"My grandparents have been married for, like, almost fifty years," Rus said with a calm demeanor, encouraging Dylan to take a breath and pause.

"The first ten years of their marriage, he was stationed halfway across the world while she stayed at home raising my mom and her sisters. Then, when he retired, my grandma became one of those traveling nurses, gone weeks or months at a time. They didn't have half the tech to keep in contact and mostly wrote letters. Still do. In fact, he's usually working with veterans while she's off helping build clinics around the world. They make it work. It's not traditional, but since when do we have to be traditional?"

"True," Kaiden added, gingerly cupping a hand around Dylan's face. "You both were the ones who reminded me we didn't have to follow the rules that others followed."

"But I hadn't even really considered things, thinking with my dick or my heart or both," Dylan said. "We could really just keep things the way they are?"

"I think right now we're all enjoying having our own space."

Truthfully, Kaiden didn't want to live with anyone again for a long time. He'd gladly make room for Rus and Dylan at his place whenever and however they wanted, but it was still his place. That distinction remained important to him after so many years trapped in his family's home.

"Well, what about kids?" Dylan asked, sparking a new panic for another random possibility of what could be. "What if you end up wanting them?"

"You know I'm not in the headspace to even consider kids," Rus said, rubbing his thumb over his Valentine's Day tattoo. "It's not something I've ever really wanted."

"You could change your mind." Dylan shrugged frantically. "Ten years from now, you might want kids. Want a picket fence."

"If in ten years I want a kid or you want one or Kaiden wants one, then we sit down and have that conversation," Rus said with a sincerity Kaiden admired. "We don't have to sabotage our relationship over what might happen in a year or five or fifty. We get to enjoy the ride right now, remember?"

Dylan dwelled on that for a minute, considering.

"I've never truly just enjoyed the ride," Dylan admitted. "I play it cool and go with the flow, but I'm a planner. I've had to be. I've wanted to be. It makes the world a better place when you're prepared for any possible outcome."

"You can still prepare for possibilities," Rus said. "Just maybe don't let them consume you, consume what we have right now."

"Instead of preparing for the worst, maybe we prepare for something good," Kaiden added.

Dylan stood silent for a moment, lost in thought. Kaiden studied his steadying breaths, the ease of tension in his stance, and believed they'd gotten through to him.

"God, you both really are the best. I love you," Dylan said, the surprise on his face revealing just how vulnerable he was by uttering those three little words.

The fear and vulnerability hummed in the quiet room, radiating off Dylan as he composed himself. Kaiden wondered if the fear on Dylan's face would flutter away as easily as those words had.

"I love you both, too." Rus kissed Dylan, soft and tender, taking his time as if to say he loved him all over again.

The pair rested their foreheads together, turning their attention to Kaiden, and offering a chance for him to make his own declaration.

"I mostly just love me, but I suppose…" Kaiden's face burned bright red. "Kidding. I don't love myself. That would involve healthy self-esteem. Kidding again. Mostly. Definitely."

Sometimes Kaiden hated himself for deflecting serious emotions with crappy humor, but at the end of the day, sarcasm helped him keep a safe distance from things that frightened him. And while he cared so deeply for Rus and Dylan, he sometimes worried what would happen when he handed them his heart entirely.

All the same, Kaiden wanted to be happy and honest.

"I do love you both." Kaiden smiled with blurry eyes. "So much so it scares me."

"Why's that?" Dylan asked.

"Because for the first time in my life, I feel complete. You both bring me to life in different ways." Kaiden's heart raced. "I feel safe with you, seen by you, and I want you both to see me. All of me."

Kaiden backstepped, leaving them on the bed as he approached the bathroom. Before either of them could speak, he raised a finger to gesture that he needed a moment. Oh God, how Kaiden needed a moment. More than a moment, really. A lifetime.

As he stood alone in the bathroom, slowly unfastening the loops of his corset vest, dread bubbled inside him. It choked him up, making each inhale that much harder. Still, he pushed through it.

Once he'd taken off his corset vest, the freedom allowed Kaiden to take a deep, shaky breath. Afterward, he sucked in his gut, already feeling ugly. And he hadn't even done the hardest part yet.

Kaiden fixated on the reflection of his buttons in the mirror. One by one, he delicately opened his dress shirt, but he couldn't bring himself to look after he'd slipped off his top. He stood alone in the bathroom, exposed from the waist up and unable to simply take in his reflection. Still, if he planned to be seen by Dylan and Rus, truly seen, then he needed to face his body, too.

Kaiden took in his reflection, at first locked onto the chest muscles below his collarbone, then the muscles of his shoulders and biceps, the parts of him that'd improved so much after years of healthy progress. But eventually, he slowly moved his gaze down to the parts of his body he rarely glimpsed. The parts of himself that he hated taking in all at once.

Yes, Kaiden saw his stomach every time he changed his shirt or hopped in a shower, but he never stared for long, never really examined himself fully, because he still carried so much shame. Despite flexing his stomach muscles as tightly as possible, there were no cute abs poking out. Only saggy skin that hung from his chest and stomach. Stretch marks added blemishes to his otherwise embarrassingly ghostly skin, pale from never even attempting to remove his shirt to tan.

What would Dylan and Rus think if they saw him naked? Saw every flaw he tried to hide from them?

Kaiden was tired of hiding himself. If he really wanted to be with Dylan and Rus, then he needed them to see who he was underneath it all.

"Since we talked about what ifs and where we see this going in the future," Kaiden said from inside the bathroom, slowly creeping out into the main corridor of the apartment. "I thought you both deserved to see who I really am underneath everything. And if you're grossed out, it's okay. There are things about my body that are permanently changed after weighing 340 pounds."

Rus and Dylan sat up on the bed, staring at Kaiden as he stepped out of the bathroom, shirtless. Even with his slacks still on, he felt completely naked in front of them for the first time. They saw his every flaw and remained speechless.

Kaiden shamefully folded his arms over his chest, hiding his saggy pecs.

"I..." He couldn't form words. The lump in his throat grew, and he knew soon enough his eyes would water.

Before he could retreat back to the bathroom, Dylan stood to his left, grabbing hold of one of his arms. It startled Kaiden, taking him aback so much so that he surrendered his hand to Dylan. Then he noticed Rus on his right side, grabbing hold of his other arm, delicately moving it back to Kaiden's side.

Kaiden stood silent, unsure how to feel having them both so close to him, invading his space, seeing his body so close up. It was a mistake, a horror show he should've never shared.

"You're beautiful," Rus said, gently kissing Kaiden's chest.

"Absolutely breathtaking," Dylan added, caressing his hand over Kaiden's stomach.

Kaiden almost collapsed right then and there, baffled by their reaction. They continued kissing his body, tracing their fingers over his skin, and Kaiden buzzed from the sensations. He'd never allowed anyone to see him shirtless. Not since he was eight years old. Not once. Not in the shower. Not at a pool. Not anywhere ever.

Slowly, they made their way back to the bed, continuing to kiss each other. Kaiden lost himself in the bliss, the pleasure of their embrace. They didn't have sex immediately. Much of what happened next involved kissing and cuddling and losing themselves in each other. It became impossible to tell where one of them started and the next one ended.

Soon, they were all naked, on top of the covers, and for the first time in Kaiden's life, he didn't feel shame over his body. Even surrounded by these two gorgeous men, he felt just as beautiful. Just as worthy.

Kaiden spent the following morning out on the balcony, staring at the all-too-scenic view of the apartment complex parking lot. A truly spectacular sight as he took deep drags from his vape. Admittedly, the huge clouds of strawberry smoke helped distract him.

The sliding glass door rattled behind him, and Rus stepped out, tucking his arms into his T-shirt sleeves.

"Burr." Rus' teeth chattered. "You realize you can smoke inside."

"Yeah," Kaiden said wistfully. "Just needed to clear my head."

"You okay?" Rus asked, poking his hands through the opening of his shirt and sparking a cigarette.

He looked kind of like a grumpy dinosaur with his tiny arms hidden beneath his horror shirt and his hands just barely sticking out underneath his chin.

"I'm fine."

"Are you sure?" Rus asked, exhaling smoke. "Is it about last night?"

"No, not at all."

Kaiden immediately noticed the concern in Rus' gaze. Perhaps he wanted to reassure Kaiden that he had nothing to be ashamed of with his appearance. Thankfully, Kaiden didn't hold any reservations for last night, finding it truly comforting to know Dylan and Rus saw him for who he was and didn't think less of him for things about his body he couldn't change.

No, the current dilemma haunting Kaiden seemed so trivial yet dire all at once. Kaiden stared at the voicemail notification on his phone, contemplating if he should just delete it outright.

"My mom left me a voicemail," he said. "It's probably just to yell at me for what happened with Sandra, but also maybe she's just worried about me since I pretty much left without a word. Or maybe she's just calling to cuss me out for being a shitty—"

"Nope," Rus interrupted. "None of that. Unless she's calling to apologize for your sister being an absolute trainwreck, or for using you for money, or to acknowledge she dropped the ball way too much, then what she has to say doesn't matter."

Kaiden gave Rus a soft smile. Rus leaned in close, huddling for warmth, but also offering Kaiden silent support. It was just the thing he needed to hit play on the unheard message.

"Hey, sweetie." His mother's voice sounded tired. "I hope wherever you are, you're doing well. I've been worried sick about you lately."

Kaiden fought the need to roll his eyes. She couldn't have been that worried since no one noticed he moved out until rent was due.

"I went through the basement and found a few of your things," she continued. "Some of your little dress-up kits."

Dress-up kits? Yes, because that made it far less effeminate than wearing makeup. Kaiden tilted his head, still listening to his mother's rambles, but trying to figure out what he'd left behind. He was certain he'd packed everything of importance. And while he hadn't managed to sort through everything around the house just yet, he hadn't noticed anything personal missing.

"Had a bit of a fall trying to lug it up those steps," his mother said with a wince. "Those rickety stairs are so dangerous."

Kaiden held his breath, waiting for his mother to add that she was okay. That she'd only stumbled a bit. That she hadn't seriously injured herself checking in on him in the basement. Instead, she wished him well and explained she had his stuff in a box for when he wanted to grab it.

"I do hope you're doing well, sweetie," she said with a haggard breath. "I might have to go to the hospital, make sure nothing's broken, but I will keep you updated. We miss you, baby."

The voicemail ended, and Kaiden spiraled.

"What's wrong?" Rus asked.

"My mom injured herself." Kaiden scrambled to get inside. "I need to head over, get some stuff I forgot, and make sure she's okay."

"Whoa, what's going on?" Dylan asked, completely oblivious to the balcony conversation.

"I have to head home—er, uh, I mean, my mom's place," Kaiden explained. "She had a fall, and I gotta get some things there."

"We packed everything," Dylan said, shaking his head slowly. "You did like three sweeps around the whole house to make sure we packed everything."

"I know, but I missed something." Kaiden frantically gathered his things and prepared to rush out the door.

"Calm down." Rus intercepted him. "Relax, deep breath."

"I'm fine, really."

"You're not," Rus said. "Let us come with you."

"No, because if Sandra is there and she sees you, she'll probably start something."

"If she sees you, she'll start something," Dylan said, stepping over to Kaiden and Rus. "She's got a short fuse."

"And so does Rus," Kaiden added. "Maybe two explosive personalities shouldn't be thrown together."

"I'll be on my best behavior, I swear." Rus crossed his heart.

Kaiden relented, realizing it would be helpful to have company, especially since Sandra would definitely guilt him for Mom's injury. Not that she needed to. Kaiden already beat himself up for not being there, for icing her out with everyone else in his family, for being so petty as to think she hadn't checked in on him because she didn't care. She had been fighting her own battle.

Dylan drove to Kaiden's former residence, and the three of them stayed piled in the car for about fifteen minutes, until Kaiden finally worked up the nerve to step inside. With a boyfriend at either side of him, Kaiden mustered the strength to knock on the door.

"I fucking knew it." Sandra swung the door wide open, hanging on the frame, and shooting her brother a dirty look.

Kaiden sheepishly went to step inside, hesitant to see if Sandra would block his entry. Instead, she sarcastically held out an arm like she was ushering him into a ballroom.

"What'd I say?" she called out to the living room, likely talking to her husband.

"Should've bet money on it, babe," Tommy shouted over the noise of his video game.

"Of course, you hear you forgot some of your precious, pricey makeup, and you run back home as fast as you can."

Kaiden froze. "I came to check on Mom."

"Why? So you can cry to her about how everyone is mean, and that's why you ran out on us?"

Rus let out this feral grumble, almost like a growl. Kaiden turned to find his fists balled and his expression furrowed, but he remained quiet and in place.

"I just want to make sure Mom's okay."

"Why wouldn't she be?" Sandra seemed oddly perplexed.

It dawned on Kaiden that his mother had lied about her fall, and he began to suspect the box of makeup, too.

"I'm an idiot," he whispered, backstepping toward the front door.

"First sensible thing you've said," Sandra snorted.

Rus took a step closer to Kaiden, glaring at Sandra, who merely smirked in response.

"Mom!" she shouted. "Kaiden's here for his stuff."

"You can drop the act," Kaiden said. "I see now I didn't forget anything."

"Oh, you forgot something all right," Kaiden's stepfather swaggered into the entryway with a beer and an open palm. "You know how much work it was getting the utilities turned back on, getting deposits, getting service fees..."

It seemed Kaiden's stunt had pissed off just about everyone.

"Now, John, let me handle this." Kaiden's mother brushed past his stepfather and sister, making her way over to Kaiden, where she tried to hug him.

When he recoiled, she paused.

"I knew you'd come home if you thought something was wrong," she said with a weak smile. "You're a good boy—one who loves his mom and his family."

Sandra scoffed. "Still say he's only here for the stuff he thought he forgot."

"I know you're upset with us and you feel that we're not respecting your space," Kaiden's mother continued, ignoring the muttered jabs from the rest of the family. "But I want you to know, we're ready to make changes around here."

"You hear that?" John chimed in. "We're accommodating you, you ungrateful…"

He quieted down when Kaiden's mother flicked her attention back to him, sending a silent message to shut up.

"We're going to clear out the basement for you," she explained. "We're going to redo it real nice. You'll need to chip in a bit, but it's going to be amazing. John's going to renovate it himself, so everything will be at cost. It'll be your very own room. Minus the laundry area, but that's no biggie. We can always just leave it at the stairs, and you can handle it and keep your space."

"So, I would do everyone's laundry?"

"Yeah, so you have privacy," Sandra snapped. "Something you keep bitching about."

"Enough of this," John snapped, taking powerful strides toward Kaiden. "Get your ass in the kitchen so we can break down payments."

"Step the fuck back," Rus snarled, blocking John's path.

"Oh, and what you going to do, little boy?" John looked down at Rus mockingly, and Kaiden knew in about two seconds, Rus would tackle his stepfather and beat the ever-living fuck out of him.

While every fiber of Kaiden's being wanted to see that, he didn't want Rus to lose his temper, he didn't want to start more drama with his family, and he certainly didn't want Rus getting assault charges.

"Well?" John stood taller, goading Rus.

Rus merely glared in response, his fists trembling at his sides.

"He's the one who's going to ask nicely." Dylan rushed in, bumping up against John's chest with his own and locking eyes with the old man. "Step the fuck back before I make you step back."

Kaiden used this opportunity to reach out and discretely hold Rus' hand. His grip was too tight at first, but with each exhale, Rus settled his nerves. He remained composed while Dylan stared down at John.

"We're not doing this," Dylan said. "I am disgusted by the way this family treats Kaiden. Can you even call yourselves that? Family? You treat him like a personal piggy bank. Like an inconvenience. You are garbage people. Liars, users, wastes of fucking space."

"Don't you dare—"

"Shut your fucking mouth, Sandra." Dylan pointed a finger in her face. "Don't think for a second I won't drag you, your daddy, and your lazy ass husband out on that front lawn and beat all your asses."

John tsked. "I'd like to see you try."

"That so?" Dylan leaned in real close, pressing his forehead to John's. "Since the day I met Kaiden, I have loved him. I have done my best to be respectful to his terrible family for his benefit, but I'll be damned if I let you fuckers manipulate him a second longer. You want to test your luck, go right ahead. I'm looking for a reason to knock some goddamn sense into that ignorant skull of yours."

Dylan didn't blink, didn't back down, didn't relent when John backstepped. He kept his eyes locked onto the old man's.

"Just get the fuck out," John snarled, finally turning away to return to the kitchen. "I said get out before I make you get out."

Kaiden's mother moved closer, trying to get her son to acknowledge her again, but Dylan intercepted.

"Not a fucking word." He jabbed a finger in her direction. "We're leaving. Do not call him until you learn how to make a sincere apology that doesn't include a selfish ulterior motive."

Sandra went to speak on her mother's behalf, but Dylan shot her a look so menacing, it silenced her immediately. Kaiden had never seen this side of Dylan—Kaiden didn't know Dylan had this side to begin with.

"Let's go." Dylan slung an arm over Kaiden and Rus' shoulders, ushering them out of the house.

This time, when Kaiden stepped out of his former home, he didn't feel like he was running away. He felt like he was dropping the anchors that had been tied around his neck all these years.

Once they got into the car, Dylan kept his intense gaze trained ahead, taking slow breaths to release his tension. Kaiden sat in the passenger seat, silently observing. Rus poked his head up from the backseat.

"I don't usually go for angry daddy vibes, but please spank me tonight with that same intensity."

Kaiden burst into laughter.

Dylan's anger washed away and was replaced by a frazzled expression.

"I can't believe I cursed them out. I'm so sorry," he said with manic puppy dog eyes. "I just couldn't take one more word of it. They were so awful and—"

Kaiden planted a kiss on Dylan's lips, silencing him. "I loved it. Every second of it."

"Me too," Rus added. "Hell, might have to let you be the assertive mean one in the relationship moving forward."

"Absolutely not," Dylan replied. "That is so stressful. Should I apologize? No, they deserved it. Total jerks. Still, Kaiden, if you need me to make amends, I can. I don't mind. I will go right up there and tell them they one hundred percent deserved to be told off but that I'm sorry for delivering the message."

"I want you to take us back to my place," Kaiden said. "I want you to prepare for a night of uninterrupted attention where I show you just how grateful I am to have you in my life."

"And I'm not kidding about that spanking." Rus squeezed Dylan's shoulders. "I want to experience that authority firsthand."

Dylan blushed, face completely red, and goofy grin growing wider.

Kaiden was proud of both the men in his life. Rus resisted his impulsivity for Kaiden's sake, and Dylan gave in to his impulsivity for Kaiden's sake. And Kaiden realized he could lean on the people in his life, people he trusted, people he loved. It wasn't weakness to accept help from them. It was commitment, devotion, and so much more that he hoped to continue exploring.

Kaiden was okay with finally walking away from his family. He wasn't abandoning them; he was simply putting himself first for a change. Putting the people in his life who truly mattered first. Kaiden had Dylan and Rus. That was enough for him.

CHAPTER 24
RUS

KAIDEN'S vulnerability had stuck with Rus over the following days, making him consider his own vulnerabilities. He still wasn't sure how much of himself he wanted to share with his boyfriends, intimately speaking, but there were other aspects of his life he wanted them to have a piece of.

"You're lucky I like you," Rus groaned as he escorted Dylan across campus to the Pride Club meeting.

The club itself wasn't a problem, and if he could latch onto Daysha the entire time he attended, it'd most certainly make the meetings bearable. Unfortunately, he still found some of the members a bit insufferable, parading their causes around like some type of competition. It did help Rus reevaluate his own angsty attitude, making him wonder if he too sounded like such a preachy cunt when discussing human rights.

He wanted to educate those teetering on the line of indifference, to bully bigots who deserved zero empathy, but he didn't want to sound like a pretentious twat stroking his own ego.

And that was the main reason some of the Pride members made it impossible for him to enjoy the club.

"Remind me to properly thank you later," Dylan said quite suggestively before they entered the meeting.

"Oh, I most certainly will," Rus whispered, slowly trailing behind his boyfriend.

Rus had found himself slipping away from campus activities. Partly because he was three years into his degree and wanted to graduate, and partly because most of his free time revolved around Dylan and Kaiden. While he had no intention of dropping time with his boyfriends, especially since Kaiden had already gotten busier with his part-time job over the holidays, he did want to make some effort in merging his worlds, so to speak.

Daysha was the only person on campus Rus actively missed, so he made time to hang out with her and Dylan—and hoped to plan some time for Kaiden to join in on a future coffee date. He wanted the three of them to kick it off well. After the Pride meeting, Daysha and Dylan babbled faster than Rus could follow, and it seemed they clicked.

"Well, right now, I'm organizing a winter fundraiser for our queer youth home," Dylan said, explaining how they try to hold a few charities a year and work with other organizations to raise funds. "Sort of our way of helping each other when we can. It's a community collective across the state. Some queer based, some not, but all great causes."

"That's amazing," Daysha said. "Reminds me of beer church."

"What?" Dylan scrunched his face in surprise.

"A bunch of bars back where I'm from would get together and host a monthly beer church charity. They'd have bar specials—usually some local brew donating samples and such—that went toward a different cause every single month. I don't know how they picked their charity or whatnot, but talk about boozing it up for a good reason."

"There's always a good reason to booze it up," Dylan said with a sultry, sly attitude.

To which Rus snorted because Dylan never drank.

"Do you guys have everything set up for your upcoming fundraiser?"

"Almost," Dylan said while fighting a grimace. "Some of our entertainment has fallen through, but some of our more theatrical teens are offering to put something together. If only they could decide on what to put together, we'd have a full show."

"Oh, that sounds stressful."

"It is, but this really is the best time to bring in donations, so I'll suck it up," Dylan explained. "Folks feel their most charitable over the holidays, whether from guilt, kindness, or strategy."

"Strategy?"

"Tax write-offs are worth as much as positive PR." Dylan chuckled.

"Well, I don't know about any of that." Daysha tapped her fingers together like some evil genius. "But I do think fate has brought us together."

"My name's not actually fate," Rus said to himself, knowing the pair were lost in their plotting. "But quite the compliment."

"Pride Club is always looking for outreach opportunities," Daysha said. "I think I could easily convince them this is a great chance to give back to our community before heading home for winter break."

"That would be amazing," Dylan gasped.

Kaiden had warned Rus that Dylan was a networking extrovert, but Rus didn't really grasp the meaning until he witnessed Daysha and Dylan coordinate in this weird gibberish half-speak as they lost themselves to the details. Suddenly, he realized Daysha was also a networking extrovert, and Rus had no idea how he surrounded himself with such people.

Next thing Rus knew, he was stuck in the meeting hall for the next hour as Daysha and Dylan brainstormed ideas to no avail. Daysha texted Pride members while Dylan contacted the teens at Dorothy's Home. So much for grabbing coffee.

"If you're thinking music, we'd probably need to find band members," Dylan said, typing away on his phone. "I could probably reach out to our current band, see if they can add your performance to their set."

"No need. Like half the Pride members have taken band all through high school," Daysha replied with a dismissive wave. "Gays and the arts, I swear."

"Nice," Dylan said. "So, maybe we do go with a song? Seems the easiest. Probably two because that'll help fill our time slot."

"We need something that won't be too much to choreograph or prepare for but will also offer the most engagement with the audience," Daysha added. "But obviously not one of those annoying go out into the audience and sing to them like some little cunt. Sorry."

"No, absolutely agree," Dylan replied with a smirk. "Also, something Christmasy without being too Jesusy. Half our donors want to feel the power of Christ compel them to give, while the other half would prefer not to see crucifixes vomited all over the winter fundraiser."

"Hmmm." Daysha's stiletto-pointed acrylic nails clicked loudly as she strummed the table deep in thought.

Rus pretended to contemplate while he picked lint off his hoodie. Dylan and Daysha continued shooting down their own ideas before even sharing more than half-mumbles aloud.

His phone buzzed, and he checked to see a message.

> Kaiden: How's the meet and greet going?

> Wish I didn't have to work all the time.

> Rus: Good. As predicted. Coffee was quickly replaced by charities.

> Kaiden: Told ya! lol

Rus huffed.

> Kaiden: Anyway...

> Can you help me with something super secret?

Rus noticed this message wasn't sent through the group chat they almost always used.

> Rus: Sure.

Kaiden replied with several screenshots of random items.

> Kaiden: Which do you think Dylan would like best?
>
> I know we discussed a price cap, ignore those. I have a discount

Rus was initially taken aback by Kaiden's inquiry, figuring he surely knew Dylan better than him.

> Rus: What does he usually like?

> Kaiden: SIGH. I don't know.
>
> Usually, I get him a gift card.
>
> Shut up.
>
> I know I'm terrible at gift giving.
>
> It's just so hard.

> Rus: That's what she said.

Kaiden replied with a GIF, responding with 'seriously' on a loop.

Rus imagined Kaiden's flustered face in the breakroom, as he awaited a response. Whether he knew Dylan better or not, Kaiden still valued Rus' opinion. Plus, he clearly sucked at picking presents since he didn't realize all his options were winners. That didn't surprise Rus too much. He'd learned all too well that Kaiden's self-doubt played a big role in his indecision. So, Rus hearted the screenshot he liked the most and gave Kaiden an answer.

> Rus: Just an FYI. If you happen to be privately messaging Dylan with similar questions, know I'm not too picky.

> Kaiden: Gift giving is the worst.

> Rus: It's fun. Just keep it low key.

> Kaiden: By low key you mean...

> Rus: Honestly, anything

> Kaiden: You're absolutely no help.

Rus chuckled and continued texting Kaiden well past his break while Dylan and Daysha continued planning.

CHAPTER 25
DYLAN

"UP, up, up," Dylan said, knocking on doors.

He'd prepared an outing this morning with a few of the residents as they lazily meandered around the house, their first day of winter vacation.

Miguel dragged himself out of his bedroom, still in his pajamas, as 10 AM rolled around. "It's too early."

"Y'all wanted lunch, part of that involves actually getting out of your bed."

"They don't even open until the afternoon," Yazmin said with a yawn as she stepped out of her bedroom.

"You do way too much." Chelsea squeezed by Yazmin, then made her way into the bathroom.

Dylan clapped enthusiastically, parading around the teens until they begrudgingly got dressed and ready.

As the only juniors in the house, Dylan planned a little getaway for them since he'd been so preoccupied with setting up for the upcoming fundraiser. Jasmine prioritized talks with several of the teens about to age out of the system. It wasn't like she wouldn't provide them a safety net if they needed it, but she preferred to work with them toward a goal, a plan for their future. Since she was going to use the bulk of the vacation days to work with the seniors on their plans for their final semester of high school, Dylan figured it'd be a good time to remind the juniors they weren't forgotten.

Plus, he could delicately pry for any details on where their minds were leaning toward for life after high school. Life after Dorothy's Home. Something Dylan himself never figured out, since he sort of wrapped himself up in keeping the house running. Although that in itself seemed to be quite a goal to set. Dylan was proud of his decision to keep his home standing strong.

"Let's get this over with so I can eat," Miguel said with a huff.

The teens followed Dylan out to his car and lounged quietly on the drive over to a nearby hiking trail. Dylan didn't pry anyone for conversation during the walk. Oh no, he smiled as they complained about the bright sun. He stayed silent as they cursed about the cold air. He stifled a few chuckles as they swore with nearly every step. But it kept them active, woke them up, and helped them bond as they collectively decided Dylan was the worst human on the planet to force them to walk this very breezy two-mile trek to earn their lunch.

By the time they left the trail, the sun had moved high in the sky and warmed everyone's frozen faces. Dylan cranked the heat up, ensuring hands and feet would thaw on the drive over to the steakhouse.

Dylan would've preferred a cheaper lunch outing, but he'd allowed the teens to pick, and since they knew they'd have to suffer through a nature trail for their food, they decided to ensure Dylan's wallet also felt the pain.

Once they got inside and placed their orders, the mood quickly shifted.

"Who you texting?"

"No one," Miguel replied, tucking his phone back into his pocket. "I made the mistake of befriending some of the AP girlies, and they're already planning ACT study groups."

There was a snarky lilt in Miguel's voice, clearly annoyed at the idea of using his break for schoolwork.

"Already preparing for ACTs, huh?" Dylan asked with an approving nod. "That's exciting. Big step."

"Well, I don't plan on living with Jailor Jazzy my entire life," Miguel said with a sigh. "The idea of helping stupid children all day sounds miserable."

"It can be pretty rewarding, too."

Miguel rolled his eyes.

"We've been considering the college," Chelsea added. "I mean, since it's right there."

She gestured, indicating that the campus was practically everyone in town, which was true.

"Well, we are," Chelsea continued, pointing to herself and Miguel. "Yaz is probably going to end up somewhere halfway across the country."

"Doubtful." Yazmin picked at her food. "Scouts today could mean nothing next year. They're always chasing the next big athlete, so who's to say they'll give a shit about me next year?"

"How many colleges have approached you?" Dylan asked.

Yazmin shrugged. "None I'm really interested in, so it doesn't matter."

"You know, if you end up picking some place close, we could get a big ass apartment and really live it up," Miguel said, nudging Yazmin and grinning at Chelsea.

"Yes, college is going to be so nice. No rules, no bullshit busy work," Chelsea added. "Though, pretty sure your itty bitty short king will finally graduate by the time you enroll."

Dylan quirked a brow but didn't say anything about their casual commentary on Rus. If he added something, chances were he'd only fan the flames.

"Blegh, I'm so over him," Miguel said with a twisted frown. "The terrible wardrobe I could work with, but the bad taste in men is simply a dealbreaker."

"Ouch," Dylan replied with a small smile.

It hadn't taken long for everyone at the house to piece together Dylan's somewhat confusing relationship status. Though no one really batted an eye at the fact that he had two boyfriends, other than to suggest they were surprised he managed to land one boyfriend.

"Oh, sweetie, it's not your fault." Miguel mockingly patted Dylan on the shoulder. "You were born this way. It can't be helped."

"I'm not exactly sure why I'm being insulted, but okay?"

"Just Miguel saving face," Chelsea said with a wicked grin.

"Gotta pretend you didn't steal his crush by acting so above it," Yazmin added.

"Shut up," Miguel hissed. "I got so many men knocking at my door, I don't have time to look down at someone else's leftovers."

Yazmin and Chelsea burst into laughter, much to Miguel's aggravation. He started swearing at them in Spanish. It didn't take long for the three of them to lose themselves in conversation, casual insults, and playful barbs as they ate.

Dylan smiled, listening intently as they enjoyed their lunch.

In the days leading up to the fundraiser, Dylan was a wreck. He always overextended himself and got a little lost on the perfect details nobody else could do. Mainly, because he so rarely trusted someone else to handle those details.

"Relax." Kaiden pressed a hand to the small of Dylan's back, centering him, pulling him back down to earth.

Kaiden always managed to soothe Dylan in the simplest ways. With a quick reminder, Kaiden went over the checklist with Dylan, he texted Rus, and they did a run-through on the performances planned for the evening.

Okay, maybe Dylan did trust some people to help with those pesky perfect details. Kaiden never let him down, and Rus turned out to be quite the talent for wrangling performers. There was a slight hiccup when Daysha called earlier about some of her Pride Club members falling through, but Rus ran interference. According to the texts, all had been resolved.

"What do you think he did?"

"Probably punched somebody," Kaiden joked.

"Oh, don't say that." Dylan chuckled, then contemplated. "You don't think he actually punched them, right? I don't want any of the performers to have black eyes or bloody noses."

"Please, black eyes would take days to show up, and a bloody nose is an easy fix." Kaiden rubbed Dylan's shoulders, grinning at him with this goading expression. "Relax. Rus knows how to behave."

"Right, right." Dylan rushed off to attend to the last touches before potential patrons showed up.

Despite his typical day-of stress, everything went quite well. Guests enjoyed the food, cocktails, and entertainment. Kaiden and Rus skirted away any headaches before they came in Dylan's direction—doing so in a way that they assumed Dylan wouldn't register. Of course, he noticed. He noticed every tiny detail, but he breathed easily, knowing he could entrust his boyfriends to handle any last-minute hiccups without causing a scene.

It allowed Dylan to bask in the fundraiser and enjoy the performances while chatting up donors between sets.

"It's such a lovely event," Jasmine said, joining Dylan at the edge of the audience as the latest singer finished their set.

"Thank you." Dylan smiled. "I try."

"You always put together such splendid parties," Jasmine continued. "I might let you continue organizing these group festivities in the future. Working with the organizations takes it out of me."

"I totally get that." Dylan chuckled. "I'll gladly keep working on these and any others for as long as you'll have me. Anything to make the world a little safer, a little happier."

Jasmine didn't reply, but her eyes studied him curiously, so Dylan elaborated.

"I talked with Kaiden and Rus," he explained, then found his mind wandering to ways to shorthand their names. Rus was already clearly a nickname, just Dylan had no inkling for what. Shortening Kaiden seemed odd. Kai or Den or just K didn't fit him well. Then he contemplated just referring to them as his boyfriends, but that seemed generic, and they were anything but. "Maybe Raiden or Kus."

"Huh?"

"Sorry, thinking aloud. Overthinking, perhaps," Dylan said. "Or under-thinking. I forgot to combine my name in there, too."

"Excuse me?" Jasmine stared quite perplexed.

"My bad." Dylan scratched the back of his head, laughing a bit at himself. "I talked with my boyfriends about our future. Who really knows where things will lead, but we're all excited for wherever that might be. We're in it together."

"That's lovely."

"But that doesn't mean I plan on stepping away from Dorothy's Home any time soon," Dylan added. "In fact, I'd stay forever if you'd keep me around."

"What about your relationship?"

"What about it?" Dylan shrugged. "They know my home is important to me, my family. They don't expect me to put it on pause just because that's conventional. We're happy just the way we are, and if things shift in the future, we'll talk about it. Me and them. And obviously, me and you. But I don't foresee changing careers or putting anything on hold just because things are getting a bit serious romantically."

Dylan's hands got sweaty from nerves, and he wiped them on his dress pants, stealthy but not nearly stealthy enough to escape Jasmine's notice.

"And yeah, I suppose this is a bit presumptuous. Assuming you want to keep me around for the long haul." Dylan laughed awkwardly. "Heck, maybe you were hoping I'd get a boyfriend and move out and start…I don't know. And here I went and got two and somehow still managed to refuse to take a hint."

"No hints were ever dropped, sweetie." Jasmine smiled at him in a way that always brought Dylan comfort, a way that said she saw him and loved him and supported him. "I just want you to follow your heart and do what makes you happy."

"Helping you, helping the home, that's what makes me happy."

"Well, then, maybe we should start discussing you taking on more responsibilities."

"More?" Dylan quirked a brow. "Like what exactly?"

"More like seeing how the home is really run," Jasmine replied, discussing things like how to network, negotiate, and navigate in a world where homes like hers were mostly unwanted. "I'm talking about balancing the books, learning how to process truckloads of paperwork, file appeals to fuck all bureaucrats who don't give a damn if you fail again and again and again."

"Wow." Dylan gave a nervous smile.

He'd worked alongside Jasmine for years, learning little things here and there, but he'd never really done the heavy lifting. The more she spoke, the more he realized just how little he knew when it came to keeping them afloat day in and day out. Jasmine was practically a superhero, refusing to let their home or anyone in it sink.

"Who knows, maybe one day you could learn the ropes so well you end up taking over." Jasmine laughed a bit, friendly and inviting. "Then I could retire. And by retire, I mean find something new to meddle with. There's easily a thousand more things to cross off my list one of these days."

"That'd be something for sure." Dylan's smile eased into something genuine.

He'd never considered running Dorothy's Home. That was easily a million years away, and perhaps only a sliver of a possibility. Dylan certainly didn't feel mature enough to handle the house. Not really. Not at this stage in his life. Then again, Jasmine was barely in her thirties when she founded the home. That was practically a blink away for Dylan. A few short years at most.

"But just a heads up that this work can put a strain on relationships," Jasmine said, once again reminding Dylan of the price that came with giving his all to Dorothy's Home.

This time her words didn't create a sinking pit in his gut or a chilling quiver of doubt running over his skin. No, this time Dylan basked in the cool confidence he had maintained since the last conversation with his boyfriends.

Dylan eyed Rus and Kaiden, who'd wandered toward the edge of the party. Based on Rus' antsy stance, he was in desperate need of a cigarette. Having them here to help made a world of difference. Having them here in his life made his world all the brighter.

"I'm not too worried about that," Dylan replied to Jasmine's comment. "Our relationship is a bit outside the box, so we should be able to weather any strain along the way."

Dylan truly believed that, believed he could have it all with Kaiden and Rus. Though he didn't know what having it all looked like or what it'd entail for them down the road, he was still eager to walk that path with them on either side.

CHAPTER 26
KAIDEN

DECEMBER turned into a busy blur, but things would slow down soon enough now that he'd reached Christmas day and put in his notice. Kaiden planned to work the rest of his shifts through New Year's, but based on what he'd heard about his managers, they had a tendency to magically remove hours from anyone who didn't stay loyal to the company and dared to quit.

Kaiden didn't care. The holiday hours gave him just enough to furnish his home with what he needed. A real mattress, a sofa, a television with a solid stand, a coffee table. Hell, a coffee pot. One of those fancy ones that made the foamy lattes Kaiden liked to treat himself with on occasion.

His phone dinged.

> Rus: Merry Christmas! Hope you're both doing great.

Rus included a selfie of him smiling in front of his Christmas tree. Kaiden grinned, always finding him so sweet when he actually smiled. Though the scowl was pretty sexy, too. Kaiden returned his own selfie, even avoiding a filter despite the fact he found his face a bit washed out without any makeup, and his hair needed a touch-up of emerald green dye.

POLITICS AND POLY

Kaiden: How's the fam?

Rus: Exhausting. My sisters are passively complaining about y'all.

Kaiden: Why?

What did we do?

Rus: Because they're single spinsters and I've got two men.

Whatever. It's kind of the highlight of the holiday to piss them off.

Kaiden: You're such a mean girl.

Rus: Damn right.

But alas, now my mom has been trying to corner me the whole time.

Kaiden: She's not a fan of two boyfriends? Or any boyfriends?

Rus: Worse. She's gonna want to have a sit down on the importance of maintaining emotional and physical intimacy in polyamory or something equally awful.

She's obnoxiously supportive of all our life choices.

Kaiden: Seriously?

> Rus: Yes. My mom can turn every conversation into some philosophical after school special on the human experience.

> Kaiden: That's sweet.

Rus replied with puking emojis.
Dylan replied with heart-eyed emojis.

> Dylan: Wait. Noooooooooooooooo!

> The heart eyes are for your sweet mom not the vomit!

> How come the send is under the vomit faces? I sent them before you puked.

> I hate techno

> Technologic*

> Technology*

> Le sigh

> Hope you're both having a good Christmas.

Dylan followed up with a frazzled faced selfie.

> Kaiden: Oh, it's so much better now, grandpa.

POLITICS AND POLY

> Rus: He is the oldest here. Maybe we have a GILF fetish?

> Dylan: I'm not old.

> What's a gilf?

> Wait are those the moving memes?

> Kaiden: That's a gif, sweetie.

> Dylan: -_-

> Maybe I am old.

> Reminder, I'm *cumming* over later today. 😳

> Rus: 👀

> Send noods.

Kaiden replied with the laughing crying emojis.

> Dylan: Hmmmm.

> Kaiden: You don't have to come over just because it's a holiday. I'm just chilling. I'd be more than happy to hang out tomorrow

> Dylan: Are you working tomorrow?

> Kaiden: Alison closed the gallery until the 28th so I'm free.

> Dylan: Perfect. Gives me a few uninterrupted days to plow you!

> Ho, ho, ho. *Insert something funny about snow.*

> Rus: Oh, you're going to insert something for sure.

> Dylan: 😊

> Rus: Now you have to send pics.

> Sad face.

Kaiden continued chiming into the group chat with some silly gifs, but focused more on cleaning up his place since Dylan actually planned on stopping by for Christmas. Usually, Dylan would be overwhelmed with how busy his place got over the holidays, so Kaiden didn't have to worry about being festive.

As he worked, his phone buzzed with another unwanted text from his mother, who'd started sending long messages expressing how much she missed him, worried for him, needed him. Her concern rang hollow in Kaiden's ear when his absence quickly turned into how he'd abandoned his family, leaving them with nothing. Funny, since he'd literally left them with most of his bulkier belongings.

Kaiden had blocked everyone else's number, blocked them on every social he could think of—even the platforms he rarely used—but he couldn't bring himself to cut off his mother entirely. Though while her sad messages did tug at his heartstrings, Kaiden refused to move back, and he continued ignoring her request for his new address. After Sandra's outburst at the gallery, after the near blows Dylan came to with his stepfather, Kaiden didn't want to chance what they'd pull on his front lawn.

Kaiden deleted the message without reading it, finding that the easiest solution when faced with wordy guilt trips, then he went back to work until the rumble of Dylan's car pulled up to his trailer.

Dylan arrived, handing Kaiden a bouquet of blue and white roses for the season. They were enchanting and almost distracted from the bags of groceries in Dylan's other hand. "Before you say anything, I only got stuff I like to cook, so really this is for me. And Rus. Basically, just us. Your fridge will just have to make room."

"I almost didn't see the bags, distracted by that sweater."

It was definitely a top-tier ugly Christmas sweater with a T-Rex Santa Claus, triceratops reindeer, and raptor elves.

"Cute, right?"

"Uh huh." Kaiden pushed the screen door open, holding it while Dylan carried easily a week's worth of food into the house.

Kaiden made a point to provide for himself, to prove he could handle this, and while he didn't find Dylan's assistance undermining, he also didn't want to become dependent on it. So much of his life revolved around believing he had no choice but to rely on his family, trust his family, believe his family when they convinced him he needed them and couldn't do anything on his own.

And yes, his relationship with Dylan and Rus was one of equals, of trust, of love. But Kaiden didn't want anything like his lack of providing for himself to sour their connection.

"So, what're you going to cook me?"

"Spaghetti and meatballs." Dylan wiggled his eyebrows. "The most suggestive dish."

"Limp noodles and squishy balls?" Kaiden countered playfully. "That is quite the suggestion."

"Oop." Dylan snorted. "I didn't think that through. Okay, we're eating hard noodles, so the suggestive dish works."

"Or we actually have a good meal, and you can show me something hard later."

"Deal."

With that, Kaiden helped put away groceries while Dylan started cooking their late lunch or early dinner. While Kaiden unpacked, he found a large gift-wrapped box.

"No," he whined. "No, no, no. You know I don't do good gifts."

"I liked your gift," Dylan replied as he cooked.

Kaiden had gotten a semi-decent gift for Rus and Dylan thanks to each of their assistance. Basically, he made them shop for each other and simply paid for the gift. Sentimentality wasn't Kaiden's best quality. And he gave them both their gifts early because he didn't like or understand the importance of waiting for the day. Plus, he was terrible at keeping secrets. Not to mention, Rus was leaving town, so he needed it early, and if Rus got his early, then it was only fair Dylan did too.

They'd actually made him wait until Christmas Day. Kaiden sort of forgot the whole gift exchange thing was happening.

"What is it?"

"It's from me and Rus," Dylan said.

"Do we wait till he's back in town?"

"No, but you do owe him a gratitude blowie for not making me film the experience."

Kaiden tsked. "Shut up."

"Maybe just a gratitude blowie for the awesome gift," Dylan said as he swaggered back and forth in front of the stove. "I'll take a gratitude blowie for sure."

"I bet." Kaiden went to unwrap the gift, finding himself carefully lifting up the tape and unpeeling the wrapping.

"Just tear it apart."

"But it looks like y'all put so much work into wrapping it."

Truthfully, the gift wrapping alone made this special enough to put on display. Maybe he didn't need to open it at all. Dylan's protests quickly changed Kaiden's mind, and he reluctantly ripped open the bundled package.

Kaiden stared in awe. "Seriously?"

"Do you not like it?" Dylan dropped what he was doing and spun around to check on Kaiden.

They'd picked out a few sketch books, some boxes of fancy pencils, colored pencils, and a cool figurine designed to be posed in different positions. Kaiden rarely thought about drawing anymore, but every now and then, he'd mention it.

"I love it." Kaiden's face fell into a perfect smile for the perfect gift. "Thank you."

"Nothing says thank you quite like a—"

"Get back to cooking before you ruin the moment," Kaiden said a bit sternly as he went to put his gift away in his bedroom, where he'd definitely be dragging Dylan later this evening.

They ate in the living room since Kaiden had never really grown up eating at a kitchen table and hadn't bothered buying one for his place yet. He still needed to get more furniture. Right now, they made do with the sofa and coffee table.

After finishing their food, Kaiden turned on the television, a small one, but big enough for Dylan and Rus to enjoy when they visited. Dylan leaned back, practically sprawling out on top of Kaiden, using him as a body pillow.

"The point of a couch is so we all have space."

"What?" Dylan rubbed his back against Kaiden's chest. "You're so cozy."

"Fine." Kaiden lay back, giving Dylan free rein to rest on him.

About halfway through the movie Dylan picked, he rolled over, sitting with his stomach between Kaiden's thighs and his head resting almost up to Kaiden's chest.

"How's the holiday been going so far?"

"Pretty good, mostly. Helped at a few charities, played an elf a few times."

"Oh?"

"Yep, you should see me in those striped tights."

"Now, that would've been a hell of a Christmas present."

"You know, you can get more than one gift." Dylan grinned.

"Hmmm. But whatever will I get you?"

"I can think of a few things."

"What'd you have in mind?"

"Let's do something to make Rus jealous that his flight is still a few days out."

"Oh? Are you going to write him a graphic text on our exploits?"

"I was thinking a snippet of our good times." Dylan had this minxy expression.

"You're not filming me."

"What about audio?" Dylan teased, wiggling side-to-side on top of Kaiden. "Just a few well-timed moans. Maybe a few slurps."

"Absolutely not."

"Fine," Dylan sighed, retrieving his phone.

"What did I just say?"

"Don't worry," Dylan said, tracing his fingers along the screen of his phone. "I'm just making do with what I got."

After a minute or so, he revealed a stick figure drawing. One stick figure was bent over while another stick figure with an absurdly giant penis—fully detailed and bigger than the two stick figures combined—stood behind the bent-over stick figure. Then there was a crying face in the background.

Kaiden burst into laughter. "Oh my God, that's horrifying."

"What? I'm not the artist in the relationship."

Kaiden's heart pattered a bit quickly there. It'd been so long since he'd considered himself an artist. Maybe he could be again. Could be for the first time. Every sketch, every painting, every attempt over the years held this hollow sensation. Practice without payoff. The skill of another person entirely. Even looking at his old work on occasion made Kaiden feel like a fraud. But he wanted to explore art all the same. All the time. The passion snuck up on him, creeping its way inside and burrowing into his veins, consuming him.

Now that he'd stopped working his second job, he might actually have the time to explore his interests. Alone in *his* home, he could take his time with artwork, explore it without judgment or expectations or condescending comments that it'd never bring him any real money. Yes, Kaiden would've loved to get rich off his passions, but that was never the point. The joy of drawing was the point. Exploring different styles. Learning new techniques. Finding his niche in a world of so much beauty.

Dylan hit send on his terribly hilarious drawing, then tossed his phone onto the floor.

"Now, about that blowie." Dylan shot Kaiden a minxy grin.

"You're so exhausting," Kaiden said with a playful sigh.

Dylan kissed Kaiden, the rough stubble tickling Kaiden's face. Dylan caressed Kaiden, running his hands under the edges of Kaiden's corset vest. For the first time, Kaiden didn't flinch or feel the need to adjust or pull back or change positions to take attention away from himself. He lay there lost on Dylan's lips.

After a few minutes, Kaiden unfastened Dylan's pants, tugging them down just enough to pull his cock out. As Kaiden stroked Dylan's dick, he let out an eager groan.

"You like that?" Kaiden whispered, bringing his hand up to his mouth and quickly licking his palm before returning to stroke Dylan off.

Dylan growled into Kaiden's ear. "You want me to wreck that pretty face of yours?"

Kaiden responded with a passionate kiss. Dylan sat up some, and Kaiden braced himself on the couch, keeping his head beside the arm of the sofa.

Dylan crawled up and straddled Kaiden's chest. The weight made Kaiden gasp, and Dylan used that opportunity to immediately shove his cock in. Kaiden gagged, choking at the suddenness, but lay there taking it in inch by inch.

As the dick hit the back of Kaiden's throat, he tried to widen his mouth, hoping to squeeze in a breath between the pumps. Dylan ran his fingers through Kaiden's hair, gently rubbing his head as he took steady strokes. Eventually, his pace increased, and his grip on Kaiden's head got firmer. He held him in place, fucking his face harder.

Each time Dylan bucked forward, his knees pushed a bit heavier onto Kaiden's shoulders. The current position made it harder for him to breathe, for him to find a comfortable position. He almost tapped out, so he could get a minute and then drop to his knees to suck Dylan off. As much as he needed a slight reprieve, he had a different idea.

Kaiden wrapped his hands around Dylan's lower back and butt, getting a firm grip while holding his cock in his mouth. It wasn't much, but he lifted himself forward and changed their position just enough so Kaiden could sit upright with his back against the sofa and Dylan's knees not weighing so heavily on him.

"Holy fuck, muscle daddy," Dylan said with a chuckle. "I know I said I was going to ride your face, but damn. Did you seriously just lift me?"

Kaiden basked in the moment, letting gravity push Dylan's cock deeper into his throat before he started to rhythmically pump in and out again.

Dylan took swift thrusts, humping Kaiden's face and only occasionally pulling his cock out to give Kaiden a breather while teasing him with the head of the dick, rubbing it along Kaiden's mouth and cheeks.

Minutes passed. Dylan grunted, his thrusts becoming more erratic as his balls continued slapping Kaiden's chin. He kept a firm grip on Dylan's hips, giving just enough resistance to encourage more assertive pumps.

"Fuck, I'm gonna cum." Dylan kept pumping into Kaiden's mouth, pushing so far, Kaiden's throat muscles ached.

Then Dylan pulled out all the way, fish hooking his thumb into Kaiden's mouth, and pulling his jaw open wide. He tugged on his dick a few times, unleashing a jet of cum onto Kaiden's face. Dylan pushed the head of his dick back into Kaiden's mouth, aiming the second and third bursts of his load more accurately onto Kaiden's tongue.

After he'd shot his load into Kaiden, Dylan pushed his semi-erect dick further into Kaiden's mouth. Kaiden sucked on Dylan's cock until it completely softened and continued sucking until Dylan eventually pulled out entirely.

He hopped off the couch, literally jumping onto the floor, and trotted off to the bathroom without a word. Then he quickly returned with a towel and wiped Kaiden's face clean.

"Thank you."

"Of course." Dylan plopped back onto the couch beside Kaiden.

He let his slacks slip off but kept his boxers on.

They sat on the couch, continuing the movie they'd lost track of. Dylan rocked his leg side to side and bopped his knee against Kaiden's a few times. The rhythmic touch was soothing. Kaiden sank into the couch, lost in this blissful little holiday he'd never cared much for before now. He supposed, perhaps in the future, he could attempt a more festive approach. Kaiden had never had much reason to celebrate before now. But he hoped to have many more lazy Christmas afternoons with his boyfriends.

Eventually, Dylan turned to Kaiden, ignoring the movie altogether. "How soon before I'm allowed to drag you back to the bedroom so I can unwrap the rest of my present?"

"Oh, I'm a gift now?" Kaiden batted his lashes playfully.

"You're a goddamn prize." Dylan gave Kaiden a peck on the cheek.

Kaiden giggled, and the pair got up, heading to the bedroom.

CHAPTER 27
RUS

WITH a new year came a new semester, and Rus remained hopeful his unwanted nemesis wouldn't end up in any of his courses. Unfortunately, that also meant he wouldn't have any classes with Daysha since her focus had shifted to courses for her business and econ major, whereas Rus had to stack his history and poli sci requirements side by side in order to obtain his double major.

Rus missed Dylan and Kaiden something fierce after nearly two weeks away from them, but he barely had time for himself as he adjusted to classes, so he told them they'd meet up soon when he could actually dedicate time to them both. And oh boy, did he want to set aside some time for them. During the holiday, he gave himself a New Year's resolution to be a bit more adventurous. His mind wandered with everything he'd thought about over the break, everything he'd missed about them, everything he wanted to explore.

But Rus quelled those curiosities as he walked across campus. He'd planned to meet Daysha for lunch between classes, making his way to the café near the student center.

Hope was dashed when he spotted Emma beeline directly toward him. Even her sorority sisters seemed agitated by her hostile demeanor. Rus rarely garnered sympathy from them since he usually berated their choices when arguing with Emma. Personally, the sorority itself never bothered Rus, aside from how dated Greek life on campus had become, but he found their presence excruciating when he knew it'd undoubtedly lead to a confrontation with the worst pick-me girl in the universe.

Rus clenched his fist, biting back his anger. A wave of heat washed over him, building frustration for the impending argument. He hadn't even thought about Emma since their last day of class together. Part of him was amused by how easily he must've gotten under her skin that she'd immediately seek him out at the start of the new semester, but his stomach sank and twisted into knots at the realization that he also relished arguments.

Of course, he'd never get through to Emma, convince her to open her tightly shut eyes. She embodied everything he despised about the country, the state of the world, and, in turn, made the perfect verbal punching bag.

As his nails dug into his palms, Rus cooled his temper. There was no point getting riled up before she'd even spouted whatever obnoxious one-liner she had planned.

"I can't believe you showed your face here, you filthy fucking whore!" Emma shouted, brushing through a small crowd and stomping right by Rus.

"The fuck?" he muttered.

The tension he'd built fizzled away as he watched Emma approach her bestie, Landon, the worst kind of self-centered, self-hating homo.

An argument broke out between the pair, with Emma threatening him in a thousand different ways, and Landon alluding to every dirty secret he held on her.

"You think I'm afraid?" Emma raged. "Scorch the earth, motherfucker. I'll gladly toss you into the flames too."

Rus half-smiled, bemused by his own arrogance in assuming Emma wanted to spar with him. It also made him late for his plans, perplexed by what could've happened between these evil besties to drive a wedge between them.

"Dick," Daysha said, side-stepping over to Rus. "It always comes down to genitals with you allosexuals."

"Huh?"

"You're trying to figure out what they're arguing over." Daysha gestured over to Emma and Landon, in no way being subtle, but the pair roared and raged so intensely they didn't notice the growing crowd of onlookers.

"Maybe I'm a little curious." Rus shoulder bumped Daysha. "What'd you hear?"

"Emma and Landon went on some resort or ski trip or something absurdly decadent," Daysha explained. "Her, the perfect picture of prestige with her man on one arm and her token gay on the other. Unfortunately, for Emma, they decided to lock arms—and a whole lotta other stuff—without her."

"Oh, shit." Rus grinned. "That's hilarious. She probably didn't even think Landon could have sex."

Emma was the type to perceive gays in two categories. Good self-deprecating gays, like Landon, who were merely eunuchs in conservative eyes, and then, of course, the bad gays that made their whole personality political and were naturally sexual deviants who obviously fetishized everything with their wicked groomer gaze.

Rus snorted, thoroughly entertained by the unfolding argument. The world was a chaotic mess, but sometimes the universe smiled down and handed you a good day by making a terrible person's life a little more miserable.

"Couldn't have happened to a better pair, if you ask me." Daysha scoffed, eyeing Emma and Landon up and down.

"Think they'll kiss and make up?" Rus asked, turning to lead Daysha into the café.

"I hope not. I want to see them drag each other online."

"Ooooh. I might have to unblock them if they post anything good." Rus laughed. "Keep me in the loop, bestie."

The pair walked off to grab a bite and discuss their new semester.

POLITICS AND POLY

The week flew by with Rus adjusting to his new schedule and finding time to spend with his boyfriends. He'd texted with Kaiden and Dylan off and on, planning a get-together after his last class on Friday. While he waited for Dylan to pick him up, Rus contemplated the interests he'd been wanting to explore.

It wasn't something they discussed much since Kaiden was more than comfortable bottoming for both men. But all the same, Rus found himself curiously considering it. Every time he fucked Kaiden, he wondered how the sensation felt. Every time he watched Dylan rail Kaiden into a breathless state, he craved the very same.

Rus took the time he had to prepare for any possibility—though he wasn't sure he'd work up the nerve to mention it, he did want to be ready if things took such a direction. After cleaning up, Rus hopped in the shower and used his favorite body wash that Kaiden had bought. A fruity scent that drove Dylan wild every time.

> Dylan: here

Rus quickly dried off, tossed on a hoodie with jeans, and walked outside. Suddenly, he regretted his outfit, feeling it didn't scream intimacy or curiosity or whatever the hell else Rus wanted to say without explicitly saying it.

But it was too late to turn around as he'd reached the railing of the stairwell and caught Dylan waving up at him. Rus went downstairs, hopped in the car, and silently rode with Dylan over to Kaiden's place.

Dylan sniffed the air, grinned at Rus suggestively, and then focused on the road.

Every time Rus went to speak, his mind wandered with all the right ways to broach the topic, yet none of them seemed correct.

"You're awfully quiet," Dylan said, turning into Kaiden's neighborhood. "Long week."

When they arrived at Kaiden's, Rus continued his internalized contemplations, trying to find a way to jump into the conversation with such a random suggestion. Usually, when they initiated something intimate, no one struggled to make a move. Hell, Rus had started things on more than one occasion, but it was easier for him to suck a dick or get sucked or even fuck an ass than it was to suggest getting fucked.

They lounged on the couch with Kaiden drawing, Dylan gaming, and Rus lost in his thoughts.

Kaiden had bought a used PS4, so they'd have something to do when visiting, especially since Rus and Dylan kept bringing over the PS5 for gaming weekends at Kaiden's place. He never cared much for games themselves, but he seemed rather content watching while he drew. Normally, Rus would hop into whatever game Dylan picked, or at least watch with some enthusiasm, but he struggled to even pretend he paid attention. Truthfully, his mind drifted too much to focus on gaming, on conversation, on much of anything.

"What's on your mind?" Kaiden asked, setting his sketchbook onto the nearby coffee table.

Dylan paused his game, tossing the controller onto the carpet and peering over Kaiden's shoulder. They were clearly curious. Rus needed to work up the nerve to say it. To express his desires. It wasn't like either of them would judge him, but Rus worried, despite how much he wanted to move things in a different direction, that he might not be ready for it. Even if his eager body suggested otherwise.

"I've just been thinking," Rus replied, adjusting so his back pressed against the arm of the couch, and he faced Kaiden and Dylan. "I'd like to be a little more open with you both. I've been thinking about it, and I wanted to share—"

"Oh my God, you're going to tell us your full name," Kaiden blurted, overly excited, and flailing a bit on the middle seat of the couch as he folded his legs crisscross in some poor effort to calm his enthusiasm. "Okay, okay, I'm ready."

An equally eager Dylan set his chin on Kaiden's shoulder and stared intently at Rus.

"I wasn't planning on that," Rus sighed. "I was thinking of something else, something bigger."

"Aauuuugh," Kaiden whined. "My heartbreak knows no bounds."

"Will I ever recover from this letdown?" Dylan collapsed onto the other side of the couch, dragging Kaiden with him as the pair feigned defeated depression.

Rus stared at them silently, then let out a deep huff of annoyance. "Fine, I will share my name, with a few stipulations."

"Anything." Kaiden immediately perked up.

"You're not allowed to call me by it. You're not allowed to share it with anyone—"

"Our secret," Kaiden interrupted.

"Even under threat of death." Dylan crossed his heart.

"You're not allowed to laugh," Rus continued. "You're not allowed to make jokes. I don't want any Greek mythology innuendos or references or any of that bullshit."

"Greek mythology?" Dylan and Kaiden turned to each other with puzzled expressions.

Rus let them dwell in their confusion, practically groaning as he went to answer them. "Rus is short for Icarus."

"Who?" Dylan quirked a brow.

"The sun god, I think," Kaiden replied. "Right?"

"That's Apollo, which I would've preferred," Rus sighed. "My folks have a big obsession with Greek mythology and tragic figures."

Rus explained a summed-up story of Icarus, who flew too close to the sun, lost his wings in the process, plummeted into the sea, and drowned. A tale of foolhardy arrogance met with a swift demise.

"And your parents thought that was a good name?"

"A cautionary tale, for sure." Rus shrugged. "You should hear what they named my siblings."

Dylan and Kaiden both stared quizzically.

"No, we're not doing a full-blown roster on my siblings and which mythical metaphor their name is a moral for."

"Amoral or a moral?" Kaiden asked, teasingly.

The coy grin on his face gave him away, and Rus almost immediately regretted divulging that piece of himself.

"Okay, so what are we doing?" Dylan asked, nudging Kaiden playfully. "You had something else you wanted to talk about, aside from a name that we shall never speak aloud."

"Well, I was thinking we could have a little fun tonight," Rus said a bit sheepishly.

This was why he leaned into the truth behind his name. Despite how difficult that was for him, Rus found it far easier than what he intended to bring up tonight. Rus had found himself becoming more and more curious sexually speaking. Normally, he dove right into his curiosities, eager to explore something new, but when it came to bottoming, he didn't know where to begin.

It didn't help that Kaiden and Dylan eyed him. Speaking the words aloud to one guy was hard enough, but to say it in front of both the men he cared for made his face flush.

"I've been thinking about exploring… Well, you know." Rus gestured wildly, in the most non-descriptive manner that certainly implied no one would 'you know' what he meant.

That much was made clear by Kaiden's dumbfounded expression as his eyes followed Rus' hands. However, Dylan merely cocked his head, seemingly studying Rus' scrunched face, which in turn made Rus blush more.

"Oh." Dylan perked up. "So when you said you wanted to be more open, you meant you wanted to be opened up?"

Rus coughed. "I wouldn't exactly phrase it that way."

"I would," Dylan teased.

"Keep it up, and you won't be opening anything."

Dylan mimed as if to zip his lips.

"Wait, are we talking about…" Kaiden asked with his jaw falling a bit slack. "I fucking knew it."

"Did you now?" Dylan asked, gripping Kaiden's knee to steady himself. His demeanor shifted from his aloof minxy face into something calmer, more reserved, then he turned his gaze back to Rus. "And what did you have in mind?"

"I thought we could…" Rus shrugged, looking away from Dylan nervously. "I mean, I did sort of get ready before coming over. You know, just in case…"

Dylan's piercing gaze seemed to lay claim on Rus, making him shudder and quake and eagerly steal a glance of eye contact. When their eyes met, Dylan rushed him, and their lips collided.

Soon, the three of them were enmeshed on the couch, kissing and touching and teasing each other. Rus found himself sinking into the couch cushions, ready to submit right then and there, but Kaiden had other plans.

"Come on." He pulled Rus up to his feet, kissing him all the way.

They took a few awkward steps; arms tangled around each other and lips pressed roughly against one another.

Rus panted, teeth biting Kaiden and hands clawing at the lacy strings of his corset vest.

There was a silent pause between them. Kaiden had this look of hesitation. Rus immediately stopped, realizing he'd gone too far, stripping away the layers of comfort Kaiden still clung to, but after a few breaths, Kaiden gave Rus a light peck and reached his arms behind his back to untangle a few of the strings.

Dylan swooped in from the side, one hand pressed between Rus' shoulder blades and another behind Kaiden's back. While Rus couldn't see Dylan work from this angle, he knew he had untied the rest of Kaiden's strings.

Rus kissed Kaiden, falling back into their passionate moment without missing a second, and Dylan moved his lips to Rus' neck, licking and biting and teasing with every breath.

Their bodies stumbled around the living room, at some point finding their way into the kitchen, but no one stopped for a moment. No one considered hitting pause long enough to make the simple walk to Kaiden's bedroom. It was so much more fun kissing their way there, even if it turned into a much longer journey.

Rus yanked the dangling strings and then pushed at the small of Kaiden's back, forcing him to follow toward the bedroom. Each backward step was more work for Rus, but he allowed Dylan's guiding caress to lead him with certainty.

Once they'd made their way into the room, Dylan gripped Rus by the shoulders and turned him away from Kaiden's sweet kisses.

There was a small yearning to continue kissing, to keep in this comfortable space leading up to what he desired.

Dylan steadied his grip, squeezing Rus' shoulders tightly. "You sure about this?"

"Yeah." Rus nodded, a bit anxious, but enthralled all the same.

Without any forewarning, Dylan shoved Rus back onto the bed. Rus bounced on the mattress a bit and sat up on his elbows while his legs hung over the edge of the bed.

"You look beautiful." Dylan stared down at Rus, then stepped closer and stood between Rus' spread legs.

Dylan's knees bumped against the edge of the bed. It unsettled Rus in the most intoxicating way, waiting for what came next. Anticipation met with exhilaration. Dylan stood there silently, slowly unfastening his belt.

Rus reached out with an arm, running his fingers over the hairs of Dylan's exposed stomach up to the frayed edges of Dylan's crop top. As he leaned forward more, ready to help undress Dylan, Kaiden pushed Rus back and waggled a finger.

"Be patient," Kaiden teased, brushing his hand under Dylan's shirt and caressing his chest beneath the fabric.

A taunting action made all the more enticing to Rus when they kissed in front of him. With their lips locked, they went to work, slowly undressing. They barely paused between sweet kisses as they stripped off layer after layer of their outfits, eventually standing naked before Rus.

"I suddenly feel overdressed." Rus grinned, reaching to unbutton his jeans.

He was met with a quick swat from Kaiden's hand before he dropped to his knees and went to work unfastening and unzipping the jeans with his teeth.

A provocative and hot action to watch, one Rus barely had time to register as Dylan slid Rus' hoodie over his head. It got tangled around his neck and covered his face. Something that seemed intentional the longer it remained, and the more Dylan's lips brushed along Rus' body.

Gentle kisses teased his skin. Each peck was deliberate and seemed to outline one of Rus' tattoos. First, Dylan kissed his neck, then his chest, ribcage, arms, and even thighs. But those kisses below his waist might've come from Kaiden.

With a quick motion, they both tugged Rus' jeans and boxers down to his knees. They inched them down slowly as they reached the edge of the bed, where his legs hung off, and pulled his slacks off entirely in a swift motion.

Now, Rus lay on the bed completely naked with his hoodie bunched over his face.

"Oh, fuck," Rus said with a muffled groan when someone licked his shaft.

Dylan lifted the hoodie so Rus could breathe, but immediately pinned his thighs over Rus' shoulders, straddling his chest. It weighed heavily on him.

"Open," Dylan demanded, pushing the head of his cock into Rus' mouth.

Obediently, he took the dick, gurgling as he went to work sucking Dylan off from this angle. Despite the pleasure he got from Kaiden deep throating him and the comfort he got from lying down, Rus struggled to take in Dylan's cock.

"That's it, baby." Dylan ran his fingers through Rus' curls, grabbing a fistful of hair and yanking his head back and forth.

Rus choked, bobbing up and down Dylan's dick, taking in inch after inch. The thicker cock proved hard to wrap his mouth around, but Dylan's assertiveness didn't relent.

Unable to hold his neck in this position, Rus pulled back just enough to ease the tension. Dylan seemed to understand, lightly caressing Rus' face as he adjusted his placement. After a moment, Dylan started pumping his hips and pushing his cock back into Rus' mouth, deeper and deeper with each thrust.

His balls slapped Rus' chin. The head of his dick pressed against the roof of Rus' mouth, pushing further back with each pump. Rus' throat constricted around Dylan's cock, barely able to handle the girth wedging its way deeper and deeper.

"This is what you want, isn't it?" Dylan bucked harder, faster. "To feel this inside you. To buckle under the command of my strokes."

Rus gurgled, hands pressed to Dylan's thighs to ease the brutal pumps into his throat. As he gagged and gasped to choke in a few breaths, Rus slowly guided his hands to Dylan's sides, cupping his ass and encouraging the rough thrusts.

Just as Rus believed he couldn't handle it any further, the face fucking eased. He prepared to quite literally tap out, informing Dylan he needed a break, but it seemed Dylan had other plans.

He hadn't climaxed, Rus didn't expect him to finish in his mouth, but a nervous part of him would've been okay to put off his curiosities a bit longer.

As Dylan slid off Rus, he retrieved a bottle of lube from the nightstand. Rus sat up, wiping drool from his chin and moaning a bit as Kaiden continued sucking him off.

"I gotta be real," Rus panted, lost in the pleasure of his blowjob. "I don't know if my ass can handle that level of enthusiasm."

"Don't worry." Dylan sat upright at the head of the bed, back pressed to the wall. "We're going to start at your pace."

Dylan continued lubing up his dick, then nodded for Rus to come closer. Kaiden stopped what he was doing and made his way to the foot of the bed. Rus crawled over to Dylan, who instructed him to sit on his lap.

With only a quick shot of his gaze, Dylan's eyes said so much. No, commanded so much.

Rus sat on Dylan's lap, quivering as the head of his lubed dick slid between his cheeks, just barely grazing his hole.

"Relax." Dylan moved one of his hands behind Rus, easing the lubed fingers into Rus' hole.

"Fuck," Rus panted, immediately taken aback by the odd sensation.

The pressure didn't hurt but did make him a bit uncomfortable. As Dylan worked his fingers in and out of him, gently helping Rus adjust, Kaiden slipped behind the nervous guy. Kaiden pressed his chest against Rus' back, helping him relax. As Rus leaned back, he allowed Kaiden to brace his stance.

Kaiden kissed Rus' neck, sweet and distracting. The leading kisses worked their way down his shoulder, over his collarbone, and along his back. The tenderness of Kaiden's affection helped relax Rus as Dylan continued fingering him deeper.

"You ready?" Dylan asked, locking his gaze onto Rus, who nodded nervously in response.

After a moment of patience, Dylan guided his dick and lined it up against Rus' hole. He clenched the second the head pressed there.

"Relax your body," Dylan instructed. "Ease your way onto it and just let it inside."

Rus tried to obey, resting on the dick. The pressure hurt something fierce in comparison to the fingers. He whimpered as the head entered him, nearly retreating altogether.

Kaiden's gentle kisses and the light touch of his hand massaging Rus' shoulders kept him in place, but goddamn how easy it'd be to jump right off Dylan's dick. Instead, he continued resting on it, letting it sink an inch or so more inside him.

"That's it, baby." Dylan wrapped a hand around Rus' back, pulling him closer.

Rus tensed as Dylan rocked his hips upward, easing his way in further. He used his hand to guide Rus' body, encouraging this small thrust back and forth.

Rus gasped, taken in by the burning that coursed inside him. "Fucking A."

"Quite literally." Dylan grinned.

The pain seemed to radiate throughout his body, making him tremble from the pressure.

When Rus winced, Kaiden kissed him, seeming to swallow the noise and the pain all in one swift motion. The distraction helped. Dylan's guidance became less terrifying. Each push up and down got easier.

Somewhere in the mix of pain and chaos and sweet kisses, the sensations shifted, and a euphoria swept across Rus' skin. The burning pulsed, and he quaked at the pleasure that came from the pressure. It swelled inside him, making every muscle of his body tingle, making his skin slick with sweat.

Kaiden continued kissing Rus, moving his hand back to Rus' cock and stroking him hard. He hadn't realized he'd gone soft. He hadn't realized because each time he bucked, he found himself throbbing. How could he be so ready to burst without being hard? Not that that lasted long. Kaiden's touch aroused him, stiffening his cock as he continued bouncing on Dylan's dick, a bit faster each time. The thrusts he took synced with Kaiden's strokes, letting his cock slide between his fisted hand.

"Fuck," Rus groaned.

"Not yet," Dylan demanded.

He ran his hands up Rus' abdomen and nodded at Kaiden, who pulled away much to Rus' displeasure. When Dylan reached Rus' shoulders, he pushed him off his dick and left Rus yearning for more.

Every part of him braced for Dylan to climb on top of him, to roll him over, and fuck him deep into the mattress the same way he'd fucked his face earlier. Rus quivered, anxious and enticed. Every cell of his body was frightened by the commanding force and equally eager to submit.

"Roll over." Dylan's commanding gaze fell to Kaiden, who obeyed.

Rus couldn't hide his disappointment, having just found the pleasure in such painful pressure, only for Dylan to grow bored with his ass.

"Get over here." Dylan nodded, and Rus obeyed.

It seemed Dylan hadn't grown tired of Rus, merely sought to shift their positions.

"Oh fuck." Rus clenched his teeth as Dylan pushed back inside him, doing his best not to clench his hole in the process.

Keeping calm in this new position on his knees was challenging, but he rested his hands on the small of Kaiden's back as Dylan pumped into him.

After sliding deep enough to stay, Dylan adjusted and helped guide Rus' cock to Kaiden's entrance. Once he slipped inside Kaiden, Rus found himself lost in the most incredible sensation of his life.

"Holy hell."

"Nice, huh?" Dylan whispered, nibbling on Rus' ears. "Told you. Vers boys have the most fun."

With that, Dylan bucked into Rus, leading each of their strokes. Rus lost himself to the pleasure of pounding Kaiden's hole as he got pounded out in equal measure.

Kaiden arched his back as Rus leaned forward, pumping faster and harder. He wasn't sure if he was chasing the pleasure of fucking Kaiden or being directed by Dylan's swift strokes. Either way, he relished it.

Rus clawed at Kaiden's back, bucking faster when Kaiden moaned into the mattress.

They continued screwing, limbs wrapping around each other, mouths gasping and kissing, hands caressing, and skin slapping until Rus lost himself to the bliss.

"I'm going to…" Rus grunted, unable to stop himself.

He shot his load deep inside of Kaiden, panting as Dylan continued pounding into him hard. It hurt so much more now that he'd climaxed, but Rus grit his teeth and braced himself against Kaiden as Dylan continued.

"Roll over." Rus guided Kaiden onto his back and scooted further up.

As Kaiden adjusted himself, Rus took his dick into his mouth and worked on sucking Kaiden off. Dylan didn't pause, just kept pounding away at Rus' rear. The back and forth of both men pumping into him from either end excited Rus.

He gagged when Kaiden shoved his head further down, holding it in place as he took quick, short thrusts. Rus knew Kaiden would finish soon by how the dick twitched in his mouth.

Dylan's thrusts became more erratic with each second. He slapped Rus' ass and got a firm grip on his cheeks as he pushed all the way inside him.

Rus moaned at the suddenness, and Kaiden used the slack jaw to push all the way into his throat.

Both men shot inside Rus at the same time.

Kaiden filled his mouth and held Rus' head in place until he'd swallowed the load.

Dylan pumped into Rus' ass slowly, seeming to hold onto the climax a bit longer with each stroke.

When both men finished, they lay on the bed sideways on either side of Rus, who could barely move. He was lost in the rush of pleasure and drained from it all too.

"Goddamn, that was something for sure." Rus wheezed.

"Just wait until I pound you out in the shower later," Dylan teased.

"My ass is going to need one to two business months to recover."

They all laughed.

"Maybe you should pound Dylan out in the shower," Kaiden suggested.

"Preferably in the bed," Rus replied, his muscles feeling like jelly, and in no mood to stand at the moment.

"Fine by me." Dylan rolled Rus onto his back and straddled him in a swift motion.

"I'm going to need a minute to recover," Rus said, practically out of breath. "And a cigarette. Goddamn, could I use a cigarette."

Dylan collapsed beside him, moving so he could pull Kaiden into their embrace.

The three of them lay there resting, then kissed and cuddled and enjoyed the night together.

CHAPTER 28
DYLAN

IN the weeks that followed, Dylan found himself busier than usual. Jasmine hadn't been kidding about giving him more responsibility. January flew by in a whirlwind of paperwork that he'd never realized stacked up oh so quickly. Bills upon bills. Permits. Hearings. Appointments. Every little thing came with an average of three reminders in Jasmine's phone, quite a literal lifeline, to ensure she never missed anything.

So, when Dylan had a free weekend at the beginning of February, he didn't hesitate to bolt. He drove over to Rus' apartment and hunkered up with no intention of leaving until Monday morning. He wouldn't even step outside for food, demanding they order takeout for the convenience.

"Stop picking fights with everyone," Rus grumbled, clicking his controller to set up his characters defensively for a battle Dylan had provoked.

He lay sprawled out on Rus' bed playing Baldur's Gate 3 and intentionally starting fights with every single NPC they encountered just to see how many surprise attacks it'd take before Rus blew a gasket.

Surprisingly, Rus kept his cool, merely sighing every time they started a new battle. He sat crisscross on the bed, which made for the perfect pillow for Dylan to rest his head on.

"Considering you're the hot-tempered one, you'd think this would be right up your alley," Kaiden said from the floor.

Dylan looked up at Rus, grinning. It helped that Kaiden unintentionally supported his teasing. With Kaiden on the floor, Dylan kept his legs stretched over Kaiden's shoulders, almost hugging him with his legs. But not too tightly, since Kaiden positioned himself there so he could draw. He camped out on the floor so he had room for his art supplies and could use the edge of the bed as a sort of brace for his back.

There was a special kind of joy Dylan found in using his boyfriends as comfy furniture. They didn't seem to mind, and Dylan enjoyed having them to prop him up as he sank deeper into the mattress.

They continued playing for hours with Rus dropping random hidden facts about the game every time they explored a new area, and Kaiden disappearing into his artwork. Occasionally, he'd hold up a sketch to a character he knew Rus or Dylan loved.

"It's terrible," Kaiden said, tossing the sheet of paper back at them.

"I love it," Dylan said, snatching up the page and studying the details.

Kaiden could profess all he wanted that he hated video games or found the fantasy stuff too confusing to keep track of, but Dylan suspected he rather enjoyed the story. Especially since he'd managed to sketch a portrait of every companion at least once.

Granted, they did play the game a lot. It helped that every time Rus and Dylan started a new game, they made entirely different choices. Mostly different choices. Dylan couldn't be evil in the game, no matter how much Rus tried to influence a little bit of chaos. Personally, Dylan suspected that was the influence of Rus' in-game murderous vampire twink boyfriend, who always wanted to stab somebody. Dylan much preferred the honorable warlock with a chivalrous heart and the chatty wizard who never stopped rambling about something. They didn't want to conquer the world, merely save it.

As conversation died down, Dylan's mind wandered to the upcoming holiday. Despite how busy he'd been as of late, he hoped to celebrate with his boyfriends.

"You know," he said as casually as possible. "I was thinking of making reservations for Valentine's Day."

He looked up to find Rus' gaze locked on the television screen. Before Dylan could continue, Kaiden flicked his leg. Yes, Dylan realized Valentine's Day wasn't Rus' favorite holiday, and for good reason. It carried memories he'd rather ignore. If Rus wanted to avoid the holiday altogether, Dylan would accept that, but he hoped to pry just enough to figure out if it was something they could explore anew.

"I've never celebrated the day," Dylan said. "I mean, maybe in school or whatever for a class, but not like actually celebrated. Pretty sure Kaiden never has either."

Kaiden responded by yanking some of the hairs on Dylan's leg.

"Ow," he muttered, before lifting his leg.

He used it to pop Kaiden in the chest with his heel. A light smack, but enough to make up for the mean tug of his leg hairs.

"I get if it's something you don't want to celebrate," Dylan said, staring up at Rus, who didn't return his gaze. "And you're probably thinking it's something we could celebrate without you. Kaiden and I having a fancy little dinner or something silly. But I don't like that idea."

"Then why bring it up?" Kaiden asked aloud, more to himself, based on his mocking tone.

"I just think if we were going to do something for Valentine's Day, it should be as a trio or not at all," Dylan continued. "To be clear, I'm cool abstaining from the holiday. It's so corporate anyway. Boo to the card companies and flower murderers."

"I don't know," Rus finally said with an aloof shrug. "I think it'd be nice to make new memories."

"Yeah?" Kaiden cocked his head curiously.

"I'm well past any feelings or regrets with Lana, and maybe I'm not entirely over the day itself," Rus explained. "I think a small part of me will always wonder what could have been. Even if I don't actually regret giving up the kid. Like I would've been in way over my head. Probably would've resented the kid or Lana or both eventually. Still, it's nice to remember him."

Rus ran his thumb over the Valentine's Day tattoo on his wrist.

"But maybe it's better to just remember him, not let the joy of the day be ruined." Rus looked down at Dylan and grinned. "And I'm here for all the flower murders. I say slaughter 'em all and drown them in delicious chocolates!"

Rus cackled loudly with obnoxious flair, imitating his favorite vampire character.

Soon after, they settled back into comfort, playing their game and enjoying each other's company. Kaiden put aside his drawings and started looking up restaurants he thought they'd all enjoy.

"Do we have to do gifts?" he asked with a twinge of concern.

"I don't think—"

"Absolutely," Rus interrupted. "I demand only the best of presents to honor me on V-Day."

Kaiden huffed. "I'm giving you a coupon book, and you better like it."

"Really?"

"Yeah," Kaiden replied. "It'll have like one free hug and one premium massage and one silly drawing and… Hmmm. Other cool stuff. I don't know. I don't want to ruin the surprise."

"I love it," Rus said.

Not long after, they paused the game and put something random on the television for background noise. Dylan enjoyed the silence. He could enjoy anything with Rus and Kaiden.

"Speaking of upcoming holidays," Rus chimed in to break the silence. "I have a three-day weekend coming up in March."

"Oh?" Dylan looked up inquisitively.

"Yeah, and I was sort of considering heading home for it," Rus said rather casually, even if the slightest crack in his voice revealed a twinge of nervousness. "I figured it might be a good time for y'all to join, too. If you wanted, of course. Not that you have to. It's short notice."

"It's like a month away," Kaiden said, perhaps perplexed by the short notice comment based on the tone of his voice.

"Yeah, I know," Rus replied. "Probably should've given a bigger warning. It's cool if you don't want—"

"I want to go," Dylan blurted.

"Me too," Kaiden said, turning around so he faced them.

He was kind enough not to knock Dylan's legs aside. Instead, he lifted them as he spun around and propped them back over his shoulders.

"A month is plenty of time," Kaiden continued. "Plus, if the three-day weekend is related to a holiday, Alison might already have plans for closing the gallery. If not, taking a Monday won't be the worst thing in the world."

Kaiden rarely worked weekends with the gallery unless they hosted some gala or banquet.

"Okay, cool," Rus said a bit sheepishly. "My mom really wants to meet you both. She keeps texting."

"Really?" Dylan looked up at Rus.

"Yeah, so I figured a three-day weekend would be a safer bet than, like, a spring break visit. A week with my family is far too cruel, and summer would be fine, too. You'd have more time to brace yourself, but then I'd have to listen to her pester every single day until the end of the semester."

"I think it's brilliant," Kaiden said. "I'd love to meet your family."

"Mostly just my parents if we're lucky. Maybe one of my sisters." Rus shrugged. "But honestly, it's just going to be my mom asking you a million and one questions. Each."

"Is she excited to meet us?" Dylan asked with a smile, then let his smile fall into a playfully stern expression. "Or is she planning to grill us?"

"No grilling you, she's vegan," Rus joked.

"Don't people grill vegetables all the time?" Kaiden asked.

"It was a cannibal joke," Rus sighed. "You murdered it, sweetie."

"Jokes are supposed to be funny, so looks like you murdered your own sense of humor," Kaiden countered, a wicked grin on his face.

Rus huffed, and Kaiden leaned forward, bending Dylan's legs well above his head, as he positioned himself close enough to give Rus a peck on the lips.

Dylan stared up at them both, his body contorted with his head pinned in Rus' lap and his legs bent in such a way by Kaiden that his ankles practically grazed Rus' shoulders.

"Well, hot damn. Aren't you a flexible one?" Rus teased.

"I should've been a gymnast," Dylan wheezed.

Kaiden playfully slapped Dylan's butt. "You should've been a bottom with a perfect pretzel eight like this."

"Nah, not quite perfect." Rus grabbed Dylan by the heels, twisting his legs ever so until they sort of crossed over each other. "There we go. Perfection."

Dylan burst into laughter, attempting to wriggle loose, but found Kaiden's muscular grip on his sides and Rus' firm hold on his feet made it impossible.

"Seriously?" Dylan panted.

"What?" Rus looked down at Dylan, batting his lashes innocently.

"Hey, if you're gonna fuck me, at least let me get comfy first." Dylan bounced a bit in place, huffing until finally they moved enough to allow him to roll over.

Before he knew it, Rus lay on top of him with his full weight.

"Feeling comfy yet?" He bit the side of Dylan's neck, kissing and licking him.

"Almost." Dylan adjusted himself, finding the more he maneuvered, the more he synced up beneath Rus.

Rus wrapped his arms underneath Dylan's arms, pinning him in place. He lined his crotch up with Dylan's butt and playfully bucked against him. The motion pushed Dylan deeper into the mattress. Rus positioned his legs between Dylan's, keeping them wider and pushing him into an almost arched position as he lay on the bed.

"Okay, okay, less comfy, but digging it."

"Think of this as my early Valentine's gift." Rus leaned forward, kissing Dylan, who craned his neck to meet Rus' lips.

The pair kissed for a while until Rus pulled away and met Kaiden. He released Dylan and began to make out with Kaiden. Before long, the three of them became entangled, kissing and cuddling and caressing each other.

Dylan had no idea where their relationship was leading, but he was thrilled to follow them on this journey. He hoped Valentine's Day led to more wonders, more celebrations. He hoped meeting Rus' family proved a treasure of an experience. Not only for him, but for Kaiden too. They each deserved to see that not all families hated their queer children.

The three of them rolled around in the bed, and Dylan lost himself to the pleasures of their company. He couldn't wait to explore everything life had to offer with his boyfriends.

EPILOGUE
KAIDEN

Three Years Later

AFTER sleeping in later than expected, Kaiden woke up and went to wake Rus before he realized it was his day off. Somehow, Kaiden had gotten used to the chaos of their schedules. His, Rus', Dylan's, and making sure they all overlapped at some point or another.

Kaiden checked his phone to find a slew of messages from Cassie and Andy. After reading through them all, he huffed. Part of him was relieved to find Rus' siblings so welcoming, while another part of him found it incredibly overwhelming to keep up with all the family expectations. He and Dylan had found themselves roped into a welcoming family since their first visit.

Cassandra and Andromeda—both of whom didn't seem to have a problem with their full names, unlike Rus—tended to arrange the family get-togethers the most, second only to their mother.

"Okay, your sisters are concerned that Dylan and I won't be able to convince you to come home for your surprise birthday party without giving away the secret," Kaiden said, standing beside Rus' side of the bed.

Kaiden wasn't ruining the surprise. Rus had forewarned that his sisters loved to plan surprise birthdays for everyone, not for the person being celebrated, but mainly as a testament to their party planning skills.

"What should I say?"

"Tell 'em to get fucked," Rus grumbled into his pillow.

Kaiden rolled his eyes. "Suppose I can figure something out later."

While Kaiden found the idea of a surprise party sweet, he understood Rus' disdain for such things. After all, he was born on a day with constant practical jokes and unwanted surprises. So, planning an April 1st surprise birthday clearly never sat well with Rus.

Kaiden sluggishly made his way to the kitchen, enjoying the lazy morning, and went to make breakfast. He was still the only one in the house who cooked, which he quite preferred.

Once he finished cooking, he fished out his phone again and texted Dylan.

> Kaiden: Look what you're missing.

Kaiden dropped a photo of his breakfast that he admittedly spent far too much time making look pretty.

> Dylan: Jealous. 😔

> Saving me a bite?

> Kaiden: Maybe.

> Dylan: If not I can always find something else to snack on when I stop by.

> 🌷🌷🌷

> Nom. Nom. Nom.

> Kaiden: lmao

> Dylan: Don't laugh it off until I get a taste at least 😉

> Kaiden: You're ridiculous lol

> We still meeting for lunch

> Not a joke.

> A reminder.

> Dylan: I'd never forget.

True. Kaiden knew more than anything that Dylan had gone to great lengths to balance his much busier schedule. All the same, Kaiden liked sending little reminders, little check-ins. If anything, it gave him a reason to talk. Plus, it made Kaiden feel helpful, even in the tiniest of ways.

Dylan's work continued playing a bigger role in his life, the more Jasmine stepped back. Technically, she still ran Dorothy's Home, but had gotten around to traveling more, helping others start up their own queer homes, whether it was for teens, homeless trans adults, disabled queer people, or just those in the community generally struggling to get by.

With Jasmine away to help these projects get up and running, that left Dylan to lead the helm and keep Dorothy's Home afloat. Which he did quite well. It seemed Dylan had learned everything over the last three years, and what he hadn't learned, his enrollment in community college helped to fill in the gaps.

> Dylan: sushi or steak?

> Kaiden: sushi 💯

POLITICS AND POLY

> Dylan: Yum.
>
> I vote for Sakura.

> Kaiden: Cool deal.

It didn't surprise Kaiden that Dylan suggested Sakura, considering it was downtown and right around the corner from his job, and Dylan knew how much Kaiden hated abandoning decent parking downtown. Now, he could walk to meet them for lunch without losing his space.

Kaiden walked over to his bedroom and shook Rus before turning to step over to the closet.

"Breakfast is ready," he said with a cheery lilt, then went to change.

Rus yawned and stretched until he shook away the sleep, groggily eyeing Kaiden as he changed out of his pajamas. It'd taken a while, even after showing Dylan and Rus what he looked like without his corset vests or compression tanks, but he'd finally gotten comfortable enough to be himself entirely around them both.

Kaiden stripped down, taking his time as he rifled through the closet, deciding which corset vest he'd wear. Eventually, he settled on crimson red since it went with his nails, then he went over to his vanity to ensure his makeup matched his outfit.

"Looking cute." Rus rolled out of bed and gave Kaiden a sloppy kiss on the cheek, intentionally smudging his makeup.

"Ass." Kaiden glared, biting back a smirk.

"I am what I love." Rus swaggered out of the bedroom and went to grab his breakfast. "Thank you, sweetie."

"Uh-huh." Kaiden fixed his face and went back to work.

Shortly after graduating, Rus had moved into the trailer, which made life easier for everyone. They didn't have to debate about whose place to go to. Sure, they dropped by Dorothy's Home from time to time to help organize donations, assist with a teen moving out, or just generally dropping by for dinner. But when Dylan wasn't running things at the home, he knew where to go for a little escape.

Plus, with the cost of Rus' master's program, even his shitty apartment seemed overly expensive, and his internships with local campaigns didn't pay. But Rus didn't really work on those for the salary, merely the chance to make the world a bit brighter without having to punch a bigot.

"We're meeting at Sakura for sushi during lunch," Kaiden said as he waltzed by Rus, who ate at the kitchen counter.

Though Kaiden never understood the purpose of dining rooms, he did settle on some barstools to make a tiny kitchenette or whatever for Rus' convenience.

"Sounds good."

Kaiden kissed Rus goodbye, the most casual and natural thing in the world, then left for work. Life with Dylan and Rus had changed Kaiden's outlook a thousand different ways, altered his routine in every which way, but had also turned into a simple normality of everyday life.

The drive downtown was quick, and he breezed by Slayer's Brush, eyeing the art gallery as he drove a few blocks away before arriving at his new job.

Wicked Ink tattoo shop was pretty empty this early.

Kaiden had fallen in love with this new chapter of his life, learning anything and everything he could about tattooing, even if that mostly involved grunt work right now. While he never considered himself a very smart person, having barely passed any of his classes in high school, it turned out Kaiden was a quick study for all things tattoo-related.

The intrigue initially came when he joined Rus for one of his new tattoos from the popular artist Anna Rojas. With a bit of luck, some surprising passion, and a whole lot of persistence, Kaiden somehow landed an apprenticeship at the Wicked Ink tattoo shop.

What started as an apprenticeship had quickly evolved into helping around in every which way. It turned out he worked under one of the best artists in the state, but his new boss sort of lacked the basic skills of keeping her business books organized.

POLITICS AND POLY

Thanks to the years Kaiden spent working under Alison at Slayer's Brush, he knew how to manage accounting, scheduling, inventory, and everything in between with a breeze. He never intended to walk away from the gallery, but Alison sort of made it impossible to stay.

When she found out about how much time he planned to dedicate to his new apprenticeship, she fired him. Not maliciously. It was her parting gift, or so she claimed when offering him a hefty severance and wishing him well on the next step in his artistic journey. Kaiden actually had to look up what a severance was, never realizing there were actual jobs that paid people after canning them. It kept him afloat during his transition to working more at the tattoo shop, and Kaiden remained grateful to everything Alison had done for him over the years.

The door alert chimed as someone stepped inside.

"Wow, your shop really is out in the middle of nowhere," said a muscular guy in a ridiculous hoodie that said CLIT.

Kaiden rolled his eyes, assuming this obnoxious dude bro was their next appointment.

"Can I help you?"

"Oh, yeah." He gave Kaiden a friendly smile. "I'm here to see Anna. We have a consult thingy. The tattoo planning stuff."

His expression was goofy, but his eyes were a piercing green. Much brighter than Kaiden's darker emerald. They caught his attention almost immediately since Kaiden rarely met someone else with green eyes.

Kaiden quickly reviewed the schedule, seeing the name Colton Lennox in the system.

"Colton, right?"

"Yep," he answered with an excited shiver.

"First tattoo?"

"Oh no. The tattoo's not for me. I don't really do tattoos. I mean, there's this one"—Colton adjusted his hood, revealing the word IMP scrawled in pink ink across his neck—"but that's my boyfriend's doing."

Boyfriend? Okay, maybe there was more to the weirdo hoodie than Kaiden realized. As Colton rambled, Kaiden glimpsed the smaller text underneath the CLIT title. It read Clinton Lloyd Institute of Technology. What an absurd name for a college.

"He's obsessed with tattoos," Colton continued. "Hell, he got a tramp stamp because of a bet. But that's a whole other story. Actually, I don't really know the full story now that I think about it. The point is, he loves 'em. Probably more than me. Just kidding. Who could love anything more than me?"

Colton shot a minxy grin that reminded Kaiden of Dylan's sass.

"But he really likes them. Hence the surprise," Colton said. "We're doing this whole road trip vacation thing—totally my idea, because if I left it up to Isaac, he'd hide in our place all day—but also it helped me set up the whole tattoo surprise."

"I see." Kaiden nodded politely.

It wasn't uncommon for people to travel from other cities or even across state lines to work with Anna. She attended a lot of conventions and was pretty popular on social media. Chances were this Isaac guy had seen her style and mentioned it to his boyfriend, who ran with it as a surprise gift.

"You're not worried he'd want to be at the consult?"

"Psht." Colton waved a dismissive hand. "Please, Isaac gets tattoos on a whim. Trust me, he's going to love it."

With that, Colton made his way to the back of the studio to join Anna for the consultation. Kaiden continued working out front, reviewing files, and checking the schedule for the next appointment he'd observe.

After four months of working under Anna, he hadn't been able to observe many tattoos. Mostly, he worked on keeping things clean and organized, along with some extra stuff he'd started to pick up the slack out of habit.

Kaiden went back to work and then let Anna know he was heading out for an hour. The cool air sent a chill through him, but he still decided to walk over to Sakura, enjoying the leisurely stroll downtown. When he arrived, he found Rus standing outside with a cigarette.

"How's work?"

"Pretty good. Got this guy getting a consult for his boyfriend's tattoo."

"Oh?"

"Yep. Meaning his boyfriend is very trusting, or the guy gifting the tattoo is very controlling," Kaiden explained, though from his brief encounter with Colton, the guy didn't seem demanding in any way. Just a chill, go with the flow kind of person. Something Kaiden admittedly strived to accomplish for himself.

"I vote trusting," Dylan called out from behind them, making his way from the alley.

He rested his hands on the small of Kaiden and Rus' back, leading them each into the restaurant.

"So, are you going to be giving this mysterious and trusting boyfriend the new tattoo?" Dylan asked.

"Not a chance," Kaiden said with a laugh. "Anna barely lets me sit in to observe her work. If I'm lucky, she might let me work on some design ideas in a month or seven thousand."

The apprenticeship seemed like it'd last an eternity, but Kaiden didn't mind. For the first time in his life, he found a job that didn't feel like work. A career he could be happy in with a family he chose to support and be supported by.

Life was good. Simple and happy. Kaiden couldn't ask for much more than that with the two men who meant more than the world to him.

THE END

ACKNOWLEDGEMENTS

I want to give you all a huge thank you for taking a chance on this story. *Politics and Poly* really was a way for me to scream about all the rage I've had for the world over the last few years. It's been building longer than that, but things have definitely taken a downward spiral as of late. Romance is such a wonderful genre where we can explore the cute fluff and sweet spice between people falling in love with each other, but there's a lot of depth to the romance genre too.

We can enjoy the romance, the banter, and the swooning while having deeper conversations about important issues. That's what makes this genre so nuanced and versatile. And you know what they say about versatility. 😉

While I'd like to believe queer identities don't have to be political, it's important to remember our rights are constantly being challenged, and our lives are often at threat. Whether you're a queer person or an ally, please remember to take in joy where you can find it, stand strong with your support, and don't let bigots bully you into silence. We're stronger together than they ever will be!

I hope you enjoyed following Rus, Dylan, and Kaiden on their journey to self-discovery as they fell in love. I know I certainly did. Exploring each of them was a challenge and a reward, one where I got to look inside myself and share a few pieces with the world.

If you enjoyed this story, it'd mean a lot if you took a moment to give it an honest rating and review. They really help with visibility. As an indie author, every little bit makes such a difference. Thank you again for joining the poly boys on their journey.

AUTHOR'S BIO

MN Bennet is a former high school teacher, writer, and reader. He lives in the mountains of Arizona, which make for really cold winters for a desert state. He's still adjusting to the cold after being born and raised in the South.

He enjoys writing paranormal and fantasy stories with huge worlds (sometimes too big), loveable romances (with so much angst and banter), and Happily Ever Afters (once he's dragged his characters through some emotional turmoil).

When he's not balancing classes, writing, or reading, he can be found binge watching anime or replaying Baldur's Gate 3 for the millionth time.

Author website:
https://www.mnbennet.com

Amazon page:
https://www.amazon.com/stores/MN-Bennet/author/B0BLJJK5NF

Goodreads page
https://www.goodreads.com/author/show/23017668.M_N_Bennet

Patreon:
patreon.com/MNBennet

Newsletter
https://subscribepage.io/zUylj7

Find All My Stuff:
https://linktr.ee/mnbennet

www.ingramcontent.com/pod-product-compliance
Lightning Source LLC
LaVergne TN
LVHW040040080526
838202LV00045B/3421